When she was at school, Julie Garratt always came top of the class for writing stories! In the early 90s Julie gained a City and Guilds qualification enabling her to teach creative writing and has since often been employed to teach courses in the county.

Julie is the author of several published romance novels and claims that her vacations serve a dual purpose—'holiday *and* research trip!' She is married with two grown-up children, and lives at the top of a steep hill, which overlooks a valley dividing Nottinghamshire and Derbyshire. Her hobbies include photography, driving, antique book fairs and music. Julie also has a much loved garden where she can 'sit under the trees and write my novels . . . or play with my dogs!'

Prologue

'Your contract *here* is with me, Thorne! Your commitment to my daughter is at the altar in a fortnight's time. Don't get the two confused.'

Oscar Herrick, team owner of Oscar-Jade Racing was a hard man who never wasted words. Today, those words were as exacting as he expected his leading driver's performance to be on the track. Winning was the name of the game. Where Herrick was concerned, the *second* driver past the chequered flag was *first* loser!

The tall man in white racing gear was not intimidated. 'I'll be here when you need me for the next test run, Oscar. I just need ten minutes to get Louise from publicity to show the girls around the place.'

'We're here to test tyres, dammit, not to show off to a bunch of pretty girls,' Oscar stormed.

Rafe Thorne kept his patience with some

difficulty. 'The engineers say they'll be at least twenty minutes with the suspension before they're ready for the next test run. And you know as well as I do that your own shareholding daughter is one of those pretty girls. Jade has a perfect right to be here.'

Oscar Herrick made a snorting noise. He was a bull of a man nearing sixty, but what he didn't know about motor racing wasn't worth knowing. He turned away abruptly now and walked over to a fresh-faced younger driver he could browbeat more easily. Both drivers were kitted out in the same Oscar-Jade colours — white driving overalls, green flash down either arm. Oscar never allowed sponsor advertising on the sleeves of his drivers. That green flash on the cars and on the sleeves was sacrosanct. The green flash represented his daughter, Jade Herrick, and Jade must forever remain unsullied in her father's eyes.

Rafe headed towards the circuit office area to find Louise Hanson, Herrick's publicity officer. He'd arranged for Jade, his fiancée, and her friends to be shown around the place today. Jade seldom visited the track. It was well known that she hated the noise and the speed of the Formula One cars. It was ironic really that she showed so little interest in the company that bore her name.

Her three colleagues who were accompanying her today though, had been nagging at her to bring them here. To those girls, Rafe realized, racing high-powered cars at breakneck speeds must seem like an exciting job — much more so than helping Jade design the wedding dresses for which she was becoming justifiably well known in the north of England.

Designing was obviously in the blood of the Herrick family, but whereas Oscar designed and raced sleek, fast racing cars, Jade's priority was fashioning dresses that would make one day at least, extra-special for many a girl whose life often lacked that extra bit of lustre.

The day was still quite warm for March, though the sun was past its height now. He pushed the heavy glass door of the office block open and walked inside.

Jade was standing in the reception area and came over to him eagerly the moment she saw him, her smile wide, her shoulder length chestnut hair gleaming, and her green eyes lighting up with the look she kept especially for him. She looked like a million dollars in her simple slim fitting suit with a jade silk scarf tucked under its collar. Jade though, had the looks, the figure and the money to achieve perfection in every area of her life.

3

'Rafe!' Her soft voice was the oasis he craved at the end of a fraught day with her father. He often wondered how she could have grown up to be so unlike Oscar. 'Are we too early, darling?'

'No! Of course not.' Behind her he could see three girls on the green leather seating round a glass topped table, and he lifted his hand to one of them — his sister, Ava, before pulling Jade close to him and allowing his lips to taste hers briefly. 'I'm looking for Louise,' he told her softly. 'She's the one who's going to show you round the place.'

'You'll be lucky to find Louise, mate.' A man dressed in Oscar-Jade overalls had just followed him through the door and had obviously overheard his last remark.

Rafe's head jerked round to him. 'Lucky? What do you mean, Geoff?'

'Louise! She's entertaining the electronics people who have come up from Gloucester. It was a last minute arrangement but they're wining and dining at the Manor. Oscar's joining them later.' He glanced at the company clock on the wall. 'He's going to be *much* later though — he reckons he's not leaving the track till we get the suspension right. Louise won't be well pleased. She had other plans.' The mechanic grinned at Jade. 'Your Dad's a slave-driver, love. But I expect you know that.' With the words he loped off towards a door at the back of the reception area, and disappeared through it.

She pulled a face. 'I should know Dad by now, shouldn't I? I've had twenty-five years of him. I suppose he argues that if he's rented this circuit exclusively for the whole day, then he's going to get his money's worth.' She was unperturbed however. Nothing much ever rattled her. She was too sweet natured to bear grudges, Rafe knew.

'Hell! This shouldn't have happened. I sorted it all out with Louise last week.'

'Hey, don't look so worried. It's not the end of the world. And anyway, sponsorship has to come first with Dad. He's probably all set to get a few million out of the electronics gang with the race season coming up.'

Rafe shook his head, worried. 'I'd show the girls round myself but I've got to take the car out again. Can you manage without a guide?'

'Sure I can. I know this place inside out. Are we okay insurance-wise though if I take them in the workshops?'

Rafe ran impatient fingers through his close-cut dark hair. 'Lord knows. I leave all that sort of thing to the powers that be. I just drive the car.'

Jade laughed softly. 'Don't forget I'm here

when you've finished with your nifty dragonfly will you? I sometimes think you're as much in love with that car as you are with me.'

'No contest,' he quipped. 'You win hands down, all the time. You're the prettier of the two.'

'Dad wouldn't agree.'

His eyes kindled as he looked down at her. 'You're wrong. It's just about the only thing Oscar and I *do* agree on. And I know for certain that if I ever damaged you the way I have done that car at times, he'd kill me.' He took hold of her hand. 'Look — I have to go now, but I'll meet you in the west stand in about an hour — okay?'

'Sure. I'll be there with the girls. They want to meet you. They think racing drivers are madly exciting people — Ava knows differently, of course. Your sister has no illusions about racing drivers.'

'I'll try not to look too haggard for the other two girls then — after a twelve hour stint fighting dragonfly — and your father.'

A disembodied voice boomed out over the tannoy system. 'Thorne! Where the hell are you?'

'Dad!' She disengaged her hand from his. 'He sounds irate.'

'Patience has never been one of Oscar's virtues!' His eyes rested on her for a moment

1

'How do I tell Dad I'm finished with Brand Motors?'

Maggie Brand shook her hair loose from the silk scarf that had been wrapped round it all day. 'What words can I use? Whatever I say, he's going to be so hurt. So disappointed in me.'

But what alternative was there? She'd never intended the job to last as long as it had, and now, at twenty-six she was having to take a good hard look at her life. It had been all right at first, working with her father in the garage, restoring the classic cars he made a living from. She'd gained lots of experience there after leaving college, and had been happy too. Now, however, things had changed.

She picked up a comb and raked it through her shoulder length blonde hair to tidy it, then she picked up the scrap of silk from the bench and looked at it pityingly.

It was the only bit of frivolity she allowed herself in her working life — that scarf, and at the end of every day it finished up smeared with oil smudges and had to be scrubbed in soapy water and put on a radiator to dry, ready for use again next morning. She felt sorry for the scarf. It didn't deserve the harsh treatment she gave it; it didn't even look like silk now, it had seen so much wear over the years.

She swung it from her hand as she walked outside through the big double doors. The April evening was cool, but on a sudden impulse she strode out the few yards it took her to reach the top of the low lying boulder cliffs, and looked at the sea. There were heavy, white-tipped waves breaking on the shore down below her, and she could feel the misty spray from them on her face. The beach was deserted. Fudge would enjoy his run tonight. A smile tilted her lips as she thought of the crazy welcome she'd get from the dog in another few minutes' time.

So what was she waiting for, she asked herself, as she turned away from the sea and went back to lock up the garage.

She could hear St Martin's church clock in the centre of the tiny village of Shorecross, chiming six as she started to walk quickly down the long straight road towards home, and her mind made up, decided to have it out with her father that very night.

She hoped he wouldn't try to persuade her to stay. Hoped too that he wouldn't think her wanting to leave was born out of weakness of character. She'd always prided herself on her strength of mind, her ability to work under pressure. And she'd proved she could do that, when after leaving college eight years ago with A-levels in maths, chemistry and physics, she'd then gone on to study mechanical engineering so that she could confidently earn her keep at Brand Motors.

But things had changed drastically after Edgar Brand's accident last year . . .

So deep in thought was she, that it wasn't until the last moment that she saw the car that was parked right outside Fox Cottage, the lovely old house she'd been born in.

She stopped dead and looked at it. She knew nobody in Shorecross who drove a Ferrari — but it was a beauty. She just stood and stared at its sleek lines, its gleaming midnight paintwork, five-star wheel trims — and then she took a peek inside and drew in a deep breath of satisfaction at the sight of an interior knee-deep in rich Conolly leather. Luxury! Impressive, unashamed luxury. All that and a 5,500cc. engine to go with it, she thought with a touch of envy.

13

With envy, however, came the realization that she couldn't just barge into the house and shake hands with what might be a prospective customer of that calibre. No! She'd just have to sneak in round the side to the kitchen door and clean herself up a bit first. She gazed down at her hands, paint smudged, oil grimed. She shuddered at the sight of her short fingernails with ruby-red paint ingrained under their tips from the paint she'd been using to re-spray the little Austin that afternoon. She'd have to change out of her greasy overalls too, and put something more appropriate on her feet than the steel toe-capped boots she wore for work.

She edged quietly up the garden path, hoping she'd be able to get round the back without anybody noticing her from a front window.

But her luck didn't hold. The front door suddenly shot open and there was Dad in his wheelchair, grinning and yelling, 'Come on Maggie — there's somebody here wants to meet you.'

And before she could answer him, he'd whizzed his motorized wheelchair round, just as deftly as he used to be able to handle a car, and was heading off back across the hall. Then, from the back of the house Fudge set up a ferocious barking.

'Pandemonium!' she muttered, chuckling under her breath. But this was always how it was at home. Organised chaos her mother called it, and Sheila Brand had often sighed and said, 'If I ran my gynae unit at the hospital like this house runs, I'd be out of a job in no time at all.'

Edgar Brand was already half way back across the hall by the time Maggie got through the front door, and she had no option but to follow him towards the sitting room which Dad, to Mother's despair, always insisted on calling the front parlour.

As he was about to disappear into the room, she whispered loudly, 'Dad, I'm a mess. I can't meet anybody important looking like this.'

Edgar Brand jerked his head round and grinned at her. 'Never mind that, love. It's good honest muck you've got on your overalls. Come and see who's here.'

She heard a deep laugh and then a voice she'd never expected to hear again in all of her life. 'Edgar! Leave the girl alone. Maggie won't remember me, after all these years.'

She halted instantly, glad that her father had disappeared into the parlour again. Then she closed her eyes tightly and prayed, 'No! No! Don't let it be him!'

But she knew it was, and every bit of breath

15

seemed to be seeping out of her body at the prospect of meeting him again.

It had to be faced however, so she opened her eyes and focused on the door ahead of her. Her feet hadn't got the message though; they'd rooted themselves into the polished floor, and her legs were giving the impression they had suddenly turned to soggy ice cream. Then her heart joined in the general chaos that was threatening, and started thumping like a mad thing, as if, she thought cynically, it was trying to emulate the speed he generated when he raced round a circuit in his million pounds' worth of Formula One racing car.

Rafe Thorne!

It was the last thing she wanted, to meet the owner of that voice again. What she should do was turn and run, but her steel toe-capped boots were still refusing to budge. She felt such a fool, anchored there, just outside the front parlour door.

'Maggie!' Edgar Brand was not the most patient of men. 'Maggie — come on in and see who's here.' He was inching round the open door in his chair and beckoning wildly to her. 'Come on, Mags. You wouldn't guess in a million years who's in here, waiting to meet you again.'

She wouldn't guess? She wanted to laugh

wildly. If only he knew . . .

She knew only too well though, who she was about to come face to face with. And that ghost from the past now propelled itself head-first into the present bringing with it poignant memories of the Silverstone circuit on a hot summer weekend — the crowd jostling her — pungent aromas spilling out of hot dog stalls — cameras clicking — and her attention riveting — the moment she saw him — the tall, handsome driver in the white and green colours of Oscar-Jade Racing.

The team had been a relatively new one all those years ago, but according to Dad — who'd known Oscar Herrick at school — shouldn't be underestimated. They had a good number one driver in Rafe Thorne, he'd told her. Oscar had sent Edgar tickets for Silverstone that year, with an invitation also to attend the barbecue afterwards.

Maggie tried to blot out the memory of that day — the day she'd fallen in love, madly, excruciatingly, and for all time, with a dazzling smile, a pair of dark eyes, close-cut hair the colour of a raven's wing, a tanned handsome face, and a lean body confined in white Nomex racing gear. It was also the day her teenage dreams had been shattered, because just after the start of the race, she overheard somebody saying that Rafe Thorne was engaged to be married to his team owner's daughter — Jade Herrick . . .

After that, the barbecue hadn't been much fun for her because she'd watched in silent anguish as the beautiful Jade monopolized Rafe for what remained of the night. And in the car home much later, she sat in the darkness beside her father and faced facts. For the first time in her life, she was in love — but he was totally out of her reach.

She had to face him again though, she told herself fiercely now. She had to act like a normal 26-year-old, and go through into the parlour and prove to herself that the years-old magic wouldn't work again. She'd almost forgotten his existence she tried to convince herself. Forgotten as much as anybody could anyway, about somebody who for six months of the year each summer was constantly in the public eye. But she wasn't a silly lovesick teenager any more, she reminded herself, and she wasn't going to go all coy and act like one in front of him.

He stood up as she entered the room and came to meet her. Her eyes swept over him, missing nothing. Still tall, still good looking, lean and self-assured. But she knew all that, of course. Never a month went by when he wasn't either in the newspaper or on the television screen. His hair was longer now though than it had been all those years ago, and a few years of living had given it the faintest hint of silver in the raven blackness, which had never looked attractive in the newspaper photos — not like it did now in real life!

She went forward, placed her hand in the one outstretched to greet her.

'I remember you now,' he said. 'Edgar said I would, but I meet so many people . . . '

'You lead a busy life, Mr Thorne.' She withdrew her hand and let it fall to her side, hoping he hadn't noticed her paint-encrusted fingernails. She wanted to crawl into a hole. She was mortifyingly aware of her stained overalls, and the silky headscarf, still in its turban shape, dangling from her other hand. It must make her look as if she'd just stepped out of a munitions factory of the 1940s, she thought. Nobody wore turbans in the 1990s, not even if they did have to keep their hair clear of all the hazards of their working environment. She made a mental note to get herself a baseball cap for future use, and shove all her hair on top of her head underneath it — either that or have all her hair cropped short.

It was too late for that now, though. And she wondered what he must think of her. Realistically though, she didn't want to know.

'Edgar tells me you're the one who's been keeping Brand Motors running since he had his accident last year.'

She forced a smile. 'Not just me. There's Mark Langham too . . . '

'Mark!' For a minute she thought her father was going to explode. 'My late partner's son,' he explained for Rafe's benefit. 'He took over from his dad when Johnnie died eighteen months ago. Johnnie Langham and me — well, we go back a long way. He bought into the business when I was struggling to set it up. He was a good worker. One of the best was Johnnie. Wish I could say the same for his blasted son though.'

'Dad! You can't expect Mark to be a carbon-copy of his father,' she chided gently.

Edgar clenched his teeth together and thrust out his chin — a gesture she knew well. It indicated that he knew he was in the right, and Maggie was forced to acknowledge that her father had a point. Mark wasn't one to get his hands dirty. Even though he'd got all the relevant qualifications for the job, sometimes he just didn't even try to be of any help in the garage. He didn't seem to care a toss about it most of the time, and was always turning up late in the mornings and leaving early each evening.

To Rafe, she said, 'Mark was dropped in at

the deep end. He thinks the classic cars we work on have had their day. Your kind of car would be more to his liking, Mr Thorne — something fast and exciting like a Formula One racing car — or that dream of a Ferrari standing outside our front gate at the moment.'

'Rafe!' he said quietly. 'Call me Rafe, Maggie.'

Her heart turned over. Shaking her blonde hair back from her face, she said, 'I don't know you.'

'You're not an old-fashioned girl though, are you? We don't have to know each other for years before using Christian names, do we?'

She felt foolish. 'No.' Suddenly her hands were in front of her and she was twisting and turning the turban between them. 'Look — I'm a mess,' she said. 'I really must go and clean myself up.'

Her father began to say, 'I don't know what I'd have done without my Maggie after I had that accident on the lifeboat . . . ' and Maggie fled.

She heard the parlour door slam behind her, and wished she hadn't yanked it so hard. She hadn't meant to make such a grand exit, but she couldn't just stand there and hear Edgar sing her praises — not when she was going to let him down so badly later on by telling him she wanted to leave the garage. She had to get away. She had no desire to spend another minute in Rafe Thorne's company, because all of a sudden, she realized that the old feeling for him was still there.

She was still in love with him!

'That is ridiculous,' she told herself as she burst into the kitchen at the back of the house and Fudge hurled himself at her.

She laughed with the dog, ruffled his giant brown head, then disengaged the leggy length of him from her overall buttons. 'Down,' she whispered. 'Stay down and we'll go for an early walk. It'll give Dad the time to get rid of Mr Rafe Thorne.'

She ran upstairs and Fudge followed. She showered quickly and then went to her bedroom and changed into a stick-of-rock-pink sweatshirt, old but presentable jeans, and the comfortable white trainer boots she always wore to walk Fudge on the sands. It was second nature then, to scoop up the small black pager that accompained her everywhere, and slip it into the pocket of her jeans.

Her hair was still damp from the shower when she let herself out of the back door, and slipped down the side of the house, scurried across the drive, and strode back down the road with Fudge on his chain. She avoided looking at the Ferrari — still parked by the gate!

When she reached the low-lying cliffs beyond the garage workshop again, she saw that there were now several fishermen casting their lines into the sea. They, and people like herself with dogs, were the only ones who used the beach at this time of the year — and at this time of day. Shorecross wasn't prominent on any map of Holderness so it didn't attract holiday makers like the larger resorts of Bridlington and Scarborough to the north.

The substantial stretch of coastline, of which Shorecross was a part, had long ago become a forgotten kingdom. It was known locally as the 'vanishing coastline' — vanishing because every year, more land was taken by the greedy tide. Shorecross village centre was now less than a mile away from the sea, whereas in the history books, it had been three. For centuries the land had been plundered, the ground crumbling away at the command of the great north sea. Every year, buildings crept closer to the edge of the cliffs, then slowly began to break up, to lean seawards, and then to topple into the waves.

She walked along the grassy clifftop and

slipped Fudge off his chain, then finding an accessible spot, scrambled down the few feet of boulder-clay to the beach below. Fudge was sure footed and eager to leap ahead of her, then race round her in huge circles on the sand before prancing away to bark at the tide and a solitary seagull. That done, he slowed down to sniff at seaweed and small boulders and pebbles along the shore line. Once clear of the fishermen, she kept an eye on him as she walked briskly beside the ocean in the wetness left by the retreating tide.

Dusk was beginning to set in. After twenty minutes or so walking, she yelled to Fudge, then turned and started back the way she'd come. And it was then that she saw the man.

He was standing in the shadow of the dark cliffs, and as she came closer, he started walking diagonally across the sands towards her. Fudge overtook her, then also saw the man and stood stock still, quivering right to the tip of his tail.

She called to the dog, slipped the chain round his neck again. He was a big dog, and some people were timid where big dogs were concerned. Even big men had been known to quake in their shoes when Fudge was around and off the leash.

He stopped about ten feet away from her,

the man. He waited for her to come up to him.

'Why did you run away?' he asked in a soft, yet understanding way.

She stood still, facing him. 'You came to see Dad, not a scruffy car mechanic. And Fudge was eager for his walk.'

His eyes narrowed. There were little lines at their corners. Laughter lines? Lines of concentration? She didn't know. All she did know, was that when he looked at her like that, it made her toes curl into the soles of her size six trainer-boots.

His firm lips twisted into a smile. 'I thought perhaps I'd scared you off.'

'I don't scare easily.' The wind was behind her, blowing her hair forward. She tossed it back, ran her fingers through it impatiently, but north sea squalls had a mind of their own, and her hair was immediately whipped back across her face, stinging her eyes.

Conversationally he said, 'You were just a kid when I saw you last. I got quite a shock when you walked in tonight and you'd grown up.'

'I *was* just a kid. It was years ago . . . I was in my teens — and feeling tongue-tied and awe-struck that so many great racing drivers had shaken me by the hand in the racing paddock that day.'

'Edgar loved showing you off. He thinks the world of you.'

'He's my Dad. Dads usually dote on their daughters, don't they?' Her laugh was intended to sound brash and off-hand.

'I guess so.' He seemed to withdraw into himself. 'I only knew one girl and her Dad before though.'

Momentarily she closed her eyes and cursed herself. Oscar-Jade! Father and daughter. She could have kicked herself for reminding him, yet he must be reminded every time he took the wheel of a racing car in his hands. She recalled the headlines, splashed across every newspaper in the country only twelve months ago —

'RACE-ACE THORNE KILLS FIANCÉE'
'TRAGIC F1 ACCIDENT'

'I — I'm sorry,' she blurted out, embarrassed. 'I shouldn't have said what I did. Me and my big mouth . . . This past year — it must have been hell for you.'

He nodded, his eyes shadowed. 'It was. It is. But another shock I had was seeing your father the way he is — in that wheelchair.'

'His legs were crushed. The lifeboat had gone out to get some kids off the rocks beyond Flamborough. Dad went in the inflatable to get a rope to them . . . '

'Yes. He told me — quite matter of factly. He blames nobody except himself for getting caught up in the swell and being hurled against the rocks.'

'The lifeboat is there to save life,' she pointed out. 'We all know the risks involved.'

'You don't appear to have much sympathy with those gallant men,' he said a trifle sarcastically.

'They don't ask for sympathy. They don't ask for thanks,' she retorted, her chin jutting defiantly and knowing that Dad had, at least, respected her wish for anonymity where her own work with the lifeboat was concerned, and had not told Rafe Thorne about it.

'They risk their lives,' he said. 'Your own father risked his life.'

She looked at him steadily. 'You risk your life every time you enter a race,' she pointed out.

'But I don't risk my life for somebody else. When I race, I race for me — or at least if not entirely for me, then for Oscar Herrick, my boss.' His voice was hard. 'I race for kicks. I race because it brings me a lot of money.'

'We all do what we believe in,' she said.

Fudge sat down on the wet sand with a huge sigh, as if he thought this conversation could go on all night.

'And you believe in being a dutiful daughter?'

'I suppose so. But I like working with cars.' She lifted her shoulders in a shrug. 'Dad can't do the things he used to now.'

'But it's safe, isn't it? Working for Daddy? Haven't you ever had the urge to branch out on your own and take a risk, Maggie?'

'It depends,' she said. 'Risks come in all shapes and sizes, don't they?' But she deliberately kept quiet about the rescues she'd been involved with since volunteering for the lifeboat service. Her fingers though, curled round the pager in her pocket.

'You inhabit a safe little world — working for your father,' he said.

She supposed he was right about that. And even the voluntary work with the lifeboat held no fears for her. Thrills, yes — she loved the sea; she'd been brought up with it and had a healthy respect for it, but it had never had the power to scare her . . .

She said thoughtfully, 'Yes, I suppose I do, but is that a crime?'

'But what do you do for excitement?' he wanted to know.

'I do what I'm doing right now. I take Fudge for a walk — three times a day. But what has that got to do with you?'

'Nothing.' He looked almost pityingly at

28

her. 'Nothing at all, Maggie. I just can't help thinking you're playing everything a bit too safe, though.'

These past few months, she'd thought the same thing herself, but she wasn't going to tell him that. 'It's my life,' she said.

'Maybe I'll see more of it.' His mood had lightened. He even managed a smile — of sorts.

'I don't think so . . . '

'I'll be living quite close. We might see each other sometime.'

'Close?'

'Heronsea. Five miles down the coast.' He indicated past her with one hand. 'I've bought the lighthouse there. Decided to give myself some roots to take over from the wheels when I'm ready to settle down.'

'You're going to live in a lighthouse?'

He pushed his hands into his pockets. 'Well, not exactly,' he said. 'I'm converting the old engine house for my own use. My sister Ava needed somewhere to set up a business though, so it's she who will be using the actual lighthouse.'

'How fascinating.' Maggie's interest was immediately caught. 'What kind of business is she in?'

'She designs and manufactures wedding dresses. She and Jade were partners, and things kind of fell apart after Jade died.'

He spoke, she noted, seriously and matter of factly about his former fiancée. She said quietly, 'And now, your sister is getting the business on its feet again?'

He nodded. 'Ava's been running the work room in Beverley for the past year — there were orders to fill, that sort of thing. Now though, the lease has run out for the showroom part of things, so she was looking round for something else when she saw the old lighthouse at Heronsea advertised for sale.'

'It's certainly an eye-catching place, perched on the headland as it is at Heronsea.'

'Yes,' he said. 'I saw at once that it had possibilities, and then Ava came up with the idea of calling it the 'Ivory Tower' and showing her creations off there.'

Maggie's mind was working quickly. Brand Motors needed new outlets to keep it going, and she'd had an idea. 'Is your sister there now?' she asked. 'All the time I mean — not right now this very instant?'

He lifted his shoulders in a shrug. 'When she's not in Beverley supervising the machinists, yes! Why? Are you looking for a wedding dress, Maggie?' His scrutiny of her face was guarded.

'Heck, no! Nothing like that,' she said. 'It's

just a thought I had, that's all.'

'Shall I ask Ava to give you a ring when she's over at Heronsea?'

'I'll ring her,' she said, not wanting to give anything more away at the moment, even though her mind was working overtime with a plan that was beginning to form.

'Suit yourself.'

She was saved from a reply by the sudden, urgent bleeping of the pager in her pocket, and Fudge leapt up with a frantic barking.

'I have to go,' she said quickly, knowing she had only between three and five minutes to get Fudge home, jump in her car and be down at the lifeboat station within that time.

As she spun away from him, she heard the laughter in his voice as he called out, 'What is it, Maggie? A stranded motorist calling the garage out to rescue him?'

She turned round as she raced towards the cliffs and laughed back at him. 'Something like that,' she yelled as she scrambled up the soft boulder clay with Fudge already prancing round on top of the cliffs.

'Get yourself a life, Maggie . . . '

Hauling herself up on to the grass at the top of the cliffs beside Fudge, she turned and gave him a last wave, deciding he could think what he liked of her.

It was obvious he'd placed her neatly in the category of 'dull-as-ditchwater' women he must know.

And wasn't interested in her the slightest little bit!

2

She returned home from the lifeboat station after half an hour, disappointed that she'd got there minutes too late to go out on this particular call. The dark blue boat with its bright orange painted hatches and wheelhouse was already thrusting its way through the waves when she arrived at the station. It had been called to the aid of a capsized yacht, and a further six crew members had already been allocated to winching operations on shore for when it returned.

She saw her father looking out for her from the parlour window. He waved as she came up the drive, and she heard Fudge give a short, sharp bark of welcome as she locked her little Ford Anglia classic in the double garage attached to the house, being careful to leave room for her mother's BMW when she should return from the hospital that night.

'What on earth made the great man, Thorne, come to visit?' she asked as Edgar switched the kettle on in the spacious kitchen at the back of the house some minutes later.

'He came with Silverstone tickets for me — from Oscar. Apparently Oscar had phoned the garage to speak to me last week, and Mark hadn't thought to let me know. He'd just told Oscar Herrick I wasn't working there any more.'

'So Rafe was merely the errand boy?' she asked lightly.

'Hardly that, love.' Edgar looked questioningly at his daughter. 'I suppose Oscar — realizing that Rafe had come to live nearby — thought he'd save himself a journey, or a first class stamp, that's all, though goodness only knows what made him think of me again after all these years.'

'News of your accident hadn't reached him then?'

'No.' Edgar laughed and patted the arms of his wheelchair. 'Rafe Throne got a shock when he saw me in this. But what did you think of him, Maggie?'

She forced herself to give a little shrug of complacency. 'What should I think of him, Dad? He's a racing driver. They come in much the same packages as other men.'

'Are you going to have your dinner now, lass? I've been keeping it hot since before you

34

came home from work. Hope it's not dried up.'

It would be. She knew that instinctively. Since voluntarily taking over the household duties, Dad had got most things right — all except the art of keeping food hot and still eatable.

Edgar brought the teapot over, poured out a cup for her and one for himself then put it down while she eased the plated-up meal out of the oven and took it to her place at the table.

'After that accident with his fiancée last year,' her father was saying conversationally now, 'Rafe apparently told Oscar Herrick he'd never drive again, but Herrick's a wily old bugger. Held him to his contract — even though it was his own daughter Rafe had killed.'

'Perhaps Oscar Herrick wanted to make him suffer, and driving those fast little cars round the track would certainly do that, wouldn't it?' She shivered slightly. 'It must bring it all back to him — what happened when Jade Herrick was killed.'

Edgar frowned. 'I never thought of that. One thing I do know — Herrick hates Rafe's guts, but he won't let the poor sod go. Oh, no. Rafe Thorne is Oscar's number one driver. And Oscar's got him right where he wants him. But only till the end of this year.'

'And then?' Maggie sat down, then glanced across the kitchen at Fudge, eating his dog-meal and cubed meat, and wondered if she could perhaps slip him her chicken too, without making it too obvious that she considered it inedible.

'Rafe's not sure what will happen then. He says he might go into consultancy but I can't see him taking to that. Racing's been his life.'

'And the death of that poor girl.' Maggie picked up her cup and took a deep swallow of tea. 'That's been his 'life' too — for the past twelve months, don't forget.'

'But that was purely accidental — though they never found out what really happened, except that some girls Jade had taken for a look round ran out on to the track for no known reason. The only one who didn't go was Rafe's sister, Ava. Apparently, she stood by and saw it all happen, she was the only witness, but even she didn't know why the others had done such a foolhardy thing.'

Maggie concentrated on the vegetables and rice on the plate in front of her. 'And Jade Herrick and another girl were killed. But if I remember rightly, the newspaper reported there were three girls involved in the accident. I wonder what happened to the third?'

Edgar pulled a face. 'Lord knows. She had a funny sort of name, didn't she?'

Maggie recalled the name quoted in the newspapers. 'Tamsin,' she said. 'Her name was Tamsin. And she was slightly injured, I think. It might have been concussion or something. But I never heard what became of her afterwards. You'd think if she had made a full recovery, she could have thrown some light on the reason they'd gone on to the track.'

'You have a good memory for news items.' Edgar chuckled.

'I have about most things, Dad.'

'Just as well.' Edgar grinned at her. 'You're my right-hand girl, Maggie. Without you, I'd never remember to pay the garage bills — without you I wouldn't have a garage any more.'

Instantly she felt guilty, and wondered if now was the right time to tell him she was going to look for another job. She wished he didn't depend on her quite so much. Wished too that she could confide in him more than she did. Just lately, it had been hell at the garage. But so far, she'd not told Edgar about the squabbles she had at work with Mark Langham. She'd have to though. She knew she couldn't put it off for ever.

Her concern must have showed in her face because Edgar said, 'Are you okay, love?'

'Of course I'm okay.' She washed down the last bit of indigestible chicken with the rest of her tea.

'What have you been doing at the garage today?'

'Working on the 1938 Austin Ruby. Mark did some work on the 1979 XJS Drophead Coupé we bought last week.'

He pulled a face. 'Trust Mark to go for the showy stuff and leave you with the modest little Austin.'

She laughed softly. 'I don't mind working on the little cars, Dad. It's all to the same end, isn't it?'

'I keep meaning to get down to the garage. I might have made it today except that your mam had an emergency call from the hospital just as she got home this afternoon, and right after that, Rafe Thorne turned up. Your dinner might have been more eatable if Mam had been in charge of it instead of me,' he said apologetically.

She hadn't the heart to tell him then. She pushed her chair away from the table and started to clear the things away.

'I'll come down to the garage tomorrow. I promise, love — now I've got the hang of this wheelchair — and how to stop and start it.'

'Look forward to seeing you there, Dad,' she said shortly.

'I do know what it must be like — down there without me. I know young Mark can be a bit stroppy, but you mustn't let him get away with things, Maggie. Pity he's not a chip off the old block. Johnnie, his dad, he didn't mind getting his hands dirty.'

She sighed. She was tired and all she wanted was to put her feet up and read a book before she went to bed. 'Dad — I'm whacked,' she said, yawning. 'And poor old Fudge is too. I think I'm going to go up and have a nice hot relaxing bath, and then an early night.'

'Aren't you going to wait and say hello to your mam, girl?'

'Not tonight, Dad. If you don't mind. If Mother's got a difficult birth on her hands, it could be midnight before she's home.'

'Well, you know where we are if you want us.'

'Dad.' She went over to him and gave him a kiss on the forehead. 'Dad, I'm not a little girl who's scared of the dark any more. I just need some sleep.'

'You're still *my* little girl, love.'

★   ★   ★

39

Mark Langham walked into the workshop late again as usual.

She looked up at him. 'Don't forget that we need the Aston Martin ready for the weekend.' Her voice was sharper than she'd intended it to sound, but she was getting fed up with him treating the garage like a holiday camp.

'Oh, for heaven's sake, let up will you, Maggie.' He pulled off his navy blue donkey jacket and hurled it across the bench. 'You're nothing but a damn slave-driver.'

'I've been here since eight,' she pointed out.

Mockingly he said, 'And now it's nine. So what?'

'I like to put in a full day.'

'Poor little you.' He turned his back on her, walked down to the end of the workshop and felt at the kettle. 'Stone cold,' he muttered. 'Do I have to do everything around here myself? Tea-making's a woman's job.'

She put down the spanner she'd been using and went over to him. 'Mark — we're going to have to talk. We can't go on like this.'

He merely turned his head a fraction and said in a bored tone, 'No. I don't intend 'going on like this'. No woman is going to tell me what to do.'

'We're partners, for heaven's sake . . . '

'No.' He turned right round and wagged a finger at her. '*You* are not a partner, Maggie Brand. Your father is *my* partner. *You* are merely an employee.'

'My dad can't carry out his duties as a partner. You know damn well he can't,' she stormed. 'I had to take his place here.'

'If Edgar can't do the job, then he ought to agree to us selling the place.' He stared at her, and when she didn't answer, he went on, 'Well, say something. Be honest for once in your life, my lovely Maggie. Say what you think — not what you know Edgar will think. These cars have had their day. We could sell up, take the money and run — or,' he said pointedly, 'you could marry me and we could run it together then. God knows, I've hinted at us getting together often enough.'

'Hinted!' She laughed. 'Is that what your groping is? Hinting we should get married?'

'I don't grope,' he looked down his nose at her. 'Believe me, Mags, I do not grope. If I want a girl, I go all out to get her. I know how to treat a woman.'

'I take it I don't come under the category of 'woman' then,' she taunted.

He looked her up and down. 'In those clothes? No, my sweet, you are most definitely not a woman. You are nothing. You are wasting your life on Edgar's dream. Why not settle for some dreams of your own?'

'I have my dreams,' she said. 'But they don't include you.' She picked up her spanner and started work again.

'You really do like playing hard to get, don't you?' He swished the kettle under a tap and splashed water everywhere. 'Why can't you see reason, Mags? Marriage would make sure we were both settled. When your dad goes, the garage would be ours. We could do what we liked with it then — sell it or employ somebody to do the dirty work. It would be ours though and we could split the proceeds fifty-fifty . . .'

'Whereas now, you only own twenty-five per cent.' She rounded on him. 'Is that all you see me as? Seventy-five per cent of Brand Motors?' She gave a hollow little laugh. 'And you're willing to sacrifice yourself on the altar of marriage merely to get the other seventy-five per cent of Dad's business — eventually?'

He looked uncomfortable. 'Mags, we're not kids, for heaven's sake. Neither of us is the romantic kind. It would be a good business move — you and me getting married.'

'No thank you,' she said in a stony voice. 'I am not interested in marriage.' And it was true, she knew. She had plans, yes. But they didn't include marriage — not at the moment.

He shrugged. 'Suit yourself. But think about it. Right now though, I'm going to have a cup of tea before I start work. How about you?'

Her voice was low. 'Don't you think you ought to leave that for an hour or so? I've told you — the Aston Martin must be ready for the weekend or else we'll lose the customer. He's already been nagging at you for a fortnight.'

He opened his mouth to argue with her again, but at that moment the phone started to ring. He ignored it, and Maggie dropped the spanner again and ran to the small office at the back of the workshop to answer it.

'Can you come over to the lighthouse, Maggie?'

'Rafe!' Her legs gave way and deposited her on a high stool next to the desk which was littered with grimy paperwork.

She heard him laugh softly. 'So you do know how to say my name, after all.'

'I — I'm working.'

'Yes. That's why I rang you there and not at home.'

'I can't see you right now. Anyway, what's wrong?'

'Nothing!'

She didn't have time for playing games, drily she asked, 'Do you want to buy a classic car? We have a sweet little Aston Martin that might be roadworthy by the end of the year.'

He had a deep, sexy kind of laugh. 'I don't think they'd let me take it on a race track — not with twenty-two Formula Ones flying around at a hundred and eighty miles an hour.'

Another wise guy! And she'd had as much as she could take with wise guys. 'I don't have time to play games,' she said loftily. 'I have work to do.'

'All work and no play, Maggie? You know what they say?'

'Makes Maggie a dull girl. Well, yes. That's what I am, Mr Thorne. A dull girl. A girl with no excitement in her life. A girl who never takes risks. Goodbye, Mr Thorne . . . '

'No,' he cut in. 'Don't hang up. I'm not really a time waster. I just wanted to tell you that Ava will be here this afternoon — at her Ivory Tower. She rang me earlier and told me she was coming over so I mentioned that you'd like to meet her.'

'Oh! Oh, I'm sorry . . . '

'No need to be,' he said easily.

It was business. And the garage could do with a new image — a new project just like the one she was working on, she decided. She made up her mind swiftly, 'I'll come over. This afternoon,' she said, 'if that's okay.'

'It all sounds very mysterious,' he said.

'It's not,' she said, 'It's not mysterious at all. But I don't want to discuss it. Not until I've talked to your sister.'

'I'll maybe see you around then? This afternoon?'

'Don't you have a madly exciting job you ought to be doing?' she asked, a trifle sarcastically. 'Like motor racing? With the season just starting?'

'My last season!' His voice had turned suddenly hard. 'My contract with Herrick runs out after October.'

'But you'll go to another team, surely . . . '

'At thirty-six? Maggie — a lot of people think thirty-six is ancient for a racing driver.'

'They say racing's in the blood though. A lot of older drivers . . . '

'Go to Indy cars, or consulting, or designing, or start up their own team? Is that what you're saying?'

'We-ell, yes.'

He gave a sober little laugh. 'Not me,' he said.

'Now you're the one being mysterious.'

He laughed softly but declined to answer, so she told him what time she'd be over to see Ava Thorne, then put the phone down and walked back into the workshop.

'Who was that?' Mark looked up from the guillotine where he was slicing up bits of metal.

She told him of the idea she'd had — cautiously. He had a right to know; he was a partner in Brand Motors. But Mark wasn't usually the sort who welcomed new ideas. The classic cars they worked with were merely bread and butter to him. He didn't really care a toss for them, she knew.

'I'll come with you,' he said, surprising her for once with his enthusiasm.

She didn't want him to go with her. But what could she do? 'I'm going to see Dad first and see what he thinks about it,' she said.

'Okay!' He gave her a brilliant smile. 'Go now. You could do with a couple of hours off. Have a manicure. Do something with your hair. If this idea of yours is going to take off, we'd better look as if we mean business.'

3

In the afternoon, she drove down the coast to Heronsea with Mark at her side in the little Ford Anglia she'd rescued years ago and had painstakingly restored to its original smartness.

Mark was sulking because he'd wanted to go in his own car which was a few years' old Porsche, but in the end he'd given up trying to persuade her when she'd pointed out that driving up in a classic — however small — would emphasize they meant business, and would also show Ava Thorne that the cars they restored were reliable enough to go on any public road.

'Did you remember to bring the photos of the other cars?' he asked as they neared the popular little town of Heronsea.

'Yes,' she said. 'They're on the back seat — in the leather folder. For starters, I brought pictures of Dad's beloved Corniche, the 1967 Rolls Phantom, and the 1935 Buick Sedan.'

'The Buick?' He laughed outright and with derision. 'You don't think anybody would want to turn up for their wedding in that, do you?'

'Well, I know it looks like something out of an Al Capone film, but I like it.' She glanced sideways at him as she drove along the sea front at Heronsea and the lighthouse came into view.

'You wouldn't get married in it yourself though, would you?'

'Maybe I would. If I decided to get married.'

'The guy who gets you down the aisle would need all the might of the Mafia behind him — not just the Al Capone car,' he jeered.

'We need something to bring money into the garage,' she said quietly, refusing to lose her temper with him, and knowing full well that if she really was going to leave Brand Motors, then she wanted to leave it as a thriving business and not just some run down little garage. If this deal came off, she was one step nearer her own ambition, she knew. It would put her in a better position to talk her dad round to her way of thinking.

'We're fighting a losing battle with that damned garage. If I had more say in it though . . .' He stared out through the side window.

'We need a new lathe, and a new workshop too. And if we pull this deal off, we might get both,' Maggie pointed out, hoping that Mark would take more interest in the place when she wasn't there any more. It couldn't be much fun for him, she realized, having to work with the boss's daughter.

He sighed heavily. 'Oh, heavens, Maggie, you're starting to talk like Al Capone now with sayings like that. Pull the deal off! Do you fancy yourself as a gangster's Moll, I wonder?'

'Mark — be serious. This idea of running a wedding car service in conjunction with the Ivory Tower could open new doors for us. When people see what gorgeous cars we've got . . . '

'So why haven't we done something like this before?' he asked. 'If it's such a money making venture why haven't we been doing it for years?'

'Because up to now, we haven't had a proper wedding emporium anywhere near Shorecross,' she said with as much patience as she could muster. 'People around here have relied on old Jack Benson's funeral cars for their weddings, and it's not ideal, is it?'

'Oh, I don't know. Jack tarts them up with white ribbons, and puts a white sheet over the back seats.'

'They're still recognizable as funeral cars though.'

She knew she was right. And as she parked on the sea front, she was determined to push her idea for all it was worth, with Ava Thorne.

Heronsea, being a medium sized town, had a sea wall to keep the cliff erosion at bay. It was a high concrete structure that swept up from the promenade to a peak of thirty metres or so above the headland where the lighthouse had been built almost two centuries ago. The place attracted a certain number of holidaymakers. It had a safe beach, donkeys in the summer months, and ice cream and hamburger stalls. Here the boulder clay cliffs petered away from the headland to nothing for a few miles before rising up again further down the coast towards Withernsea.

A woman came towards them from the base of the lighthouse. She looked in her early thirties, attractive with wispy brown straight hair that was blowing across her face in the stiff sea breeze. Did any woman living on this bracing north east coast ever manage to keep her hair in place, Maggie wondered? Ava Thorne was wearing huge pearl and gilt ear-rings, a sober black suit, white blouse and high heels.

'Hi,' she yelled above the booming of the

waves below them. 'You must be Maggie Brand.'

Maggie liked her. She laughed easily and readily. She had lovely manicured hands which made Maggie glad that she was wearing her leather driving gloves because her own nails had to be kept permanently short when working in the garage.

Maggie introduced Mark when they were inside the smoothly rounded building that instantly made Maggie think of being inside a baked bean can.

'Mark is my father's partner,' she said. And then she outlined briefly to Ava the reason they were there as they stood in the cavernous, empty room, with stairs curving up round one side to the floor above.

Ava's eyes lit up as Maggie produced the photographs of her father's best loved cars, the ones she'd thought would be suitable for use as wedding cars.

'I'm impressed,' she said. 'Could you leave the pictures with me? Just for a day or two?'

Maggie nodded. 'Of course. I don't expect you to jump at the idea of us cashing in on your own project without giving it some thought. If we could come to some sort of agreement though, it could benefit us both.'

'Cars are something I've never had much to do with,' Ava said. 'Up to now, I've merely concentrated on turning out dresses and accessories — that sort of thing. I can see how this idea might take off though. If I could offer a complete 'get-me-to-the-church' service — cars thrown in as well as the dresses and flowers — yes. I like it, Maggie.'

'I'll leave you to think about it, then.' Maggie was happy. It looked as if Ava was definitely receptive to the idea.

'Don't go,' Ava said, scooping the photographs up carefully and putting them away in the folder again, to place them on top of one of many large cardboard boxes that were lying around. 'Stay and have a look round my Ivory Tower.'

'I'd love to,' Maggie said, glancing enquiringly at Mark.

'It won't always look like this,' Ava cut in. 'This ground floor room will be the main showroom, and upstairs there's quite a bit of space for living accommodation.' She tilted her head back and looked at the ceiling and Maggie's eyes followed her gaze.

It wasn't the conventional hollow lighthouse with stairs spiralling round and round above your head in a dizzying way. This lighthouse had been altered and given floors. Maggie remembered it had been in use as a museum for some years now, but there had been reports in the local newspapers about it not paying its way. Heronsea was only a small seaside resort, and it wasn't everybody who wanted to climb up hundreds of stairs when they were on holiday.

'There must be a fantastic view from the top,' she said to Ava.

'There is. Would you like to see it?'

Mark groaned. 'Count me out! I went up to the top once — when it was the museum. It's not something I want to repeat, thank you very much.'

Maggie said, 'I like the name you've given the lighthouse — the Ivory Tower.'

Ava gave an expressive shrug. 'It seemed appropriate for weddings — just romantic sounding enough without going over the top.'

Mark said patronizingly, 'But I thought that was what all women wanted — romance with a capital 'R' — bags of romance to keep the little dears happy.'

Ava directed a level look at him. 'I hope you won't be talking like that to prospective customers — if I decide I like your wedding cars,' she said pointedly.

Mark, to his credit, looked a little sheepish, 'We-ell,' he said, 'Romance does play a large part in the life of any woman, surely?'

Ava said, 'Romance has its place — but that place is not in business.'

With a swagger and a direct glare at

Maggie, Mark replied, 'But any normal girl dreams of being swept off her feet by a man who can take charge, make the big decisions for her. Wasn't it the romantic Lord Byron who said, 'love is of man's life a thing apart, but 'tis woman's whole existence'?'

Ava said sweetly, 'Do you really read Byron's poetry, Mr Langham?' And then she promptly ignored him and turned her back on him so she could direct any further conversation in Maggie's direction.

Maggie saw that Mark's face had turned scarlet. She gave him a warning look which left him in no doubt that he should let the matter drop there. And, unusually for Mark, he took the hint and sauntered away, his hands thrust deep into his trouser pockets, his back ramrod straight. He'd be hell to live with for the rest of the day, she realized. Mark never liked being put in his place — and especially not by a woman.

Ava flashed her a smile. 'I think you and I shall get along well, Maggie,' she said. 'Your father obviously trusts your decisions, and my brother Rafe speaks very highly of him. They've known each other for some years, I believe.'

'Yes. Dad's interested in anything at all to do with cars — even racing cars, though he's limited now to watching them on television.'

'Well — how about that climb then — up the Ivory Tower?'

Maggie looked round for Mark but he was nowhere to be seen. The outside door was open however.

'Leave him. He'll guess where we are,' Ava said, leading the way to the staircase that Maggie had first noticed, hugging one side of the great curved wall of the building.

They climbed the first sixteen steps to the first floor. 'This is a slightly smaller room than the ground floor,' Ava explained. 'It's due to the tapering of the tower. It's here that I plan to store a lot of the dresses. Come over here — let me show you the banana bunks. First though, did you ever come here when it was a museum?'

'No,' Maggie had to admit. 'I never did.'

'Well,' Ava said, 'The borough council did a pretty thorough job of kitting this on-shore place out to look just like an off-shore lighthouse would have done in the early part of this century.' She swished aside a red cotton curtain. 'These are the banana bunks I mentioned — see? They curve round the wall of the lighthouse. The real things must have been pretty uncomfortable to sleep in. I can imagine the lighthouse men walking around bent double after a few nights in them.' She laughed. 'For my purpose though, these bunks are ideal for hanging wedding dresses in.'

Maggie drew in her breath, amazed at the sight of four curved bunks, all looking exactly as if somebody had been sleeping in them the previous night. Blankets were awry. Small shelves held personal belongings. A mug and razor, a photograph, a prayer book engraved with the words 'Heronsea Light'.

'As a museum, I suppose it was unique,' Ava said. 'But so few people came to visit it became a liability to the council. That's why it came up for sale.'

'You were lucky — knowing about it.'

'Yes. It was quite by chance I saw it advertised, and mentioned it to Rafe.'

'You should get quite a lot of dresses in here.' Maggie looked round the room, not wanting at the moment to be reminded of Rafe Thorne. He was best kept out of the conversation!

'Forty or fifty I'd reckoned on.'

'Yes,' Maggie said, making a mental note of how many dresses she thought would fit into the banana-shaped bunks. 'And I suppose the cupboards underneath could be used to store accessories — shoes, head-dresses, veils, etcetera.'

'My thoughts exactly.' Ava was obviously enthusiastic about her venture. 'But come on up the next set of stairs, let me show you the living quarters.'

Maggie followed Ava up the curved staircase to the next floor and was surprised at how much space there was as this room had been completely cleared of clutter of any kind.

Ava walked over to one of the deeply recessed windows — a replica of the ones downstairs and those on the winding staircase, except that this one had shutters across it. She called out, 'Come and look at this,' and opened the shutters to expose slatted shelves that had been built right across the window space.

'What is it?' Maggie was nonplussed as she stared at what could have been a small cupboard, had the back of it not been a plain glass window through which the bleak coast of Holderness could be seen, stretching away for miles upon miles to the north.

'In an off-shore lighthouse, this would have been used as a larder,' Ava said. 'And that's what I intend to use it for too. See these shelves — they'll be ideal for storing fruit and veg, tomatoes, potatoes, oranges and apples, it's so cool in the window recess — facing north as it does.'

'It's certainly an idea. Inventive and ingenious.' Maggie laughed. 'But,' she frowned as a sudden thought hit her, 'won't you be lonely up here? With only the sea as your neighbour?'

'I won't be alone.' Ava turned to face her. 'I have a partner in this wedding business. Her name's Tamsin. Tamsin Curtis. We've known each other ever since we both worked with Jade Herrick — you've heard of Jade?'

Maggie drew in a breath. So that's what had happened to the Tamsin who had featured in the newspaper article. Tamsin was the third girl who had run out on to the track in front of Rafe Thorne's car. She wondered again about the accident, and how it had been caused. Wondered too, if Tamsin knew the answer. Open verdicts had been recorded on the other two deaths — Jade Herrick's and her friend. She hesitated slightly before replying to Ava, then said, 'Yes, I've heard of Jade Herrick. I read about the accident in the newspapers last year. Dad and Oscar Herrick knew each other from the old days when they were at school. Since then, they've kept in touch — Christmas cards and all that mainly. But Dad has met Oscar Herrick once or twice — at Silverstone and the other circuits in this country.' She gave a small laugh. 'I often think Dad had a secret ambition — to be a racing driver, but he turned out a bit too portly to get in those little cockpits, so he had to settle for working with classic cars.'

'Jade and my brother Rafe were going to be married.' Slowly, Ava walked over to a second window, one that looked out over the town, and gazed out. 'It made it doubly hard on Rafe when Jade was killed, and it was thought at first that Tamsin had suffered brain damage when his car hit her too,' she said at last. 'Both Rafe and I knew we'd have to take care of Tammy after that.'

'But she's all right now? Your partner?' Maggie too walked across the room to stand beside Ava and look out over the streets far below them.

Ava's shoulders moved in the merest hint of a shrug. Then she turned back to Maggie, her smile wide and her eyes like two cold chips of aquamarine. 'Tam's okay.' The words were abruptly spoken, and Maggie suddenly felt as if Ava regretted bringing up the subject of the accident and didn't want to talk about it any more, when she spun away from the window and asked brightly, 'Do you think you can manage another three floors to the top of the lighthouse? And then a few more steps up to the lantern platform?'

Maggie replied, 'Just try and stop me. Do you know, I've lived on the coast all my life, but I've never ever been to the top of a lighthouse before.'

At the top, she found the view was stupendous. She just stood and stared out at the sparkling sea and took in deep breaths of the heady fresh air.

'Hang on to the rail,' Ava said. 'And don't look down if you're squeamish about heights. Also,' she added, leaning past Maggie to retrieve a key from the door they'd just gone through, 'watch that door. It slams shut behind you sometimes — that's why I always like to take the key out — so I can get back in if the wind catches it. It wouldn't do to be locked out on this little balcony in a howling gale.' She pulled a face. 'It might be exhilarating for a while, but you could freeze to death up here.'

'I don't mind heights.' Maggie stood on the metal platform and gazed out at the sea so far below her, entranced.

'You don't?' Ava's hair, loose around her shoulders, was blowing into her eyes and all but taking off into the stiff breeze whistling round the top of the tower.

'I've done a bit of rock climbing. Dad taught me how to take care of myself when I was just a teenager.'

Ava faced her. 'How does Mark Langham fit into the picture?'

'His father owned a quarter share of Brand Motors, so when Johnnie died it was only natural for Mark to come into the business with Dad.'

'I get the feeling he's not all that keen though.'

'Classic cars have never interested Mark like they do Dad, but now he's got shares in the firm, he comes into the garage.'

'How does the land lie between you and Mark, Maggie?' The question was direct and to the point.

Maggie said, 'We work together. Nothing more than that.'

'And you don't want anything more?'

'From Mark?' Maggie gave a forced little laugh. 'No, I don't want any other sort of relationship with Mark. We're opposites. Mark likes to think of himself as a go-ahead executive while I've never wanted to do anything except work with cars. I love cars and driving. Anything to do with engines, in fact.'

'You do?'

Maggie knew she oughtn't to say too much on the subject of her working with her father — not when she'd already determined to move on the minute she could find something suitable. 'Mark says I'm crazy, doing such a dirty job,' she said, laughing. 'He reckons it's no job for a woman.'

'Tell him he has no right to interfere in

your life,' Ava said.

Maggie let out a huge sigh. 'I suppose he doesn't. It would be nice though — to stand on my own two feet. Mark often seems to resent the fact that, being Dad's daughter, I have such an interest in the garage — and that Dad relies on me so much.'

'And that causes problems?'

'Yes. Sometimes.' Maggie smiled. 'Don't worry,' she said, 'one day, I shall sort my life out.'

'Would you really like to do something else?' Ava tipped her head on one side and considered her seriously.

'Maybe. One day.'

'But you don't want to tell me your secret hopes and ambitions,' Ava said in a practical voice.

'It's something I have to work out myself.'

Ava nodded understandingly. 'Tell me when you've worked it out then, will you?'

Maggie smiled. 'Yes.'

They went back down the stairs and found Mark lounging against the smooth white wall directly opposite the stairway, waiting for them to reappear. Before any of them could speak, however, there was the sound of a car drawing up outside, then a door being slammed shut, and a girl's easy laughter was heard.

'Tamsin's back. Now you can meet her,' Ava said.

Mark looked questioningly, to first one, then the other of them.

Ava explained that Tamsin was in partnership with her. 'As well as her exquisite embroidery talents, Tam has a flair for flowers,' she said.

The door burst open, ushering in a rush of cold air and two people — one a slim, vivacious girl with a mass of pale gold curly hair that was blowing wildly around her face. She was slender and small, and had wide grey eyes and petite and perfect features.

But it was the other person who followed this whirlwind into the building who held Maggie's attention.

For that person was Rafe Thorne.

And from where she was standing, it looked as if Rafe and Tamsin were very much 'a pair'!

4

'We meet again!' He made Maggie a little mock bow as he came up to her, smiling that twisted little smile at her that made her go weak at the knees.

Ava seemed to take his greeting at face value, but Tamsin whirled round to him accusingly. 'You know these people?' Her glance flew first of all to Ava, then back to Rafe again.

Ava made the introductions, but Tamsin seemed rather put out. 'I didn't know we were expecting company,' she said.

Rafe said easily, 'I knew Maggie's father from way back.'

Tamsin seemed to accept the situation then.

Conversationally, and with a meaningful glance at Maggie first, Rafe turned to Mark and said, 'I heard quite a bit about you from Edgar when I called to see him the other day.'

'All good things, I hope.' Mark beamed.

Rafe raised one eyebrow, and this time a look of amusement was shot at Maggie as he lied convincingly, 'But of course.'

Maggie felt the air was charged with a certain amount of antagonism as Tamsin sidled up to Rafe and looked at him, her eyes adoring. 'Why didn't you take Ava and me along too, when you went to see Maggie's father?'

'Edgar's an old acquaintance of mine. We had a long chat about Formula One, and classic cars. You would have been bored out of your mind, Tamsin.'

Tamsin's exquisite little chin came up in a defiant gesture. 'Did it interest you Maggie?' she asked pointedly.

Maggie felt bound to explain, 'I wasn't there. I was at work on the cars in Dad's garage. I only had time to pop in and say hello before taking my dog for his evening walk.'

'A dog!' Tamsin shuddered delicately.

Rafe's laugh rang out. 'You see, you wouldn't have liked it if you'd come with me. Fudge is a great brute of a beast.'

'I dislike dogs intensely,' Tamsin said, moving away from Rafe at last and wandering over to where Ava stood.

Rafe sauntered further into the room, his eyes questioning. 'Is anybody going to enlighten me? About this visit?' He glanced first at Ava, then at Maggie.

Ava said quietly, 'Maggie's interested in hiring out her father's cars for the weddings I organize. She and Mark have brought some photographs. We haven't got round to terms and conditions yet. I'm sure we will though, after I've talked it over with Tamsin.' She smiled brightly at Maggie. 'We never make any decisions without consulting each other. You do understand?'

Maggie nodded. 'Of course.'

Mark, for once, seemed to have nothing to say. Maggie noticed that his attention was firmly fixed on Tamsin the whole time, however. He watched her every move, his gaze darting to her face each time she spoke, his eyes all but devouring her.

Maggie decided it was time to make an exit. 'We ought to be getting back,' she said firmly, avoiding Rafe's dark glance.

Ava seemed glad to distance herself from Tamsin and walk to the door with them. 'I'll be in touch,' she promised. 'But you can take it from me, I am very, very interested in your ideas, Maggie.'

'Thank you.'

Rafe called out, 'Give my regards to your father . . .'

Mark grabbed hold of her elbow and

pushed her outside.

In the car he slid down in the seat and glowered at her. 'This car does my street-cred no good at all,' he complained.

Laughing softly at him, she said, 'I don't suppose for one minute that the gorgeous Tamsin thought my little Ford Anglia belonged to you.'

His scowl deepened. 'I should have brought the Porsche.'

'Bring it next time.' She started up the engine. Mark's Porsche might not be new, but it was his most treasured possession.

'Then she'll think I'm just doing that to impress her.'

'Well, you will be, won't you?'

He glared at her. 'Sometimes I hate you, Maggie Brand.'

She turned and laughed at him as she pulled away from the lighthouse.

★ ★ ★

A couple of weeks passed, during which time Ava signed, and was well pleased with, the contract with Brand Motors. It was now early May, and the inside of the lighthouse was clean and sparkling after being given a major facelift.

Tamsin was not in the best of moods as she

sat at Ava's kitchen table opposite her partner and asked, 'Why does your precious brother always have to be rushing off somewhere?'

Ava, making a sketch of an Elizabethan style wedding dress on an oversized drawing pad, looked up and shook her head at the girl. 'It's not just 'somewhere', Tam. It's Rafe's job. He's got a big race almost every fortnight throughout the summer, you know that, and with Monaco coming up . . . '

'I sometimes think it's just an excuse he gives us — saying he's testing those blessed cars. Surely he could spend a bit more time here with us. We hardly ever see him these days.'

'He does have to test them.' Ava was fast losing all patience with Tamsin. She pushed her drawing pad away and laid down her pencil, realizing she'd get nothing done at all this morning unless she placated Tamsin. 'How else are they going to get the things right?' she wanted to know. 'Who but the driver can tell if something's wrong with the car?'

Tamsin propped her chin on her hands at the table, 'The big Fl teams have test drivers who stand in for the real drivers, don't they?'

'Yes. But even so, the 'real' drivers as you call them, have to test the cars too. They're the ones who are going to be driving them in the big races. Oscar-Jade isn't considered all that big — not when you think of the real giants like Williams, or Ferrari, and McLaren.' Ava sighed. 'Tam, you know that Rafe thinks the world of you. He doesn't keep going away just to spite you or anything like that.'

'I miss him though — when he isn't here.' She pouted, then added — slyly, Ava thought — 'And I still keep having those bad dreams.'

'He's my brother. I miss him too.' Ava rose to her feet and pushed back her hair. She'd heard everything there was to hear about Tam's 'bad dreams', and while not wishing to be uncharitable, she didn't want reminding again of them just now. Tam's dreams were the reason the girl was here, living with her and Rafe. The dreams had started after the accident last year, and Tam had become terrified of living alone. 'Look love,' she said, 'we've got work to do if we're going to get everything ready and ship-shape for the Wedding Fayre next month.'

'We shan't have people traipsing all over *our living rooms* shall we?'

'No! The Fayre will be downstairs on the ground floor, and outside too if the weather holds good. I thought I might ask Maggie Brand to bring those cars over and you can decorate them up. What do you think of the idea?'

Tamsin's interest was caught. 'I'll enjoy doing that — providing I can use real flowers.'

Ava smiled. 'You know I wouldn't use anything else for one of my weddings.'

'That sinister black Buick they left the photo of would look really great with delicate arrangements inside — clusters of pansies on the back of the seats! It's such a masculine type of car, pansies would soften it up — and gypsophila too . . . ' Tamsin tapped a finger to her lips, and her eyes held a far-away expression.

Ava leaned against the table. 'You love them, don't you?'

'Flowers?' Tamsin's gaze flew up to meet hers. 'Yes. I do. And they seem to love me too, because I can do almost anything with them. Flowers never let you down, do they? You know just where you stand with them. And when they don't please you any longer, you just chuck them away.'

'Ouch!' Ava laughed. 'That's a hard thing to say.'

'It's a pity we can't do the same with people.' Tamsin got up from the table and caught at Ava's hand, laughing too. 'Oh, come on, let's go downstairs and start making plans

70

then, shall we? And then I'll help you distribute those posters advertising the Fayre all over town if it'll make you happy.'

Tamsin, for the moment had forgotten about Rafe, and Ava was glad because she'd seen how Tam had been trying to wheedle herself into his affections just lately. And it wasn't fair — Rafe had his career to think about, and it wouldn't do him any good having a clingy, dependent girl hanging on to him.

As they reached the bottom of the stairs, Ava stopped for a moment and looked round the showroom. She breathed in a deep sigh of contentment. 'It really is something, isn't it?'

And it was. She was pleased with the conversion. Wedding dresses were discreetly hidden behind dustproof dark curtains round one half of the circular room. The colour scheme was just right, she decided, bracken-brown velvet hangings, with upholstered gilt chairs to match. The inside walls of the lighthouse had been painted a warm cream, the effect being to make it softer, more intimate than the stark white outer shell of the 'Ivory Tower'. A single glass chandelier with gold hangings illuminated the room with five-hundred-candle-power electric lighting. Gold-leaf had been used to outline the panelling on the cream coloured doors, and gold, too, edged the full-length mirrors that were positioned around the room where the light would give fullest advantage.

She went down the last step on to thick carpeting that was a blended echo of each one of the colours — cream, gold, and darkest brown — and then she saw the flowers, a flamboyant arrangement of gold, flame and white on the circular oak table against the door.

Tamsin said softly, 'Do you like them? I thought they'd look nice for customers coming in the door.'

Ava turned, placed an arm around Tamsin's shoulders and hugged the girl. Sometimes, just when you were at the end of your tether with her, Tam could do the nicest things. 'They are . . . ' her voice broke off on a sob and she stepped away from Tamsin and brushed her hand across her eyes. 'Oh, Tam,' she sniffed, 'It's just so perfect, isn't it? And it's all ours. We can't fail to make a go of it, can we?'

'We'll do our damnedest to make it work. Everybody knows we're open for business now.' Tam pulled a face at her friend. 'It might help though if you don't dissolve into tears when our first customer walks through the door, huh?'

'I'm an idiot, aren't I?'

'Yes, partner, you are. You should be more like me — tough! Weddings mean money in the bank for us, and don't you forget it. Why, even the flowers have been specially designed to lure the poor, unwary, scared little bride into our sanctum and make her want to spend, spend, spend.'

'The flowers?' Ava glanced across the room again.

'White carnations for purity — a woman's love. Flame-red for the heart. Big gold daisies for innocence. Who could resist buying a frock from us.'

Ava gave a shaky laugh. 'And there was me thinking you'd taken the whole colour scheme into account, and the flowers were just . . . well flowers, to brighten the place up.'

Tamsin walked solemnly into the centre of the room, spread out her arms and did a little twirl. 'It all has to say something though. And flowers have a language all their own.'

'Purity, innocence and love. Yes, I see what you mean. First they see the flowers, then the . . . '

' . . . the simplicity of the place,' Tamsin said nodding. 'The clear, uncluttered smooth round lines of the walls. And hopefully, by then they'll be hooked! They think this is a nice place to be. It's classy so they won't get ripped off.' Tamsin spluttered with helpless laughter. 'They don't really notice the gold-leaf on the chairs, the doors and the chandelier until they've parted with their cash.'

'You minx. Are you utterly heartless?' Ava followed her across the room and leaned against the glass topped counter where veils and head-dresses of purest white peeped out.

'It's business. Just business. Just like a fish and chip shop,' Tamsin replied flippantly. 'You expect the best when you buy fish. You don't want something old and smelly. And girls coming here will want the best — the best of everything for their big day. Poor fools.'

'Oh, Tam!'

'Oh, Tam!' Tamsin mimicked. 'Oh, come off it, Ava. We're offering a service for which we expect to be paid — handsomely. That's what all these trappings are about. We've got to make a living. And there's no sentiment allowed.'

'It is lovely though.' Ava let her gaze roam round the room again.

'Paint! Fabric!' Tamsin shrugged. 'You're a good designer. Just pull back those hangings and look at the dresses that have come out of your imagination. We, dear child, have spent good money having those designs made up in our very own workrooms. Now it's our turn to make a profit. Okay?'

'I'll try to look at it your way.' Ava grimaced. 'I tend to get all dewy-eyed though at weddings.'

'You're in the wrong job then,' Tamsin said. Then her voice altered to a wheedling note. 'On another subject though — why don't we give ourselves a couple of days off before we really get into this too deeply? We've earned a break.'

Ava's laugh was sharp. 'We've only just opened up, for heaven's sake, love. Why would we want to take time off?'

'It's May! And you know what happens in May, don't you?' Tamsin stared down at the head-dresses arrayed inside the glass counter, then turned to say abruptly, 'Monaco!' and her eyes danced and her face took on an animated expression. 'We could go to Monaco, and watch Rafe drive in the Grand Prix.'

Ava almost choked. 'You are quite mad,' she said. 'We'd never get accommodation or seats or anything at such short notice — and anyway — we've got a Wedding Fayre to arrange.'

'It's all arranged though, isn't it? And it's not happening until June.' Tamsin sighed. 'Oh, come on, Ava. You know you'd enjoy it.'

'I can't. You know it's impossible.'

'I know nothing of the sort.' Tamsin's face darkened. 'You never want to go and watch Rafe in a race. And it's not fair . . . '

'You go if you want to.' Ava turned away from the pleading eyes, the agitated wrangling of the girl. Watching Rafe tearing round a race track wasn't her idea of fun. She hadn't been near the tracks since the day of the accident — more than a year ago now — and she knew Rafe didn't want her, or anybody else who was close to him, getting involved with Formula One racing.

'We never go *anywhere* exciting. It's getting so it's all work. And sometimes I can't stand it. You know what I'm like if I get over-tired — those dreams start up again — all blood and mangled bodies . . . ' she shivered visibly, 'and that car coming at me like it did . . . '

Ava's mouth had gone dry. Did the girl have to describe it all so graphically, she wondered. Was Tamsin perhaps revelling a bit too much in recalling the accident in such detail. Putting on her most practical voice, Ava said, 'We do have a living to earn.' And though she realized she was sounding like a real old killjoy, she knew that what she said was true. It was time they started picking up the pieces of Jade Herrick's broken empire. Jade wasn't there any more, but the workforce was and those girls who made up the dresses needed their jobs. That was why Ava had tried to salvage what was left of Jade's company. That was why she was still designing, and those girls in Beverley still had jobs, cutting and machining wedding dresses. Some good had to come out of this sorry mess! Ava knew she'd never cope otherwise.

'You're just being a spoilsport . . . '

She rounded on Tamsin. 'No, I'm not. But just remember Tam, we're not only responsible for the mortgage on this place, we also have the workrooms and the wages of the machinists to pay — back in our old home town of Beverley.'

Tam sighed again. 'Rafe bought the lighthouse. We didn't.'

'But we agreed to pay our way. The building was taken out in my name as well as Rafe's, you know that.'

'Rafe wouldn't hold you to it. He paid for it outright. He could afford to do that. And you *are* his sister, for heaven's sake. Anyway, big brothers like to look after their sisters, don't they?'

Ava turned away uneasily. 'I don't like looking at it that way. I intend paying Rafe back for our share in the place. I can't let him support us. We have to be self-supporting. The wedding dresses have got to earn enough for us to keep the girls at Beverley in work and enable us to carry on here.'

'You're much too independent for your own good.' Tamsin scowled at her. 'Look at you — you've got it all made — a brother who adores you — who goes all out to buy this place for you — and here you are, making excuses not to spare him two days out of your life, to watch him race — maybe even to win the Monaco Grand Prix.'

'You know I hate anything to do with racing cars.'

'Just because of the accident.' Tamsin threw her hands in the air. 'It's time to let bygones be bygones, and start afresh. You weren't even injured. You didn't get a scratch. If anybody ought to be scared of racing cars it should be me. I, at least, came out of it as a victim.'

'You shouldn't have been on the track . . . ' The words were out and nothing could bring them back. Instantly, Ava bit them off and cursed herself for ever uttering them.

Slowly, Tamsin lifted her head to stare at the other girl. 'That's a rotten thing to say. I only went on to the track to try and save Sue. She'd dashed out in an effort to knock Jade out of the way of the car. You know damn well what happened.'

Ava shook her head, bewildered at the way the conversation had turned. 'I'm sorry,' she heard herself mutter. 'I'm sorry, Tam. But I don't *know damn well what happened*. I'd glanced away — just for a moment. I told them at the inquest that I never saw a thing — not until you were all out there on the track and Rafe's car was thundering towards you . . . '

'It was an accident, for heaven's sake . . . ' Tears were glittering in Tamsin's eyes now. 'You know it was an accident,' she stated with vehemence. 'You could have told them it was an accident, but you were too stubborn . . . '

'But I didn't know what happened.' Ava held out one hand in a pleading gesture. 'I couldn't lie, Tam. Not at the enquiry into my partner's death. I've told you a hundred times . . . I'd just glanced away, and when I turned back, you were all out there on the track.' Ava too was now biting back the tears.

'So you didn't see who tossed Jade's scarf on to the track? You really didn't see who did it?' Tam said warily.

'Of course I didn't. Look — I've gone over and over this in my mind, and the only conclusion I can come to is that a sudden gust of wind must have whipped the scarf from under Jade's collar and blown it towards Rafe's car.'

The silence that ensued was suddenly broken by the soft burring of the telephone on the glass topped counter. Tamsin, being the nearest to it, picked it up, and her face broke into a wide smile.

'Rafe!'

Ava dashed a quick hand across her eyes, fixed a smile on her own lips and reached out her hand for the phone. Tamsin backed away, holding up one hand as she spoke to Rafe. 'Yes. She's here. Just one thing though, Rafe, before I hand you over . . . I've got a favour to ask.' Tamsin flashed a defiant glance at Ava.

Ava whispered softly, 'No. Oh, no . . . '

But Tamsin was speaking into the phone again, and there was the light of battle in her eyes. 'We want to come to Monaco . . . yes . . . that's right . . . both of us . . . can you arrange it?'

5

'We can't afford another fiasco like Imola in Italy.' Rafe was standing looking down at the computer screen in the Oscar-Jade garage. Behind him, a Formula One car screamed down the pit lane to where its own mechanics and engineers were waiting to jack it up, strip it down and, like Rafe and Oscar Herrick were doing now, check the telemetry.

Oscar Herrick — never a man to hold inquests over what couldn't be helped, said, 'Well, we went out in a cloud of smoke — if not a blaze of glory in Italy, but nobody's blaming you, Rafe, lad. It was that blessed engine at fault again — that and the downforce.'

Rafe balanced the green helmet with the white 'T' for Thorne emblazoned on it in his hands, and glanced back at the car. 'All the same, I want to do a lot more testing on the engine before we take it to Monaco, Oscar.'

'My words exactly.' Oscar turned aside

from the screens where zig-zag lines and complicated looking graphs were on show, to say to his number one driver, 'But let up a bit, will you. It's looking good now.'

'But is it good enough?' Rafe was still studying the screens, and another car rushed past the open door of the garage at 75 miles an hour to be checked by its team manager.

The engineers were working on Rafe's own car. It was barely recognizable as a car at the moment though. The instant it had been hauled into the garage by the mechanics it had been swooped on, jacked up, its nose unscrewed, its back cowling taken off and placed on stands just outside the garage door. The carbon-fibre shell of the car was being polished now, while the engine was being fine-turned, the drive shaft examined and the tyres changed. The garage had the appearance of an out-of-this-world operating theatre where the only doctors present were technicians whose prime job was to remove organs and transplant others, giving a boost here, a new wing there, an oil seal replaced and minute adjustments made to moving parts. Everything was aseptic and clean. There were no oil splashes, no dirty hands or uniforms. When the car eventually went out on test again, there would be an all male army of what amounted to scrub-nurses with sweeping brushes removing all trace of it ever having been there. Its discarded, worn and gritty racing slick-tyres would be silently wheeled away to be piled high on top of each other in front of the mass of gleaming transporters and buses lined up like a defending army outside the long range of pit garages.

Oscar walked outside and Rafe followed him to lean on a pile of scrubbed slicks. Oscar perched on one of the steps leading up into the nearest transporter emblazoned with the green and white swirling colours of Oscar-Jade, and the names of their sponsors.

'Did you notice any drift on that last bend?'

Rafe nodded. 'It's still too light on the back end.'

Oscar looked up at him. 'A different kind of wing, do you think?'

'Is there time? To design something new. We've tried most things in the past, yet still we can't fathom that lightness.'

'I'll get Ian on to it.' Oscar glanced at his watch. 'He'll be back this afternoon, I should think — it can't take that long for your wife to give birth to twins, can it?'

'You're the expert in that department,' Rafe said in a deliberate way.

Herrick's eyes grew hard. 'No need to rub it in, but you know as well as I do that both my kids are dead.'

'Not both, Oscar. Only the one. Jade.'

Herrick swung his greying head aside for a moment, and just for that split second, Rafe felt compassion for the man. It had been hard for Oscar, losing his only daughter. But he still had a son, even if he did have to be constantly reminded of that fact.

When Herrick made no reply, Rafe said softly, 'Why not make it up with Vaughn, Oscar? You're hurting like hell, and all it takes is for you to . . . '

'Apologize?' Herrick swung round to him again. 'Will you get it into your thick head, Thorne, that I've got nothing to apologize for?'

'Does it matter after all these years who makes the first move — you or Vaughn? Wouldn't it be better to bury the hatchet rather than sharpen it at every opportunity?'

'He made his choice.' Oscar set his jaw in a firm uncompromising line. 'He could have driven for me — given time. But he was too impatient to wait till he had more experience. You know what the youngsters are like these days — they want it all, and they want it now! He was like that. Impatient. Couldn't bear to take 'no' for an answer.'

'He! You never mention him by name.'

'I've forgotten his name,' Herrick leered.

'You're a stubborn old fool.'

'And you're talking out of turn, Thorne,' Herrick blazed with sudden passion flaring in his eyes. 'You never had a son,' he went on, 'and I sure as hell hope that if ever you do have one, he doesn't turn out to be an ungrateful, pig-headed sod like Vaughn Herrick did. There! Does that suit you? I've mentioned his name — and it must be the first time in years I've done that. Are you satisfied, man?'

'No,' Rafe had to smile at the indignation in Oscar's face. 'No — I won't be satisfied till you've made your peace with Vaughn, but,' he laughed softly, 'it's a start, isn't it? Getting that name rolling off your tongue again. I bet it leaves a bitter taste in your mouth to do it though.'

Oscar flapped his hand up and down. 'A-ah, get away with you. You make it sound like a major milestone, and it's not that at all. I haven't got it in me to forgive — as you should well know. Vaughn left me of his own free will. He said he never wanted to see me again. He was nineteen, for heaven's sake. What father wants to hear a kid of that age slamming into him like that?'

'He only wanted you to give him a chance,

Oscar.' Rafe was serious now.

'He was too young.' Oscar flung away and strode out of the garage. Rafe tried to catch up with him as he dodged round the raggle-taggle of motor-homes, transporters, bits of cars, and spectators milling around at the back of the long line of garages of the pit lane.

'Oscar!'

'What now? Look, Thorne, if you're thinking of putting any more of my world to rights, just back off, will you. If you're thinking of having egg and chips with me at the Pit-stop Diner however, that's another matter altogether. You're welcome to join me.'

'You wouldn't let me have egg and chips if I went down on my knees to you,' Rafe said, rocking with laughter.

'Okay! I'll have the chips, you can have the Nell Gwynne special — chicken breast followed by a couple of oranges. Just keep that weight stable till the end of the year, huh? Then, if you're still intent on retiring, you can have all the chips you want.'

Over lunch, Rafe wondered how to bring up the subject of Oscar's son again, but the opportunity seemed to have been lost now, and he was fast despairing of ever healing the rift between the old man and Vaughn. They were two volatile people, he realized, but he hated seeing a life being wasted, and that's what Vaughn was doing right now. Tom Blanchard's team would never be up to Oscar-Jade standard. He knew that, and Oscar knew that. Vaughn Herrick knew it too, but Vaughn was too proud to admit it.

In the end, just as he was peeling the second of his two oranges, Rafe jerked up his head as Oscar, across the table from him, said, 'Would he come back, do you think?'

'Vaughn?' Carefully, Rafe pulled off the last remaining bit of orange peel, held it suspended between finger and thumb and looked at Herrick.

'Who else, you dunderhead.' Oscar was fretful and snappish. He'd rushed his meal, wolfed it down as if he hadn't eaten in an age, but his mind had been elsewhere all the time they'd been in the Pit-stop Diner, Rafe could tell.

'He'd need some careful handling.' Rafe said at last. 'Not your usual bull in a china shop approach.'

'A prima-donna — that's what Blanchard's made of him.'

'Tom Blanchard won't want to lose him. It's one in the eye for you each year Vaughn stays with his team. You know damn well you and he have always been arch enemies, Oscar.'

'I'd like my lad back though. I'm not getting any younger.' Oscar wagged his fork across the table. 'Don't you tell anybody I said that though. Pit-stop Diner revelations are strictly off the record. Understand?'

It was a start, and Rafe felt himself grinning. 'I expect it's the indigestion talking,' he said softly. 'But you can depend on me, Oscar.'

⋆ ⋆ ⋆

'Monaco!' Tamsin squealed, waving the letter in the air as she rushed down the lighthouse stairs and into the showroom. 'Ava — look! Air tickets to Nice, then a car to Monte Carlo, and rooms at a top hotel.' She slapped the letter, envelope and tickets down on the counter in front of Ava, and Ava felt as if a huge cloud had just descended on her.

'He — he didn't do this, did he? I never thought he'd be able to find anywhere for us to stay in Monaco at such short notice . . . '

'Well — you might sound more pleased about it.' Tamsin's fingers gripped the edge of the glass counter. She let go of it just to shove all the paperwork she'd received in that morning's post across the top of it towards Ava. 'Read it. There's a note from Rafe. And the air tickets and . . . '

'Yes. I think I get the picture.' Ava scooped up a pile of white tissue paper and pearl beading and deposited it on a shelf under the counter. Then she gave her attention to Tamsin. 'Tam — is this really a good idea, do you think? Won't it bring back all those awful memories watching Rafe race round a track again . . . ?'

'No. Monaco doesn't have a proper race track. They race the cars in the streets. It won't be at all like it was when Jade . . . ' she swallowed a little before concluding, 'when Jade was killed at the test circuit.'

'I know, love, but . . . '

Tamsin pleaded, 'Oh, don't go and make a fuss, darling. Please, *please*, let's just go and enjoy ourselves. Look, you don't even have to watch the race if you don't want to. You could go shopping, or sightseeing. There are plenty of places you could get away to. Places like Menton — where you could stroll along the Soleil and imagine you were a gentle English maiden of the late 1800s, or else take a ride over the Grande Corniche . . . '

'Hey! Steady on.' Ava held up one hand to ward off the barrage of enthusiasm. 'Just let me read Rafe's letter, will you?'

'He says he won't be able to see much of us.' Tamsin frowned. 'They have practice runs on the Thursday, and a 'qualifying' day on

Saturday when they find out whose time is the fastest and decide on starting points on the grid for each driver and car.'

Ava sorted through the various papers and odds and ends of literature Rafe had sent Tamsin — hotel and restaurant brochures, a map of Monte Carlo, another of the surrounding hill country. It all looked exciting and despite her fears, she began to feel just a little bit keyed-up about it herself.

'It will be marvellous. It's making my spine tingle already.' Tamsin could hardly keep still. 'Aren't you just the teeniest bit looking forward to it?' she asked when Ava eventually stacked all the bits and pieces together and slipped them back inside the envelope.

'I suppose we do need a bit of a break — after all the work we've put in on this place.' Ava let her gaze wander round the interior of the 'Ivory Tower', but had to admit to herself that this gave her the greatest buzz of all time — knowing that at last she was her own boss, and there was so much in life to look forward to again.

'Of course we need a break. If I had my way, we'd spend a month on the Riviera.' It was settled, it seemed, as far as Tamsin was concerned, and Ava had to admit that after the trouble Rafe must have gone to in order to get them accommodation, it was the least she could do — to be pleased about it.

Although she'd travelled extensively, she had never been to Monte Carlo before, and, she decided, it would give her the chance to see what was in fashion at the moment at the most expensive place of all on the Cote d' Azur. Having had no real holiday for the last twelve months, it really was time she went out into the world again.

She gave a little breathless laugh. 'I must remember to pack my sketch pad,' she said. 'If nothing else — I can always sit in the sun and people-watch. That should ensure I bring home a few inspiring ideas — fashionwise — shouldn't it?'

6

If it had wheels, it had a number on it. If it had feet, its eagle eyes were busy hunting out a bargain. Mobile phones were a must, jeans and T-shirts optional, yet still they remained the universal uniform of the classic car enthusiast.

The bidding was hotting up, though it had been a slow start. Rain had bucketed down on the Lincolnshire fens since early morning. Obviously nobody had told the weather that this was one of the most important days of the year!

Now though, the sun was shining, and for May, it was warm. 'It's going to be hot as hell driving back up to Yorkshire,' Mark Langham grumbled, but Maggie only laughed at him, grabbed hold of his hand and made him hurry with her towards the auction room again.

'I've decided we must have the little Hornet,' she said, 'and the two seater

Sunbeam Tiger sport that has a full history — invoices, bills and old MOTs.'

'And the E-type Jag?' he asked as they reached the hangar doors.

'If it's the right price, and you've checked it out, maybe,' she agreed.

'That goes for all of them,' he said loftily. 'By the way, did Edgar give you a limit? Or is it left to me?'

'We have six-thousand to play with,' she said. 'Not a penny more.'

He gave a sulky laugh. 'And Edgar wants four or five cars taking back — for a measly six thou?'

'They don't have to be in mint condition,' she argued, facing him and letting go of his hand. 'We do expect to have to work on them to get them up to saleable standard.'

'At the price you want them for they probably won't even have engines,' he snapped.

'Oh, don't be so sour,' she pleaded, determined that he wasn't going to spoil the day for her. 'Come on — let your hair down and enjoy yourself.'

'Enjoy myself! While you hold the purse strings. Is that it?'

She shoved her hands into the pockets of her jeans and shrugged. 'If you feel like that, why don't you do the bidding. Dad's made it so I can sign cheques for him, but if you're so insecure about me making a decision, go ahead. Do it yourself — you're a partner, you can be the second signatory instead of me.' One hand shot out of her pocket, holding a chequebook. 'Here!' She thrust it into his hand. 'Go and get on with it. You don't mind if I just stand by and watch, do you?'

'Aw, Maggie. Don't be like that . . . '

She'd pushed her hand back into her jeans pocket. She swung away from him then and went into the auction room. It was crowded inside and the auctioneer's voice was booming out over the loudspeakers, echoing hollowly round the place which had once, in its prime, been an aircraft hangar.

She pushed her way to a spot near the front, then took out from where she'd had it tucked under her arm, the catalogue listing the cars for sale that day. It was as she stood reading it, and mentally marking off where the selling had got to on it, that Mark came and stood beside her.

'I'm sorry,' he said in a stilted, stiff voice.

She held up the catalogue. 'Here,' she said. 'Have it. You'd better mark the ones you're interested in.'

'Look Maggie — Edgar said I'd got to let you have some say in this . . . '

Inwardly, she was seething. It couldn't go

on, she realized, this hate-hate relationship — for that was what it amounted to. Mark resented her being Edgar Brand's daughter, resented too, the fact that Edgar trusted her judgement. Mark was never going to accept her. She bit back the angry words she could have spat at him, and said in a perfectly calm voice instead. 'It was a mistake — us coming here. If you don't want to get the cars Dad asked us to bid for, let's call it a day and go home.'

'Oh, yes!' he came back at her. 'And then what? Edgar will hit the roof if we go back empty handed. He's got customers asking for . . . '

'A Wolseley Hornet — and a Sunbeam Tiger, both of which I've given a thorough going over. I've checked bonnet and boot, quality of oil in the sump, pressure gauge and . . . ' She turned away from him, and fixed her gaze on the auctioneer. What was the use of trying to explain things to Mark? He had his own fixed ideas on what would sell and what wouldn't. In truth though, she had the feeling he couldn't care less about what happened to her father's business. And while he felt like that, she knew she couldn't leave Edgar in the lurch.

'Okay! We go for the two of them then.'

She refused to be drawn any further, and

declined to answer him.

'Well, say something,' he spluttered. 'For heaven's sake — they're bringing the Hornet in now — it'll only be another five minutes before it's going under the hammer.'

She turned slowly and smiled up at him. 'I'm going for a cup of tea,' she said. 'I'll see you later, Mark. Do just as you please.'

'Hell, no. You can't do this. I don't know how much to bid. I can't be expected to guess at Edgar's profit margins, can I?'

'Maybe you should spare the time to go through the books with Dad and me sometime,' she said. 'Bye, Mark. You'll find me in the canteen when you're ready to go home.'

She pushed past him and stalked out of the hanger, taking in a huge gulp of clean fresh air when she got outside again. Inside it had been hot and airless, the whole place choked with the fumes from revving up engines. She was glad to be away from it all. When Dad had been able to come, it had been different. Now though, it was a chore — as was every day she had to spend with Mark. Dad would be disappointed, she thought guiltily, especially if they went back to Shorecross empty handed, but there'd be other auctions, other days. And somehow, come hell or high water, she was determined that next time they'd bring Dad along with them — wheelchair or no wheelchair.

She sat and waited for Mark in the canteen, sipping scalding hot tea and listening to the far-off drone of the auctioneer's voice as she searched her mind for a solution to the problem she was facing every day now. It just wasn't working — her and Mark together in the garage. And sadly, she came to the conclusion that Dad would have to be told just how things stood. She hated the thought of letting him down, but Edgar needed a man at the garage to do the heavy jobs. Thinking back to when her father had been an able and working partner, she recalled that he and Mark had got along famously together. It was only after the accident at sea, that the trouble had started — and that, she told herself firmly, was when she and Mark had been thrown together. She wondered if she'd become too bossy. But no. She shook her head. It wasn't that. It was Mark's whole attitude towards her. Even when Edgar Brand had been there, Mark had expected her to fetch and carry for him. 'Pass me the spanner, Maggie,' — 'Put the kettle on, Mags,' — 'We need some parts picking up from Appleby's — be a good girl and pop over there in the van, Maggie.'

And to keep the peace, she'd done his

bidding. But now — now that they were one man short — she couldn't just be the fetch-and-carryer. Now, she had to pull her weight, and do the jobs her father used to do.

She looked up and Mark was there, staring down at her. 'I hope you enjoyed your cups of tea,' he said pointedly, almost making an issue of looking at the three polystyrene beakers in front of her.

She resolved not to lose her temper. 'Yes, thank you,' she said.

'We lost the cars.' He threw up his hands. 'I didn't feel justified in going over the thousand mark for any of them.'

She shrugged. 'It was your decision, Mark.'

'I got the Jaguar, though.'

'Yes,' she said in a tired voice, pushing her chair back and getting to her feet. 'Yes! Somehow I thought you would.'

★ ★ ★

Edgar was mildly disappointed. 'Maggie, love. What went wrong? Were the prices too high?'

The journey back home had been disastrous. Mark had been surly and ill at ease. 'You'll tell Edgar it wasn't my fault, won't you? He can't blame me . . . '

It had been no good telling him to come and see Edgar and explain for himself why they had come back with another Jaguar, and none of the cars Edgar himself had wanted. Mark said he just didn't have either the time or the inclination to do that.

So, it was left to Maggie.

'Dad!' She flopped down into the kitchen rocking chair beside the Aga, 'Dad — I just don't know what happened. I can't get on with Mark. We argued, and I left him in the auction room by himself.'

'You can't get on with him?' Edgar whirled his wheelchair into the middle of the tiled floor and fixed her with his stare. 'Maggie! He's all we've got between us and starvation. You'll *have* to get on with him.'

She sat forward in the chair, balancing it at a point where it couldn't rock any more. She clasped her hands between her knees, 'I've tried and tried,' she stated. 'But I'm a woman, Dad, and that means, in Mark-language, that I don't count for much.'

'Well, love, I know he can be a bit of a bore, but . . . '

'Dad,' she broke in impatiently, 'You have no idea what I have to put up with. He's late every morning and he goes early every night. In between those times, he goads me every minute he's around . . . '

'Goads you?' Edgar's keen eyes narrowed. 'What do you mean by that, girl. Goads you

. . . he doesn't harass you — you know what I mean, lass — he doesn't try any hanky-panky does he?'

Maggie had to smile to herself. Hanky-panky, in Edgar's eyes, meant sex, but what did it matter about a few pinched bottoms, a few crude remarks about certain parts of her anatomy. And she'd managed to put a stop to Mark's semi-amorous approaches — once with a slap, and another time with a well aimed knee. She thought he'd finally got the message after that — until the niggling and the wrangling had started — the hints he'd thrown out that she wasn't capable of doing a man's job, that she didn't have the proper mentality to even work alongside a man because she couldn't make or take jokes with a sexual or smutty undertone.

'Dad, I can take care of myself in that department,' she said. 'It's the other stuff that worries me — Mark's timekeeping, and the everlasting innuendoes about me only being your daughter, so I have no rights whatever in the workshop.'

'But you're there in my place, love. Mark knows that.'

'Maybe he does know it. But he can't accept it, Dad.' She shook her head and her fair hair cascaded around her face. She pushed it back with an impatient hand. 'Dad

— I don't want to let you down, but I'm really beginning to feel you should employ somebody else and let me go.'

'Let you go?' Edgar stared at her astounded. 'Mags, love, what are you saying. You were born to work with cars. You love cars . . . you're a first class mechanic and you know it.'

She stood up and stretched. 'Dad, I agree with you. I do love cars, and that's why I have to say this to you.' She took a deep breath and plunged in. 'Dad — I want something more. I want you to think about getting another mechanic in to replace me — a man this time — somebody Mark can respect and work with.'

Edgar looked stricken. 'I — I had no idea you felt like this, Mags.'

She'd started now so she knew she would have to tell him everything. 'Dad — I want you to understand — more than anything I want you to understand that I'm not turning my back on you or Brand Motors. I'll do anything I can to help — but not in the garage. I can do the book-keeping, type the invoices, that sort of thing, but . . . '

'But,' Edgar said in a tense voice, 'You want to go and work for somebody else? Is that it?'

Slowly she shook her head. 'I don't know,

Dad. I honestly don't know what I want. I just need time to think things out.'

He frowned and looked closely at her.

She forced a smile. 'Don't look like that,' she said. 'I haven't taken leave of my senses.'

'Talk to your mam,' her father suggested kindly as she slipped the chain on Fudge. 'Yes, that's it. Talk to her. She might be able to suggest some of those women's pills.' He looked a bit embarrassed, and went on hurriedly, 'You know — those that get your hormones back in working order so you know what's what.'

'Dad, my hormones are in good working order. I don't need pills. I need to be my own person.'

'Then what's all this nonsense about, love?' Edgar fondled Fudge's big brown head as the dog nuzzled up to his wheelchair.

'It's not something that's going to go away.' She let go of Fudge, walked over to the window and looked out at the garden, then turned round to face him again. 'Dad, your business will suffer if I don't get out. Mark is so dead-set against me being there that we're falling behind with orders — you know we are.'

He chewed absently on one side of his mouth, thought about her words for a few moments then said, 'You're right. I know you're right, love. There have been complaints about jobs not done — cars not ready on time. I'll see what I can do.'

★   ★   ★

The late evening sun sent shadows slanting down towards the water's edge. Fudge rolled and tumbled in the clean soft sand, sneezing and sending up showers of it as he dug frantically for dog-treasure — rotting fish, seaweed, or the unexpected unearthing of a seashell which he would toss into the air, then chase after as it came back down to earth with a thud.

Maggie laughed as he skidded in the wet sand where waves were breaking gently and almost lapping at her feet. It was only here that she could relax. She loved the sea and the sand — every bit of this bleak and desolate coastline in fact. It put things into perspective, watching those great rolling waves out there in the ocean. It brought a sense of tranquillity to her mind, and made her wonder if she'd been perhaps making too much of things at the garage just lately. It didn't make any difference to her plans though. She'd thought of nothing else for months — but what she was going to do when she left Brand Motors, she just didn't know. It was a big step she was contemplating, and there were a lot of things to be weighed up. But she had made the first move. The only work she was familiar with was cars and engines, so somehow, it seemed idiotic to give it all up. For some time now though she had been worried about Mark's attitude to herself and to his work. After Edgar's accident Mark had resented working with a woman who knew more than he did about the cars, and now it was affecting his relationship with customers. A couldn't-careless attitude was bad for business. And Mark had already fouled up on more than one deal.

'Oh, forget the cars,' she told herself. 'Enjoy your walk with Fudge.' Fudge never argued. Dog's didn't. Dogs accepted you — warts and all — as her dad would say. And surely something would present itself. She made a resolution to scour the situations vacant columns in the local papers, meanwhile she stood looking out to sea. Alone. This was peace. This was utter bliss.

Fudge set up a furious barking. She looked up.

He came racing back to her. 'It's only somebody out for a jog,' she told him. 'You don't own the beach, you know.'

The figure came nearer, running from the south, too far away for her to see his features clearly. He was dressed in black jog pants, black sweatshirt and white shoes. He had hair that was a bit too long to be fashionable . . .

She couldn't drag her eyes away. She recognized who it was now. He was gorgeous. She'd loved him in his white fireproof driving suit all those years ago. It was a dream she'd cherished. Now he was here again, and she marvelled at the wide shoulders that she knew he must have to cramp up like mad to get inside the cockpit of that fast little car he raced. He came up to her, not a bit out of breath.

'You must be in peak condition,' she said. 'I'd be gasping by now if I'd run all the way from Heronsea.'

'I didn't run all the way,' he said. 'I walked some of it.'

He raked both his hands through his thick dark hair. Behind him the sun picked out the silver bits in it. He had big hands. Strong hands. Strong like his face, hardboned and decisive. Rock-like and safe. He turned his head to watch Fudge who was racing off again after the seagull he could never catch.

She liked his profile. It was chiselled and clean cut. There was a hint of black stubble round his jaw. 'It's a long way to come — walking or running.'

'I guessed you'd be here with that dog of

yours, and I decided the long haul was worth it.'

Her heart gave a jump. It wasn't accidental then. This meeting, the meeting she'd dreamed of, day and night for the past seven-and-a-half years. Those dreams seemed childish things now, born of a need to see him again — to meet him on a deserted beach, just like this one, or on an island in the South Seas, or a space ship to Mars. It really didn't matter. He was here, in the flesh. Or at least in a sweatshirt that covered most of the flesh, yet still couldn't disguise the sex appeal, the magnetism that oozed out of him, and grabbed her and held her prisoner — maybe for the rest of her life. She didn't know. She couldn't guess, but just at the moment, time was her friend. It was standing still and she was a willing prisoner for as long as he wanted to stand and talk to her.

'Did you want me?' The words sounded banal, unreal to her ears. 'I mean . . . you said you thought I'd be here, with Fudge . . . '

'Did I want you?' he echoed softly, then laughed in that same deep, dark way she remembered.

She laughed. 'I meant . . . was there something you wanted to see me about? The wedding cars? Your sister — she signed the contract with Dad and Mark, and . . . ' she stopped suddenly, realizing she was babbling on about nothing in particular.

He twisted his lips into a half-smile, half-grimace. 'Nothing like that. I just felt like talking to you again, and I need to keep in training. So ... ' he lifted one hand expressively, 'I decided to train on the beach tonight — the machines in the gym were impersonal things all of a sudden.'

He just wanted to talk to her. To make some sort of intelligent conversation. She said, 'It was bad luck for you in Italy. I watched it on television with Dad.'

He gave a grim smile. 'The engine blew up.'

'Yes.' She nodded. 'It made Dad swear — especially as you were gaining on the leading car.'

'It happens,' he said with a tiny shrug.

'Better luck next time.' Now he was here, now her dream had come true, and she didn't want it to end — ever. She turned and saw Fudge a long way off. She called to him and he came bounding back.

'Shall we walk?'

She set off beside him with Fudge keeping a good distance away from the water.

'Why doesn't he go in?' Rafe wanted to know.

'He hates water. When he was a pup, he

went head first into it — thinking it was something nice and cuddly, I think. When he found it was cold and wet he dashed out yelping. He's never forgotten it. The sand he loves, but not the water.'

He laughed, and the sound was a good one. He was completely at ease with her. 'I've often wondered what it would be like to have a dog,' he said.

'You should get one. They're great company. They help you meet people on lonely beaches,' she said.

'Maybe I will get one. One day.'

She glanced across at him. 'I suppose it would be awkward just at the moment. You're out of the country for so much of the time.'

'Only for the next few months. Then my contract with Oscar Herrick runs out.'

'You'll miss it though, I suppose, if you give it up. Motor racing. It's been your life for a long time.'

'I shan't let go of it completely.' He smiled down at her. 'It's not something you pick up and put down at will.'

'Have you decided what you will do?'

'Something on the fringe of motor racing, I suppose. I've thought about management — or test driving. I might even have a go at commentating if I can get an opening into television. Designing I'm not so hot on. We're bugged at the moment by a problem we can't seem to get over, and I wish I had the time to sit down at a computer and work it out.' He laughed then and said, 'I didn't come here tonight though to talk about me. What are your ambitions, Maggie? What's your burning desire in life?'

At that precise moment she had only one burning desire. It had been a funny old day. She'd been made to feel inadequate by Mark, she'd found no answer to her problem from Dad, and now, here she was, doing the one thing she wanted in life, walking on a deserted beach with a man she'd worshipped from afar for almost the whole of her adult life.

Yes, she had a burning desire.

'What's the matter?' he said.

She pulled a face at him, stood still and looked at him. 'That burning desire you were talking about,' she said. 'Some of us never even see it start to materialize, do we?'

His face was very near her own. 'You have to know how to make the most of opportunity,' he said softly. 'I told you once before you were playing everything a bit too much on the safe side.'

He was so near she could have touched him if she wanted. Tilting her head on one side, she said, 'Do you mean it? About me playing everything too safe?'

His eyes were very serious. 'You have something on your mind, don't you?'

Solemnly she nodded.

'Then do what your heart tells you to do.'

'Mmm.' She nodded, thinking of the plans she'd made for leaving Brand Motors, but already another plan was forming in her mind. 'Do what my heart tells me,' she said softly, looking up into his face. 'You really mean that?'

'Whatever the cost,' he said steadily.

Fudge raced away again. The seagull was back.

A picture of Rafe and Tamsin flashed into Maggie's mind. That day as they'd come into the lighthouse together. They were a pair. He was lost to her.

She had nothing to lose. He was already out of her reach. But Tamsin wasn't here to see, and she knew he was too much of a gentleman to ever tell Tamsin what she'd done — if she dare do it.

'Your dog takes every opportunity to catch that bird,' he said, laughing down at her. 'And he doesn't stand a chance you know, of ever catching it. It's too fast for him.'

Her hands reached out to him and touched his arms, her fingers closing round the soft black material of his sweatshirt. She could feel the muscles, the tense, hard muscles under her hands and through that soft black stuff. And then she was right up against him, and her hands slipped up to his shoulders, then to his head, threading themselves through the thick black hair and pulling his face down to hers. She'd never taken the initiative with a man in her life before, but what was it he'd said? *'Make the most of opportunity . . . do what your heart tells you . . .'*

It was too late to stop now.

He didn't resist, not even when her mouth found his. She could feel the tensile strength of him, the lean hard length of his body against her through the cotton sweatshirt. He became aroused quickly; she could feel that too.

And suddenly it wasn't Maggie making the running. His arms went right round her, moulding her to him, his fingers, his hard, strong fingers gentle now on her waist, then sliding under her T-shirt and touching her skin in a manner that brought shivers to her spine and made her feel almost intoxicated. His tongue forced her mouth apart. She could taste the salt from the sea on his skin, could smell the shower-fresh scent of his hair twisting round her fingers . . .

The kiss burned deep down into the very

heart of her — and he was enjoying it too.

She pulled away a little, tilted her head back and looked up into his eyes. What she saw there excited her and brought an aching longing for him, for all of him.

'Is this what you meant?' she whispered against his mouth. 'When you said I should make the most of opportunity?'

His eyes were deep wells of desire. His hands came up and cupped her face between them, and he held her there, gazing hungrily into her face. 'It's a start,' he said at last, and he brushed his lips across her forehead.

Fudge came dashing up, barking ferociously. He laughed and said, 'Is he trying to protect you? Does he think I'm harming you, Maggie?'

She shook her head and Rafe's hands fell to her shoulders. They both turned towards the dog.

'Oh, no,' she groaned as she saw another figure bearing down on them. 'Oh, heck. I ought to have recognized Fudge's bark — it's the one he keeps for somebody he knows well.'

'Mark Langham!' He made the name sound like a curse as he uttered it under his breath.

'Ma-a-ggie . . . ' Mark was no more than twenty or thirty yards away from them and he stopped suddenly when he realized what he had interrupted.

'Well, well!' he said, seconds later as he sauntered up to them. 'I never took you for that sort of girl, Maggie.'

'Just what does that mean?' Rafe's voice was very low and very dangerous.

Mark's easy laughter rang out. 'Oh, I think you know quite well what sort I mean,' he said, his lip curling as he looked at Maggie as if she were a piece of flotsam flung up by the tide.

Rafe put her away from him and walked towards Mark. 'Spell it out,' he said, coming up directly in front of Mark.

Mark laughed again, but this time not so confidently. 'I believe in motor racing circles they're commonly known as 'screwdrivers' — because they do just that. Or in some cases the name is 'paddock ponies' — ladies who hang around the circuit paddocks to give rides, though not in the cars if you get my meaning. I'd have thought you'd have known both terms pretty well, Thorne . . . '

He got no further because by then he was flat out on his back on the sand, and Rafe was rubbing the knuckles of his right hand.

And Maggie was slipping the chain back on Fudge, and then her hand flew to her mouth as Rafe whirled round to face her again.

'Oh, no,' she said huskily, as Rafe strode back to her, put his arm round her shoulders and forcibly propelled her round the groaning figure of Mark who was staggering to his feet and then without a backward glance, stumbling back away up the beach.

'What have I done?' she asked in horror.

7

Tamsin was standing at the hotel window looking at the stupendous view of mountains towards the Italian borderlands.

'Rain! Oh, no. It looks like rain.'

Ava struggled to sit up in her bed. 'What? Heavens! Is that the time? Why didn't you wake me sooner?'

Tamsin half-turned. She was newly showered and had put on a simple but elegant pink linen dress. Her legs were bare and her skimpy sandals almost non-existent. 'It's only ten o'clock — and as we didn't get to bed until three this morning, I though you might appreciate a lie in. It is, after all, a Sunday — even if we are in Monte Carlo, and not back home in Heronsea.'

Ava groaned. 'The Casino! Now I remember. And those drinks afterwards in the American Bar . . . What time did Rafe leave us? I remember him saying he had to get an early night.'

Tamsin grinned across the room. 'Rafe went very early. Don't you remember? He's got a big day today.'

Ava screwed up her eyes against the light coming in at the window and almost shrieked, 'The race! Oh, Tam. You should have shaken me awake or something. I wanted to wish him luck before the race began.'

'Well, you can't.' Tamsin went over to Ava's bed and sat on the end of it, crossing her legs. 'Rafe did tell us that he wouldn't be seeing us again until after the Grand Prix.' She gave an exaggerated sigh before asking, 'Don't you remember *anything* about last night?'

'Not much.' Ava swung her legs out of bed and groaned at the sudden movement. 'Oh, my head. It feels like I've got a hundred golf-balls smashing themselves against my brain. What on earth did I have to drink last night?'

Tamsin laughed. 'Only a couple of cocktails — but you're not used to the good life, are you?'

'Apparently not,' Ava said ruefully, 'But what was it you were saying when I dragged myself away from that fabulous dream I was having?' she asked as an afterthought.

'I said it looks like rain. There's a heavy mist over the hills.' Tamsin's head jerked up then and she said with sudden interest, 'What's all this about a fabulous dream, then? You never mentioned before that you were having a fabulous dream? Was it about all those gorgeous hunky men Rafe introduced us to last night?'

Ava got gingerly to her feet, and looked down at Tamsin in a pitying way. 'They weren't hunky. Racing drivers are so fit and healthy they don't need to turn into the conventional 'film-star' hunk in order to get themselves noticed. Anyway, the dream doesn't matter, but rain *does*, my girl.' She walked over to the window and stared out, a worried little frown deepening between her eyes. 'I hope you're wrong,' she said. 'I hate it when Rafe drives in the rain at speeds of nearly two hundred miles an hour. They can't see a thing you know — on the track if it rains. Rafe says it's just a mass of spray coming up from the tyres and you're driving blind.'

'Don't they have lights?'

Ava gave a small smile. 'Just one on the back of the car, but even that doesn't help much with all that spray being chucked up.'

'Well, they might go and cancel the whole darn thing if the rain is so bad,' Tamsin said flippantly. 'And if they re-schedule it for later in the week — well, that will just mean an extra few days holiday for us, won't it.'

'My dear Tam, that kind of logic doesn't work in Formula One circles,' Ava said. 'They won't re-schedule, they'll merely change the tyres and things if it gets too dangerous to drive on slicks.'

Tamsin sighed. 'Slicks! Do you have to be so know-it-all boring by using all the right words for what are, after all, common or garden car tyres?'

'They aren't ordinary tyres, Tam. You know they're not.'

Tamsin bounced further on to the bed, kicking off her sandals and curling her legs up under her to get more comfortable. 'Well, you might know all the right terms, but you don't know a damn thing about handling men, hunky or otherwise, do you? Can't you see that if you act helpless and innocent, the drivers talk to you more and explain about things like tyres — which might be boring, but it does get them talking to you.'

Ava glanced up at the ceiling. 'Oh, trust you to know that the easiest way to a racing driver's heart is through his car!'

Tamsin pouted. 'Don't put them all in the same bracket, Ava darling. Your dear brother sees through my little wiles. I can't get round him the way I do with most men. Sometimes I'm really jealous of the way you and he talk

118

together.' She stared defiantly at Ava. 'Rafe talks to you about important things, like his career, doesn't he?'

Ava hesitated as she was about to turn and go to the bathroom. 'We-ell, yes, I suppose he does,' she said.

'Is he really going to give up motor racing at the end of the year?' Tamsin cocked her head on one side as she asked the question.

Ava shrugged. 'I leave Rafe to make his own decisions, love. Motor racing is important to him, and though I hate him doing it, I wouldn't ever try to stop him.'

'I hope he doesn't give it up. I hope Oscar Herrick renews his contract, or else one of the other team owners snaps him up.' Tamsin sighed in a melodramatic way. 'It would be heaven, wouldn't it if he went to drive for one of the big teams? Just think — I could be rubbing shoulders with the crème-de-la-crème of motor racing if he went to Williams or Jordan, or . . . '

'Oh, for heaven's sake!' Ava cut in, 'Stop day-dreaming, Tam. Rafe's thirty-six years old. He's been in this game for as long as most drivers already. They usually step down from racing around the age he is now.'

'But it's so exciting — being a racing driver — and for me to be seen in the company of a racing driver. I mean — Rafe's quite well-off financially, isn't he? And he's famous too — and good looking. He gets his photo in the newspapers, and the television commentator's know him. And it's been fantastic this last year — living with you, and knowing he's your brother, and I can see him and talk to him at almost any time I want to . . .'

Ava sounded bored. 'I hadn't noticed that this year was any more exciting than any other year.' She lifted her shoulders in a little helpless gesture, 'But I suppose I'm accustomed to having a racing driver brother. It doesn't really mean all that much to me.'

'But it must do,' Tam insisted. 'Of course it must. We wouldn't be here at this minute in this fabulous place, would we, if Rafe wasn't your brother. And I like it when he takes me out somewhere, and everybody recognizes him. I feel important. Like I'm a film star or something, because people have seen him in the newspapers and on television.' Tamsin paused for breath, then blurted out, 'Do you think he'll ever get married?'

'So that's what you're getting at is it, you minx?' Ava shot her a frosty smile, then said, 'Oh, for heaven's sake, Tam, give him time to get over Jade, will you? It's only twelve months since he lost her.'

'But he must have got over the first shock of that by now. He talks about her quite naturally, doesn't he? And he gets on with his job. He doesn't go around with haunted eyes and looking tragic. He must be getting over her by now.'

Quietly, Ava said, 'He will always blame himself for her death though, love. And as far as I know, he's never taken up with another woman since Jade.'

'But he has us. Why should he want anybody else?' Tamsin reasoned. 'He has you to talk to about his work, and he has me to take out shopping and to restaurants. And we both go to the theatre with him, don't we? And now we're all living together — just one big happy family.'

Ava walked back to the bed and sat down opposite the girl. 'We aren't all living together. We have the lighthouse, and Rafe is completely separate in the house next to it. Look, Tam,' she said, 'Don't go getting all dopey over him, will you? I wouldn't like to see you get hurt.'

Tam's pretty face clouded over. 'But he likes me,' she insisted, and she knew what she said was true. She could make Rafe laugh — and not many people had been able to do that this past year.

'Yes. I know he does. But that's as far as it goes. Don't go reading romance into what's only friendship, love.'

'It might not be only friendship.' Tamsin was suddenly irritated by her friend's words. 'How do you know what he's feeling, deep inside?'

'Tam, it is only friendship. Believe me. I know my brother.'

Tamsin tossed back her head. 'And if I prove you wrong?' she asked with defiance.

'I'd be the first to admit I was speaking out of turn if you could do that. But I don't think you can. Tam, you're not his type. He's not your type either. If he did give up racing, you'd be bored with him before a month was out. You have very little in common, you know. You like to have a good time, and Rafe is the . . . '

' . . . strong, silent type?' Tam broke in impatiently. 'Is that what you were going to say? Well, if it was, maybe he's what I need. A good, steadying influence.'

Ava reached out and squeezed her hand. 'Don't pin your hopes on him,' she warned gently.

Tamsin dragged her hand away and leapt up off the bed. 'I'm going out,' she said in a petulant voice. 'I'm going to go and see where our seats are for this afternoon's race. Are you coming or not?'

'Later. When I've showered.' Ava rose to her feet again.

'Nothing you say will make me back off. You do know that, don't you?'

Ava sighed. 'All I know is that once you set your heart on something you hang on like a dog with a bone, Tam. But in this instant, you're just chasing rainbows. Jade Herrick was the only woman for him, and he's not going to forget her in a hurry I can promise you.'

★   ★   ★

The grid was awash with engineers, mechanics, drivers, team managers, and anybody and everybody who had a hand in tuning, repairing, polishing, taking apart and rebuilding those narrow-bodied, wide-wheeled monstrosities called racing cars.

A steady drizzle that had started earlier was now turning into a sharp shower that was confusing everybody and causing havoc. Tyres were the biggest problem. Some cars were still on the dry weather slicks because earlier the rain had only been hinted at. Others were on rain tyres. Rafe was satisfied he'd made the right choice in having intermediates fitted, but there were still twenty minutes to go before the race started — time enough for everybody to change their minds again regarding tyres if the rain should let up.

Rain aside though, Rafe knew there was still one more duty to perform now that Oscar was occupied with checking the computers. Oscar would guess where he'd gone. He knew that for sure. As he strode away from the Oscar-Jade pitch, Rafe ducked past a press photographer, but waved to the kids clinging like bats to the high meshed barriers beside the grid. They'd been there for some time, the massed spectators, craning their necks for the best view of the drivers and their millions of pounds worth of cars that would soon be screaming round the circuit.

Sponsor names were emblazoned everywhere — tobacco sponsors, tyre manufacturers, oil, and ale. They all had a place — on the hoardings, on the cars, and on the drivers' Nomex driving gear.

Despite the rain there was plenty of colour about too. Ferrari red was prominent — while Williams blue was less so, mainly because a lot of the teams favoured blue for their cars. The distinctive silver of McLaren vied with the vivid yellow of Jordan, and as drivers from several of the teams started settling into their cars there was little but their uniforms to tell them apart. Team mates could only be distinguished by their helmets — every one of which was different and usually designed by their owner. Most of them bore at least one individual characteristic such as an initial capital letter, or part of the team logo.

Position-wise on the grid, both of Tom Blanchard's drivers were about as far away from Oscar-Jade positions as they could possibly get. Blanchard's cars had been sluggish on qualifying day, and Rafe knew their engines were not in the same league as Herrick's. As he pushed a way through the various teams and mechanics, he silently wondered why Vaughn Herrick couldn't see sense and come back to his old man. In reality though, he knew why Vaughn wouldn't do that. It was basically the same reason Oscar wouldn't put an end to the old enmity between himself and his son. They were both stubborn people — Vaughn — to the point of rebellion, and Oscar, a martyr to his reputation of never admitting he was wrong.

Vaughn was kitted up and standing gazing worriedly down at his car while mechanics swarmed over it. He was nothing like his father in appearance; he was small for a start, and short-sighted too. Out of the car he wore pale, steel-framed spectacles. He had them on now and they gave him a chubby, baby-faced appearance, but there was nothing babyish about Vaughn. He was tough. And as hard — if not harder — than Oscar, in some ways.

He worked hard, and he played hard too. Under that soft looking exterior, that smooth-shaven, dapper appearance, was a heart that Rafe knew could have been made from titanium — it was so unyielding.

Vaughn was the darling of the track 'ladies' though. He had a string of them — and he kept them on strings too. 'Puppets,' he'd laugh. 'Puppets dancing to my tune.'

His mechanics were finished with the car now, and Vaughn looked as if he might be going to get into the smart little magenta racer when Rafe walked up to him.

On seeing his old friend, Vaughn yelled to an engineer, 'Give me a couple of minutes!' and dashed forward, hand outstretched. 'I've been looking for you, Rafe you old devil. But you were always tied up with Dad when I got anywhere near.'

Rafe's hand smacked into that of the younger man. 'And it'd never do to come over and say 'hello' to Oscar, would it?' he chaffed in a good-natured way.

'Dad wouldn't want me saying 'hello'! Dad would want me saying 'yes-sir, no-sir, three bags full-sir' and you know it.' The bluer than blue eyes of young Herrick were full of amusement. 'Life's a game, and according to Dad, there's only one name for his particular game. Winning!'

'That makes two of you.' Rafe's words were tempered with a touch of humour. 'You're so alike it's uncanny — you and your dad.'

'Hell, don't say that. He's the last person on earth I want to be like.'

Vaughn though, was hard. And Rafe knew it was Oscar who had made him hard. Oscar had brought him up in a tough school — the Oscar Herrick school of discipline — more commonly known as 'home'! Oscar had old-fashioned ideas, coupled with old-fashioned values. The only difference between father and son was that Vaughn had a sense of humour, while Oscar had none.

Vaughn's grin was infectious now — infectious but well-practiced.

Rafe said, 'You're a cynical bastard. Oscar would be proud of you. But enough of Oscar, I just came over to wish you all the best.'

'Sure! You too.' That outsize grin was there again. 'But keep out of my way on the track, remember, take your time, eh?'

'No speeding,' Rafe's easy laughter rang out. 'Do we have a deal? I'll take my time — and you remember to keep below the ton.'

Somebody tapped Vaughn on the shoulder. 'Got to go.' He sobered suddenly. 'Take care, huh? You're the only one who can keep Dad in order. Don't forget that.'

He swung away. Rafe yelled, 'I'll give him

your regards, shall I?' then shook with silent laughter as the younger man made a vulgar sign with his finger without even bothering to look round again at him.

★   ★   ★

Oscar was in a het-up mood. He was charging up and down the grid, headphones on, waving his hands wildly as Rafe came up to him.

'Where the hell have you been?'

Rafe gave him a steady look. 'You know damn well where. I've been where I always go before a race. Where you yourself should have been if you had any decent feelings for your own son in that refrigerated heart of yours.' Rafe shook his head in a bewildered fashion. 'Would it hurt?' he asked softly. 'Oscar, would it really hurt you to go over and wish the lad luck?'

'Pah!' Oscar waved him away, obviously disinclined to react to Rafe's words. 'Get in the damn car,' he ordered brusquely. 'And win, damn you! And if you can't win — at least try to finish the course. We need points this season and I'm pinning every hope I've got on you.'

'There's another ten minutes.'

'Get in the blasted car. Get the feel of it.'

'Yeah! The feel of all the bumps, the feel of all the bruises I get trying to fit my long legs in that carbon-fibre sardine tin, the feel of my elbows sticking in my ribs. Oscar — you don't know you're born. When you were driving racing cars, they did at least have a bit of space in them.'

'What's up with you?' Oscar growled. 'You going all soft in your old age, Thorne?'

Rafe stepped up into the car, pulled on his white Nomex balaclava and his helmet, then slid easily down into the cockpit, arms extended above his head — it was so cramped in there. He glanced up at Oscar. 'I wished him luck for you,' he muttered, as Oscar scowled.

'Whose side are you on — his or mine?' Oscar Herrick's voice rasped back.

There was no time for a reply. Rafe saw that his team mate was already belted into his car, and his own engineers and mechanics descended on him then, threading seat belts round his arms, reaching into the cockpit, drawing the other belts together to anchor him in. When the belts were fastened, he adjusted them to his liking himself, making sure they were snug — tight even, and would hold him in the event of a smash.

Gloves on then, the steering wheel clipped into position, and the adrenaline starting to flow, he raised his hand to signify he was ready, felt the jolt from behind as the starter motor was activated by a mechanic. Engines all along the grid burst into life, tyre trolleys were trundled away, girls with colourful umbrellas gave them one last twirl towards the television cameras to show off the sponsor names, then moved off the track.

It all worked as if by magic, the clearing of the grid. Rafe never failed to marvel at how fast it could be achieved, that melting away of so many people when the race was due to start.

In a long line then, the cars started off on their formation lap of the circuit. On this lap there was no overtaking; everybody had — by Formula One ruling — to get back on the grid in their original position after the lap was over.

The Monte Carlo circuit was just over two miles in length. Consequently, the cars were back in their positions within minutes, and a breathless silence descended on the crowd in every part of Monaco. Away from the grid, in other positions along the circuit, huge television screens had been erected. Every balcony, every window, every doorway of every hotel in the place, was filled with spectators. And there were thousands more too who filled the specially constructed stands all along the circuit.

The rain came down steadily. This was one race where nobody could predict who the winner would be. The streets of Monte Carlo had little provision for overtaking. The corners were tight. Strong barriers had been erected to protect the onlookers.

All eyes now though, were on the banks of lights in front of the Formula One drivers sitting — or to be more accurate — almost lying flat out in their cars, waiting on the grid — waiting, and watching, for the red lights to disappear — and the Monaco Grand Prix to get off to a start . . .

8

Maggie popped her head round the parlour door and informed her father, 'Sorry, Dad, I won't be able to watch the race with you on television this afternoon.'

Edgar swung round from the television screen in his wheelchair, irate. 'What the heck are you talking about, our Mags. Look — the race is just about to start. You're cutting it fine, aren't you?'

'Dad!' She pushed a hand through her windswept hair. 'I can't come and watch it with you. Mom's car — it's out of action!'

'Your mam's gone to the hospital, love. There was some sort of emergency. She was muttering about blood groups and caesareans when she set off about five minutes ago.' Edgar frowned. 'What are you talking about, girl? I saw her drive away with my own two eyes. I waved to her out of that very window.' Impatiently he pointed to the large bay window that overlooked the front garden.

'Mom just rang. Didn't you hear the phone? I was just coming back up the drive with Fudge. I heard it and raced into the kitchen.'

'No! I never heard the blessed phone . . . '

And no wonder he hadn't heard the phone, Maggie thought, a smile touching her lips, nobody would hear a phone ringing when they had the television blasting away as it was doing at the moment. Edgar loved watching cars though. It didn't seem to matter to him what kind they were either. Formula One, classics, Indy — if there happened to be a programme on any of the television channels with 'car' in the title, then he'd watch it.

Today though, Maggie too had been quite eager to watch the Grand Prix, because Rafe would be racing on the Monaco circuit. And yesterday he'd been in the top seven when the qualifying had come to an end. She was glad he was near the front of the grid. Monaco was a hazardous circuit and she knew how virtually impossible overtaking was along the narrow, winding streets of Monte Carlo.

'Maggie! What's going on,' Edgar's voice bellowed out way above that of Murray Walker the commentator on the television set.

'Mom's car! She's got a puncture.' She tried to be patient with him, but it wasn't easy, knowing that her mother would be pacing up and down restlessly waiting for her to get her to the hospital with the minimum waste of time.

At last he aimed the remote control at the television set and turned the volume down, but only to say, 'Your mam's dues to the get-you-home people have been paid. Why didn't she call them out?'

'It's Sunday, Dad; Mom could be waiting ages for somebody to go out to her — and she's needed urgently at the hospital. Anyway, she's only just a mile down the road.'

Edgar started nodding his head up and down. 'Okay,' he said, 'Okay, you'd better go and see to her, love. Leave it to me.' He chuckled. 'I'll make sure you don't miss any of the race. I'll slip a video in and record it for you.'

'Thanks, Dad.' She hurried out of the room.

As she slid behind the wheel of the Anglia, she began to relax a little. Maybe it was better this way. At least she'd be able to watch the recording of the race in the privacy of her own room later on. Yesterday had been bad enough as she and her father had watched the qualifying session together on TV. Then it had taken all her effort to stop herself biting her nails as she sat holding her breath and watching Rafe's timings coming up on the screen. Yes, she'd definitely prefer to watch the actual race on her own.

★ ★ ★

Sheila Brand didn't have time to wait while Maggie changed a tyre. 'Run me to Queens in your car, will you darling,' she said as Maggie drew up beside her with the car window wound down. 'This is an emergency. A difficult birth imminent, I'm afraid.'

'Hop in then, Mom.' Maggie already had her car door open.

'I managed to park the car safely, but I skidded all over the place when the dratted tyre blew out.' Her mother glanced out of the side window at the dark grey BMW parked near the grass verge on the country road. 'A beer bottle.' She pulled a wry face. 'Somebody had a skinful last night, I expect, and just couldn't manage to get home without a last drink on the way. Too bad he hurled the bottle into the middle of the road afterwards.'

'I'll clear the glass away when I get back,' Maggie promised.

'I kicked most of it to one side while I was waiting for you.' Her mother settled herself more comfortably beside Maggie and said, 'But now if we could just hurry? There's a baby waiting to come into this world, and he's not going to make it without my help, I'm afraid.'

★   ★   ★

The rain was not going to stop, Rafe decided, as he completed the twenty-first lap in a haze of grey mist and spray sent up by the other cars. He braked for the hill he was now accustomed to after his practice session three days earlier, dropping down to seventy for the apex. The green, yellow and red lights on the dash in front of him in the cockpit flashed constantly; they told him when to change up or down gears, but he seldom needed a reminder. He drove primarily by the sound of the engine and the feel of it through his bones; it was an automatic reflex after so many years of driving, to change gear when the sound and feel of the car told him to.

There was no hope of avoiding the welded-down manhole covers on the run up to Casino Square, but all the same he braced himself for the expected bumps. F1 cars were not built for comfort he'd long since discovered.

There was a car up ahead of him, he could see the tail light through the greyness. Then suddenly it wasn't there. His mind flashed into overdrive wondering if the unseen driver had hit his brakes and spun the car round in which case that car could now be slewed across the track.

He lost precious seconds slowing in the name of safety until he glimpsed the tail light again. Then he breathed a sigh of relief. If the car up front had spun out of control on the greasy road surface, the driver had obviously been able to control it and put it back on course.

The circuit and its hazards were imprinted on his brain.

Casino square. Up to a hundred miles an hour again. Now — hug the barrier — downhill, the road's heavily cambered. Mirabeau. Watch that bend. Second gear. The next one's the worst though — Loews!

He took the hairpin safely and in low gear. All the cars racing today had been adapted especially for Monaco and these tight corners. Nothing was left to chance. Everything had to be accounted for. The tunnel posed no problem — sixth gear — flat out . . .

'Hell' He almost lost it. Oil. It had to be oil on the track. Oil and water.

Out in the daylight again and the rain seemed not so heavy. It was clearer here.

Downhill! Alongside the harbour. Tabac

— the bend before the swimming pool.

Everything flashed past in a blur. No time to see faces eagerly straining to watch for who was coming.

Up to a hundred and forty now. Watch those barriers. Easy to hit!

That swerve in the tunnel still worried him. Oil was a killer. His own LCD screens showed no abnormality in oil or water pressure though. The guy in front. It had to be the guy in front.

Foot down. La Rascasse, and then the last corner — Antony Noghes. Watch it — don't lose the back end.

He felt his breath easing as he went into the straight again — and that tail light was there again.

He caught a glimpse of magenta up front.

'Herrick!' He had no idea if it had been Vaughn in front of him in the tunnel though, or some other driver. Whoever it was though, must surely have noticed the oil warning light in the cockpit by now. And the engineers in the pits — they'd have picked up the fact too.

Rafe swallowed, his mouth was dry. He had a distinctly uneasy feeling that it *was* Vaughn who had the oil leak, and he knew only too well that it wouldn't be the first time Vaughn had taken a risk . . . What was the fool trying to achieve though? At the very most, he could only be on his eighteenth or nineteenth lap — he'd spun off at the beginning and had only just managed to hang on and keep the engine going; it had cost him some time to manoeuvre the car round and get back on the track.

The race was a two-hour one now, due to the weather conditions. And there was still over an hour to go . . .

It came to Rafe in a flash then, that Vaughn would be determined to finish. It could be foolhardiness — it could be that he wanted to impress Oscar, but driving a car with a dangerous fault on it wouldn't do that. Oscar would curse the lad for putting himself and all the other drivers at risk.

Who knew which way Vaughn's mind was working though? Blanchard's hadn't even come close to a win in the last two seasons, so maybe Vaughn was in danger of being dropped by Tom Blanchard if he didn't score points this season.

He was close on Vaughn Herrick's tail now and the spray was blinding him again. Every so often though, he caught sight of that brilliant magenta flash as a rear wing loomed up in the fog ahead of him.

Through gritted teeth he muttered, 'Pull in, Vaughn, pull into the damn pits and get it sorted . . .'

He was amazed they hadn't summoned Vaughn in. Something must have shown up by now on the computers.

But Vaughn kept on. And the tunnel was coming up again . . .

Loews hairpin . . .

The magenta was lurching around like a drunk in an alley.

Slow. Two more bends before . . .

A flash of orange! No sign of magenta any more. Just orange! Bright red!

Flames!

The tunnel was a gaping mouth.

'Stop . . . ' Rafe's voice was hoarse in his own ears, but by then, Vaughn's car was just a ball of fire being swallowed up by that ugly, great black mouth.

Rafe swerved to the right, coming to a violent, screaming halt just outside the tunnel. His car shouldn't be a problem there. All the drivers swung to the left before entering the tunnel . . . Anyway, the red flags would be out now, and the lights on. Nobody would be fool enough to carry on . . .

He raced across the track towards the flames, aware all the time of the roar and scream of the other cars coming down from Portier. They'd stop though. They had to stop. In his mind, he knew that the lights and red flags would stop them. The ones already up front — in the tunnel ahead of Vaughn were by now fast disappearing towards daylight at the other end.

Heat from the inferno beat him back as he approached the car. There was no sign of Vaughn. He *must* have got out by now . . .

'No!'

Through the smoke he saw him. Still in the car. Struggling with the steering wheel. He couldn't get it off, and the cockpit was so cramped, that wheel just *had* to come off if Vaughn was going to be saved.

Vaughn was trapped!

The drivers' suits were designed for an accident such as this — but even they couldn't hold back the flames for ever.

He dived at the car, hands up in front of his visor. He grabbed the wheel, and knocking Vaughn's hands aside, was able to release the catch that had been the problem. He flung the wheel aside then and leapt away as Vaughn rolled out of the car, then lurched to his feet and started running, yelling, 'Get away from the car, man . . . save yourself . . . '

There was oil everywhere, burning, pooling. Black smoke engulfed them and Vaughn disappeared into it. Rafe felt the skid of oil beneath his feet and over the roar of the flames heard what sounded like a car coming into the tunnel.

The idiot. Couldn't he see the flames . . .

He wrenched off his helmet and instantly started choking on the smoke. He couldn't see a thing, it was so dense. He wheeled away from the burning car. And it was then that he overbalanced. He cursed himself as he threw out his arms but clutched vainly at the air. By the time he'd righted himself the car was screeching down on him . . .

It felt like no more than a dull thud against his leg. No damage he thought thankfully as he hit the ground and bits of carbon fibre showered over and around him.

But as he rolled over and over, the pain hit him . . .

★ ★ ★

Maggie was devastated as she listened to Edgar relating the events of that afternoon's television coverage of the Manaco Grand Prix.

'Dad . . . No . . . ' she whispered hoarsely. 'No . . . '

'Sit down, lass. Look — I've put the kettle on. Sit down and I'll make us both a cup of tea.'

'But . . . tell me again — and slowly, what happened?'

'It was like I told you, love. There was a

142

fire. Herrick's son's car. The lad escaped — thanks to Rafe Thorne.'

'But Rafe . . . you said Rafe . . . '

'Got hit by a car — one that shouldn't have gone into the tunnel — not when he saw what was going on in there. There was no excuse for it — that driver behind must have seen the red flag, but he deliberately ignored it.'

'But didn't they say on television whether Rafe was badly injured? Dad . . . ' she banged her clenched fists down on the kitchen work-top and almost yelled at him, 'Dad — tell me . . . you would tell me, wouldn't you . . . if . . . if . . . ' Her voice broke off. She made an effort to stay calm. It wasn't easy. Not when everything inside her was screaming.

'They don't tell you nothing, girl. Not on the telly. They pan to another scene. You know how it is. They don't want people alarmed. The picture went blank for just a split second, and then there they were — the commentators — sitting on the boat in the harbour — stalling, I suppose you'd call it, till there was some news of what had happened. Next thing they showed was young Herrick's car being hoisted off the track by a crane — somehow they'd pulled it out of the tunnel and got the circuit clear enough for the race to carry on.' Edgar shook his head slowly.

'And the other car — the one that hit Rafe — well that came out in bits and pieces, but the driver was okay. Looked a bit shaken like . . . He'll face a hefty fine — five thousand dollars I should think, or else he'll be disqualified from the next Grand Prix which is Spain, because he definitely ignored that red flag . . . '

'But Rafe . . . ?' She was almost sobbing now in her frustration. She didn't care about fines and disqualifications. All she did care about was Rafe Thorne. 'Dad,' she pleaded, grasping at his arm, 'Dad, we've got to find out what's happened to him . . . '

'Calm down, girl. What's it to you?' Edgar looked puzzled, but patted her hand as he said, 'Well — it's not as if he means all that much to us, is it? I mean — he's practically a stranger. Even I don't know him all that well. Anyway, all that the television people said was that he'd been rushed off to hospital. No more than that. And as for us finding out anything — well that's impossible, love. They won't tell you a thing. Not unless you're family. And they did say that his family was there — at Monaco — watching the race. I suppose they meant his sister. That's all the family he's got as far as I know.'

'I could telephone her . . . Ava would tell me . . . '

'Where would you phone her, love?' Edgar spread his hands helplessly. 'There are dozens of hotels, and we don't know where she was staying. Anyway, I suppose she's with him — wherever they've taken him. We'll just have to wait.'

'Wait!' Maggie stared at her father as, unperturbed, he began to make a pot of tea. 'Wait?' Suddenly her legs gave way and she sank down on to a chair against the kitchen table as she realized her father was right. They couldn't do anything but wait, could they?

Edgar brought cups and saucers to the table, then looked at her squarely. 'It's all we can do, Mags. We're not family. We can't just force ourselves in where we might not be wanted. And anyway — it's too far away for us to do anything about it. It's the south of France, for heaven's sake. And here we are — stuck in Yorkshire. There's no way we can get to know how badly injured he is at the moment. P'raps there'll be something on the television news tonight — or else tomorrow morning in the newspapers . . .'

'Morning?' She couldn't wait till morning. Not when he was lying injured somewhere . . .

Memory came flooding back and she recalled the last time she'd seen him. Rafe Thorne — amusement in his eyes —

145

matching that in her own. Both of them down on the beach. She in his arms, he in hers. The kiss that had started as a spur of the moment had finished up as something entirely different. To her it had, anyway.

But the moment had passed. Mark had made sure of that, even if it had culminated in him lying in the sand, nursing a bruised jaw.

It hadn't ended there though. Rafe had walked back with her and Fudge, and they'd scrambled up the shallow cliffs — all three of them, the man, the girl and the dog. And she'd said to him, 'What about Mark?'

'He asked for it.' He was calm and cool. His anger against Mark had soon evaporated. 'He gets away with too much where you're concerned,' he added. 'But I couldn't stand there and hear him insult you the way he did — and do nothing about it.'

She said, 'I can take care of myself . . . '

He cut in sharply, 'I'd be no sort of a man to let him get away with it, Maggie.' Then his voice had softened and he'd said, 'You shouldn't have to take insults from somebody like Mark Langham — not a girl like you.' His eyes had said much more than that though, and she remembered thinking to herself, he can't be talking about ME! Can he?

She'd felt warm inside. And then guilty about Mark who was staggering up the beach and trying to find a spot where he could clamber up the cliffs and not run into them again. In a way she felt sorry for Mark, but Rafe was right. He had asked for that punch on the jaw. He had insulted her, but she'd come to accept Mark's snide remarks and innuendoes as the normal things that happened each day. And no matter what he said, she still thought Rafe had over-reacted somewhat.

'We'll meet up again, Maggie. And talk.' His eyes searched her own. 'I wish I didn't have to go away — there's so much I want to know about you. So much to say,' he pulled a rueful face. 'So little time . . . '

Her heart gave a wobble. She felt suddenly breathless. She couldn't answer him, she just looked up at him. Was this just a line with him? She didn't think so. He wasn't that sort of man. Maybe she was reading too much into his words though.

'When I come back from Monaco — I'll call you? Okay?'

'Okay.'

He'd bent and kissed her lightly on the lips, lingering there a little longer than was necessary. Fudge barked at him, warning him off, but with a last deep searching of her eyes, he laughed softly at the dog and then went down on his haunches, took the great furry face between his hands and said, 'What's up with you? Do you want a kiss as well?'

Fudge had looked foolish, and then licked Rafe's hand.

Rafe stood up then and said huskily, 'He likes me. Your dog likes me.'

His eyes never left her face for a moment. He stared hungrily at her. Then he was gone, descending the shallow cliffs, then running lightly down the beach beside the fast-incoming tide.

He never looked back, and Maggie didn't expect him to. Racing drivers had their sights set on what was ahead, she thought, not what they'd left behind.

He was running back now to where he belonged. Back to the Ivory Tower. And back to Tamsin . . .

Her thoughts came crashing back to the present with the ringing of the telephone. She was half way across the kitchen before she even realized she'd moved.

Edgar said, 'Sit down. I'll answer it.' And he wheeled away towards the wall phone hanging by the kitchen door.

She heard him laughing, then saying, 'Well done.' And, 'Yes. Yes. She's here.'

She rushed across the kitchen, tore the

phone out of his hand. 'Rafe . . . '

But it wasn't Rafe's voice that answered her. It was her mother's. 'What's that you said, love?'

'Mom!' All the breath left her body. 'Oh, Mom. Sorry — I thought — I thought . . . ' Her hand fell to her side, the phone dangling there uselessly. Edgar took it out of her nerveless fingers and spoke into it.

'Mags thought it was somebody for her,' she heard her father saying, then he went on, 'Oh, aye, love. The car's all right now. Back in the garage, good as new. Well, you know our Mags. She'd never let anybody down, would she?'

He turned and winked at her, and slowly, Maggie felt her world coming the right way round again. Dad was right. They were in an impossible situation. And there wasn't any-thing they could do about Rafe — not at the moment, anyway.

Edgar was talking to her mother again. 'Our Mags is one in a million. She cleared up all that glass on the road — and changed the tyre before bringing her own car back, then she walked nigh on a mile back there to fetch yours as well . . . '

Maggie's insides were still churning. She wished her father would get off the phone. Anybody, just anybody could be trying to get

149

through while he was making small talk with her mother.

He beamed up at her, half-covered the mouthpiece of the phone with one hand and said in a loud whisper. 'Mam's finished at the hospital, love. The baby's been born okay, and his mum's fine too! Can you go over to Queens right now and bring Mam home?'

It was the last thing she wanted to do. She wanted to sit beside the phone and wait for it to ring. Wait for him to ring and tell her he was all right.

But Dad wouldn't understand how she was feeling. How could he?

She nodded. 'All right, Dad. Tell Mom I'm on my way.'

Slowly she walked out of the room. Then, like an automaton, she went outside and got into her car, worried slightly that Dad depended on her so much. And Mom too — though to a lesser extent, it was true. She wished they didn't. She wished at this moment that she could be tearing off to catch a plane to Monaco. If she were doing something like that, at least it might ease this awful hollow feeling inside her.

She started up the engine, her thoughts still full of the dreadful thing that had happened, and as she drove away from the house, she wondered how she would ever sleep that night, not knowing whether Rafe was still alive or not.

It was so awful — not knowing, and feeling so helpless.

9

Maggie was mystified next morning when Edgar informed her he was going down to the garage on the sea-front with her.

'Why, Dad? What's wrong?'

Edgar faced her at the foot of the stairs, sitting in his wheelchair and dressed in mechanic's overalls and a woolly jumper.

'You're doing too much. Look at you — pale faced and bleary eyed, love. And I blame myself for it. You've got no life of your own. You're at my beck and call all the blessed time. Even on Sundays. Yesterday you spent the entire afternoon going out to your mam's aid. I said to her last night, 'Our Mags is doing too much. And I'm going to go and sort things out at the garage'.'

'We manage, Dad.' Maggie hesitated three steps from the bottom of the stairs and looked down at her father as he sat in his chair beside the front door of Fox Cottage waiting for her.

'Managing is not what it's all about,' Edgar stated in a dogged voice. 'You used to enjoy your job when I was working, and now it's not the same, is it? You're all in this morning, girl. Just take a look at yourself in the mirror.'

'I — I didn't sleep well, Dad.'

'No! You took it badly — Rafe Thorne's accident on the telly, didn't you? You see, Mags, you're taking the worries of the world on your shoulders, and at your age you shouldn't be doing that. I've decided.' He nodded his head more violently than was necessary, and went on, 'I have decided to take up the reins again. And you — you, Mags, are going to have a lot more time to yourself than you've enjoyed these past few months, I promise you.'

'Well!' She managed a little laugh. 'What can I say?' In her heart, she rejoiced. It was good to see Dad with some enthusiasm for his cars again, but it changed nothing really. She was still determined to leave Brand Motors, but her conscience shirked from leaving Edgar in the lurch. Somewhere, somehow, there had to be a solution.

'I'm not complaining, love.' His voice was gentler now. 'I appreciate everything you've done to keep the place ticking over for me.' He gave a heavy sigh. 'I also know how little Mark has helped. He's that sort of man though — the sort who thinks a woman's place is in the kitchen. He's got to buckle down, Maggie. We can't afford hangers on, and if necessary I'll buy him out of the partnership — he only has a quarter share in it anyway. He knows I hold the major part of Brand Motors.'

She smiled and went down the remainder of the stairs. 'Well,' she said, 'What are we waiting for?'

'Don't forget the dog,' Edgar said drily.

'Fudge has already had his morning walk.'

'Aye! Well, take him for another one, will you, lass. I want to have a serious talk with young Mark Langham — and I don't want you around when I give him a good bollo . . . '

'Okay, Dad. You don't have to spell it out.' She pulled open the front door and allowed him to get outside with the wheelchair. Then she turned towards the kitchen and yelled, 'Come on, Fudge. Double walkies this morning.'

Fudge appeared in the doorway, ears pricked but with a mournful look in his brown eyes.

Edgar laughed. 'He looks knackered.'

'He is. We did a couple of miles this morning.' She grinned at her father.

The dog loped towards them.

'Good lad,' Edgar said, patting him.

Maggie fetched his chain. 'How long shall I leave you alone with Mark?' she wanted to know of Edgar.

He gave a great shrug. 'Half an hour? I reckon I can say all I want to in half an hour, don't you?'

'Will that be enough time?'

He pulled a face at her. 'Just keep an eye on the garage roof,' he joked solemnly. 'If you see young Mark whizzing up through it, you'll know he's taken it badly. If you see me flying through the air, you'll know he's taken his telling off very badly.'

★ ★ ★

Maggie went back to the garage around ten that morning, after she'd taken Fudge back to the house and settled him in the kitchen yet again, after his second walk that day.

There was no sign of her father, but Mark was bending over the engine of a 1950s Triumph Herald as she walked through the door of the garage.

'You're late.' Mark straightened up and scowled at her. 'Did Daddy give you orders to keep out of the way this morning?'

'I gave Fudge an extra-long walk,' she replied, going past him and towards the back of the garage.

'No need to put the kettle on. Edgar's doing that in the back kitchen.'

'Oh,' she spun round to Mark again.

'He's also taken the law into his own hands and rung the employment agency, asking them to send him a mechanic.'

'Oh,' she said again, but in a hollow tone this time.

Smiling, but in a snarling voice, Mark said, 'Have you been telling tales about me to Daddy — to cover up the fact that you haven't been pulling your weight, my sweet . . .'

But Edgar's voice suddenly bellowed out behind her, making her whirl round to face the back of the garage. 'That's not the case, Mark — and you know it. It's you who has been lax in the weight-pulling department. I've watched what time you've been driving past my house in a morning — and it's not good enough. Now, with all this work on we're way behind schedule with the cars we have clients for. That's why I'm asking for a new mechanic.'

Mark looked surly. 'We could manage with a lad. A kid. A school leaver. We just need somebody to tidy the place up and learn the ropes. There's no need to employ another man on a full time basis.'

'I disagree.' Edgar was adamant, 'We need

somebody who knows this job inside out, but if this one starts shirking he'll be out on his ear before he can count to ten, I promise you.'

'Are you hinting that's what you'd do to me if I wasn't a partner?' Mark asked, obviously ruffled.

'Take it any way you like,' Edgar's voice was like ice.

Maggie could see Mark's temper was rising. 'I think I should have been consulted before you decided to employ somebody else,' he snapped at her father.

'You've been consulted, lad. This morning.' Edgar spun the wheelchair with expertise and trundled back into the kitchen. He yelled back over his shoulder, 'Tea's almost mashed. We'll have a ten minute break and fill Maggie in on what's happening.'

'Ten minutes!' Mark muttered slamming down the screwdriver he'd been using. 'I don't see why I should be taking orders like this.'

Maggie ignored him and went over to the little Austin she'd been working on for the past fortnight. It was coming along nicely. She loved the Austins for their sturdy shapes and their ability to become roadworthy again after years of neglect. Of all the cars she worked with, these were her favourites. And now this one just needed polishing, and its seats waxing, and all the final touches putting to it that would make it a good buy for the customer they already had for it.

'I'll be sorry to see this one go.' She made a light-hearted attempt to make civilized conversation with Mark.

His lips twisted. 'You treat them like your babies. You're not normal. You need proper babies, Maggie. At your age you should be married and with real kids.'

His comments hurt. They always did, even though she'd steeled herself to them over the past months. She made no reply, and this seemed to irk him even more than a reply would have done.

He came over and stood beside her as she applied a soft cloth to the chromework. 'You really are the end. You know that, don't you?' he sneered.

'Mark.' She straightened and gave him her full attention. 'Mark — I don't want to fall out with you.'

Edgar shouted from the back of the garage, 'Tea-up, you two.'

'Make him change his mind,' Mark muttered. 'We don't want anybody else around here. He'll take notice of you. Tell him we can manage without somebody else coming in to share the profits.'

'But we can't manage, Mark.' She looked him steadily in the eyes. 'We need a good worker. I agree with Dad.'

'You would,' he said, snapping at her, 'Daddy's little girl. What you want is a real man to show you what life's all about.'

★   ★   ★

The radio had been on in the garage all morning, and at each hourly news bulletin, she'd listened avidly for possible details about Rafe's accident. At lunch time, it was reported on the longer programme, but she learned nothing except that Rafe had been taken to hospital in Monaco but no press release had been given as to his condition.

By three in the afternoon, the little Austin car was gleaming and preening itself from the good going over it had been given. Maggie had expended all her energy on it, finding some small relief from the worry of Rafe in hard work and elbow grease.

At ten past three, Edgar made another three mugs of tea-bag tea and yelled to them from the back of the garage.

And then, from outside the garage came the sound of two quick-fire explosions.

Maggie downed tools immediately and yelled across the workshop to her father. 'It's the lifeboat, Dad. I have to go.'

'Now who's shirking?' Mark said as she raced past him towards the open door.

She ignored the jibe. Mark knew full well that when the summons went out, all lifeboat crew had to drop whatever they were doing and answer it. As she climbed into the little Anglia and set off down into the village and then along the coast road, she knew instinctively that Edgar would be giving Mark the telling off of his life for his inappropriate remark to her. Next to his beloved cars, the lifeboat service had been the love of her father's life — until that accident last year.

It had been after the accident that Maggie, on a shopping trip down to the village, had learned that the crew — already understaffed when her father had been there — were in danger of being disbanded if they couldn't find other volunteers.

It would be tragic, she'd realized then, if this part of the coast was left without a lifeboat.

She remembered staring at the little notice pinned up in the post office. It had caught her eye with its red, white and blue colouring, and the huge centralized heading:

VOLUNTEERS WANTED URGENTLY

It had seemed the appropriate thing to do at that moment — to offer her services. And she'd never regretted it . . .

Now though, time was precious and couldn't be wasted on thinking of the day she had joined the lifeboat service. She drove fast, and within minutes she'd parked her car at the far end of Shorecross on the little gravelled piece of land next to the slipway from which the boat would be launched, and was charging into the lifeboat station.

A cheer went up from half a dozen men already shrugging themselves into orange coloured water-proofs and lifejackets as she burst through the door.

'Thank goodness you've come,' Bill Fretwell — a crew member who was also the village butcher — shouted to her. 'Josh is a bit under the weather.'

Josh Martin, the only full-time crew member was the mechanic, and looking at him now as she hastily changed into her own protective orange suit, Maggie realized that age was creeping up fast on Josh. He didn't look at all well, and he hadn't done for some considerable time now.

'Want me to help with the launch, Josh?' she asked as the elderly man started up the engines.

'Aye, lass. I reckon you'd better.' He shot a pale grin at her.

Several other men had joined them now. When the lifeboat was launched, everybody knew their job and went to it as quickly as possible.

The Coxswain was issuing orders, telling them that a small boat had capsized in Heronsea bay.

Maggie was the only female member of the crew. Being a mechanic herself, she had soon tagged on to Josh, and found that a boat engine responded in exactly the same way as a car engine did if it had plenty of loving care and attention lavished on it. The only difference was that work which needed doing on a lifeboat engine couldn't wait around for the same amount of time that a car often could. The lifeboat had to be ready to launch twenty-four hours a day, three hundred and sixty-five days a year. Josh was responsible for all the mechanical equipment on board, and Maggie had learned a lot from him.

A thought came to her, but she dashed it away as impractical. It returned however as, beside her, Josh mopped at his forehead with a red hanky and said, 'Eh, lass, I'm gettin' too old for this lark.'

Josh was the only full-time member of the crew. It was necessary for the mechanic to occupy the only paid position. It was important that the lifeboat engines were kept in tip-top condition.

All thoughts of Rafe and the upset at the garage that morning were pushed from her mind now, as she took over from Josh and made ready to go to the rescue of that other boat in Heronsea bay. Personal worries had to be left behind on shore once the boat took to the sea.

It did so a few minutes later when a shore member of the crew, the launcher, struck the coupling mechanism that released the lifeboat from its mooring, and sent it hurtling down the seventy metre long slipway. It hit the water with a tremendous force, and amid a half-circle of foaming spray. Maggie always loved the moment they became seaborne, and only one thing ever marred the event — that being the knowledge that her father could never again be a part of the team.

At first, it had been a novelty for the men to have a woman on board, but they'd soon found out that she asked for no favours because of her sex. She became accepted by the men, most of whom had known her for all of her life. They were local, ordinary men who delivered milk in the mornings, kept local shops, and farmed the land or fished the sea. There was a dentist, a chemist, twins from a nearby printers — two lads who were full of energy and enthusiasm, and Lloyd Rogers, a serious young man who'd set up an estate agency in the village only six months earlier.

It was a small crew of less than twenty, which meant that if only one man dropped out, they had to make up the deficit as soon as possible. Not all the members could attend every call out, but six were needed to man the boat, and another six had to be left on shore to help with the launch and then be there to operate the winch that pulled the boat back up the slipway when it returned.

One member on board the boat operated the radio, another was in charge of first aid, while the cox at the helm made all the important decisions regarding the rescue, and kept in constant contact with the second cox who worked out the course they would take using charts and navigational aids.

They were soon out in deep water and heading towards Heronsea, and it took no time at all to pinpoint the spot where the capsized boat was being tossed about on the choppy sea. There were two people in the sea, keeping well clear of the wreckage, and it was a fairly easy rescue. No first aid was required, other than to wrap the survivors in warm blankets and then head back to base.

When Josh was feeling better, she managed a few minutes' break, and as she looked back across the bay she saw Heronsea lighthouse towering above the town on its concrete headland. It was the first time since boarding the boat that she'd had time to think about Rafe, and seeing the lighthouse brought a sick feeling to her stomach as she wondered again what had happened to him.

★　★　★

It was after five when Maggie got back to the garage, and as she parked her little Anglia outside it, Mark walked out to get into his own car.

'Enjoy the trip?' he asked glibly.

She forced a smile. 'It was successful — nobody injured.'

'You look a real mess.'

She raked the fingers of both hands through her hair which was snarled and tangled from being at sea on an open boat. She could feel the salt in it — sticky and making it stiff. 'Thanks! You say the nicest things.' She pulled a face at him and strode over to the garage, hearing his car engine spring into life as she went in through the tall doors, her mind made up on one thing at least.

Her father was just preparing to lock up for the night.

'Hi, Dad!'

He wheeled round in his chair to face her.

'I watched the boat going out from the clifftop.' He beamed broadly at her. 'I saw the rescue through my binoculars.'

'You miss going out with the lads, don't you, Dad?'

'Aye!' His smile faded. 'I do.'

'Dad . . . '

'What is it, lass?'

'Dad — can you manage without me for a while?'

'A while, love? How long would that be then?'

She lifted her shoulders in a little shrug. 'Days! Maybe a week?'

He nodded. 'You could do with a holiday. And the agency rang me. They're sending a man in the morning. He sounds okay. Mark's got a real bag on about it though.'

She took a deep breath and plunged in. 'I'm going to France, Dad. I've decided.'

His eyes narrowed. 'Rafe Thorne. That's what this is about, isn't it?'

She said, 'Yes. I have to find out what's happened.'

'Aye,' he said. 'I reckoned you would.'

She leaned against the bench and looked

round the garage. 'I'm going to ring Oscar Herrick's team base in the Midlands. They should at least be able to tell me which hospital he's in.'

'And a phone call to the hospital won't do for you, will it?' Edgar was remarkably astute, she realized.

'No, Dad. It won't. I want to see him. I can't rest until I know what's happened to him.'

'Then go,' he said. 'Follow your heart, love. You have my blessing.'

10

It was three days later, and Mark was in a foul mood.

The film he'd been to see at a cinema ten miles from home had been a total waste of time. He'd spent two hours and five minutes in the darkness thinking of her — Maggie Brand — and realizing he was missing her like hell. He silently cursed himself for making her believe he didn't care about her, whereas the truth was that he did care, and he knew now that the old saying was right. The truth hurt. And it was his own fault that he'd lost her.

He strode across the cinema car park and yanked open the door of his car. Around him, couples were also getting into cars, laughing, arguing, kissing — but couples all the same. Two people together in a crowd, all of them only *two people*, with eyes for each other. Two people who loved or tolerated, but stayed together no matter what. There were hundreds of couples, and he was the odd one out. A man alone.

He slammed down into his seat, telling himself that he hated them because the majority of them wouldn't be going home to darkened, cold houses as he was. They were maybe going for a pizza, or on to a club, or back to a bedsit — but together. Not alone, like him.

He felt like a drink. Maybe that would make him forget. He looked at the dashboard clock.

He stared at the illuminated figures in front of him. 'Eleven!' A pub was out of the question at this time of night. Anyway, he was driving. 'Damn!' He thumped the steering wheel with his fist, and he wondered where she was now. Probably already half way to the Cote d'Azur — or else held up in an airport lounge somewhere. He hoped it was the latter. His lip curled. She had no right to go off like that — and at a minute's notice.

He started up the engine and shot out of the car park ahead of all the other twosomes. It was a twenty-minute drive home to Rothwold down the coast road. On a clear night, he recalled, when he'd been younger, he used to look for the light shining from the top of the lighthouse at Heronsea just before he turned inland. Now there was no light to look for. Now, the proud white tower had been turned into what amounted to little more than a shop. Oh, it was quite a grand shop, give those two girls their due — they'd made a real good job of it, whilst still retaining the majesty of the lighthouse from the outside. He could have thought of better things to do with a lovely old lighthouse though, except at the moment he didn't want to think about buildings. All he wanted to think about was Maggie Brand, and wonder if it really was too late to tell her how he felt about her.

Ahead of him the road was dark. There were no street lamps along this stretch of open country. A pale moon shone down on the brilliant yellow of the rape fields beside him as he drove northwards. There were lights in a barn off to his left. He frowned. That barn was derelict, surely? He slowed the pace of the car almost to crawling, then leaned across the passenger seat and stared across the yellow fields. There was a steady thumping in the air, repetitive, not music exactly, but with the same heavy beat that some tunes had. He stopped the car but left the engine idling and rested his hand on the frame of the open window. The beat went on and on, never ending. He let the car go forward again, his foot just touching the accelerator till he was opposite a five barred wooden gate.

Then he saw the crudely scrawled notice. '*Rape-Rave — ten till dawn*'!

'Hell what'll they think of next.' It was sick. 'Rape-rave'! He yawned, and pitied the poor sods who would crawl home to their beds the next morning stoned out of their skulls, hypnotized by the drum-drum-drum of soul-less 'music', drenched in sweat, wide-eyed but lifeless with excesses of caffeine and who knew what besides. There had been a crack-down on illegal 'raves' such as this one. The do-gooders of Heronsea, Rothwold, and other towns and villages in the locality had voiced their concern at the harm being done to their teenagers. They'd made a feeble attempt to organize 'legal' and 'good-honest' raves where the young folks could meet up on a Friday or Saturday night from eight till eleven and drink lemonade and cola, and dance in an orderly fashion under the watchful eye of the 'Neighbourhood Teen-scene Committee'!

It hadn't worked — the NTC. He gave a mirthless little laugh. Of course it wouldn't work. The name itself was enough to send the young-bloods of Holderness screaming into the cornfields. It smacked of the fifties and sixties and 'flower-power' and 'peace-man-peace'! And the youngsters of the nineties wanted more than that. They wanted power, and sex, and excitement enough to fly them over the moon.

Mark thanked heaven he was thirty — and not a teenager any more. Even cigarettes had been frowned on in the Langham household when Dad was alive so he'd never got into even that dubious habit. Mother had liked 'social' smoking though, and it had caused no end of bickerings.

The house at Rothwold was his now though — his to do with as he pleased. Mother was off in Australia with a new husband and a new home since Dad had died. It had hurt him — how fast she'd managed to find somebody else. But now, the old house was his, and he was finding it a lonely place in which to live, he mused. It needed that bickering back again to wake the house up, and once awake, to keep it alive.

He set off again, the roads were narrow and winding. It was impossible to speed knowing that only a foot or so of tarmac separated him from the deep ditches on either side of the road. The pale strip of tarmac ahead of him twisted and turned every few yards, and the moon had disappeared now, turning the yellow fields into a dull and lifeless grey.

For a few minutes the road straightened, and up front, just before the next corner, he saw something white fluttering about on the road. He peered into the glare of the headlights. It looked like a plastic bag, dancing this way and that, bobbing up and down, then flattening itself down to the ground again before bouncing up once more.

He approached the corner with caution. There was no wind. It couldn't be a plastic bag. The night was still and airless. He felt prickles down the back of his spine. It was weird — it was scary . . .

It was a girl!

At the last minute she lurched into the path of the car and sprawled across the road. He stood on the brake. The back end of the Porsche slewed sideways. Rubber screeched sickeningly on cold tarmac. The front wheels stopped only inches away from the inert body in front of him.

He was out of the car and on his knees beside her before he even realized he'd killed the engine. She was lying face down, her gold hair spread out around her head. The white dress was diaphanous. It was up around her thighs. She had good legs — slender, shapely, her feet were bare.

Carefully he eased her over on to her back. The car had missed her. There was no danger of any serious injury. She must just have passed out cold. He looked down into her face and then sat back on his heels and drew in a deep breath.

'Tamsin!'

Her eyes flicked open the instant her name was mentioned. She looked up into his face and giggled. 'I can fly.'

'Yeah!' he said. 'And I can do a belly flop, my lovely, but you can't stay here.'

'It's comfortable. I like your bed.'

'Have you been drinking?' he asked, gazing down at her.

Still flat on her back and illuminated by the car headlights she rolled her head from side to side. 'Water,' she said in a prim and precise voice. 'They said I should take water with it.'

His heart froze. 'Take water with what?' he asked, knowing full well what the answer would be.

'The stuff. They called it 'stuff', but I think it was aspirin and icing sugar mixed together.'

'You don't say.'

'Yes, I do.' She looked huffy. She pouted. 'I had a headache. Nobody had any pills though.'

'Nobody. Who is nobody?' he asked guardedly.

'The kids. The kids from the NTC. The rebels that the Neighbourhood Teen-scene Committee tried to tame.' She began to giggle again and squirmed around on the

174

ground. 'The music gave me a headache.' She pushed herself up to a sitting position and hugged her knees like a flopped over rag doll. Her gold hair fell forward around her face. When she glanced up at him he saw that her eyes were heavily ringed with black mascara, but apart from that, she wore no lipstick or make-up. She looked unreal and sexy in the harsh light of the car headlamps.

'Did they hurt you? The rebels?' he asked gently.

'Hurt?' She wrinkled up her nose, then shook her head. 'I had a good time — best time of my life — except for the headache. The music was too loud.'

'Do you still have a headache?'

'No. I flew it away.' She leaned her head back and stared up into the dark, star-studded sky. 'I flew it away up there.'

'You can't fly, honey. Believe me, you can't fly,' he said drily.

She stared at him. 'I can,' she said in a solemn voice. 'I'll show you when I get home. I shall fly from the top of the Ivory Tower. Then you'll believe me.'

'Oh, no,' he groaned.

'Yes,' she insisted. 'It's mine — all mine tonight.'

'Your partner — Ava Thorne. Where is she? Won't she be home if I take you there?'

With a pensive, almost childish look at him, she said, 'Ava went out. She said she was fed up with my tantrums. I don't have tantrums. I have bad dreams though . . . ' Her voice tailed away.

'Bad dreams?' Mark sat back on his heels and looked questioningly at her.

She nodded and a tear trickled down her cheek. 'Bad dreams you wouldn't understand about.'

Mark didn't know what to say. He just crouched there looking at her, feeling incredibly sorry for her. She made him feel infinitely protective towards her. He wanted to put his arm round her and mop up that tear . . .

She said, 'Ava wouldn't let me stay in France. She said I had to come back with her. There's the Wedding Fayre, you see . . . '

Mark nodded slowly. 'Yes. I know about that. Brand Motors are sending some cars over next week.'

She sniffed and brushed the tear away with the back of her hand. 'I wanted to stay in France.'

'You did?'

She stared hard at him. 'You don't understand a damned thing,' she snapped in a childish way, and her mouth drooped into a pout.

'I understand that you can't stay here in the middle of the road,' he stated. 'As to the rest — no, you're not making much sense.'

'I wanted to stay with him. He needs somebody. And now, that girl, that girl from Brand Motors, she's gone to him.'

At last, light was beginning to dawn. Tamsin had wanted to stay with Rafe Thorne after his accident, that much was obvious. 'Yes,' he said softly, 'Maggie's gone to him. It's like you say. Now I'm starting to understand.'

'No,' she shook her head vigorously. 'You don't understand. Nobody understands.'

'You're in love with him.'

She leaned her chin on her cupped hands, then swept them slowly through her hair and brought them back to either side of her face to stare, wide-eyed at him. Her face began to crumple then and the tears started in earnest.

Mark's voice was husky with compassion. 'Don't cry,' he said.

'I'll cry if I want to.' She buried her head in her knees.

'Come on. Let's get you up. Into the car.' He went round the back of her and dragged her to her feet with his hands under her arms. She looked frail and thin, with the flimsy dress clinging to her body when she was upright. He led her over to the passenger side of the car and somehow got her inside. It was hopeless trying to get the seat belt on her, she just crumpled up like a rag doll and sagged down in the seat.

His mind was working overtime as he drove home. It would do no good taking her back to Heronsea, he argued to himself. If Ava Thorne was indeed away for the night, who knew what might happen — always supposing of course that Tamsin could get into the lighthouse. She had no bag, no purse, not even a pocket that he could see in that sexy, see-through dress.

'Do you have a key?' he asked.

She looked at him as if he'd asked her for the moon. 'Why?'

He kept his attention firmly on the road. 'Because if you want to go home to the Ivory Tower, you'll need a key to get in,' he said.

She'd stopped weeping now. 'No key.' She shook her head.

'Where is it?'

She lifted her slender shoulders in an elegant little shrug.

He sighed and tried again. 'Where do you want to spend the night.'

'Bed,' she said firmly. 'I want to go to bed.'

'You don't still want to jump out of the window then?'

'What window?' She turned those great

innocent eyes on him again.

'You don't want to fly?'

'Yes.'

'You can't! You do realize that, don't you? You can't fly, Tamsin.'

'I know. Ava said I couldn't. She won't let me go back to him.' Her voice ended on the tiniest of sobs. 'I could make him happy. I can make him laugh.'

'Honey — you could make any man happy — in that dress,' he muttered, glancing sideways at her nipples that were prominent and taut under the gauzy material.

'Make you happy?'

'Yes,' he growled. 'You make me happy. But not while you still think you can fly, my sweet.'

'I remembered,' she said suddenly.

'What have you remembered?' He glanced at her again.

'The key.'

'Yes. What did you do with the key?' He'd take her back to Heronsea, he decided, and if necessary, he'd stay the night there just in case she took it into her head to jump off the lantern platform. He'd go up there himself and bed down across the door. That way she'd be safe till morning.

She started to giggle. 'I threw it in a ditch.'

He groaned, 'Oh, no.'

'I want to go to bed.'

He turned inland, and towards his own home. There was nothing for it but to oblige the lady, he told himself. And if bed was what she wanted, bed was what she'd get.

11

Mark was stampeded awake by a fury smashing away at him with a feather pillow . . .

'You louse! You absolute louse! What the hell right did you have to bring me here . . . '

Mark rolled away from her, curling his legs up tightly to his chest, covering his head with his elbows, his mind not at first aware that it was a pillow laying into him and not a hammer. When his sleep-befuddled brain eventually did realize what was going on though, he began to see the funny side of things, and he rolled over on to his back then, all tangled up in the duvet, and laughed up into her face as he expertly dodged each thud of the pillow she was aiming with such force.

She was kneeling on the edge of the bed, precariously balanced, and her language would have made a strong man cringe.

'You're an absolute bastard! You're a swine, Mark Langham!' Every syllable she uttered was emphasized by another swipe, another flurry of feathers coming loose from their former safe little bagged existence. 'You'll — be — so — rry — for — this . . . ' She scored a direct hit every time she opened her mouth.

Her hair was dishevelled, but he didn't care. He loved her hair, all golden and fuzzy around her head, untamed and unmanageable at eight o'clock in the morning. She looked wanton and sexy, and unbelievably desirable even though her gamin little face was contorted with rage.

He reached up and grabbed at her hands as she made ready for another attack. The pillow was between them now, not a weapon any more, it was merely wobbling about as her small wiry body trembled with the pent-up passion that had been unleashed when she'd imagined herself a prisoner in his house.

'Let — me — go,' she hissed.

'No!' He laughed up into her face.

Her eyes blazed down at him. She raised herself up on her knees, but with a subtle twist of her wrists he forced her to let go of the pillow. Deprived of it, she lost her balance and fell on top of him with only the tumbled duvet making an insubstantial barrier between them.

'Rapist!' she hurled at him. 'Kidnapper!

Barbarian! Is this how you get your thrills — luring helpless females to your . . . '

'Helpless!' He was helpless himself now — helpless with laughter as he tossed her over on to her back, held both her hands immobile against her shoulders, and leaned up on the bed to look down into her face. When he managed to compose himself a little, he asked her again, with incredulity in his voice, 'Helpless! Is that how you see yourself, you Hell-cat?'

She was still fully clothed, he noted, though the white flimsy dress was up around her thighs by now. It was the ultimate turn-on as far as Mark was concerned, being woken up first thing in the morning by a raging maniac with a face like an angel and a body like a dream-goddess. First things first though.

'I did not rape you,' he stated. 'And I did not kidnap you.'

'You brought me here — and God knows where *here* is,' she snapped back at him. 'You made me get into your car — I can remember that. And then the next thing I remember is waking up in a strange bed, a house I don't know, maybe I'm in a different country to the one I went to sleep in . . . '

'You're in Yorkshire,' he said.

'How the hell do *I* know that?' Her eyes were spitting sparks now.

'If you'd taken the trouble to look out of the window . . . '

'I did.' She wriggled to free herself. 'All I could see were trees and fields.'

'Did it look like Siberia?' he asked sarcastically. 'Or Egypt, or Japan?'

He felt her suddenly go limp. 'No . . . ' she admitted, 'But . . . '

'Did you pass a harem as you came down the passage from your room to mine?' he asked, struggling to keep his face straight and his voice stern.

'No, but . . . '

'Ah, but you must have seen the chains on the doors, heard the ferocious barking of the guard dogs, and noticed of course that all the windows had bars on them,' he said in a smug voice.

'No, you idiot!' She aimed a kick at him that he was quick to avoid as he moved his legs away under the duvet.

Calmly he said, 'But you've been raped, have you?'

'We-ell . . . '

'I didn't even undress you,' he yelled into her face. And with the words, he let her go. He pushed himself to a sitting position then and linked his hands loosely together in front of him to let her know she was in no danger from him. Maggie Brand, he thought grimly, might think him a lecher and a sex pest, but one thing he wasn't — he certainly wasn't a rapist or any of the things Tamsin had accused him of being.

She rolled off the bed, then just stood there looking at him, 'Why did you bring me here?' she said, her face as unyielding as if it had been carved out of stone.

'Think back, lady,' he said. 'You told me you'd chucked the key to your Ivory Tower away. You also told me nobody would be at home if I took you back there. What was I supposed to do? Leave you there on the road? Stoned out of your skull with dope?'

Her head jerked up. 'I don't do drugs.'

'You did last night,' he said drily. 'Believe me — you did.'

'B- but . . . ' Her lips trembled, then she bit down hard on them, compressing them tightly together as if in an effort not to say anything that might incriminate her.

'A one-off,' he said, in a more gentle tone than he'd hitherto used with her. 'Is that what you're telling me?'

She nodded. 'I've never even been to a 'rave' before. I saw the notice pinned on a farm gate, and I thought what the hell . . . '

'You needed excitement. Is that it?'

She hung her head, then lifted it just to give him a hostile stare. 'No. I was going crazy because Ava said the girl — Maggie Brand — would be good for Rafe.'

His eyes narrowed. 'That damn racing driver.'

'I hate him.' Her eyes blazed again. She faced him with defiance.

'Not from where I'm sitting — you don't hate him,' Mark said.

She looked away again. 'What do you know about love anyway?'

He leaned back, placed his hands behind his head and said, 'What indeed? Why should a rapist, a kidnapper and a bastard know anything about love?'

She seemed all of a sudden to realize that the bit of him she could see from the waist up, was naked. 'Why don't you put something on,' she snapped. 'It's not decent — sleeping like that — not when you've got a visitor in the house.'

'A victim,' he corrected her. 'You're a victim remember? Not a visitor.'

She raised her eyes to the ceiling. 'Bastard!' she said again.

'A nice polite 'thank you' might be more in keeping with what I did for you,' he said silkily. 'At least you slept soundly and in complete safety last night.'

She seemed flustered and twisted her hands together in front of her. Then, abruptly she flung away from him and walked over to the window, turning her back firmly on him as she yelled, 'Get up. Get out of that damned bed. And for heaven's sake get some clothes on, will you?'

'If that's what you want.' He tossed the duvet aside, swung his legs out of bed and reached for his pants and a shirt. He stood up then and pulled on a pair of jeans then raked his hands through his hair. 'Okay,' he said, 'You can turn round now. I'm decent.'

She was scowling as she looked him up and down. 'Well, it's an improvement.'

'Look — I need a shower. Do you think you could possibly find a crumb of domesticity in that tousled head of yours that would enable you to go down to the kitchen and make a pot of coffee?'

'Black or white?' she snapped as she stormed across to the door.

'Black. And strong.' He was in no mood for further argument.

'I'll do my best,' she said in a sugary insincere voice as she reached the door and flounced through it.

'Nice one, Langham,' he muttered to himself as she went. 'You finally get a dame under your roof who looks like she was made in heaven, and what do you ask her for?

Coffee. Strong and black.' He shook his head as he made his way to the bathroom.

★ ★ ★

He couldn't fault her coffee. He couldn't fault the two slices of toast either that were smoking hot, golden brown and heavily buttered, and were at the moment he entered the kitchen, being put down on a china plate on the table for him.

She sat down opposite him with a dish of cereal.

'Is that all you're having?' He picked up his mug of coffee and took a swig of it. It was delicious. Just how he liked it.

She nodded and carried on eating.

'There's bacon and eggs in the fridge.'

'I'm not your servant. If you want bacon and eggs you can get them yourself.' Unperturbed she gave him a smoky glance. 'My job stops here. I don't do dishes either. When I've had something to eat, I'm going home.'

Suddenly he didn't want her to go. It was nice having somebody else in the house in a morning for a change, he was realizing. 'There's no hurry.' He crunched into a neatly sliced up piece of toast.

'Ava will be frantic.' She scooped up the

last of her cornflakes, then pushed the dish away.

'Call her.' He waved a hand towards the door. 'There's the phone.'

'I already have done.'

'Oh!' He sat back in his chair and considered her. 'Did you ring the police as well? Did you tell them you'd been kidnapped?'

'No, I just called Ava. The answerphone was on so I left a message.' She lifted her shoulders in a shrug. 'I didn't know what to tell her so I just said I was all right and I'd be back later this morning. If she didn't get up early, she probably doesn't even know I've been out all night. I don't suppose she would have looked in on my room last night when she came in.'

'What are you going to tell her?' he asked interestedly.

'I'll think of something.'

'Do you often stay out all night with strange men?'

She looked uncomfortable for a moment, but that moment soon passed. He was beginning to find out that Tamsin was rarely at a loss for words. 'That's none of your business,' she hedged.

He pulled a nonchalant face at her. 'I agree,' he said. 'I was merely interested.'

'Why?'

'I like to think I saved you from a fate worse than death last night,' he said. 'After all, anybody — just anybody could have come along and picked you up, couldn't they?'

'They did,' she said. 'You did.'

'Insult taken,' he said, getting up and carrying his plate and mug over to the sink, but inside he was feeling a bit fragile. Didn't the bitch know how to hold a civilized conversation? Didn't she realize how she could hurt a guy by her continuous insults?

'Don't get in a huff,' she said as she came up to him with her own breakfast pots.

'I'm not in a huff.'

'Yes you are.' She moved away, across the kitchen again, to stand beside the door. 'Come and show me your garden,' she said. 'I've seen the rest of the house and I'm not really interested in houses. I like flowers, and gardens.'

'Go see it yourself.' He never looked round at her. He ran hot water over the two mugs, the plate, cutlery and the dish, scrubbed at them, then placed them on the draining board, upside down.

'Oh, for heaven's sake, stop sulking,' she yelled at him. 'You're not a child so don't act like one.'

Nobody, but nobody had got away with

talking to him like that — not since he was six years old. He spun round to face her, drew in a deep breath preparatory to telling her just what he thought of her, then decided against it, and walked over to her.

'Okay,' he said smoothly. 'Let's go and look at the damn garden. What do I care if I'm late for work and Edgar Brand threatens me with redundancy?'

'It's Saturday,' she pointed out. 'You don't work on a Saturday, surely?' Her blue eyes were questioning. Her delicate little features animated.

'Yes,' he said. 'I work Saturdays — until twelve when I'm needed.'

'But I need you. Here.' She walked ahead of him down the long passage to the front door. 'Come on.' She turned. 'Slowcoach.' And for the first time that day, she smiled at him.

It was like the sun coming out through a stormcloud. In that moment he was hooked. Her evil temper was a thing of the past. Her impatience and her ability for jumping to all the wrong conclusions could be overlooked in a second when she smiled at him like that. She wasn't so bad, he decided. At least she could make good coffee and toast, and sitting across the breakfast table from her had been like nothing he'd ever experienced before.

'You've got no shoes on,' he said, looking down at her bare feet.

She bent her head and gazed down. 'I hate wearing shoes,' she said.

'There are stones in the garden . . . '

'I'm not made of china.' She stuck her tongue out at him. 'Sometimes we have to take risks,' she said, 'b-i-i-i-g risks like walking without shoes. Don't you ever walk around without shoes?'

She was the end. The absolute end. 'In the garage?' he asked, slightly annoyed with her.

'No, stupid. Here at home.'

He pulled open the front door and she went outside into the bright May morning. She looked at him interestedly as he came and stood beside her.

'Take them off now,' she said. 'Show me you can live dangerously. Take your shoes off.'

'No,' he said, glowering at her. 'Don't be silly.'

She considered him for several seconds then shrugged. Then, without warning she dived at his legs and before he knew it she'd wrestled one of his shoes off and had flung it back towards the house. It hit the front door with a thud.

He yelled at her, 'Get off me . . . ' but she already had hold of his other leg and was trying her hardest to lift it off the ground.

She was shrieking with laughter, her hands hard and her fingers digging into his calf muscles and his shins as she shook and tugged and behaved for all the world as if she were a terrier worrying a bone.

Mark's temper snapped. He kicked out at her. He shouted at her. 'For goodness' sake — act your age, woman . . . '

But she tumbled in the dust at his feet, triumphantly raising one hand aloft with his second shoe grasped tightly in it.

She sprang up like a monkey then, agile and prancing, waving his shoe at him as she ran out into the garden, on to the neatly edged lawn and then round the side of the large detached house towards the back.

He swore softly under his breath as she disappeared. 'Hell!' Then he was racing after her, yelping in pain as the white limestone paths cut into his feet, cursing afresh because they'd made no impression on her. Her feet must be as hard as her heart, he reasoned as he limped, hopped and hobbled after her.

He found her eventually by the rose beds. She seemed to hear him coming up behind her on the soft, dew-laden grass, and she turned to him eagerly, her hand cupping one exquisite red rose. Gone was the teasing and the jeering; she was stroking the petals gently with the thumb of the hand holding it, and her eyes were misty and faraway as she looked at him.

He stood stock still, a couple of yards away from her, shaken by her beauty, her complete naturalness in that place of thorns. Her gold hair was being lifted by the light breeze of the morning. Her eyes were wide and luminous, her lips as red as the rose she was holding. The soft stuff her dress was made of moulded itself to her and with the sun coming up behind her emphasized each delicious curve and arch of the sylph-like body beneath.

And in that moment, Mark knew that this girl was the one he wanted to spend his entire life with. The knowledge caught him unawares. It made him jittery, and tongue-tied. He tried to speak, 'Tamsin . . . ' but there were no words adequate to follow that one, trivial little one. 'Tamsin . . . ' He couldn't believe this. Would never have believed it if somebody else had told him that love could strike like that. She'd exasperated him all morning, intrigued him too though. But coming across her holding the rose as she was doing right now had dazed him. She seemed so at home. It was as if she had been there all the time and he'd only just noticed her.

She tilted her head on one side. 'What's the matter with you?' She gazed down at his feet and started to laugh. Her laughter rose higher and higher, spiralling to join the song of the blackbird above her in the shrubbery. And like the blackbird, Mark thought worriedly, she might just take off into the blue, blue, sky above and never be seen again, she was so insubstantial — like a thread of gossamer or a wispy twirl of silk caught up on a thorn.

'Tamsin . . . stay here,' he blurted out, his voice harsh with emotion.

Her eyes played over him till he felt he was drowning in them. Her mouth tilted in a little smile of derision. Then, without warning, the hand holding the red rose gave a sudden jerk, snapping the rose off the bush with a violent motion. She came towards him then, holding it by its stem; the sharp thorns didn't seem to worry her. She held the rose up to his nose.

'No scent,' she said in a most practical tone. 'It just goes to show, doesn't it, that we can be taken in by the most beautiful of things. You'd imagine it would have a scent to match its looks, wouldn't you?'

He shook his head, still dazed.

'The first ever rosary beads were made of rose petals — did you know that?'

Again he shook his head; he was incapable of speech.

She held the rose a few inches away from him and said, 'If I gave you this rose the way it grows . . . ' she twirled it upright, 'it would mean I loved you.'

Mark swallowed painfully and sought in his mind for some glib reply. Nothing presented itself though. He cleared his throat and muttered, 'Tamsin . . . '

She laughed in his face, twisted the rose upside down and with the back of its petals towards him. 'However, if I gave it to you this way, it would mean there was absolutely no hope for you at all.'

Very deliberately then, she moved in on him and pushed the stem of the rose through one of his shirt buttonholes, upside down and back to front. She whirled away from him then and snapped her fingers in his face.

'You're mad,' he roared, ripping the rose away from his shirt and then flinging it to the ground as the thorns tore into his fingers.

He shook his hand. 'Damn!' The magic had gone. 'That hurt.'

She caught hold of his hand, turned it over in both her own and looked at the red blood seeping down into his palm.

She watched it for some moments, and he held his breath and tilted back his head and closed his eyes, savouring the exquisite touch of her hands, the nearness of her, the fresh scent of the morning in her hair.

He felt a soft nuzzling movement then, and

opening his eyes, jerked his head down to see what she was doing.

Her head was bent over his hand, and her little pink tongue was curling into his palm, lapping at the blood the rose had drawn.

He shuddered and pulled his hand away. It wasn't right for her to do that. It was pagan — uncivilized.

She lifted her head and looked up into his face. There was a red smudge on her chin. His blood.

Her smile was wide and mysterious. And then she was gone, heading back to the house, her footprints leaving only the faintest indentation in the soft green grass as she went.

He walked back slowly, not bothering to wonder where his second shoe had gone. It didn't matter. It was only a shoe.

When he reached the house he searched it from top to bottom for her, but she'd gone.

It was five miles to Heronsea.

He locked up the house, went and got in his car and crawled along the country lanes till he reached the small town with the lighthouse, but he saw no sign of her.

She wouldn't have gone home by road though, he suddenly knew beyond all shadow of a doubt. She was a free spirit, and like no girl he'd ever known before. She would have gone the fields and hedgerows way, the way of the seagull, the way of the fox and the butterfly.

She would go her own way — no matter what. Nobody would ever be able to keep her on a leash.

It was a sobering thought, and one that filled Mark's heart with an aching loneliness.

12

For such a small principality, the light-coloured buildings of Monte Carlo were enormous things — tower blocks built one on top of another, sprawling all over the hillsides around the picturesque harbour. There were boats too, hundreds of them all anchored in straight lines against little jetties, boats, cruisers and luxury yachts, and bronzed rich people strolling betwixt blue sea and lush greenery, with those tall buildings and the mountains beyond, a lavish backcloth.

Maggie hadn't expected to come this way — not right through the middle of Monte Carlo, but her driver was bronzed and French and garrulous; he also insisted on showing her all the sights.

Monaco, she had to admit — and despite her worry over Rafe — was a fabulous place. A few days ago, she wouldn't have believed she'd be actually driving through France, admiring panoramic views of the coastline, the dazzling blue Mediterranean, and the blink-of-an-eye blackness as the road slipped in and out of tunnels through the sheer rocks beneath old villages perched on dizzy crags.

But though the drive was enchanting, her mind was busy all the time, wondering, questioning, hoping, and also fearing what she'd find at the end of it all.

She regretted nothing however. One simple phone call to Oscar-Jade Racing headquarters had resulted in her being given Oscar's number in France. In turn that had led to Oscar putting her on to Ava who was just about to fly back to England. Ava had explained that Rafe had a badly crushed ankle, but he had discharged himself from hospital and was now recuperating in a villa in the mountains beyond Monte Carlo.

Ava was the one who suggested that Maggie should go to him.

'You'll be good for him. He mentioned your name several times when he was coming out of the anaesthetic after the operation on his ankle.'

'He did?' Maggie had held her breath.

'Maggie — just go to him,' Ava said. 'Believe me — you'll be doing me a big favour if you do.'

She hadn't explained further, but had gone on to give instructions on how to get to the place in the mountainous country around Peira-Cava and Luceram where the villa was situated.

But would he remember asking for her, Maggie wondered? And would he still want her around if he was making a good recovery? And then there was Tamsin. Ava had said that Tamsin had been absolutely livid when she had to return home.

'We had to be practical though,' Ava had said. 'We've got the Wedding Fayre in less than a month, and when it turned out that Rafe wasn't as badly injured as we first thought . . . '

The rest was left unsaid, but Maggie had the distinct impression that Ava was desperate for the Ivory Tower to be a success. And why not? It was her livelihood, after all — hers and Tamsin's.

The car was climbing out of Monte Carlo now and behind it as Maggie turned to look, she saw the blue sea glinting in the afternoon's hot sun. Soon though the coast was left behind and after another half hour had passed, Maggie asked, 'How much further?'

The leather-like features of the driver screwed into an elfish smile as he told her in almost perfect English that it was no more than a few kilometres.

The hill villages were awesome. Maggie marvelled at the tiny stone houses perched precariously on rocky outcrops, with hundreds of steps winding up the hillsides to the terraces. Mist hung in the hollows of the mountains, and in places the road was edged with only low stone walls that bordered steep ravines with precipitous drops away to the side of her.

She clung on to her seat and held her breath, glad that she hadn't urged the driver to go any faster. It was hair-raising on some of those bends, to see the road almost falling away into nothing.

And then after almost an hour, the driver was pointing through the windscreen and telling her to look ahead.

And above them, at the top of a fairly straight road that was hugging a mountainside, she saw the house. It was made of white stone, and from here she could see several arches above a palisaded patio.

As they drew closer, she saw also that there was a courtyard through one of the arches, then they were through it, and the car drew to a halt at the foot of a flight of stone steps. There was wrought ironwork on an outside balcony, where there were chairs with flowered cushions. The villa itself had deeply recessed windows, and was built on several different levels, each one topped with a pink pantiled roof. There were white plant pots with brilliant geraniums in them, a small terraced garden, and twisted trees. Her eyes were drawn again to the balcony where yellow roses clambered and tumbled all over it.

She got out of the car and he brought her baggage out and dumped it on the ground.

'I take it inside? Yes?'

A voice above him, at the top of the steps called down, 'No. Leave it there. I'll see to it.'

Maggie didn't recognize the voice. She looked up as a young man came into view and ran quickly down the steps. When he was level with her, she found herself looking into a pair of steady grey eyes that stared out with undisguised interest from behind a pair of steel-framed spectacles. He was young — maybe twenty-four or twenty-five, she'd guess. He had mousy brown hair and was quite good looking. He wasn't over tall, just about her own height which was roughly five feet five and a half inches. He was slim and straight as a sapling. His smile was genuine. 'I'm glad you made it.'

She found herself smiling back at him; she recognized him now from pictures in newspapers and television interviews.

'I'm Maggie.' She held out her hand. 'And you're Vaughn Herrick.'

The driver was back in his cab and starting up the engine again as the young man shook hands with her.

He kept hold of her hand longer than was necessary. 'My fame goeth before me.'

She slipped her hand free. He was very much a ladies' man — that was obvious from his frank and admiring appraisal of her.

He said, 'You must be whacked after that long journey.'

'No. It's been much too interesting. But Rafe . . . How is Rafe . . . ?'

'Asleep.'

This was the man who had caused the crash, she realized. This was Vaughn Herrick whose car had been on fire, Vaughn Herrick who Rafe had risked his own life to save. And he was here. But why? She drew in a deep breath, then let it out again slowly as he picked up her luggage. He glanced at her.

'I know what you're thinking.' He stood and looked at her steadily with the sun blazing down on them both in the hot courtyard.

'I don't think you do.' It took all the strength she could muster to be polite to him. Dad had told her that young Herrick faced a race ban for entering the tunnel on the Monte Carlo circuit when his car was unsafe. And if it hadn't been for Herrick being so foolhardy, Rafe wouldn't have stopped to save the young man's life. It was doing that which had put his own life in danger, and she could never forgive Vaughn Herrick for that . . .

'It was my fault.' He gazed at her for a second or two more, then said, 'Okay — it was my fault. Now — can we just get inside and forego the post mortems till later?'

She followed him up the steep steps and into the house. Inside it was cool and quiet. The walls were made up of great blocks of stone that were painted white. The ceiling was wood, varnished to a high gloss. On the flagged floor were little cotton mats with tassels. She had an overall impression of wooden chairs, a simple wooden table, fat cushions on a couch, and then more stairs.

A woman was there too, a round little woman with white hair scraped back from her scrubbed face — a kind face with barely a wrinkle or a line in it.

Vaughn whisked her luggage into a room on a balcony above the sitting room through which they'd just come. He reappeared almost immediately to say, 'Maggie, this is Theresa. She's acting as housekeeper for a while. She looks after us all.'

Maggie was relieved she could speak French — in a fashion. It was a long time since she'd had to though. She held out her hand, 'Bonjour Theresa . . . '

'Eh, lass — I dunna understand any o' that there French stuff.' Maggie's hand was shaken vigorously.

In the background, Vaughn's low laughter was a grumble of sound. He broke in, 'Theresa used to be our housekeeper in Yorkshire when Mum was alive and I was just a kid.'

'And when you and your dad were still pals,' Theresa said with a knowing shake of her head.

'I'm pleased to meet you,' Maggie said, 'Relieved too because my French is a bit rusty.'

Theresa must have been in her late sixties. She said confidently, 'You'll like your room, lass. They've all got nice views mind. One thing more though.' She shook a finger warningly first at Vaughn, then at Maggie. 'No more of this Theresa stuff. I'm Tess! Understand?'

Maggie laughed softly. 'I'll remember that.'

'You can see him when you've had a cuppa.' The old woman bustled away.

'He's sleeping,' Vaughn said.

'He's all right though?'

'He — he'll mend.' Vaughn shoved his hands in his jeans pockets, rocked on his heels, then looked solemnly at her. 'His leg

— his ankle — it's a mess. He's in a lot of pain but he never lets on.'

'But — he's not in any danger? They wouldn't have let him out of hospital if he'd been in danger?'

'He's okay.' Vaughn chewed on his bottom lip. Thought about his words for several seconds more, then said, 'Yes. He's okay.'

'Can I see him? Just for a minute? I won't wake him.'

Vaughn cocked his head on one side and considered her for a moment. Then, seeming to make up his mind, he said, 'Come on then — while Tess is busy in the kitchen.'

She followed him away from the balcony and down a tiny passage. At the end of it he pushed open a door and held it open while she stepped past him and stood on the threshold of a bedroom.

She looked inside. Drew in a deep breath.

Rafe was lying sprawled across a stark white cotton bedspread. He was dressed in an Oscar-Jade T-shirt — green and white, and blue denim shorts.

Her gaze was riveted on his right leg which was in plaster up to the knee. The leg above it was swollen. Her eyes swept to his face, and tentatively she took a few steps inside the room. His head was turned away from her.

Restless, he jerked over on to his side and

she gasped as she saw his face — bruised and battered, with a deep cut over his left eye that had several stitches in it. His dark hair was singed almost down to his scalp on the other side of his head.

Pain as he tried to move his leg made him groan in his sleep. His forehead creased into a deep frown.

She spun round to Vaughn. 'Leave me alone with him,' she whispered.

'No! He gave strict instructions — I was to wake him — let him make himself a bit more presentable before you saw him.'

'Please . . . '

The figure on the bed stirred again. 'Oscar . . . is that you . . . ?'

Vaughn pushed past her and went over to the bed. 'Dad went back to England yesterday, old man. Don't you remember? I wouldn't be here if he was, now would I?'

'Hell! Did they have to remove my brain cells in that damned hospital?'

'It's the pain killers. They said you'd feel pretty lousy if you insisted on discharging yourself from the clinic, and coming off the morphine.'

'Damned doctors!'

Maggie watched as Rafe pulled himself up against the pile of pillows. Now she could see dark circles under eyes that were dull and pain-wracked. She could understand now why he hadn't wanted her to see him like this, and her heart went out to him. She tried to edge away into the shadows, tried to get back through the door without him noticing her.

He heard the scrape of her shoe on the flagged floor though. His head shot up. He peered across the room. 'Who's there? Vaughn — who the hell is there? I'm not having hallucinations, am I?'

Vaughn sighed and turned round to her. 'You'd better let him see you, Maggie.' He grinned but it didn't hide the worry on his face.

'Maggie!' Rafe exploded. 'No! I told you — I can't see her like this!'

Maggie went over to the bed. 'I'm here,' she said. 'Whether you like it or not, I'm here.'

Vaughn backed out of the room and closed the door.

'Hell!'

She perched on the edge of the bed. 'Don't keep saying 'hell'!'

'It feels like hell.'

'It's been hell for me too.'

'Has it?' He stared hard at her. 'Has it, Maggie?'

She nodded solemnly. 'I couldn't get any news of you for two days — Sunday and

Monday. I was out of my mind with worry, but even after I found out you were still alive, it still took the rest of the week to arrange a flight. It's been the longest week of my life.'

'Wish I could have made myself beautiful for you.' He managed a ghost of a smile. 'Wish I'd had a wash and a shave and was sitting in my wheelchair to welcome you when you arrived.'

'You're here. That's all that matters.'

'You too.' He reached out to her, took hold of her hand and brought it up to his lips.

13

'You came. Did Ava ask you to?' His dark eyes sought hers, his fingers curling round her hands and holding them very tight as he asked the question.

'No. I made a thousand phone calls. I couldn't stand the not knowing any longer. When I eventually did get in touch with your sister, I was almost out of my mind with worry.'

'So she didn't bully you into it?'

She laughed softly. 'Not a bit of it. I think I would have searched the whole of the south of France for you if I hadn't managed to locate Ava to get news of you.'

At last he let her go, and allowed his gaze to sweep round the spacious sunlit room. 'Oscar brought me here. The villa belongs to him. He didn't take kindly to Vaughn turning up though.'

'I hated Vaughn too when I realized who he was.' She looked down at her hands. 'I've never hated anybody so much in my whole life as I did when it hit home what he could have done to you.'

Rafe moved his position slightly. 'Don't hate, Maggie. It could have been anybody in that burning car.'

'But . . . '

He leaned forward, touched a finger to her lips, 'But nothing,' he said gently, 'It's done now. I had a choice — a choice whether to plunge in and do what I thought was right at the time, or else drive past and just be glad it wasn't me who was trapped in that holocaust.'

She thought about his words for some seconds then said, 'I plunged in too, though at the time I never realized I could 'drive past' and ignore what was happening to me.'

'Are you talking about coming out here to me?'

She lifted her head a little and decided the time had come to be honest with him. 'No. It was years ago,' she said. 'I plunged in that long-ago day at Silverstone when I was just a teenager. I plunged in and fell head over heels in love with a man in Oscar-Jade driving colours, a man who loved another girl.'

He looked dazed. 'I never knew.'

Solemnly she said, 'You never would have known if you hadn't looked Dad up again a few weeks ago.'

'But — you knew about Jade? Knew I'd killed her?'

She nodded. 'I read about the accident. I knew she'd died.'

'I killed her, Maggie.' He leaned back against the pillows looking very tired and pale, and she knew it wasn't his own accident that was causing the pallor. 'I killed my own fiancée and another girl as well. I also wrecked Tamsin's life.' He directed his glance at her again. 'You knew that Tamsin was injured in the smash?'

Again she nodded. 'She's all right now though?'

'Hell, no. She has these nightmares. She goes off the rails at times.' He swallowed, was silent for a while, then went on, 'I feel responsible for her, Maggie. I have to be honest with you — I don't think I can enter into any kind of a commitment with anybody else just at the moment.'

Maggie felt her heart plunging. Was he going to tell her to go back home to England? Was he also, in a fumbling sort of way trying to tell her that there was something between him and Tamsin, as she'd suspected herself at the lighthouse that day when she and Mark had been there?

'Do you want me to go?' she asked quietly.

He sat up, took hold of her hand again and

said, 'No. Don't go. I just wanted you to be aware of how things stand — at the moment.'

'At the moment?' Hope flared briefly.

'Maggie . . . ' He seemed to be stumbling over words, 'Maggie . . . it's not what you think . . . Oh, hell! I'm making a mess of this . . . What I want to say . . . is that when I met you again — at your father's house . . . ' He stopped, unable to go on.

She tried to make light of that meeting. 'I was a mess,' she said. 'Dirty working overalls, steel toe-cap boots and a turban swinging from my hand.'

'Listen to me, Maggie — please.' He let go of her hand again and said, 'Those things don't matter. Do you think I can't see beyond a few paint smears? A tousled head and mucky hands? No! Up to that point I had almost made up my mind to marry Tam.'

She gripped her hands together tightly on her lap, but said nothing, although somewhere deep inside her a tiny voice was screaming for him to stop telling her about Tamsin.

He went on in a steady voice now, 'I didn't love her — not the same way I loved Jade. I felt responsible though, and I liked her. I thought in time that liking could turn into something else.'

'But . . . ?' she said.

'But I met you, and everything changed.'

'Not love at first sight, though?'

'No! Not love. Attraction. Attraction such as I'd never felt towards Tam. Maggie, I want to be completely honest with you. I wanted you — wanted to hold you, to feel a real woman in my arms again. A year's a long time to be alone . . . '

Slowly, she pushed herself up from the bed and walked over to the window so her back was towards him. Did she want to hear this? she asked herself. Did she want her dreams shattered? Did she really need reminding that nobody could ever take the place of Jade Herrick in his heart?

'Maggie?'

She half-turned towards him. She'd made an idol of him in her heart, and now she was discovering he was just a man, not an idol, not a god, but just a man who had been deeply hurt and was struggling to put his life back together again.

'Have I hurt you?'

Had he hurt her? Thinking about it logically, no, he hadn't hurt her. She'd expected something more though, she supposed.

'I'm grateful you came . . . '

She spun round to face him fiercely, 'I don't want gratitude.'

'No,' he said in a low voice. 'No — I shouldn't have said that. What I mean is, it's nice seeing you, Maggie. I'm glad you came.'

But not ecstatic, Maggie thought. And why should he be? She decided in that moment to make the best of things.

'I can be quite good company,' she said, forcing a laugh. 'I'm good at card games and Scrabble, if that's what you want.'

'Oh, hell! I really have made a mess of this, haven't I?' He swung his legs to the side of the bed, reached for a couple of walking sticks that were within reach of it, and levered himself off the bed. With a great deal of balancing and with pain etched on his features he eventually stood up.

'Should you be doing that?' she said, compassion for him coming to the fore.

'With practice it gets better by the day,' he quipped. 'But walking is difficult so why don't you just come back over here and save me the trouble of coming over there?'

She went back to him. 'Okay,' she said. 'We know where we stand now. I won't ask for hearts and flowers. And in a fortnight I'll be gone. Sooner if we find we can't stand the sight of each other, okay?'

Standing in front of her he was not as tall as she remembered him from their last meeting — he was stooping over the two

216

sticks that were keeping him upright and he was leaning forward looking down at the floor. She could see beads of sweat on his forehead and knew he was in a good deal of pain. He seemed intent on proving he could fight back though. 'You know what Oscar says?' he said eventually, still keeping his gaze on the ground, 'He says winning is the name of the game.'

'He's right, isn't he?'

'Maybe.' He tried to straighten, and looked up into her face. 'Love's not a game though, is it? We don't set our sights on it like a winning post. If it happens, it happens, but I look on it more as a game of chance than anything more substantial.'

'I don't know,' she said. 'I don't know what it takes to make it work. I'm new to this particular game.'

Steadily, he observed her. Carefully he chose his words. 'Don't turn and run Maggie,' he said at last, 'But I have to be honest with you. I still feel the same way I did at your father's house, and on the beach — remember?'

She nodded. 'What are you trying to say?'

'I wanted you then. I want you now. It's like I said before. 'I need a woman in my arms again, there's nothing on this earth that compares to another warm, living body close

217

up against you, making life bearable, becoming a part of you. Can you understand that, Maggie?'

Sadly, she had to tell him, 'No. I can't understand it. To be that close to another human being I'd have to love them, truly, deeply and for all time. It's the only thing that lifts 'wanting' out of the animal world, isn't it? Love!'

'With animals it's a basic instinct to stop their breeds dying out,' he said. 'With humans it's different, I agree, though the same basic instinct must be there, I suppose.'

'We must agree to differ then?'

'And satisfy ourselves with games of cards, and Scrabble?' There was a lightness in his pain-shadowed eyes that hadn't been there before.

She'd settle for that. She had to. A stillness came over her. He wasn't going to send her back to England after all. She was glad.

'I still want you,' he said.

'You say that as if there's a 'but' to be added,' she stated with a smile.

'There is. I wasn't going to say it though.'

'You can say anything to me. It's best to be honest with each other, Rafe.'

He looked at her hard and long, then said softly, and it seemed with a genuine regret, ' . . . 'but' — I don't love you, Maggie.'

Two weeks sped by, and Maggie saw a distinct improvement in Rafe with every day that passed. He was getting about more easily now and had taken up a limited fitness regime again alongside Vaughn in the gym in the basement of Oscar's villa. Maggie often joined them; it was important, she knew, to keep in the peak of condition for her work with the lifeboat crew back home.

Vaughn had been given a two-race ban by the Federation Internationale de I'Automobile — the oft dreaded FIA which was the ruling body of motor racing. He'd been really cut up about it, but realized all the same that he deserved the ban.

She came to understand that Oscar would not visit the house while his son was there. She'd learned something about the stormy relationship between the two Herricks from Rafe.

Vaughn himself rarely left her and Rafe together, and she wondered whether it was at Rafe's insistence that the younger man was always tagging along with them when they walked in the gorgeous gardens of the villa, or merely sat on the veranda talking or playing the million games of cards that whiled away the hours.

Her last day at the villa was, like most of the others she'd spent there, scorching hot. On the wide balcony overlooking the parched valley with its little outcrops of limestone that was so typical of this part of France, Vaughn was joking about his father.

'I bet Dad's real pleased I shan't be racing for a month. He won't have to go out of his way to avoid me at the circuits, so some good's come out of all this.'

'Yet he obviously doesn't mind you being here — in his house,' Maggie said.

Rafe laughed. 'Oscar has more on his mind than Vaughn, there's the next big race for a start.'

Vaughn sighed and sank back in his cushioned wrought iron chair. 'Don't remind me about Montreal. You know darn well I'm really in the doghouse with the FIA. Two race bans! Well, I expected one, of course. It was a damn silly thing to do — entering that tunnel at Monte knowing about that blasted oil leak. I don't know what came over me.' He sighed again. 'No need to tell you — yet again — how I regret it now though. Every time I look at your gammy leg, I'm reminded that I did that to you . . .'

'We can't turn the clock back so forget about it will you?' Rafe turned his attention to Maggie who was pouring out a glass of iced lemon at the little marble topped table on the end of the balcony. 'Maggie — tell him, will you, to stop harping on about the accident.'

Maggie came over to the other two and sat down with them. It was an idyllic day with just a mild, balmy breeze wafting the scent of the yellow climbing rose around them. She was cool in shorts and cotton shirt though — as were both the others.

'Rafe's right,' she said. 'It's done now, and you're paying the price by having missed the Barcelona Grand Prix at the end of May, and now the Canadian one coming up in a week's time.'

Vaughn downed a whole glass of juice in one go, then stood up and stretched. 'I ought to be jogging — not sitting here,' he said.

'Quite right.' Maggie felt her spirits lifting. 'You should be getting in trim for the Magny Cours race . . . '

'And then good old Silverstone,' Rafe said. 'I want to be home for that one. In fact, I intend taking Maggie to watch you race there.'

Vaughn joked, 'Well — at least there are no tunnels at Silverstone.'

'No risks now.' Laughingly, Rafe shook a clenched fist at him. 'Promise me, huh? Just do your stuff and keep your head down. No

221

heroics, no showing off.'

Vaughn grimaced. 'Not even to prove to Dad what a good driver I can be when I put my mind to it?'

Rafe leaned his head back and looked up at the sky. 'Oscar knows your limits. You don't have to prove anything there, my lad, but it won't do you any good getting on the wrong side of the FIA again.'

'Dad hates my guts.' Suddenly, the usually effervescent Vaughn was serious.

'He's not an enemy.' Rafe said quietly.

Vaughn pulled in a deep breath and then blew it out through gritted teeth. He glanced at Maggie then, 'You're right though, Mags. I ought to be doing my stuff — getting in trim, as you said.'

She grinned at him. 'It's too hot for me to join you in the gym this afternoon,' she said. 'I shall leave it until later.'

'And I shall miss that pleasure,' Vaughn said. 'I've decided to get me a bit of night-life tonight. I'm going down into Monte. Like to come with me?'

'No.' She laughed. 'I'm having an early night. I leave tomorrow — or had you forgotten?'

'I hadn't forgotten. That's why I'm going out. I thought you two might have things to talk about. I'm being tactful, see — leaving you together.'

Maggie spluttered with laughter. 'So your plans would have come unstuck if I'd said yes to your invitation to come to Monte Carlo then?'

He gave her a serious look. 'I knew you wouldn't come. That's why I asked you.'

Rafe sighed. 'Have you two quite finished?'

Vaughn held up a hand. 'Okay. I'm off. Running. I must be mad but I'll make it to the top of old smokey there.' He tilted his head back and looked up at a chiselled peak half a mile or so away.

Rafe laughed as Vaughn jogged off the veranda and into the house, and a few minutes later emerged down below them on the geranium-decked patio. His voice floated up to them, singing the lyrics to a country and western favourite of the fifties, 'On top of old smokey . . . '

'I wish he and Oscar would make up that stupid quarrel.'

Maggie said, 'I've heard so much about Oscar Herrick — I'd love to meet him.'

'You will, Maggie. I promise. But it will be Silverstone now, I'd think. He's too busy to be out here at the moment. There's a lot of work to be done on the cars, and he's making a play for one of Bassetti's drivers to take my place.'

'Do you realize I knew next to nothing

about motor racing when I came out here, and now I'm learning more than I ever knew there was to know about it with listening to you and Vaughn talking.' She laughed.

'I expect you get bored with us talking cars, tyres and engines all the time, don't you, Maggie?'

She shook her head. 'No. I'm used to a certain amount of car-talk at home, remember? Though Dad's classics aren't quite in the same league as Formula One.'

'And your dad isn't as devious as Oscar.'

'No! From what I've heard about Oscar Herrick, he sounds someone to be reckoned with.'

'He is. At the moment he's intent on breaking Phillipe Angelis's contract with Bassetti, and he's playing with fire.'

'Will he get him? The driver he wants?'

'It will cost him.' Rafe grimaced. 'And he won't manage it this side of the season's half way mark. Still,' he lifted his shoulders in a little shrug, 'there are still eight more races after Silverstone, so he might think it's worth the risk.'

She considered him seriously. 'You're going to miss all this, aren't you? If you give up racing?'

He leaned forward in his chair and put his injured leg in a more comfortable position before he answered. Then he looked at her and said wryly, 'I'll miss it like I'll miss this great hunk of plaster when it's finally taken off.'

'Joking aside,' she said, 'You will miss racing, Rafe.'

He was silent for a few minutes as he focused his gaze on the village across the valley — and the hundred or so little white, pink and yellow houses with pantiled roofs, rising up out of the rock face. Then he turned to her again and said, 'But this is the life, isn't it? This is real. Motor racing isn't real. Being a driver is acting a part. On show for all the world to see.'

'Risking your life,' she said softly, almost inaudibly.

His gaze raked over her face. 'I never consciously think about the danger,' he said.

'I suppose you'd be a nervous wreck every time you got in a car if you did.'

'We're getting morbid. You should have gone jogging with Vaughn.'

'I don't think I could stand the singing.'

'You like him? You seem to get on well together.'

She nodded slowly. 'Yes. He can be a lot of fun.'

'I can't, Maggie. Not like this.' He looked down at his leg.

'I needed a break. I've enjoyed these two weeks. It's been different — like having two brothers.'

'Nothing's changed though, has it?'

No. Nothing had changed, she realized. She'd merely spent two weeks in the company of two men she hardly knew. He was right. But she was glad she'd come all the same. She wasn't worried about him any more. She knew what was happening to him, whereas back home, it had been all guesswork, and wondering if he was at death's door, and if he'd be paralysed or brain damaged . . .

'Did you expect it to?' She kept her gaze fixed firmly on the houses on the opposite hillside.

'I'm glad you came, Maggie.'

'How about a walk?' she asked.

'I'm game if you are. Let's not stay in the garden today though. Let's go a bit further afield, huh?'

'The ground's very stony . . . and uneven on the road out there.'

'I have to start somewhere.' He sounded irate. 'I hate being an invalid. I want to be a man again.'

She laughed gently. 'You are a man.'

'I feel like a babe in arms. Coddled. Wrapped in cotton wool.' He struggled to his feet. 'I want to be *normal* for heaven's sake — like Vaughn — I want to run.'

'Okay! Okay! Let's walk then.' She held up a hand, laughing.

'We'll go and meet Vaughn — I hope in this heat he's finding it heavy going. It would make my day to see him struggling up that hill,' he teased.

'Spoken like a true Oscar Herrick.'

'Hell! I've spent so much time with the man these past years some of his temperament must be rubbing off on me.'

They went back inside the house; it was slow progress for the inside was on several different levels and there were steps to all of them. He managed though, and she tried not to let her anxiety show when he had to get across the polished wooden floors of some of the rooms.

Outside it was even worse; again there were steps, this time roughly hewn ones though, and dry as dust gravel to skid on. But once they reached the end of the driveway, the road was at least smoother to walk on.

He looked at his watch fastened round his wrist. His arms were tanned from being out in the constant sun. 'Five already.'

'Ought we to start back?' She glanced at him and saw beads of sweat on his forehead. He was pushing himself too much. It had taken it out of him, coming even this far — and not yet a couple of hundred yards from the house.

His face was healing well though. The stitches over his eye had been taken out by a doctor sent from Monte Carlo by Oscar. The bruises were barely noticeable now. Each time she looked at him, she loved him a little bit more.

He stopped walking and leaned on both sticks, then nodded in the direction of a gnarled and twisted leafless tree a bit farther down the road. 'See that tree?'

She nodded.

'I want to make it that far today.'

'Okay.'

'And each day after that I'll go a bit further.'

She faced him, happy that he was getting on so well.

'You should wear yellow more often,' he said, glancing admiringly at her bright loose-fitting top.

'I should?'

'You look like the yellow rose clambering over the balcony back there.' He jerked his head towards the villa.

Just then there was a sound above them.

A voice called out. 'Hi-i-i-i-i! Look at me-e-e-e!'

Beside them the steep side of the mountain towered, a saucer shaped limestone hillside with not much growing on it except coarse brown grass and a few scrappy shrubs. Most of it consisted of limestone scree, pebbles and chips of sharp limestone that had broken away from the topmost rocks and trickled down making the whole hill look like a giant ski-run.

Maggie shaded her eyes, recognizing the voice. 'Vaughn!' She turned to Rafe. 'What on earth is he doing up there?'

'He's on the top road, the road that forks off this one and heads towards St Martin. It leads nowhere though; it's little more than a track up there. And look at the idiot — balancing on that narrow wall . . . ' Placing both his walking sticks in one hand he cupped the other to his mouth and yelled up to Vaughn, 'Get down. Get down. It's unstable.' Then turning to Maggie, he explained, 'It's limestone scree — nothing more than loose chippings, holding those few stones up there.'

'The view from up here's amazing . . . ' Vaughn shouted back.

'Come down, you fool.' Rafe was looking concerned.

Maggie held her breath as Vaughn, imitating a tight-rope walker started prancing along the wall, arms outstretched. 'Oh, no,' she breathed, 'doesn't he realize . . . ?'

'It's a hundred foot drop from that level to this one.' Rafe's mouth was drawn in a straight line. 'Honestly — he'll go too far one of these days.'

He did.

Just at that precise moment, Maggie heard a surprised yelp from above and a scattering of scree careered downwards.

Rafe pushed her to the other side of the road as the cascading stones bounced towards them, but rolled harmlessly into a bed of scree at the bottom of the hill — ten feet or more away from them.

They both looked up.

Maggie's hand flew to her lips.

'The idiot. I warned him!'

'Help — get me out of this — what the hell . . . '

Vaughn had slipped off the wall and had rolled several feet down the hill. He was caught up now by his bright blue T-shirt which had hooked itself over a sticking out piece of rock. His legs were dangling in mid air and he was wriggling around like a fly caught in a spider's web, trying to free himself.

'He'll have the whole lot down on top of him if he's not careful.'

'No. Not if I can help it.'

'Wha-at?' He was staring at her as she took matters into her own hands and raced towards the hillside.

'Maggie! Come back!'

She twisted round just long enough to say, 'Keep clear in case he falls.'

Then she was shinning up the hillside, stopping ten feet above him just to call out to Vaughn, 'Keep still. I'm coming. You'll never get yourself off that rock.'

Vaughn looked down, obviously shocked to find himself in such a perilous position. She heard him moan, 'Maggie — Maggie, go back. Go back to the house and call somebody — anybody . . . '

She was hanging on to tussocks of grass, finding footholds in minute hollows in the scree, hauling herself upwards, ever upwards, and never putting a foot wrong. She smiled grimly to herself. The shallow boulder-clay cliffs along the coast back home had never posed a problem, so why should she let this French mountain scare her?

Below her, Rafe kept shouting, urging her to come back down, while above her, Vaughn was haranguing her to go and get help.

She had to ignore both men; to keep stopping to answer them would distract her from looking for footholds. And it would do no good at all, she knew, to explain that you just couldn't dial 999 out here like you could in England, and have a rescue team leaping into action. They were in too remote a spot, and Vaughn up above her, obviously realized that too. Eventually he fell silent, but she was aware of him watching her all the time, and seeming to know that his slightest movement might send small rocks showering down to dislodge her.

★ ★ ★

Rafe felt absolutely helpless. His heart was pounding, threatening to choke him as he watched her scrambling like an agile cat up the hillside. He daren't let his mind dwell on the danger she was putting herself in. Under his breath however, he was cursing Vaughn. The man was a walking disaster — as well as a driving disaster! In a lucid moment, he wondered if Vaughn had been such a handful as a child, then realized he couldn't possibly have been as much trouble as he was these days — he would never have made it to adulthood if he had been.

For the first time ever though, he could understand why Oscar had very little patience with his son. After this, he doubted if even he himself would ever look kindly on Vaughn again.

She was getting nearer to Vaughn now. Rafe swallowed, leaning heavily on both his walking sticks. His leg was hurting like hell. His mouth was dry. He felt cold and clammy all over, where a moment ago he'd been scorching in the hot sun. He couldn't understand this awful feeling that had crept over him. He'd never experienced anything like it before, he was sure — and yet — that feeling *was* familiar.

Fear! It must be fear.

If she fell . . . If he lost her . . . What was he thinking of? You couldn't lose something you'd never had . . .

That feeling — he remembered it now. It wasn't something new. A year ago he'd felt like this — helpless, angry. It was on that race track in the Midlands . . .

Memory was bitter. A green scarf twirling around in the breeze — dancing along the track towards him — slamming itself into the visor of his driving helmet.

Jade! Tossed in the air. Then her body smashing down into the hard tarmac behind him.

'No-o-o,' he whispered in a broken voice. 'No! Not again. Not again.'

He'd tried hard to keep his feelings at bay

these past two weeks. And it hadn't been all that hard — not with Vaughn around, and the three of them being together for most of the time. It had suited him, being one of a threesome because he'd sworn to himself he would never love another woman like he'd loved Jade Herrick in the whole of his life again. Love destroyed. Love hurt. He didn't want to hurt like that ever again. It was one game he'd had enough of.

Maggie had kissed him though. On that quiet beach in England, she'd kissed him. But even before that, he'd known — known as soon as she walked through the door into her dad's old-fashioned parlour that there was something different about this girl. She had no airs and false graces. She had dirty hands, a smudge of red paint on her cheek; she'd been wearing a man's overalls and boots with steel toe-caps.

And even in such a state she was beautiful.

'Maggie . . . ' he breathed, watching her as she inched towards Vaughn. 'Maggie — Oh, Maggie — take care.'

He heard laughter. Saw her perched up there, tugging at Vaughn's shirt, stretching the thin cotton material to double its length as she carefully unhooked it from round the sharp little outcrop of rock.

'Hold on to these clumps of grass,' he

heard her telling Vaughn.

And Herrick was laughing too now and teasing her, 'I never thought I'd find myself taking orders from a woman . . . '

A flurry of scree rattled down the hillside.

'Maggie . . . ' Rafe yelled. 'Maggie — watch out!'

Too late.

Vaughn cried out as the clumps of grass came away from the hillside in his hand and he started slipping and sliding. Maggie tried to grab at him. She had a firm handhold, but she leaned over too far and the grass slid through her fingers.

And then both of them were falling, tumbling over and over, sliding, arms and legs flailing like windmills, bodies skimming down the scree face of the mountain, bumping together, then jolting apart again.

Vaughn was yelling for all he was worth. Maggie never made a sound.

If he could catch her . . . Before she hit the bottom . . .

His leg was on fire as he dragged himself towards the two bouncing, gliding, plunging figures, and the spot where he thought they could reasonably be expected to land.

They veered off course at the very last moment, ultimately coming to an ungainly halt at the bottom of the hill. Vaughn Herrick was flat out on his back, winded and gasping for breath. Maggie landed neatly on top of him, face down, panting.

Somehow, through a mist of pain, and full of anger at her foolhardiness, he reached them.

They disentangled themselves from each other, broke away, their combined laughter ringing out on the still air and echoing around the valley walls.

Laughing! How the hell could they laugh?

'I don't find it funny,' he snarled, glaring down at them.

Vaughn started dusting himself down. Then he turned to Maggie and slapped the dirt away from her white shorts.

Her legs were scratched and bleeding.

Rafe stared at them both.

Vaughn loped to his feet and hauled Maggie up with him. The force of pulling her up sent her sprawling into his arms, and Vaughn seemed to think this was a great joke.

They both started laughing again. Like a couple of kids.

Rafe was furious.

She could have been killed!

He told her so. He yelled it at the top of his voice at her.

She turned, surprised, towards him.

'I'm okay,' she said, brushing her hair back

from her face with her hand. The hilarity faded from her face, the light from her eyes. 'Rafe — I'm okay.' She reached out to him.

He felt like he was a volcano — ready to blow. He knew if he stayed, he'd say something he would regret.

He gave her one last meaningful stare. Both of them. They looked good together standing there. A pair. And she'd never laughed like that with him . . .

He swung away, back towards the house, uphill. He was impatient with himself because he couldn't move as fast as he would have liked.

Out of earshot of them, he cursed, 'Damn this leg. Damn Vaughn Herrick. Damn! Damn! Damn the whole lot!'

Well, she could go, he decided. And what did he care? There was no future for either of them together. He'd tell her that. Yes, he'd tell her that tonight, when they were alone. She could take it with her as a parting shot when she went back to England tomorrow.

Love was for fools. Love destroyed you. Love hurt you. You could never trust it. He wanted nothing more to do with love.

14

Ava placed the phone down with a sigh, then looked up and faced Tamsin.

The girl whirled away from the glass topped counter in the showroom of the Ivory Tower and busied herself arranging the folds of a wedding dress on a plastic model bride in the middle of the floor.

'Tamsin!'

'Mmm?' Tam turned round, a pin-cushion in her hand.

'Tam — why won't you speak to him? Why are you acting like this?'

Tamsin turned back to the dress and inserted another pin. 'I just don't have anything to say to Mark Langham,' she muttered. 'I've told you — if he rings, I'm not here. Just tell him that.'

'But he's getting to be a real pest, love.' Ava walked round into the main body of the showroom. 'That's the third time he's phoned today, and I've lost count of how many other times he's tried to speak to you during the last fortnight.'

'Well, if he wants to waste his money on telephone calls, let him,' Tamsin snapped. 'Now — let's change the subject, shall we? How many more of these dollies are we going to have hanging around the place for the weekend?'

'Only two more. We agreed, didn't we, not to clutter the place up too much. We don't want people falling over plastic brides, although they shouldn't exactly *fall over* a platform measuring five feet square that's a good twelve inches off the floor.'

'Just a handy size for squalling kids to climb all over.' Tamsin grimaced. 'And the dresses will get all grubby, you can count on that. Everybody will be fingering the silk, and the dresses will be ruined by the end of the weekend. We ought to have put the dresses in glass cases.'

'It would have been too impersonal,' Ava pointed out. 'People want to know what the dresses feel like as well as seeing them. And if they do get handled too much we can always sell them off cheaply as shop-soiled.' Ava was determined that Tamsin's ill-humour was not going to spoil the Wedding Fayre for her. Too much work had gone into it for that. She was looking forward to it.

'I'll be glad when it's over.' Tamsin stepped back off the small dais to admire her handiwork. 'There! All ready and waiting for the mob.' She turned to her partner, 'Have you decided which of the dresses are going on the other stands?'

'I thought perhaps the 'twenties-style' — that short silk jersey one with the side fastening, and then probably the traditional satin and guipure lace . . . '

Tamsin broke in impatiently, 'We have a dozen satin and guipure lace . . . '

'The one I called *Daisy* when I was designing it,' Ava said, 'If you'd let me finish the sentence without biting my head off, I would have said which one! Honestly, Tam — I don't know what's got into you just lately. You seem to have no patience at all for anybody.'

The girl rounded on her. 'Well, you only have yourself to blame,' she stormed. 'You know damn well what's wrong. You made me come back here while that Brand girl goes off to France to be with Rafe. You should have put her off. You had absolutely no right to make me come back to England with you either.'

'We have a business to run,' Ava stated.

'That wasn't the reason. You just wanted me out of his way.'

Ava didn't know how she was hanging on to what shreds of patience she had left, Tamsin had been so awkward to work with these past weeks. 'Shall we just get on with preparations for the weekend,' she said, 'And leave personal feelings out of things until after work hours?'

'There's nobody here to hear us.' Tamsin spread her arms wide. 'Look at it. All this money spent — and for what? We've been open since ten this morning and we haven't had a single customer today.'

'But we are breaking even . . . '

Tamsin's voice rose to a screech. 'We don't want to just *break even* though. We want to make a profit.'

'That's the whole point of advertising ourselves with this Wedding Fayre.' Ava raised her own voice too now. 'But I can well do without interruptions like we've been getting from Mark Langham. Look, Tam, I don't mind him ringing up, but I do draw the line at having to make excuses for you. If he rings again, you can talk to him yourself. I am not going to be a go-between any longer.'

'Well, thank you very much,' Tam snarled. 'At least we know where we stand now. And I thought you were my friend . . . '

'I am.'

'But I'm not good enough to be a member

of the precious Thorne family? Is that it? Is that why you whisked me away from your darling brother in Monaco? Did you think in his fragile, weakened state, he might go and fall for me?'

Wearily, Ava said, 'You've got it all wrong, Tam. Rafe knew we had to get back to England. He realized how much work there was still to do before the Wedding Fayre.'

'Excuses,' Tam flung at her. 'Excuses. You thought I was getting too close to him. You took matters into your own hands . . . '

'No!' Ava said heatedly. 'Maggie just happened to ring me, and you know what he was like when he came out of that anaesthetic — he kept muttering her name, over and over. I just assumed it was the best thing to do — to tell Maggie to go to him.'

'And get me out of the way.' Tam was sulking now. She glared at Ava. 'You won't get away with it though. When Rafe and I are married . . . '

Ava laughed. She had to. She had a feeling that Tam was living in cloud cuckoo land where romance with Rafe was concerned. She wasn't his type. Rafe had never gone for clingy sorts of girls. And anyway, she didn't think Rafe had ever thought of Tam in that way — she hoped not anyway.

'He will,' Tam said in a hard voice. 'You'll

see. He'll marry me.'

'Well,' Ava said, sobering, 'In the meantime, do something about Mark Langham will you?'

* * *

In Edgar's workshop on top of the cliffs at Shorecross, the new mechanic was shaping up well for his age.

Mark slammed down the phone in the office and stormed back into the garage.

'Woman trouble, mate?' Jack Orgill, a thickset man who resembled a bull mastiff asked.

'Jack-O — mind your own damned business,' Mark said, returning to the Triumph Herald he'd been working on before he'd tried one more time to get hold of Tamsin.

'Only asking.' Jack started whistling as he sanded down a wheel trim on the bench. 'Only asking.'

'Where's the old man got to?'

'Mister Brand's seeing somebody about a couple of Rollers. Some woman rang up this morning. Said her old man had snuffed it. Wanted to get rid of some stuff. Edgar said he'd go over after dinner and see her. Lives somewhere up Brid. way.'

'He's gone in his wheelchair? All that way?'

'Nah, mate. His old lady's taking him. She's a doctor, ain't she? Got the afternoon off. So he said.'

Mark was getting used to Jack-O's way of stating the obvious in as few words as possible. It didn't always come out in the right order, but usually the message got across eventually.

'He never said anything to me about buying Rolls-Royce cars.'

'You wasn't 'ere. Overslept, didn'tya? When you don't turn up till twelve, and then bugger off phonin' all over the place, what d'ya expect?'

'But Edgar wasn't here when I came in today. You could have mentioned the fact to me that he wasn't just off on his lunch break, but would be away for the best part of the day.'

'Why? Would you have gone back to bed? If you'd known the gaffer wasn't coming in?'

'What do you take me for . . . ?'

Jack-O burst out laughing. 'Well, mate, you don't exactly put yourself out, do ya?'

'I happen to be a partner in Brand Motors. I'll have you know that . . . '

'Quarter-share. That's what I 'eard. Is that all it takes to make you a partner?'

'It's enough.' Mark scowled.

'I'ad a win on the pools. Coupl'a years ago. Banked it. Every penny. Bet I've got enough saved up to buy a quarter share. Don't go all 'igh and mighty on me, mate.' Jack-O held up the wheel trim. 'Beautiful. Don't you think so? Beauties these old cars? I love 'em.'

Mark picked up an oily rag, wiped his hands on it then threw it down. 'Look,' he said, 'I'm going out. Urgent business. I'll be about an hour, if that's all right with you.'

'Okay with me, mate.' Jack-O shrugged. 'But I'm not the boss around here.'

Mark went into the back kitchen, washed his hands and face, then stripped off his overalls and changed into a decent pair of trousers and a shirt.

Within minutes then, he was driving towards Heronsea.

★   ★   ★

When he walked into the showroom, both girls were there. Ava looked up quickly as the door opened, and Tamsin spun round from a floral display she was putting the finishing touches to on a square dais beside a bridal mannequin decked out in miles of satin and lace.

She was not pleased to see him, he could tell that from the start, and he suddenly realized that his phone calls had been in vain.

'What the hell do *you* want?' Her pert little face had turned ugly at the sight of him.

Mark had a momentary urge to pick her up, throw her over his shoulder and march out of the place with her. He resisted the temptation however.

'I came to see the senior partner,' he said with a disarming smile. 'Not you, my sweet.'

Ava stopped what she was doing and came forward. 'Me?' she asked brightly. 'What can I do for you, Mark?'

'It's about the cars,' he said. 'We might — I only say *might* — I can't make any promises, but there's a chance we shall have a couple more by the weekend, and I wondered . . . '

'What kind?' Ava asked.

'Rollers. I've no idea at the moment which models, or what colours. Edgar's gone to see them this afternoon, but I thought I'd come along and find out if you'd have room for them at the Fayre if we manage to pull the deal off?'

'Rolls! Hmm! Pricey!' Ava grimaced.

'We'd do them for the same price as the Buick, I'm sure,' Mark said, realizing he was overstepping the mark somewhat before conferring with either Edgar or Maggie, but what the hell. He was here, he'd got a foothold again, and he was at the moment

246

shutting out the gorgeous gal he'd come here to see.

Tamsin was pouting in the background right now. And serve her right too, he thought, giving Ava all his attention.

'What do you think, Tam?' Ava shot the question at the girl.

Tamsin shrugged her elegant shoulders. She was wearing a simple black jersey dress with a low cut neckline and a huge silk burgundy rose nestling in her cleavage. That dress was doing things to Mark. He felt himself coming out in a sweat just looking at her pale cloud of gold hair, tendrils of which were drizzling down into that neckline and wisping themselves inside the black jersey stuff. Her huge eyes were soulful, her lips wide and full and red.

He dragged his gaze away from her and back to Ava. That was better. There was no guile about this one. Ava Thorne was tough. Attractive, but tough, and not in the same league as the petulant Tamsin in the sex stakes.

'Maybe we could talk about it over dinner.' Mark beamed widely at Ava. 'I might be in a better position this evening to let you know more about the Rollers.'

'You're inviting *me* out to dinner?' Ava said, a stilted little laugh escaping.

'Well, yes. As I said, Edgar's making a bid for the cars this afternoon, and I thought . . . '

'What about me?'

Tamsin had inched forward and at that moment placed herself between Mark and Ava.

Mark kept a straight face. 'What about you?'

'Ava and I are partners. Am I included in the dinner date?'

He pretended to be surprised at the question. He gave a little shrug. 'By all means, come if you want to,' he said, smiling seductively at Ava as he did so.

'Do you want me to come?' Tamsin all but shrieked.

'I didn't think you'd be interested,' he said. 'In fact, I didn't expect you to be here. I've been trying to get you on the telephone for quite some time to talk about the flowers and things you're going to put in the cars.'

'That's all you wanted me for?'

He smiled benignly, 'What else would I want? I just wanted to mention that we'd prefer it if you didn't use those big white lilies in the black cars. They have such stubborn pollen if it gets on to the upholstery or the carpets.'

Tamsin scowled darkly at him. 'I do know that,' she snapped. 'And if it's the Buick you're talking about . . . '

'Just thought I'd give it a mention,' Mark said. 'No offence taken, I hope?'

'None at all.' Tamsin, he could see, was perplexed by his apparent disinterest in her as a person, and he was glad his plan had worked to his satisfaction.

Turning back to Ava again, he asked, 'Shall we try that new place on the York Road — I've been there for lunch several times, but not for an evening meal.' It was an expensive restaurant, exclusive too. He saw Tam raise her eyebrows. 'Do you want me to pick you up or . . . '

'We'll meet you there,' Ava said.

'Eight-thirty?' He ignored Tamsin's presence. Time enough to pay attention to her when he next got her to himself, he decided.

For the moment though, it was enough that she was coming. She was interested.

And outside, round the side of the lighthouse where he'd parked his car, Mark punched a clenched fist into the air and growled. 'Yes! Yes!'

The impromptu visit to the lighthouse had been a success.

15

The villa was very quiet. It was early morning and Maggie lay in bed with sunlight streaming through the window. Usually she was woken by Tess singing down in the kitchen — or by Vaughn teasing the old woman. Today though, there was no noise except that of birds twittering outside of her window. It must be very early — too early for Vaughn to be up, at any rate or she'd have heard him knocking about by now. Usually, once Vaughn was awake, everybody else had to be too.

She turned her head on the pillow. Picked up her watch from the bedside table and winced at the ache and soreness of her shoulders and back — a grim reminder of her tumble down the hillside yesterday.

She pushed back the sheet and cotton throwover and swung her legs out of bed. She looked down at them ruefully; they were covered in scratches, and a few bruises were making themselves felt too.

She'd slept soundly. Tess had made her hot milk laced with whisky last night to ease her aching bits and pieces. She had to smile though when she thought of her and Vaughn skidding and slithering down that mountain side yesterday, though she sobered somewhat when she remembered Rafe's sullenness for the rest of the day.

She'd slept naked after retiring to bed early. It had been a hot and humid night, filled with the scent of geraniums from the overflowing flower tubs on the patio below her window. Now, she padded across the room to the bathroom, showered leisurely, then slipped into a cool silky wrap that she'd brought with her from home — short and white, and reaching barely to her knees.

Glancing over towards the door, she saw her main luggage standing there, already packed and waiting for her departure which wasn't till the afternoon. The silk wrap would crush up easily into her hand luggage, she decided. There'd be no need to open the big suitcase again. She wondered if she'd see him before she left the villa, or if he'd still be angry with her and avoid coming down today.

There was still no sound from downstairs. She made her way down to the kitchen, worried a little because she couldn't hear

Theresa singing. The place was deserted as well as being spick and span and not a thing out of place.

Then she saw the note. It was from Vaughn. Her eyes scanned it swiftly. She read:

Darling Maggie, I'm making myself scarce today. I hate goodbyes and Tess feels the same so I'm taking her with me to see the changing of the guard at the Grimaldi palace even though two visits to Monte Carlo in the space of two days is too much for a country boy like me! Don't let old sourpuss bite you. He was in a hell of a mood when I returned last night. If he doesn't get his morning orange juice he starts breathing fire and brimstone by the way. Take it up to him if you and he are still on speaking terms, will you? Hope to see you in good old England sometime. Luv and kisses, Vaughn.

Maggie had to smile as she walked over to a tall refrigerator in the corner of the kitchen, knowing how Vaughn must be feeling. They had both of them been in the dog-house as far as Rafe was concerned for what remained of the previous day after their disastrous little adventure.

She wondered how he would be feeling this

morning. Still mad with her for shinning up the mountain side like she had done? Well, she didn't care, she told herself, but she didn't feel quite convinced on that score. She *did* care. That was the trouble — she cared desperately. Heaven alone knew that she'd been absolute sweetness and light towards him for two whole weeks, so why should he take off at her just because she'd tried to help Vaughn?

In the fridge, she found a jug of freshly squeezed orange juice. She poured herself a glass and drank it down. It was good. She was hungry too, but she decided making herself some breakfast would have to wait until she'd 'bearded the lion in his den' with the orange juice.

She placed the jug and a glass on a small wooden tray, then added a white napkin from the cupboard where she knew Tess kept the table linen. She could make some breakfast for both of them, she decided, while he drank his orange juice in bed.

Along the passage from her own room, she knocked on his door. There was no reply.

She knocked again. Louder this time. Still no answer. A frisson of panic edged her voice as she called out, 'Rafe? Are you in there?'

Still no answer. Carefully, balancing the

tray on one hand, she opened the door and peeped inside.

The room was full of bright sunshine, the empty bed was unmade, tousled and tumbled. He'd obviously had a restless night.

There was the sound of running water coming from the other side of the room beyond a door. Relief flooded over her. He must be taking a shower.

Then she heard an irate voice. 'For heaven's sake . . . ' and a thud.

She put the tray down on a small table and ran across the room, put her ear to the door and listened. She could hear him muttering.

She called out softly, 'Rafe — are you all right?'

There was silence — not even the sound of water now.

Then his voice. 'Maggie? Is that you?'

'Are you all right?' she asked again.

After a moment's hesitation, his voice came to her again. 'No. I've skidded on the damn floor. I can't get up. Fetch Vaughn.'

'He's not here.'

'Then find him.' His voice rose on an impatient note.

'He's gone to Monaco and taken Tess with him.'

A groan greeted this piece of information. 'Rafe . . . '

'Go away.'

'Somebody's got to help you. I'm coming in.'

'No . . . '

She opened the door. He snatched at a towel from his wedged position between the bath and the shower cubicle. His plastered-up right leg was the problem, she saw. He couldn't bend the ankle to get any leverage.

She crouched beside him. 'Put your weight on my shoulder,' she ordered, 'and when I count to three, you push down with your free hand and I'll push up.'

'You're mad,' he said, looking her straight in the eye.

She slipped her arm round his naked waist. 'Do as I say,' she said. 'After three, push . . . '

'Down,' he stated. 'Yes, I heard you.'

'Okay. One, two . . . '

'I'll be too heavy for you.'

She didn't argue, she just said 'Three!' and heaved with all her might to get him up off the floor.

It worked. She knew it would. She and her mother had once found Dad in much the same position at home. Short of getting a block and tackle, Mum had said this was the only way.

'You've done this before,' he said.

She nodded, noting he was balancing on

one leg and wrapping the towel more securely round his waist now. 'With Dad,' she said. 'Mum and I have had one or two hairy moments with him at times.'

He didn't even manage a smile. 'You should be in the rescue business,' he snapped.

It was on the tip of her tongue to tell him she was — at home — several times a year when the lifeboat was called out. But she didn't say a word. She just smiled and said, 'All in a day's work. Are you okay now? Can you get back to bed by yourself?'

'I was getting up, not going to bed,' he said, dripping all over the tiled floor. Rivers of water were trickling down his shoulders and over his chest, getting caught up in the fine mass of black curling hair that started just below the hollow in his throat, and reached down to the towel.

She suddenly felt awkward and in the way. 'I brought you some orange juice,' she said. 'Vaughn's taken Tess to Monaco for the day — he left a note saying they were going to see the changing of the guard.'

'Thank heaven for that,' he said sarcastically, 'I don't think I could have managed to be civil to him today after what he put you through yesterday.'

'Don't be a bear,' she said.

His head came up, his dark brooding

glance rested on her face. 'What did you say?'

'I said, don't be a bear.' She stood her ground — if ground it could be called, this little cubicle of steam and glass, and water puddling on the floor round his feet.

'Maggie Brand . . . ' he started to say.

' . . . I'll be glad to see the back of you when you go home today,' she finished for him.

'What?'

'You heard,' she said drily. 'I blotted my copybook well and truly yesterday, didn't I? You must be counting the minutes to me leaving this place.'

It was finished, she realized. This tiny idyll she'd enjoyed for two short weeks. It was ended. It would tear her apart to say goodbye to him on bad terms, she decided, but judging from his attitude towards her this morning, he was not going to relent and be friends again. She turned away from him and walked out of the small bathroom, and was almost half way across his bedroom, walking towards the door when she heard him fling back the door of the small bathroom and yell, 'Maggie! Stop!'

She hesitated, half turned, then asked, 'Why?'

'Because . . . '

She turned fully then, and saw him

hovering in the doorway, balancing again on one leg, leaning on one of his walking sticks, gazing at her.

She looked him slowly up and down. 'You're going to drip all over the bedroom floor . . . '

'Help me then,' he said in a quiet voice.

'Help you?' Her eyes met his. She didn't understand. She'd been here two whole weeks, and in that time he'd never looked at her like that before, and nor had he ever asked her for help.

'I don't want you to go like this — with bad feeling between us.'

Colour flared to her cheeks. 'You don't?'

'You and Vaughn — you've been getting on so well together . . . ' He made a restless little movement with his free hand. 'And yesterday — you risked your life for him.'

She gave a shaky little laugh. 'I did not risk my life,' she stated. 'I've scaled higher cliffs than that along the Yorkshire coast and come to no harm.'

'I felt so helpless — watching you.'

'Rafe!' Slowly she walked back across the room towards him, and he hopped a couple of steps towards her too.

'Rafe!' she faced him as she came close to him. 'You once told me I was playing everything just a bit too safe. Do you remember?'

He nodded, and for the first time in minutes couldn't meet her gaze.

'If you want me — you have to accept me as I am,' she said. 'My life is totally different to yours. I can't get into a racing car and drive at two hundred miles an hour to show how brave I am.'

'It's not being brave to do that,' he muttered, 'It's just an ego trip when you put it that way.'

Again he said, 'Maggie — I don't want you to go.'

'I have to. Dad's expecting me back today. And I think I ought to go anyway. Don't you?'

'Haven't you ever been insanely jealous?' he asked her quietly.

'No,' she said. 'I never have. I've been envious maybe . . . '

'Envious?' His voice was a whisper. He was frowning darkly at her, not comprehending.

'Yes. Envious.' She held his gaze.

'Envious of . . . ' He let the sentence hang in the air.

She gave a little shrug. 'Jade Herrick. Who else?'

She never moved. She'd said all it was possible to say. If he wanted her, he would have to come to her, she decided.

He did, and her heart went out to him as

he struggled across the room to her, relying heavily on the walking stick.

They were standing close. He brought his hand up and touched her cheek. 'I want you, Maggie,' he said softly. 'Maybe when . . . '

She tiptoed up towards him and planted her lips on his to stop the rest of the words being said. She wanted no false promises. The kiss deepened, she gave herself up to it and when it was over she said, 'Don't say anything more. If you want me, show me now.'

His hand curled round the back of her neck, he drew her towards him and kissed her full on the lips, then drew away from her, looked down into her eyes and muttered, '*If* I want you?'

It was madness, utter madness, she knew that, yet still she slipped her arm round his damp waist where the towel was tucked in firmly, and drew him towards the bed.

The only way he could get on to it was to fall heavily on to it, and in falling he dropped the walking stick and pulled Maggie down with him, and in doing that the belt that was tied loosely around her waist uncoiled itself and allowed her robe to fall open.

She was half-propped up on his pillows, leaning towards him and laughing down into his face. He was flat on his back looking up at her.

She dug her elbow into the soft pillows and rested her hand against her head, her other hand was flat against his chest.

The humour left his face and left him looking tense and worried.

'Now what's the matter?' she said.

He gazed at her, his eyes blazing a trail down from her face, the length of her nakedness that was showing now the robe was unfastened. It was too late for modesty, she decided. This was what she'd dreamed about. This was what she wanted. Once. Just once, she silently prayed, as she relaxed against him.

He reached up with both hands and gently prised the robe off her shoulders. She shrugged her arms out of it. And then his hands were on her skin, making her tingle all over. She tilted her head back, and drew in her breath at his touch. It was turning her to molten fire, and silently, smoothly she glided down on to the pillows to cradle his head against her breast. With one hand then, she unknotted the towel that was still around his waist and when she'd done that he eased his body up and flung the towel on to the floor.

'Nothing to hinder us,' he whispered, as his lips covered hers again and he pulled her close.

As his arms went round her he must have

felt the grazes on her back, for instantly he jerked away from her. Then his hands were on her shoulders again and he was turning her away from him with concern. 'Your poor back,' he muttered.

'It's just scratched.' She turned her head to look at him over her shoulder. 'It doesn't hurt.'

His hands smoothed down the entire length of her spine, over her buttocks and down her sleek sun-browned thighs. 'You're bruised all over.'

'It was a hard hillside.' She wriggled back to face him so he couldn't see her injuries any more. She gave a soft little laugh. 'We're a pair of crocks, aren't we? You with your leg, and me with all these bruises.'

'I won't hurt you. I just want to hold you. Maggie — if I'd known you'd been hurt like this . . . '

'It's nothing. Honestly. I'll survive. I've had worse after romps on the beach with Fudge, I promise you.'

'Fudge!' He was lying facing her now, both of them lying straight down the bed on top of the white throw-over looking at each other. She touched his smooth shoulders, then ran her hands down into the matt blackness of the hairs covering his chest. 'That dog,' he said, 'I've never been able to make friends with dogs before. Fudge was something different though.'

'Yes,' she said. 'Fudge is a great dog.'

For long moments they stayed in that position, looking, touching, finding ways to give each other pleasure.

'This leg of mine,' he said, 'is a problem, Maggie.'

She grinned. 'Yes. I guessed it would be.'

'I can't put any weight on it.'

'You don't have to.' She nuzzled into his neck, planting little kisses all the way up to the hollow beneath his ear, then down again to his throat, his shoulders, and down to his waist.

She could feel his response with every indrawn deep breath he took. And she was ready when he carefully eased her over on top of his own body at waist level, then slowly, sensuously, stroking her legs, drew her down even further.

Sitting astride him, she leaned forward and shuddered in exquisite anticipation as his mouth closed over one taut hard nipple at a time. His hands became bolder then, sliding over her thighs and moving to more intimate parts of her to caress and stroke her until her breathing deepened into a desperate moan of aching desire for him.

It was everything she'd ever dreamed of

— and more besides. She could understand perfectly when it was over, why he had said he wanted somebody to hold, a warm living body up close against him, becoming a part of him again. But he was quiet. Too quiet.

In the circle of his arms, she lifted her head to look at him, and saw that his eyes were stricken.

'Why didn't you tell me?' he said. 'Why did I have to find out like that?'

'Because,' she said steadily, 'You wouldn't have done it if you'd known you were the first, would you?'

His voice was hoarse. 'No,' he said. 'I wouldn't, Maggie.'

'It had to be you,' she said softly. 'It always had to be you. There was never anybody else.'

He rolled his head away from her persistent gaze. 'I feel like I've just committed a crime — Maggie . . . ' he looked at her again. 'Maggie — can't you understand?'

She sighed heavily and flopped onto her back, staring up at the ceiling. 'Don't spoil it,' she said. 'Please don't go and spoil the best damn thing that ever happened to me in my whole life.'

He was silent again for some minutes, then he raised himself up on one elbow and said, 'Do you really mean that?'

And there was such a look of surprise on

his face that she couldn't stop a little laugh escaping her lips.

'Did I act like it was pure torture?' she asked him.

'No, but . . . '

'Was it real hard work on your part to get me in the mood for sex?'

'No . . . '

She dragged a pillow out from under his head, 'If you say 'no, but . . . ' again, I shall biff you with this.' She leaned up and held the pillow over him in a threatening manner, laughing down into his face.

'Maggie — it was great sex.'

'Yes,' she said. 'It was.'

Softly, he said, 'You have nothing to compare me to. It was the first time for you.'

She sank down beside him, sitting there, hugging the pillow to her body and just looking at him. 'I don't need to compare you to anyone, Rafe. All I know is that you were right when you once told me I played everything too safe. Well, now I've taken a chance — and I don't regret it. Whatever happens now, I know I won't do that.'

He never took his eyes off her, and he seemed worried somehow, his gaze was dark and brooding.

'What is it?' she said.

'Maggie — don't take this the wrong way,'

he said softly, 'But . . . '

'But?' she asked.

'Let's keep this to ourselves for a while, huh?'

'I wasn't going to run to the nearest newspaper with the story,' she said, taken aback.

He shook his head at her. 'I know you wouldn't do that, Maggie, I didn't mean to imply . . . '

'You mean — Tamsin, don't you?' she cut in sharply as warm colour flooded her cheeks. 'You don't want Tamsin to know about us, do you?'

'Maggie . . . ' he reached out and tried to touch her, but she thrust the pillow at him, and slid off the bed. She picked up her robe and slipped it on, belting it securely at the waist before she looked at him again. 'Maggie, it's not what you think, but I don't want complications just at the moment.'

'No?' she said.

'No. Not at any price.'

Stiffly, she said, 'Nobody will get to know about this from me, Rafe.'

'Maggie . . . '

'I'll be out of here before anybody gets back anyway.'

'Oh, Maggie! I'm making a real mess of this!'

'Don't worry about it,' she said, making for the door where she turned at the last moment before going through it and flung at him, 'I can be very discreet. Believe me.'

And then she was out in the passage and hurrying towards her own room, with her mind whirling round with a thousand unanswered questions.

She'd been a fool, she decided. A silly love-sick fool. But it was no good crying over spilt milk, or she thought irritably, over her lost virginity. What did it matter anyway? She hadn't been saving herself for anybody else but him.

Sitting down at her dressing table mirror after a quick shower, she stared at herself and wondered why she wasn't crying her eyes out. But she knew why, of course.

'I don't regret it,' she told her reflection. 'I don't regret a damn thing.' And it was true. Smiling ruefully, she had to admit to herself that he'd been right on one point.

It had been great sex!

The trouble was, she still loved him, and she knew she always would, despite his rejection of her, once it was all over.

16

Mark was shaking a can of aerosol paint just inside the door of the garage when he caught a faint whiff of roses. He frowned, glared at the can in his hand. His back was to the open door. As far as he could remember though there were no roses within half a mile of the cliff tops.

'Well!' a voice said behind him. 'Are you going to explain?'

He spun round. She was standing, hands on slim hips, just outside the garage. She had on a swirling orange frock in a dazzling Aztec design. It was a muslin-type fabric that he could almost see through. Almost, but not quite. There was a huge cream cabbage rose at the waistline, another on her shoulder.

'Tamsin!'

Her smile was absolute, pure, ice. 'You rat!'

He placed the can of paint on the bonnet of the car he'd been working on, and walked outside to her. He held out both hands in appeal to her, 'What have I done?'

'You ignored me. For the whole of last night you ignored me.'

'I did not ignore you. I took you out . . . '

'Ava!' she broke in. 'It was Ava you were really interested in, not me.'

He ignored her outburst. 'I wined and dined you . . . '

'Ava!' she said with more emphasis.

'I even danced with you . . . '

'And all the time you couldn't keep your eyes off *her*.'

'Maybe I found out which side my bread is buttered,' he said easily. 'She is the one who makes all the decisions at the Ivory Tower, isn't she? And I've a more than vague feeling that it's her money that's been chucked into this venture.'

'So that's it.' She turned and marched away towards the cliff tops, then stood there, a good ten feet from the edge, looking out to sea as he came up to her.

He was wiping his hands on a duster which he shoved into his overall pocket as she rounded on him. 'You couldn't get Maggie Brand,' she accused, 'So you saw Ava as the next best thing, did you?'

He stood looking at her then shook his head. 'Who said I couldn't get Maggie Brand?'

'So that's it!' she stated with vehemence. 'You and Maggie are an item. I might have guessed it. But one woman isn't enough for you, is it? You had to go and pick me up, and then you saw Ava as another conquest.'

'You're right about one thing,' he drawled. 'I did pick you up. Literally. You were flat out on the ground, in front of my car, stoned. God only knows what you'd been on that night — drink or drugs, but you were way out of this world, my girl.'

'So you couldn't wait to humiliate me.'

'Oh, come off it, Tamsin. You just like to bask in male attention. Be honest now. When I had you at my house, you couldn't care less about me. Now though — now that Maggie has gone to Monaco, to Mister Rafe Thorne, you're feeling neglected so any poor sod will do for you — even me!'

'I thought you cared about me. Why didn't you just leave me on that country road when I was — as you so delicately put it — '*stoned*' — if you didn't care what happened to me?' She turned a pathetic look on him.

'You thought wrong. I found out in time what you're like, Tamsin.'

'Don't you care about me at all?'

'Nope!' he said. 'Now — if you don't mind — I have work to do.'

He would have turned away, but without

warning she just whirled round, ran to the cliff edge and jumped.

'Bitch!' he yelled, racing to the edge and looking over, but what he saw had him scrambling down the shallow boulder cliffs and racing towards her. Though she'd leapt no more than seven or eight feet, at the shallowest part of the cliffs, she had obviously injured herself.

She was lying face up, in the soft sand, the swirling Aztec skirt snarled around her legs. Her arms were outstretched and her eyes were closed.

'No!' He knelt beside her not daring to move her. 'Tamsin,' he gasped. 'Oh, hell — Tamsin!'

There was no response. Carefully, he felt each arm, then her legs. Nothing seemed to be broken. There was still her back and neck though, and he daren't even think about moving those parts of her. He'd never had the slightest interest in learning about first aid, but now he silently cursed himself for not knowing what to do.

'Hell! Hell!' His breath was coming in great gulps. 'Tamsin. Why did you have to go and do that?'

Suddenly he remembered his phone, and fumbled in one deep pocket of his overalls. 'Phone!' he muttered. 'Ambulance!' Then, pulling the mobile phone out he closed his eyes and muttered, 'This can't be happening . . . '

'That was nice,' she murmured, and her eyes flew open, mocking him lazily.

He stared down at her, phone in one hand, the other raised to jab out the emergency numbers, and his mouth just sagged open.

'Check me for breaks again,' she said wriggling her lithe body in the sand. 'It was nice having you touch me. You have nice hands considering you're nothing more than a mucky motor mechanic.'

He ignored the jibe which he knew had been meant to rile him. 'Are you all right?' He sat back on his heels and watched her warily.

She eased herself up tentatively, and he breathed a sigh of pure relief. Then without warning, she screamed out loud, 'Oh, my back. My shoulders. Oh, oh, oh . . . '

He flung himself to her side, and thrust his arm round her shoulders, cradling her against him, and muttering, 'Don't move, don't try to move, love. I'll get somebody . . . '

She twisted her head. Her face was very close to his. She hung on to the pained expression for a few seconds more, her wide innocent looking eyes gazing deeply into his. Then, she gave him a push and laughed into his face. 'I don't want anybody.' She sprang away from him, leapt to her feet and her laughter pealed out again. 'So,' she said, placing her hands on her hips provocatively once more, 'You do care about poor little Tamsin.'

He still crouched there, at her feet, and groaning, he put his head into his hands, then after a moment or two, he lifted his face to her and said softly, 'You bitch, you silly bitch. Do you realize what you've done to my blood pressure?'

She came towards him. He pushed his mobile phone back into his pocket and made as if to stand up. She reached out and grabbed at his hands and started pulling. Her heels dug into the soft thick sand as she tugged, and after a brief period of resistance he gave up and staggered to his feet.

'You do care about me, don't you?' She cocked her head on one side, her hand still locked round his.

'If I say yes, you're going to hold it against me for the rest of my life. You're going to make a hell on earth for me.'

'So say 'yes',' she wheedled. 'Hell on earth is better than just stagnating like you've been doing, Mark Langham.'

'Okay! I care about you. I care like I would for a stray cat I'd taken in off the streets. Is that what you want to hear?'

'It'll do for a start.' Her effortless laughter rang out crystal clear on that deserted beach with only the crashing of waves and the cry of gulls as a background.

'It will?' He was surprised. He'd imagined she would be full of rage at being put in the same category as a stray cat.

'I like cats. Any kind of cats.' She brought her face close up to his and made a soft purring noise, then said, 'Miaow, Mark — are you going to be my pet Tom?'

He dashed her hands away. 'I don't have time to play games,' he said. 'I have work to do. And I am nobody's 'pet', my sweet.'

From under lowered lashes she asked, 'Can't you abscond for a few hours. Your keeper will never know; she's away in Monaco, stealing my man.'

'Maggie is not my keeper,' he said. 'According to you, Maggie and I are an item. That makes us equal.'

'But while Maggie's away, my Tom can play.'

Mark let out a long sigh. 'Tamsin — stop this. Just tell me what you want — why you've come here today.'

'I wanted to tell you I'm willing to give it a try if you are.'

'Give what a try?' he asked guardedly.

'You know — boy and girl stuff.' She lifted

her shoulders expressively.

He narrowed his eyes at her. 'Come off it, Tamsin. You don't want me. You're just looking for a stand-in while lover boy's laid up with that injury in France. When he comes home, you'll dump me.'

'But when he comes home, your darling Maggie will come too.'

Mark laughed out loud. 'You really do believe this stuff about Maggie and me, don't you?'

'You're right for each other — just like Rafe's right for me.' She spun away from him and ran round him in dizzying circles on the sand.

'Stop it,' he yelled. 'Stop it and explain.'

She came to a halt in front of him. 'Explain what? What is it you don't understand?'

'I can't make you out,' he said, shaking his head at her. 'What makes you think Rafe Thorne would ever consider taking up with you?'

'I know a secret,' she said in a mysterious, hushed voice.

'You're crazy,' Mark said.

'No.' She shook her head, and the teasing note vanished from her voice. 'He'll marry me.' Her chin came up in a defiant gesture. 'He nearly killed me, you know. He owes me something for that.'

'Then sue him,' he said with a short laugh. 'Sue the bugger and get some money out of him if he was to blame.'

'He wasn't to blame.' She gave a little grimace of distaste. 'And anyway, I don't just want his cash. I want him. I want what Jade Herrick had.'

'The girl's dead,' he said. 'It was in all the newspapers.'

'She had so much though.'

'But not any more. She was only human, and no match for a Formula One car. When it came to a contest, the car won.'

'We were all to blame. We shouldn't have been on the track.'

'No,' he said quietly. 'You shouldn't.'

'You don't know anything about it,' she said. 'You don't know where the real blame lies.'

'Does anybody?' Mark, like thousands of others interested in motor sport, had read the reports of the accident at the time it happened, and no conclusion had ever been reached as to why the two girls had been killed. No blame had been attached to Rafe however, even though he had been reported as saying it was all his fault for inviting his fiancée and her friends to the test session that day.

'No,' she replied. 'Only one person knows that.'

'One person?' He frowned.

'One person *must* know,' she said. 'One person tossed Jade's scarf on to the track, didn't they? One person wanted to stir things up a bit at the very least.'

Mark felt shivers running up his spine. She was so matter of fact in the telling of the tale. Didn't she feel any of the normal emotions a person should feel when two of their friends had been killed, he wondered?

'Hey! You look like I just walked over your grave,' she said.

Mark muttered, 'I feel like you did. You're completely heartless.'

She laughed again. 'It's over and done with. Forget it,' she said.

'You're a cold-hearted bitch. You never uttered one word of sympathy for Thorne, or his sister, or those two girls who were killed.'

'But they've ceased to exist — the girls! What would they want with sympathy now? It's the living ones who have to carry on and remember . . . '

'Or gloat,' he broke in, not liking her very much now he was getting to know her a bit better.

Passionately she cried, 'I don't gloat. I'm a realist that's all. What good is pity to those girls? And what does it matter now who threw Jade's scarf on to the track? It won't bring her back, will it?'

'It might clear somebody's conscience though,' Mark said. 'If that person owned up to doing it.'

She sighed. 'Yes. It might. And then again — it might not. Best to let sleeping dogs lie. Best to forget it. And as for a conscience — well some people don't believe conscience exists.'

'People like you?' he asked, broodingly.

She stared wide eyed at him, her face taut with remembrance, her eyes haunted. 'I re-live that day most nights,' she said. 'You wouldn't believe the dreams I have — going over, and over, and over it all.'

'And you say you don't have a conscience?' Mark was convinced by now that Tamsin had been to blame for the horrendous accident.

'No,' she replied. 'I never said that, did I?'

'You implied it.'

She shook her head slowly at him. 'You don't understand, do you? You just don't want to understand.'

She turned away from him and started scrambling up the shallow cliffs again, and he followed her, catching up with her at the top, where she whirled to face him.

'Do I see you again? Or is Maggie the answer to your prayers?'

He was stumped for an answer. He just looked at her. Was she crazy? He didn't know what to say. Did he really want to get mixed up with her? Wouldn't it be best to leave things as they were? He had a feeling it might be dangerous — knowing her. Maggie, on the other hand, was safe. But Maggie had shown him only too clearly that she wasn't interested in him.

'Well?'

The scent of roses was overpowering as she moved closer to him. Miraculously, the two flowers had stayed put on her dress despite her jumping down off the cliffs and rolling over in the sand.

'Is there any point?'

'In taking up with me?' she asked. 'Is that what you're saying?'

He hunched his hands into the pockets of his grimy overalls. 'I suppose so.'

'Does it always take you so long to make a decision, Mark?'

His name on her lips made it sound like nectar. He remembered her walking in his garden, telling him about flowers. And then disappearing like she had done.

'Will you run out on me again? Like last time?'

She lifted her shoulders. 'Who knows? There are no guarantees in this life.'

'What do you want from me?'

Her eyes danced for a second, then she

sobered and said, 'Friendship will do for a start.'

'Okay! I'll go for that.' It was on the tip of his tongue to suggest they went to a film, or out for a meal, or just a drink.

She forestalled him. 'Will you take me to the flower market in Rothwold?'

'When?'

'Next Friday morning?'

'Why Friday morning? I'll be working Friday morning.'

'Next weekend's the Wedding Fayre. I need some flowers on Friday morning. Anyway, you can take a day off work — you are a partner in Brand Motors, aren't you?'

'Can't you order the damn flowers and have them delivered?'

'No.' She gave him a precocious smile. 'I have to have the ones I want — not the ones the shops want to send me. I want to see what's on offer.'

'Okay. I'll pick you up — Friday morning.'

'Ten,' she said. 'I'm not an early riser.'

He said, 'All right. Ten. But how about a film first — one night — or a meal?'

'Just the market — if you don't mind.'

'It's hardly the boy-girl stuff you were talking about — going to a flower market. We'll never get to know each other that way.'

'If you want sex, a good looker like you

— with a Porsche in tow — you can get that anywhere,' she said. 'Maybe even Maggie might oblige — if she hasn't already done so.'

Mark reddened, 'I never said a word about sex. And Maggie, if she's 'obliging' anybody, will be obliging our friendly neighbourhood race driver.'

Her eyes spat sparks at him. 'Just what is that supposed to mean?'

'Oh, weeks ago,' he said, 'I caught them locked in a fond embrace. It was on the beach back there.'

There was a note of alarm in her voice. 'You lying bastard.'

'I don't lie.' He looked at her steadily.

'I don't believe you. Rafe wouldn't. He hardly knows her.'

Mark played his ace. 'He met her years ago,' he said. 'And Maggie — she's hankered after him all this time.'

'I hate you.'

'You won't need me at the flower market then.'

She pouted, glared at him, then plucked a rose from her waistband and threw it to him.

Clumsily, he caught it. And when he looked up again she was dancing light-heartedly away from him, across the cliff tops towards Heronsea, and calling out, 'I need somebody to drive me to Rothwold. I haven't got round to buying a car yet, and I hate taxis.'

He watched her for several seconds, until she seemed to remember he was there and spun round to face him again. She lifted a hand to him, and set off again, but twisted her head round merely to call out to him, 'I bet nobody ever gave you a rose before in the whole of your life, did they, Mark Langham?'

And he had to admit to himself. No. Nobody ever had.

17

Fudge's walk took a different direction the first day Maggie was back home. She walked him down to the lifeboat station at Shorecross, where she knew Jim Farmer, the lifeboat coxswain would be. The message had been waiting when she got home, and she was glad of the distraction. Just at that moment she didn't want to talk about her time in France; her emotions were still tender on that point.

'Don't know what it's all about,' her father had said. 'Jim sounded very mysterious about it. Wouldn't give me a clue.'

Maggie had phoned Jim, and he was just as cagey with her as he had been with Edgar. He merely said he'd explain everything when he saw her.

It was an intriguing homecoming.

Jim welcomed her warmly in the lifeboat station's community room which was part of the small building on Shorecross sea-front's tiny promenade.

'Come and sit down, Maggie. And bring Fudge in too. There's nothing he can harm in here. Have you had a good holiday?' His hand made a general sweeping movement round the place, inviting her to sit wherever she liked.

The room was bright and cheerful, with old black and white photographs of boats and presentations to the crew pinned on a cork board together with a colourful calendar of lifeboats, and various pinned-up notes and typed letters. There was an assortment of donated furniture and chairs around the place, most of the chairs being sturdy kitchen types, but there were also two lumpy cushioned armchairs whose bottoms had sagged almost to the floor. A long, medium and short wave radio that had seen better days was set on a shelf beside the door. The room was familiar to her. It was here, after a call out, that the crew drank tea and relaxed while Jim made out his report at the bureau in the corner. It was a man's room — cluttered — with tea-stained mugs on the fold-down table standing beside a square red tin of biscuits. It was unpretentious, but interesting and, best of all, it had a lived in look about it.

She chose a high bar stool, and Fudge flopped out on the hard-wearing square of cord carpeting in the middle of the room.

Jim stayed standing, but leaned heavily against the table as he said, 'No good beating about the bush, Maggie. We're in danger of being closed down if we can't get a replacement mechanic. Josh is down with bronchitis again, and his doctor's told him to pack the lifeboat in before the job kills him.'

'Poor old Josh. He loves his job.' Maggie forced herself to give Jim her full attention. It wasn't easy. The past two weeks had been like something out of a not-so-happy-ending fairy tale, and returning to Shorecross had resembled falling out of a hot-air balloon — very much a coming down to earth with a bump!

And Rafe was still in France which, though not all that far away really seemed to Maggie, just at that moment, as far away as the moon. She was glad in a way though that he hadn't returned to England. Knowing that he was just five miles away down the coast would have been unbearable. Her heart still felt bruised, but she'd steadfastly refused to shed any tears. Tears were for regret — and she didn't regret what she'd done.

'Maggie — are you listening to me?'

'Yes. Of course I am. What are we going to do, Jim? We can't let the boat be made redundant, can we?' She was glad she had something to focus her attention on. Something other than Rafe to worry about.

'That's just the point, love. We can't. Just think of all the rescues we've been involved in. If Shorecross loses her boat, then this coast will be a killer. We're the only lifeboat station between Spurn and Brid. That means there's about sixty miles of coastline unprotected.'

'Have you advertised? What I mean is, Josh's job is the only paid job, isn't it? Surely you could get somebody.'

Jim said, 'We need somebody local. Somebody who knows the coast around here.' He threw his hands up with impatience, then said, 'Maggie — I'll be honest with you. The person we want doesn't exist. Not in Shorecross. It looks very much as though we'll be closing the old lifeboat station down. I've already told the lads, and they agree with me. By the end of the month, we'll have no boat.'

'I could do the job.'

He stared at her. 'You, Maggie?'

She nodded eagerly. 'You know I can, Jim.'

'But — your dad, love? He needs you.'

'Dad knows I want to leave the garage. He's already taken on another mechanic while I've been away.'

'But I thought that was only temporary

— while you'd gone on holiday.'

She shook her head. 'Jack Orgill is a permanent fixture at the garage. I told Dad that I wanted something different.'

Jim shook his head slowly. 'Well, if it were up to me . . . but the lads — how would they take it, I wonder?'

'Let me talk to them, Jim,' she pleaded. 'Give me a chance. I know what needs doing, and you know you can rely on me. I've been assisting Josh for the best part of a year now. I know the boat's little hiccups, and I know how to put them right.' She sat with her hands clasped tightly together on her lap, with Fudge's chain wrapped round her fingers. 'Jim,' she said softly, 'give me a chance, that's all I ask. Put me on trial — a week, a month, I don't care. But just give me the chance to show you I can do it.'

He sighed. 'I'd do it myself, but — I have a business to run. I also have a family. Darren's at university, and Katie wants her own hairdressing salon when she's finished training. The caravan park doesn't run itself, either. I've got two hundred statics on it now, and already I could do with forty-eight hours in a day. I just couldn't take on a full-time job.'

'But *I'm* here,' she insisted. 'Jim! What's the matter? Is it because I'm a woman?'

He looked long and hard at her. Then he nodded. 'I'd have to put it to the crew,' he said. 'And then clear it with the higher-ups. I've never heard of a woman being given the job of mechanic on a lifeboat before.'

'Give me a chance, Jim.'

'Aye, lass,' he said. 'I'd give you the chance any day of the week, you know that.'

'I can do it! I won't let anybody down, Jim.'

'I'll make sure you get an interview.' Jim suddenly looked up at her and grinned.

She slid down from the stool, ran across to him and hugged him.

He held her away from him. 'Just an interview, okay? The rest is up to you.'

She nodded, her eyes alight. 'It's all I need. I'll convince them I'm right for the job,' she said.

'Good for you, girl.'

'What about living accommodation?' she asked quickly.

Jim scratched his head. 'It could be arranged — though the old coastguard cottage next door is a bit of a ruin, it was originally intended for the mechanic to live in. It's been empty though for the last ten years because Josh already had his own house when he took the job on. There'll be some cobwebs.'

'But it has possibilities?'

Jim thought about it for a minute or two, then said, 'Definitely! And one thing's certain, you can depend on me and the lads helping you to do it up. They like you, Maggie.'

'I'm going to go for it, Jim.' Suddenly she was brimming over with enthusiasm.

'Hey — talk to your mam and dad about it first. It's a big step for a girl like you to take — after all, you've never left home before.'

'Always played things a bit too safe, eh, Jim? Well, I think it's time I put an end to all that. It's time I started taking charge of my life, making my own decisions. I'm twenty-six and I've leaned on Mum and Dad all these years and never taken a chance in my life. This is just what I need.'

Jim went over to a cupboard where the tea and coffee was kept, and brought out two small glasses. Then reaching into the far depths of it, he brought out a half bottle of brandy, and poured out two tots. He came with them over to the table and handed her one.

'Cheers, then love. Let's hope you're successful. If you are, you'll have saved our bacon. Let's drink to the Shorecross boat — and long may she live, huh?'

'Long indeed, Jim.' Maggie downed the drink in one go, then pulled a sour face. 'Hells bells — was that brandy or ship's fuel?'

'Local shop. 'Pinch-penny-super-saver' — as my Misses calls it.' Jim grinned. 'It's foul stuff, isn't it?'

★　★　★

Fair and square, and pitting her knowledge against two other mechanics who had applied for the job, but were underqualified, Maggie was the one who landed it.

The rest of that month was then spent doing up the little house that stood alongside the lifeboat station, and all the crew of the boat mucked in, splashing gallons of white paint around all the inside walls, and yellow gloss on all the window frames and doors.

'At least it looks cheerful,' her father said, inspecting it at the end of one exceptionally busy day when the lifeboat had had two call outs in the space of a few hours.

'I shall love it.' Maggie, in jeans and wellingtons, was mopping out the kitchen, and Fudge was nosing around after the mop, trying to catch it.

'I've never seen you with such a sparkle in your eyes, girl,' Edgar said. 'I reckon this is the best thing you've ever done.'

'I'm happy, Dad.' She shooed Fudge away, but he pounced again and started barking at the mop.

'I never thought you'd get this old place ship-shape in a month.' Edgar looked round approvingly. 'It's a bit draughty though.'

'It will be warm with the storage heaters though, Dad. And it's been completely rewired and had a new roof. I'll be snug enough.'

'And happy?'

'That too.'

'What about the racing driver?' Edgar said.

'He's fine, Dad. Ava phoned and just said briefly that he was back home. At Heronsea.' Her brows drew together in a frown. 'She didn't say much else though. She seemed in quite a hurry to get off the phone.'

'You've not been over there though.'

'No.'

'He doesn't know about you coming to live here then?'

She shook her head. 'No — and I'm not going out of my way to tell him, Dad.'

'Why not, girl?'

'It's my life. I want it to stay that way. I don't want interference, and I don't want advice.'

'Was going to France a mistake, lass?'

She leaned on the mop handle and said, 'I found myself there, Dad. I needed to get away from the garage and Mark. And when I got back, all this happened so quickly, I didn't have time to think.'

'He's not been in touch with you though.'

'He can't drive — not with that ankle.'

'There's the phone . . . '

'Dad — I don't want to hold an inquest on my trip to France. I went because I knew I had to. I thought Rafe was at death's door. It turned out he wasn't, and I was glad about that. Really, there was no need for me to go. It was just an impulsive thing to do.'

'And now it's over.'

She gave a shaky laugh. 'What's over? There was nothing to *be* over, was there? Heck, Dad — until a couple of months ago I'd almost forgotten he existed.'

Edgar wagged a finger at her. 'One thing about you, Mags — you could never tell a convincing fib when you were a little lass. And things haven't changed, have they?'

★ ★ ★

Maggie moved into the cottage a week later. It was the middle of a hot July and Shorecross was attracting more than its usual number of summer visitors. The lifeboat had been called out two or three times — but mainly it was the inflatable inshore rescue boat that was used to go to the aid of holidaymakers who had taken risks with small boats and air beds, and had got themselves into difficulties. Maggie found she was enjoying her job, keeping the engines in perfect order, restocking the boat when stores were used, refuelling it and making constant checks to keep everything in working order. She ran the engines at least once a week to ensure they were always ready for the next call out, and the station itself got a good going over after being used for the Tuesday evening meeting that Jim had always held.

She hadn't seen or heard from Rafe, and felt disinclined herself to make the first move. France had been another world away, a world where magic was worked and the mundane didn't exist. She wondered about him constantly though — when she was alone in the cottage at nights, or when she was walking on the beach with Fudge. But she kept busy, and refused to let her mind dwell on what had happened in that villa in the mountains. Now it seemed a long time ago, and it was obvious to her from his silence that he had no intention of wanting to further the relationship that had sprung up between them at the villa.

At times she felt hurt by his silence, but mostly she was far too busy to make much of it. She settled into a routine, and when she was off duty, called in to see her parents, or else dropped in at the garage with Fudge as she was doing today.

Edgar had already told her that Mark was getting on well with the new man, Jack-O. And she could tell that her father was happy to be back and supervising his garage again. She went over to say hello to Mark, but he was snappy and looked as if he might have lost quite a bit of weight.

'I reckon he's got woman trouble,' Jack-O said, winking at her. 'He'll never learn to leave them alone.'

Vaguely, she wondered who Mark had taken up with. He'd never been much of a womanizer. She'd realized long ago that he was more talk than action in that department when he'd made passes at her in the past. He just didn't seem to know how to deal with women.

Mark rounded on the man. 'Leave it, Jack-O,' he said, his voice surly.

Quietly, Maggie said, 'What's wrong, Mark? You don't look at all well.'

'And what's that to you?' Mark ground out, walking away from her and over to the bench at the back of the garage.

She followed him. 'Look, it's none of my business, but I only asked a simple question, and I expected a civil answer.'

'You're not the boss here any longer,' he

said, rounding on her.

'I never was that,' she stated.

'You would have liked to be though.'

'I just wanted to keep the garage going till Dad could take over again.'

'Yeah!'

'Okay — so maybe I was a bit bossy at times . . .'

He pushed past her and went back to the Jaguar he'd been fixing.

She sighed, determined that she wasn't going to run after him again, and walked back to the garage door where her father was sitting in his wheelchair in the sunshine, polishing wheel hubs on a rug laid across his knees, with Fudge for company.

He looked up as she came abreast of him. 'Off already, lass?'

'My lunch break's up, Dad.' She grinned at him.

'Young fella-me-lad back there's a moody swine just lately. Did you have a chat with him?'

'Mark? Yes. And I agree with you — but I've grown quite used to his moods this past year.' She grimaced. 'You just have to leave him to come out of them in his own good time, I've found.'

'Depends how long he needs though — and it's getting longer and longer of late.

On top of that, I had a complaint from Ava Thorne last week about him.'

'You did?'

'Aye! Could have been something and nothing, I suppose, but apparently he went and made a scene over at the lighthouse — in front of customers. She was quite upset about it, and you can't blame her really.'

'I can't understand why he should do that, Dad.'

'It's like Jack-O says — woman trouble. He fancies himself a bit with that young lass over there, but she seems to have got it into her head he only has eyes for you.'

'Tamsin? She thinks that? But it's ridiculous, Dad. Mark means nothing to me, nor I to him.'

'Aye! Well, maybe somebody's jumping to conclusions.'

'I didn't know . . . '

A voice behind her said softly, 'What didn't you know, Maggie?'

She looked up and Mark was standing there. How long he'd been there or what he'd overheard of the conversation, she couldn't tell.

'If what you're getting up to is affecting Dad's business, then I have a right to ask questions,' she said icily.

Mark grabbed hold of her arm and

frog-marched her out of earshot of Edgar, and away towards the cliff tops. Once there, he let go of her and said, 'Just mind your own business, will you Maggie? And don't come pushing your nose in where it isn't wanted. Thorne's sister had no right to object to me trying to get some sense out of Tamsin.'

'You are not going to give Brand Motors a bad name just for the sake of your love life,' she stormed. 'Not if I can help it.'

'You, dear Maggie, have no say at all in what goes on at the garage,' he said. 'You made your choice and left the place. And I'd remind you that I still own part of Brand Motors, so I'm not likely to want to see it go under, am I?'

'Then what's wrong, Mark? What's going on that I don't know about?'

'As if you care,' he sneered.

'I wouldn't be asking if I didn't care.' She faced him and shoved her hands into the pockets of her jeans. The sun was beating down and below them, the beach was quite well populated with holidaymakers.

'There's something funny going on at that place in Heronsea . . . ' he started to say, when a beach ball soared up from below them and landed at his feet.

She laughed and kicked it back down to the kiddies yelling up to them for it.

Mark scowled. 'Damned kids.'

'Mark! Do you hate the whole world?' She looked at him closely and was shocked to see stark misery in his eyes.

'Mark,' she said, laying a hand on his arm. 'Tell me what you mean by something funny going on at Heronsea. Do you mean at the lighthouse?'

He pulled his arm away from her, looked out to sea for some minutes then brought his gaze back to her. 'What is it about me?' he asked. 'Why do I always go for the wrong women? There was a time when I thought you and I might have a future together, then it all went wrong. Now though — when I meet a girl who's like no other I've ever known . . . ' He threw up his hands despairingly.

'Tamsin!' she said. 'But I asked you what you meant, Mark . . . '

He glared at her. 'Things started going wrong the minute they came to Heronsea,' he said. 'First there was you and that racing chap — and then I had to go and pick that bitch up.' With words falling over themselves he gave her a quick explanation of how he'd found Tamsin on the road the night of the rave, and then told her of the scare Tamsin had given him when she'd leapt off the edge of the cliff.

'She's crazy,' he said at last. 'I really thought I might be getting somewhere with her, but it fizzled out after the trip to the flower market. She just doesn't want to know, Maggie, and she seems so under the thumb of Thorne's sister. None of it makes sense.'

Carefully she said, 'I don't know what to say, Mark. I must admit, I found Tamsin a bit . . . odd when I met her.'

'What's wrong with me, Mags?' All anger had left him now, he just seemed desperately unhappy. 'Am I reading too much into a simple friendship with the girl? And honestly, Mags, I didn't make a scene — no matter what Ava Thorne said. I merely wanted to see Tamsin again, but the pair of them just seemed to gang up on me.'

'There's nothing wrong with you,' she said, 'but maybe you should let things ride for a while, hmm? You know how important that contract for the cars is to Dad.'

'I suppose your love life is great?' he sneered.

The question caught her by surprise. She felt her face warming as colour rushed to her cheeks. She didn't answer him.

He gave a short little laugh. 'Well, you did go rushing off to France when he was injured in that smash, didn't you?'

She didn't know what to say, except, 'I

haven't seen Rafe — or anybody from the Ivory Tower — since I got back, Mark. I've been too busy doing up my little house down by the lifeboat station.'

He gave her a grim smile. 'Seems like the Thornes of this world are bad news for us both. The Thornes and anybody connected with them — Tamsin Curtis for example.'

She didn't want him starting on that subject again, she said, 'I must go,' and glanced at her watch. 'Look though,' she said on a sudden impulse, 'why don't you come down and see the house? You're obviously at a loose end — and I could do with a bit of help clearing the front garden — if you feel so inclined.'

His face lightened a fraction. 'I've got nothing better to do.'

'Okay then. Give me a ring — or just turn up one evening.'

'Sorry I snapped at you, Mags.'

'That's okay.' She grinned and held out a hand. 'Are we pals again?'

He grasped her hand and gave it a hard shake, then nodded. 'It would never have worked between you and me, would it? A love affair?'

She laughed. 'No! It wouldn't,' she agreed.

As Mark trudged back to the workshop, she shouted for Fudge, and then waved goodbye to her father as the dog came bounding up. But as she walked back along the beach to the lifeboat station at Shorecross she couldn't help feeling a little uneasy.

Things certainly didn't seem right at Heronsea. And she wondered what could have happened to make Ava so stand-offish with both herself and Mark.

18

Tamsin wanted to be alone, and to that end had lugged a folding chair up the endless sets of winding stairs to reach the lantern platform of the lighthouse. She needed solitude just at that moment — time to sort things out in her mind, and with Ava away at the workrooms in Beverley for the day, this seemed a good enough reason for Tam to close up shop downstairs for an hour and take a breather.

The platform was narrow. She unfolded the chair and positioned it in the open doorway, mindful of what Ava had told her about the door slamming shut if you didn't do something to stop it. Then she sat down unsteadily. Usually, she hated it up here. It was so high up — so completely out of touch with reality.

It was a blustery, showery day, and altogether the very opposite to what an August day should be. On the beach below her, people were huddled in windcheaters and rainwear. Kiddies were still building sand-castles though, and their thin cries rose up on the wind to her, sounding like ghost-children in a lost world.

She huddled into the thick mohair jacket she'd put on for warmth over her clinging black dress that reached down to her ankles. Tamsin was seldom seen without the addition of a flower of some sort on her outfit, and today was no exception. Today though, the flower wasn't real, it was an artificial silk Camellia she'd picked out of the trays full of such flowers downstairs in the showroom. She looked down at it in disdain and wished now that she hadn't bothered pinning it against the deep vee of her neckline. Black and white were Ava's colours, Tamsin preferred something with more warmth. Ava insisted though on them wearing black in the showroom. It was classy, she said. It was a foil for the white dresses. It was businesslike.

Tam sighed and tried to ignore the cries of the children below her on the sands. She felt very near to tears, because *he* was leaving tomorrow, and she didn't know how she was going to be able to say goodbye to him.

The hollow clang of a door deep down in the heart of the lighthouse had her stomach churning. She'd slipped him a key last night, told him Ava wouldn't be here. She hoped he'd come, but she hadn't been sure he would.

She heard his soft footfall on the steps, coming nearer with every second that passed. He took the stairs easily, running almost, but then he would. He was in the peak of condition, and she knew when he reached the top of the tower he wouldn't be the slightest bit out of breath.

'Hi!' he said.

She felt his hand on her shoulder, but didn't answer him or turn round. He was standing in the doorway, unable to get through because her chair was blocking the way. 'Are you going to make room for me?' he asked, bending down low over her and burrowing through her hair with his chin and his nose so he could kiss her cheek.

She scuffed the chair to one side, just enough for him to squeeze through and he did, then sat down on the platform itself at her feet, his knees drawn up to his chest as he looked up at her.

'You're not sulking are you?'

She looked down at him. 'No. Why should I do that?'

'Because I have to go,' he said.

'This time for good.' Watery eyes that had wept through a night of frustration, glared at him. 'It doesn't matter to you that you're leaving me, does it?'

'I have a job to do,' he said with infinite patience in his voice. 'I'm back in racing again now, Tam.'

'I wish they'd banned you for life — not just those two races,' she flung at him.

'I still wouldn't be staying here, even if they'd done that,' Vaughn said solemnly. 'It's a dead-end place, Tam. No place for you.'

'If I were more a woman of the world I could take that as an invitation to come with you,' she said.

'No you couldn't. A race track is no place for a woman to hang around waiting for her man.'

'You're not my man though, are you?'

'Darling Tam! I've been yours for all the time I've been here. What more do you want?'

'Nothing,' she said quietly. 'We agreed at the start, didn't we? No strings attached.'

'It's what I always insist on,' he said. 'Marriage is not for me, Tam. I'm married to my job.'

'What you *always* insist on?' she said in a quiet voice. 'You must have had an awful lot of women if you've got a list of conditions drawn up for them.'

He looked at her seriously. 'I never lied to you, Tam. You knew from the start how it had to be. I don't want a woman clinging round my neck.'

She stared at him, loving him for that absorbed expression he always wore, made all the more attractive with the wearing of those round, steel-rimmed spectacles. He rarely smiled, but when he did, it was like a flame had been kindled inside him, and when that happened, Tamsin felt as if her own world, her own life, had been lit up too. She knew she was going to miss him terribly. She always did when he went away to race. Now though it was different because this time he wouldn't be coming back. She wondered how she would ever bear it.

He reached out and touched her chin with one finger. 'So serious,' he said in little more than a whisper. 'So serious, my Tam.'

She felt something wet on her cheek.

'Don't cry,' he said huskily. 'It was good.'

'While it lasted,' she whispered, her heart breaking.

'We had some good times. I've been coming back for the past two months between races.'

Her lips trembled. 'Not long enough.' Inside, she was choking on words that couldn't be uttered. He hated scenes, he'd told her so. He hated clinging women. She had to let him go.

'Better a little time like this that was perfect, than a lifetime of regrets and quarrels.'

'I'd never quarrel . . . '

'Tam. You would. You wouldn't fit into my life. I could never be faithful to just one woman.'

'So you'll go — and never come back again?'

'I only came because I felt responsible for what happened to Rafe. I thought I might be of some use here if I could drop in between races, till he got more mobile.'

'You came initially because you had a two-race ban,' she said. 'Be honest now. You were at a loose end. Your popularity was at a low ebb because you'd broken FIA rules.'

His hand dropped to his lap and he stared out to sea. Then he glanced at her again and said, 'See? We're starting to argue. Already you're criticizing.'

She slid off the chair so she was sitting beside him, and she laid her head against his shoulder. 'Don't,' she whispered. 'Don't.'

His arm went round her shoulders and he hugged her close to him. 'I'm an easy going guy.' He dropped a kiss on her hair. 'I take life as it comes, Tammy. And you came along . . . '

'So you took me.' She sighed.

Softly he said in a practical voice against

her hair, 'You were willing.'

She buried her face against the silver-grey sweatshirt with his team's logo across the front. 'Hold me . . . '

He held her, his arms encompassing her, rocking her gently to and fro on the narrow metal platform a hundred feet above the ground where nobody could see, and nobody cared anyway.

'I want you,' she said in a muffled voice.

'Here?' He gave a jerky little laugh.

She nodded violently. 'I want to remember the last time . . . '

'The last time was last night,' he said, raising her tear-stained face to his with one hand, and tilting her chin up towards him. 'We agreed. We said our goodbyes, Tam, in the best possible way.'

'I want to say goodbye again.'

'We won't be alone again. Tonight it's a foursome — you, me, Ava and Rafe. A meal — out on the town.'

'We're alone now.' She stared up into his eyes, then her hands came up slowly and removed his glasses. She folded the legs down neatly and handed them to him. 'We're alone,' she insisted.

'We could go to your room? Is that what you mean?' He pushed the spectacles into a back pocket.

'No,' she said. 'It's appropriate here, isn't it?'

'Not very comfortable though.' He looked round. 'A metal platform?'

She pushed him away from her and stood up, then leaned against the door frame. 'We don't have to be down there on the platform.'

He got to his feet and stood facing her, then put both his hands on her shoulders. It was very cramped on the platform. 'You want it here?'

She nodded, her eyes direct as she stared into his. 'It's the nearest to heaven I'll ever get.' She gave a little hysterical giggle.

'It's heaven you want, Tam?'

Demurely she said, 'Yes please.'

'You're a funny girl.'

'Heaven,' she pleaded. 'Like all the other times.' And she wound her arms round his neck and pulled him towards her.

His hands slid down the length of her. He had hard hands that she loved, hard and big and used to taking charge of things. She closed her eyes and imagined his hands on the wheel of his racing car, making it obey him, teaching it to do his bidding — just like he had done with her.

His whole body was up against her then, and that was hard too. He kept himself fit by working out every day, running, weights, swimming. Each morning he'd been here he was away somewhere — training. When he'd first come back from France with Rafe, he'd spent most of his two-race ban time getting himself ready for when he could drive again.

Physical things were interfering with her thoughts though, because right up against her now, she could feel his need of her . . .

He was covering her face with kisses, she was drowning in them. Kisses and tears. He was an expert on finding his way round flowing skirts, she'd found. His hands were hard and hot on her bare legs now, stroking, gliding upwards.

Hoarsely, he said, 'There's nothing under this black stuff . . . '

She tilted her head back as far as it would go as she strained towards him. 'Just me,' she said. 'I wore nothing underneath except just me.'

'That's my Tam,' he groaned. 'Oh, yes! That's my Tam.'

★ ★ ★

Maggie had asked Jim Farmer about her manning the lifeboat shop, and he'd said okay — if that's what she wanted to do, she could. Usually it was only open on Saturdays throughout the summer if one of the crew volunteered to be there, but if she wanted to have a go weekdays, he couldn't see there'd be any problem.

The shop wasn't really a shop. It was just a little bit of space partitioned off at the front of the station, and on opening it up, she found it cluttered with cardboard boxes full of lifeboat T-shirts, lifeboat baseball caps, lifeboat badges, postcards, stickers, Christmas cards, pens, notebooks, erasers, key rings, comb-cases, purses and tea-towels.

Jim popped his head round the door with a small radio-cassette player in his hand and said, 'Wow! You've got a real job on there, Maggie.'

She grinned up at him from where she was kneeling on the floor opening up even more boxes. 'Don't worry, Jim. Out of chaos will come . . .'

'More chaos?' he asked innocently as she sat back on her heels and groaned because the box in front of her held more T-shirts.

'I've had a thought,' she said. 'We could hire a stall at Shorecross Autumn Gala in October. We might get rid of some Christmas cards that way.'

'And the T-shirts?' he asked. 'October is hardly T-shirt weather.'

She shrugged. 'I'll get on to the manufacturers, shall I, and ask if they'll swap us a box of T-shirts for a box of sweatshirts?'

'Good thinking, Maggie. Worth a try. You'll probably have cleared a way through all those boxes by October. Meanwhile I've brought you this to keep you company.' He swung the little radio across to her. 'Keep it as long as you like. It must be a bit lonely in here.'

'Thanks, Jim.' She placed the radio on the shop counter, then mused, 'It's August now, almost the the end of August. I wonder if I ought to ask them to swap all the T-shirts for sweatshirts.'

'I'll leave it to you,' Jim said, backing out of the shop. 'You look like you need something the size of a department store to house that lot — not just the rabbit-hutch-shop we've got here.'

★ ★ ★

The taxi dropped Rafe down by the lifeboat station in Shorecross, and he asked the driver to wait. Then, leaning heavily on his stick, he looked across the road at the small brick-built building on the sea-front.

It was the first time he'd ever been down to the centre of the village, the first time he'd seen the lifeboat station, and he wasn't vastly impressed.

The boathouse was another matter altogether though. It was positioned 20 yards away from the station, and built out over the sea on a spindle arrangement of stanchions. It was an elaborate Victorian type structure of iron girders with a wooden walkway leading to it from the shore, and on the sea side, at the other end of the boathouse, a long ramp led directly into the water — the slipway down which the lifeboat was always launched. It was an interesting structure, and one he'd have liked to look at in more detail — if he'd had the time, and if there had been anybody there to show him round.

At the moment though, it was the actual lifeboat station that interested him, because it was there he'd been told he'd find her. Though God alone knew what she could be doing there!

He'd called at the garage first, expecting her to be there, but she wasn't. And Mark hadn't been all that communicative — merely saying she didn't work for her father any more, but could be found at Shorecross lifeboat station.

As he approached the place now, and tentatively tried the door beside the dusty shop window, he could hear music coming from somewhere inside.

Wagner! 'Lohengrin'. Rousing music, but

hardly the sort of accompaniment he needed for what he wanted to say.

He tried the door again. In the window to the side of him there was a faded notice that said, *Shop Open* but obviously it wasn't. Yet somebody was in there.

He rapped on the wooden door with the handle of his walking stick. Wagner continued blasting out, but scarcely a couple of seconds had passed before the door in front of him was jerked open.

She stood there, with laughter in her eyes and a wide grin on her face. She was wearing a baseball cap with a lifeboat badge pinned drunkenly on the front of it. She'd obviously been expecting somebody — but not him, he realized.

Her face took on a frozen expression as the smile faded. 'Oh,' she said.

'You were expecting somebody else?' he asked mildly.

She swallowed. Looked past him, up and down the tiny promenade, then said, 'Jim Farmer. I thought it was Jim coming back.'

'Jim Farmer.'

'The lifeboat cox.'

Behind her, Act three of 'Lohengrin' was hotting up. She put her hands over her ears and said, 'Sorry about the racket. Jim left me his portable for company and there happened to be a cassette of Wagner in it. I thought he might be missing it.'

'Look,' he said quietly. 'Can I come inside?'

She glanced across the road at the taxi with its engine still running. 'Is that yours?'

'Yes,' he said.

'You won't be staying long then?'

'Not if I'm in the way.'

'There are only boxes to sit on, I'm afraid — though if you like we could go into the community room at the back . . .'

'A box will be okay.'

She opened the door wider and stood back to let him in. 'You've got rid of the plaster foot, I see.'

'Yes.' He nodded. 'I still feel like a toddler learning to walk again though.'

'Is it painful?' she asked in a stilted fashion, and he could see she was having difficulty trying to make conversation with him after all this time — and after what had passed between them on their last meeting.

He paused in the doorway, halted for just a second opposite her and said, 'No. Not any more.'

She closed the door and said, 'First door on the left.'

He went through it and into the shop. She'd obviously been cleaning down the shelves in there, and the glass fronted display units, for a bucket of soapy water was steaming away on the floor and a pair of small steps were standing against the wall.

She switched the music off and faced him. 'How did you know where to find me?'

'I called at the garage. What's the mystery, Maggie? Why was Mark so tight-lipped about where you were?'

She ignored the question. 'What do you want?' she asked.

'I — needed to see you again.'

She spread her hands wide. 'Well, here I am. You've seen me.' She turned away and bent over the soapy water in the bucket to wring out a cloth. She glanced up at him. 'You don't mind if I carry on, do you? There's a lot to be done in here before we can open up at the weekend.'

'Maggie . . .'

She was climbing up the stepladder, wiping the shelves inside the glass cabinets, her back to him. It occurred to him that she didn't care whether he was there or not.

'Maggie,' he said again, softly. 'Maggie — can't you leave that for a while?'

She turned on the top of the steps and looked directly at him. 'No,' she said, 'I have a job to do. It doesn't include standing around talking to you.'

'A job? You work here? I didn't believe

Langham when he said you didn't work for your father any longer.'

'He was telling the truth,' she said, coming back down the steps and rinsing out the cloth again.

'You get paid for doing this?' His hand swept in an arc round the little room.

'Yes,' she said.

'But . . . you're wasting your life,' he said. 'You're a trained mechanic, Maggie.'

'So?' She stared hard at him.

'This is just seasonal stuff,' he said, mystified by her behaviour. 'What are you going to do through the winter months?'

'I'll manage,' she said. 'They're paying me a wage, and then there's the house, of course.'

'The house?'

'Didn't you see it?' she said brightly. 'It's right next door. I live there.'

He shook his head. 'I didn't see a house. I was looking for you, dammit, not a house.'

'We go together — the house and me.'

'What are you saying, Maggie?'

She dropped the cleaning cloth in the bucket and said, 'Look — I've left the garage — and with Dad's blessing as it happens. I've got a new life, Rafe. I got tired of playing it safe so I did what you suggested — I stopped leaning on Mom and Dad. And it's the best thing I ever did. It's working out.'

'And you're happy?'

'Yes,' she said. 'I'm happy. Does it meet with your approval?'

'Maggie . . . ' he was horrified. What had she done? Had he inadvertently pushed her into this with his outspokenness, he wondered?

Quietly she stood and asked the question, 'Why have you come here?'

'I wanted to see you. I've been through hell since you left me . . . wondering if you were okay.'

'Is there any reason why I shouldn't be?'

She sounded hard. Tougher than he'd ever heard her sound before. 'I — I guess I hurt you, Maggie,' he said. 'And now I'm back on my feet, I wanted to see you and make sure . . . '

She gave a harsh laugh. 'Make sure what, Rafe? That I wasn't pregnant or anything like that? You want a clear conscience? Is that it? Well, be my guest — get out of here with your conscience intact. There are no lasting reminders of our little blunder for you to worry about.'

'You've become hard, Maggie . . . ' He was dazed, he didn't know what to say. Didn't understand what had come over her. He'd come here to apologize, to beg her forgiveness. He'd expected . . . Hell! What had he expected? Tears? Maybe. Tantrums? Never — not from his gentle Maggie.

Tears and tantrums he could have handled, but this . . . this indifference, he just couldn't cope with. He wanted to take her in his arms, tell her things had changed — but they hadn't changed, had they? He couldn't do that. Not yet. Maybe not ever. To do so would perhaps put her in danger. But how could he explain?

There was no way of explaining, he realized. It had been a mistake from the start to come here.

He said awkwardly, 'Look — I'd better go. This was a mistake. I should never have come.' He swung round to the door, went through it into the little passage and hurried — as much as he could hurry with that damned ankle — towards the front of the place.

She followed him at a slower pace and when he was outside, she said, 'I trust I get your approval for standing on my own two feet, Rafe.' And there was a twisted little smile on her lips that did not sit naturally there.

Just then, from the house next door to the lifeboat station he heard a yell. 'Hi, Mags,' and he turned to see Mark just walking down the front garden path.

He swung to face her and saw she was smiling at the newcomer. 'Hi, Mark,' she greeted the young man.

Mark sauntered up. 'You found her then?'

Rafe was seething, but he managed to hide his feelings with the greatest difficulty. 'No problem,' he said.

'Have you brought the takeaway?' Maggie asked Mark.

'In the car, Mags.' Mark jerked his head towards the Porsche drawn up outside her house.

'You were expecting him?' Rafe asked her, aghast.

'Yes.' She bestowed on him one of her sweetest smiles but to his imagination it was laced with vinegar. 'Yes, Rafe. Mark's going to help with the weeds in my garden. 'People have been so nice — all of them rallying round to assist.'

Mark sidled up to her. 'Are you ready then?'

'Sure!' She delved in her pocket and threw him a bunch of keys. 'Go and put the kettle on, will you? I'll be with you in a couple of minutes.'

Mark went back to the house and let himself in, and Rafe watched him, then he looked at Maggie. 'They were right,' he said. 'And yet I never believed them.'

'Them?' She looked puzzled.

'Tam! And Ava. They said you'd taken up

with that . . . that . . . Him!' he finished at last.

She gave a harsh laugh. 'You should never believe everything you hear,' she said, seeming to relent a little.

'No,' he said quietly. 'Usually I don't. But I can't ignore what my own eyes are telling me, can I, Maggie?'

'Suit yourself,' she said, closing the door of the lifeboat station behind her with a click. Then walking past him, she said, 'Look after yourself, Rafe.' But there was no sincerity in her voice.

19

Ava couldn't understand where Tam could be. Five minutes ago she'd been in the showroom, now she was nowhere to be seen. She went to the bottom of the stairs and called up, 'Tam! Tam! Are you up there?'

There was no reply, and then Ava noticed the outside door was slightly open. She sighed and marched across to it, pulled it wide and looked outside.

It was the last day of September, and a glorious day — one of those sunny warm days that made you think summer was going to go on for ever. She walked round the front of the lighthouse and stood on the headland. Tam couldn't have gone far surely. Ava leaned on the rail above the sea wall, glad of a break from routine herself. The past few months had been busy, but all the hard work had been worth it. The Ivory Tower was proving to be a success, and as word got around people were coming from further and further away for a dress specifically designed for them from the Ava Thorne range. And it wasn't just in the East Riding that Ava's wedding dresses were selling themselves — two weeks ago a prominent fashion magazine had approached her with a view to a feature in their Christmas edition, which should ensure a full order book for next year's wedding dresses too. At last, she could finally see things taking off the way she'd intended them to, and she was well satisfied with her project.

The beach had a scattering of late holidaymakers enjoying the balmy weather. A heat haze hung over the sea, blurring the horizon, and overhead the sky was blue with wispy white clouds so still they could have been painted there.

And then Ava saw Tam, sitting on one of the wooden breakwaters down near the edge of the sea, just sitting, her head bowed, her hands clasped in front of her.

'Oh, no . . . ' Not another of Tam's moods, Ava thought despairingly. 'I can't take much more of this,' she muttered to herself as she ran back to the lighthouse and locked the door. Then, with her keys still in her hand she hurried back to the headland and down the long, narrow ramp that led to the beach.

She swore softly as her shoes sank into the

sand. 'Damn!' The heels would be ruined if they were scratched by the bands of shingle nearer the sea, she thought. She called out to the girl. 'Tamsin! Ta-a-am!'

She muttered, 'Damn!' again. Tam must have heard her, yet she was apparently deliberately ignoring her. That meant she'd have to risk her shoes on that shingle. 'Like hell I will!' She could see no point at all in ruining them. Better a pair of tights than a hundred and fifty pounds worth of shoes, she thought irritably, stepping out of them and then bending down and picking them up.

She made her way carefully across the beach then, knowing she must look conspicuous in her black tailored suit and faultless make up, yet scuppering across the sands dangling a pair of shoes in her hand like some wayward toddler.

She was burning up with humiliation when she eventually reached Tamsin, and her anger overflowed. 'Why didn't you answer me? For goodness' sake, girl — you must have heard me calling you? And why didn't you tell me you were coming out here?'

Tamsin looked up slowly. The mass of tiny knife pleats in her black georgette skirt were dangling on to the sand. Ava was furious. 'You'll ruin that skirt,' she said, 'Just look at it

— sand ingrained in it and . . . '

'Oh — it doesn't matter,' Tamsin snapped.

'Maybe not to you but I, madam, have a business to think about. I don't want sand trampling in all over the salon . . . '

'Showroom!' Tamsin's huge eyes were turned on to Ava's face now. 'Showroom!' she said again. 'It's been a showroom ever since we opened, so why does it have to turn into a 'salon' now?'

'Because it sounds more in keeping,' Ava said.

'It sounds common. It sounds like a third rate, back street hairdressers.'

'Tamsin! How dare you?'

'You're going way over the top, Ava. I just had to get out of there this morning or I would have screamed the place down.'

Ava drew in a deep breath, then suddenly all her anger left her. Tamsin hadn't been herself of late. She'd been quiet — and sullen on occasion. She knew Tam was missing Rafe though, now he'd gone back to Oscar-Jade. Racing was still out of the question for him, but he said he wanted to be back on the scene — back where the action was. And at least he seemed more settled now he was working with Herrick again, even if it was only in a consulting capacity.

It had meant however, that she and Tamsin

saw very little of him these days. He stayed down in Northampton most of the time to be near the Silverstone track on test days. Oscar — he'd told her over the phone — had given him the run of his home, Starthe Manor, so he could be on hand to give advice on testing for the last three Grand Prix races of the season, the European, the Japanese and Portuguese.

Slowly, she walked towards Tam and perched herself on the breakwater at the side of her. 'Tam,' she said, 'I know you're missing him . . . '

Tam stared at her. Quietly she said, 'You know nothing, Ava. You can't possibly know how I'm feeling.'

'Well, maybe not exactly,' Ava said. 'But look love, we're keeping busy. Things are taking off for us at last. We're starting to make something of our little empire.'

'*Our* little empire,' Tam turned her head to look at the sea again. 'It was Jade's empire,' she said. 'We have merely cashed in on it.'

'But it's what Jade would have wanted.'

Tam didn't answer.

Ava laid a hand on the girl's arm, and felt Tamsin flinch. 'There's something you're not telling me, isn't there? Why are you like this, Tam?'

Tamsin moved away from her, stood up

and dusted down her skirt. 'There,' she said, 'Is that all right?'

'Where are your shoes?'

Tam — still looking out to sea — said, 'I didn't bring them. I left them in the cloakroom back at the lighthouse.'

Gently, Ava corrected her. 'The Ivory Tower.'

Tam turned and stared at her. 'The lighthouse,' she said.

Ava stood up. 'Why?' she wanted to know, 'Why are you doing this?'

'I've had enough of it.'

'Wha-a-t?'

'The lighthouse. Wedding dresses. Flowers. I've had enough.'

'But . . . you can't . . . '

'It's your little empire, Ava. Not mine. I was never more than a decoration around the place. It's not what I want any more.'

Ava closed her eyes for a second or two and then said, 'But I need you, Tam.'

Tamsin started to walk towards the sea and Ava yelled, 'Stop. Come back here. We need to talk.'

Tamsin gathered up her skirt and pulled it high around her thighs as she started walking into the frothy surf. When the water came up to her knees, she stopped and just stood there.

Ava was at a loss as to what to do next. 'Tam,' she called out. 'Don't be stupid. Come back.'

But Tam just turned towards the south then, and kept on walking, kicking up water as she went until her georgette skirt was soaked and clinging to her.

Ava fumed silently for the next two hours at the Ivory Tower, dealing with customers in her usual pleasant manner but constantly watching the clock and wondering when Tamsin would return. It nagged at her, however, that Tam was being so unreasonable. It frightened her too, that Tam had said she'd had enough of it all. It was their life, their livelihood, and if Tam went — well, there was only one place she'd head for, or rather only one *person* she'd head for. And that person was Rafe.

It was after five when she did turn up, wet and bedraggled. By that time, the heat haze had turned into a full blown Yorkshire sea-fret that shrouded all of Heronsea and the coast in its thick, grey clammy blanket. Tam's hair was damp and clinging forlornly to her head, her skirt was dripping, and her once-pristine white blouse was bedraggled.

'I waited till all the customers had gone,' she said. 'I didn't want to make marks on the carpet or anything.'

Ava put her arm round the girl and drew her over to the stairs. 'You're soaking. You'll get pneumonia. For heaven's sake, Tam — why didn't you come back earlier?'

Somehow she got the shivering Tamsin upstairs and into her own living quarters. There she rubbed her head and her arms with a dry towel. Then she headed her towards the shower room and told her to strip off and get under some hot water.

She left her then, and went to boil a kettle for some tea.

When Tamsin came out of the shower, wrapped round in a thick white towelling robe belonging to Ava, there was a steaming drink waiting for her on the table.

'Sit down,' Ava called from somewhere near the microwave oven. 'Sit down and drink that tea.'

Tamsin did as she was told and picked up the china mug. 'It smells funny,' she said.

'Whisky!' Ava came over to the table. 'I laced it — liberally — with whisky to warm you up.'

Tamsin drank the tea, then sat on the dining chair with her eyes closed until Ava put a plate in front of her.

Her eyes opened then and she said, 'I'm not hungry.'

'You never are just lately.' Ava sat down opposite her with her own plate. 'Oh, come on,' she said, 'It's only a ready-meal thing — salmon and something or other sauce. Surely you can manage that.'

Tam picked at the food and managed a good half of it before shoving her plate away from her. 'I'm tired,' she said. 'So tired you wouldn't believe it.'

'But you're warm?'

Tamsin nodded sleepily.

'Go and curl up on my bed if you like.'

Tamsin shook her head. 'I'll go and crawl into my own little bunk upstairs.'

'You can't be comfortable in that banana shaped thing.' Ava sighed heavily. 'Honestly, Tam. You try my patience. Why didn't you let me get you a proper bed when we moved in here?'

Tam managed a grin. 'I like to be different. I like my banana bed.'

'You're crazy.'

'Mmm. I suppose I am. I don't want to go to bed though. I don't want to be alone just yet.'

Ava went and crouched down in front of her. 'You're not alone. You're never alone. I'm always here.'

'Yes.' Tam yawned and smiled.

'Look — if you don't want to go to bed,

330

how about us watching a video or something?'

'Mmm. That would be nice.'

'You'll sleep better then.'

'And dream . . . '

'No. You mustn't think of those dreams . . . '

'They come whether I think of them or not.' Tam levered herself up from the table and collapsed, yawning again, on to Ava's comfy sofa that she'd had specially made to curve gently round the other side of the circular room.

'But you haven't had so many nightmares these past few weeks have you?'

'Only since . . . ' Tam looked away.

Ava knew how the sentence would have ended. Tam was going to say — 'Only since Rafe went away' — for the dreams had started up again the very first night that Rafe and Vaughn had left Heronsea.

Ava cleared the tea things away, then, looking at Tam who was dozing quietly by now, went over to the television cabinet, selected a recording, slipped it into the machine and started it playing. That done, she went and sat beside Tam on the sofa.

Tamsin was vaguely aware that people were talking in the background. Girls were laughing . . .

She forced her eyes open and blinked at the

screen half way across the room from her. Then she groaned, 'Oh, no. Not that old thing again.'

Ava said, 'I like to watch it sometimes — to remind me of the way Jade used to run her business.'

Tamsin pushed herself up to a sitting position and glowered. 'Jade's place wasn't anything to write home about. What do you find so interesting about an old warehouse packed with sewing machines and girls having a Christmas fling.'

'It's all we've got left of her. Jade. This bit of film showing the Christmas party a few months before she died.'

Tam cowered into her seat, but found she couldn't take her eyes off the screen.

Ava gave a little laugh. 'I always like this bit coming up now — where Jade dresses up in one of the wedding gowns she'd spent all morning decorating with holly and mistletoe . . . '

'And then proceeds to pour pink champagne for everybody.' Tam started to relax, then laughed softly. 'That was Jade! She could be a scream at times, couldn't she?'

Jade Herrick filled the screen at that moment, her laughing face full of happiness, her chestnut hair flying out from her head as she twirled in front of the camera then came to a graceful, swirling stop, lifted her glass and said, 'Happy Christmas everybody — and don't forget, you're all invited to the wedding in three months' time.'

A cheer went up from all the machinists and cutters. The camera picked up on Tamsin next, placing her glass of champagne on one of the benches in the workroom, then flitted on past several more girls.

Ava was naming each one as they came on screen. 'Look, there's Jayne, and Tracy, and Rebecca . . . Becca's put on a lot of weight since then. Marriage must suit her.'

'Mmm.' Tamsin was getting bored. She'd seen the video so many times by now, she knew every scene of it off by heart. It didn't seem real to her though. When she remembered Jade, it wasn't as this happy, laughing girl, twirling round the workroom and drinking champagne — it was something entirely different. It was the Jade of her dreams . . . Jade, and blood, and her lovely face battered . . .

She eased herself off the couch. 'I think I'll go to bed,' she said quietly, moving towards the door.

'Are you sure, love? Don't you want to finish the film — there's only about another ten minutes.'

Tam said in a firm voice, 'No. I don't think

I could take it — watching Jade whipping you all up to sing Silent Night round that little battered artificial Christmas tree we'd put up that year.'

Ava got up off the sofa and came over to her. 'Take some pills,' she said. 'Do you have any paracetamol or aspirin? You got a right soaking this afternoon.'

'I'll be okay.'

Ava said, 'Wait a minute,' and reached out to her shoulder bag that was hanging on the back of the door. She took it down, opened it and shook a couple of pills out of a small brown pharmacist's bottle.

'Here. Take these.'

'They're your headache pills. I don't have a headache.' Tam laughed softly. 'Stop treating me like a baby.'

'You might get a headache from that whisky.' Ava smiled.

'Oh, okay.' Tamsin pushed the pills into the pocket of Ava's robe that she was still wearing.

'Take them. They won't do you any good if you leave them in the pocket.'

'Okay. All right.' Tamsin held up her hands. 'I'll do as you say.'

'And Tam . . . '

'Now what?'

'I'm sorry, love. About this afternoon. I

shouldn't have gone on at you like I did.'

Tam pulled a face at her. 'I'm a moody bitch. Sorry, Ava.'

'Rafe will be coming back soon,' Ava placated.

Tam laughed. Oh, if only she knew, she thought. If only Ava knew — it wasn't Rafe she was missing. It was Vaughn, and yet Ava didn't have a clue about what had gone on between them when he was here.

'You've got it all wrong, you know,' she started to say, but Ava grasped hold of her shoulders firmly and turned her towards the door again.

'I don't think so,' she said in a dry, matter of fact voice. 'I think I know you, my girl, and I think I'm right in thinking that you are head over heels in love . . . '

Tam sobered. 'Well, maybe,' she said. 'But I've told you — you've got it all wrong, Ava . . . ' She bit the words off, chewed down silently on her bottom lip, and before she could make up her mind whether to tell Ava the truth, Ava had said, 'Don't worry, you'll get over it.'

To which Tam just shrugged, and said, 'Maybe. Maybe not.' But thinking of Vaughn, she knew it wouldn't be easy — getting over him.

★   ★   ★

Tamsin slept soundly without taking Ava's pills, but just before midnight she woke with a blinding headache. The night was warm and she'd curled up in her semi-circular bunk still wearing Ava's towelling robe. It had been too hot for a quilt, or even a sheet. Now though, she was shivering, and her head was throbbing. She sat up then, and after holding her head in her hands for several minutes, decided to get up and have a drink.

As her feet touched the floor, pain shot through her head and she groaned. She padded quietly across the room, crying out when her toe stubbed into a chair leg, but feeling around for her fridge, took a small bottle of mineral water out of it, then made for the little square of semi-brightness that was the window. She stared out but there was nothing to see. The grey sea-fret was swirling round her window and there was no moon. A pale haze still lingered where street lights were lit in the town though, and the reflection from them bathed the room in a pearly blackness rather than leaving it in total darkness — now that her eyes were getting used to it.

She unscrewed the top of the bottle and took a long drink of the cool water. Then, feeling in her pocket, her fingers found the pills. She swallowed them quickly, put the top back on the bottle, and carried it over to the bunk where she placed it on the floor.

Back in her bunk she listened to the silence and knew that Ava must be in bed by now. It was quiet. So quiet . . .

She must have fallen into a heavy sleep, for the next thing she heard was Heronsea's church clock chiming. She kept her eyes closed and counted to three. She hated it when she woke so early, usually it took her ages to get off again. She was drifting off to sleep again when she heard a noise — a creak . . .

Her eyes flew open. There was nothing now. She closed them again.

She was drifting . . . drifting . . .

The car came out of nowhere, silently, long, low and white. Inside, she started to panic. She turned away from it and started walking along the track, but could hear its tyres now, swishing behind her. She couldn't look round. She wouldn't look round. She knew what she would see. But the dream was always the same, and she knew that eventually she would have to look behind. When she heard the scream, that's when she would look round. And it would be any second now. Her heart was pounding, choking her in her throat. This time, she was determined, she wouldn't look, she would run. *She began to run, gasping, panting. She heard the voice. Jade's voice. 'Tammy — no!' She had to obey the voice. But not tonight. Tonight she would argue with the voice. 'Tammy — no-o-o!' Then the screech of hot tyres on tarmac, the scream of the engine. It was coming for her. It was going to get her. 'Tammy — no-o-o-o!'*

She had to wake up. She had to wake up or die. She couldn't look round. She knew what was behind her. Jade was behind her . . .

She forced herself into wakefulness, sobbing, tears streaming down her cheeks and into her hair, wetting her pillow. She buried her head in it and let the sobs die away. It wouldn't come back now. Not now she was wide awake. Sometimes it fooled her though into thinking she was awake, and at times like that it would creep up on her again the minute she shut her eyes.

She remembered the water beside her bunk. She leaned out of bed, her hair cascading round her face, her fingers groping in the darkness . . .

Darkness! It wasn't dark — not entirely dark. There was an eerie green glow. Green . . . ?

Hanging half-in, half-out of the bunk, she lifted her head slowly, pushing aside the curtain of gold curls that were splayed out across her face.

And then she froze.

In the centre of the circular room a figure was moving. A bride. Swaying. She could hear the faint swish of silk, and smell the sweet floral scent of perfume every time the figure moved.

Jade Herrick's perfume!

Her mouth formed a word. 'No-o-o.' But no sound came out.

The figure was swaying back and forth, back and forth. It had its back to her, and there was that horrible green glimmer . . .

It was turning to face her now. Slowly. Inch by inch.

Tamsin tried to scream but the scream stayed locked inside her.

She closed her eyes tight, then began to moan as her vocal chords unlocked themselves. 'No . . . no . . . no . . . '

The green was getting through her eyelids. She could sense it coming closer. Jade was coming for her. Jade was tired of being on her own. She wanted her friend again . . .

Tam heard herself wailing, 'No . . . no . . . no . . . ' and all the time she felt guilty because Jade was locked away in an eternity with no one to help her because nobody could get across that gap in time.

Her eyes flew open again, and what she saw made her flesh creep and the hairs stand up along her spine.

It had a green face. The bride. A green scarf — Jade's scarf was flattened across its face, and a white veil obscured its hair. The face was unreal, unearthly. It glowed with a light that seemed to be coming from below. But as it came nearer, she saw its green lips were pulled back in an evil, almost transparent green grin.

And it was then that Tamsin found the strength to leap out of the bunk, and make for the door.

She never stopped to look if the figure was following. She just bolted blindly to the stairs, and saw in the half light coming through the tiny windows, the steps curving down and away from her . . .

And then she was falling. And the Ivory Tower echoed and re-echoed with her screams as she hit every step between her room and the one below.

But long before then, a terrible blackness had swallowed her up.

20

Tamsin came to in the semi-darkness feeling wretched. When she tried to move, pain washed over her in agonizing waves. There was no light except that which glimmered through one tiny window above her on the steps of the lighthouse, and she had no way of knowing how long she'd been lying there. All she did know was that she had to summon help, and Ava's door was only feet away from her.

It was harrowing, crawling across the space of the small stone landing, but when she reached the door, she found she couldn't get to her feet no matter how much she tried. Each time she attempted to haul herself up, the pain was there, slamming into her, bringing her back to her knees, until exhausted, she curled against the foot of the door and battered on it for all she was worth with the flat of her hands. But each time she tried to shout, with every breath she took, the pain seared through her afresh, and at last she realized that no help would be forthcoming from Ava. The walls of the lighthouse were solid stone, the doors constructed from thick, seasoned oak. She sat with her back against the door with tears streaming down her face, too weak from pain to do anything more than weep.

When the tears had dried on her cheeks though, she began to realize that she needed help. With dawn breaking, there was more light on the stairs and with terror in her heart, she saw an ominous trail of red that had followed her across the landing. Looking down at the white robe she was wearing, she saw that it too had turned red in parts, and blood was pooling beneath her.

Weakly she whispered, 'The alarm system . . . if only . . . ' And feeling helpless as a baby, she dragged herself to the top of the stairs and looked down.

There were two more floors below her, and the thought of getting down to ground level was daunting. She knew she would have to try, though, and she pushed the memory of that haunting, horrible dream behind her and set off on hands and knees. If only she could reach the showroom, she knew her very presence there would activate the burglar alarm. As soon as the security alarm picked up her presence, it would trigger the sensor and the local police would be alerted. It had, however, been a condition of the system — laid down by local bylaws — that no piercing alarm would be activated in the vicinity of the lighthouse itself if a break-in should occur. Ava had said it made sense, for it effectively meant that intruders would not be warned that the alarm had been set off.

Before she'd negotiated half a dozen stairs, Tamsin was breathless and bathed in perspiration. Even so, she was shivering almost uncontrollably because now that she was actively moving about the pain was worse. Her breath was sobbing in her throat, as, reaching the next landing she felt her head begin to spin, and the lighthouse walls seemed to be moving in and out each side of her. She had the sense to know that lack of blood was probably the cause of these hallucinations, and accordingly she sat and rested a while outside the first floor store-room to prepare herself for the final set of stairs.

There was no easy way of getting down them though. She managed a few of the stone steps, but pain was searing through her, and finally in desperation she curled herself up into a tight ball and rolled forward.

It was a soft landing on the showroom

carpet. Even so, she was hurting so much now that it was as much as she could do to keep conscious. She lay exhausted, flat out on the floor and held on to her sanity as best she could, until she heard the wail of a police siren . . .

★   ★   ★

They were fussing over her — people in green shapeless garments, while others in dark uniforms spread themselves out, some racing up the stairs, others swarming all over the showroom swishing curtains aside, searching for . . .

'What are they looking for?' she asked weakly.

'Intruders, love. It seems you were attacked . . . '

'No!' Weakly she swung her head from side to side as they started to lift her on the stretcher. 'No . . . I fell down the stairs . . . I had a bad dream . . . '

Ava suddenly appeared at her side looking ashen, her hair tousled from sleep, and her eyes full of horror. Tamsin gazed up at her. 'I tried to wake you . . . '

'Oh, no!' Ava pushed back her hair with both hands, 'I had a headache — I took some of my pills. Tam . . . I always sleep heavily

344

when I do that. What happened?'

'The dream . . . it was worse this time . . . ' Tears flooded Tamsin's eyes.

A female paramedic beside her as they wheeled her gently outside into the waiting ambulance, took hold of her hand and said, 'It's over and done with now, love. Just try to forget it.'

The girl's compassion was too much for Tamsin, she just broke down and cried noisily. She had a vague recollection of somebody asking Ava if she wanted to ride in the ambulance with her, and hearing Ava refuse, saying she'd follow in her car, when she was dressed.

★ ★ ★

For once in his life, Mark was early for work and wasn't having to hard pedal the accelerator as he drove through the country lanes towards Shorecross. As he drove through the village, and then out on to the coast road leading up past Fox Cottage, he smiled to himself. It was eight-fifteen. Today, he'd probably even arrive before Edgar. That would surprise the old man.

He was driving leisurely when, from round the bend ahead of him, the car came careering towards him on his side of the road.

Mark yelled, 'What the hell . . . '

The unknown driver swerved, brakes squealing. Mark too hit the brakes, and in his rear-view mirror saw the car speeding back towards Shorecross village centre. He sat, hanging on to the steering wheel for a moment or two, catching his breath, then he muttered, 'Ava Thorne! What the hell was she doing up here at this time in the morning?'

He soon found out. There was a note shoved under the garage door with his name on it. Unfolding the single sheet of paper he read: *Tamsin's in Queen's hospital — please go to her.*

There was no signature. Obviously the note had been written by someone in a hurry. And Ava Thorne had certainly been that. She'd been in one hell of a hurry.

He wondered what to do. But that was only for a moment. He knew damn well what he was going to do. Racing across the yard, he slid back behind the wheel of his Porsche, and started up the engine.

★ ★ ★

He sat beside Tam and held her hand. She didn't know of course. She was still too drowsy from the anaesthetic to realize anybody was there. Nobody had told him

346

anything about what had happened. A nurse merely said that the doctor would explain. Later!

A curtain screened Tamsin from the rest of the ward. Her bed was against a window that looked out on to a crowded car park. Mark watched the cars coming and going. It took his attention away from the blood that was dripping down the tube into her arm. He'd always hated hospitals.

There was the squeak of wheels behind the curtain as the rest of the ward prepared to take its medicine from the two nurses doling it out. Tamsin stirred, and opened her eyes.

'What are you doing here?'

'Ava — I suppose it was Ava — left a note for me at the garage.'

'Ava?' Her forehead creased up into a frown. 'Where is she?'

'Damned if I know, sweetheart.' He was troubled by the black bruising round her jaw, the cut across her cheek that was held together with tiny plaster strips. He was worried too by the fact that she'd been brought here — to the gynae unit. Something didn't add up.

'What happened?' he heard himself saying. 'Can you remember? Nobody here will tell me a damn thing.'

'I fell down the stairs. Hell! I feel so

helpless. I want to sit up.'

He put pressure on her fingers. 'Wait till they say you can.'

She pulled a face at him. 'They! What do they know. They haven't got this awful backache. They don't have nightmares about ghosts with green faces.'

'Ghosts.'

'One ghost. It was enough,' she muttered angrily. 'I was a fool. I should have realized it was just a dream — but it was so real . . . '

There were footsteps coming across the ward now, and the curtain was swished aside.

'Doctor to see you,' a nurse whispered, 'but I think you can stay, Mr Langham.'

Mark didn't particularly want to stay — not if Tamsin was going to be examined. He said to her, 'Do you want me to stay? I can just as easily wait outside in the corridor.'

'You might as well stay,' she said, a trifle ungraciously, he thought.

'Mark!' He hadn't taken much notice of the white-coated figure beside him, now, at the sound of the familiar voice, his head shot up.

'Mrs Brand!' He gave a great sigh of relief. Working with Edgar and the two families being friends for years, he knew that Sheila Brand wouldn't beat about the bush.

'I didn't know you'd got a girl friend, Mark.'

'I'm not his . . . ' Tam started to say, but Mark squeezed her hand again and she just scowled at him.

'We haven't known each other long,' he said.

Sheila asked the nurse to leave them, then she perched on the side of the bed. 'Well,' she said quietly, 'I'm glad you're here, Mark. Glad you're giving Tamsin some support. She's going to be okay — but,' she shook her head a little sadly as she looked at Tamsin, 'I'm afraid you lost the baby, my dear.'

21

Maggie said quite calmly, 'You've got yourself into a right old mess, haven't you?' But there was no bitterness in her tone. No reproach.

Mark had turned up at the lifeboat station in a state of absolute shock and told her about Tamsin. It wasn't up to her to judge though, she told herself. He had wanted her to listen to his side of the story and now she had done.

They were sitting in the community room and she'd made him a cup of tea.

'I felt awful, Mags. It was your mother who'd sorted Tam out, you see, and naturally, when she saw me sitting there at Tam's bedside, she assumed that Tam and me . . . well, goodness only knows what she must have thought.'

'Mom would only have Tamsin's well-being on her mind,' she said firmly. 'You mustn't think she was blaming you.'

'I hope not. Edgar would give me a right

earful if he thinks I'm the sort of bloke who gets a girl pregnant and then leaves her to sort herself out.'

'Dad,' she broke in, 'won't know a thing about what happened at the hospital, Mark. Mom doesn't mention names when she tells us about her day. She'd be struck off if she went round telling all and sundry about her patients.'

'But the baby wasn't mine, Mags. That's all I'm saying. I never . . . ' he reddened and looked uncomfortable, then went on, 'I never slept with Tam. We didn't ever have sex — our relationship wasn't all that close, even if I did want it to be.'

'I believe you,' she said. 'Mark — I believe you.'

He dropped his head into his hands as he sat in one of the easy chairs.

Maggie was perched on the edge of a chair against the table. She picked up her own drink and sipped it as she considered him. He glanced up at her uneasily, 'Trouble is,' he said, 'She won't say who it was had got her into that mess.'

So that she didn't have to look him in the eye, Maggie placed her mug of tea on the table and gave it all her attention. 'Who do you think it was?' she asked in a distant voice, knowing full well what he was going to reply.

Mark was silent for a moment, then said, 'Well — we both know who she was carrying a torch for, don't we? It was pretty obvious that day at the lighthouse when she came in with him. She was acting as if she owned him.'

'Rafe Thorne!' she said, and there was a queasy feeling in the pit of her stomach. Surely it couldn't have been Rafe's child that Tamsin had been carrying? And yet . . .

'Mags!' he held out a hand to her, imploring her to look at him. 'Mags — I don't like the fellow, you know that, but I can't see him taking advantage of a girl like Tam. Heavens, she's so naïve — she's like a kid in some respects — easily led and all that.'

Trying to keep the hard edge from her voice, she said, 'Tam is not a child, Mark. She must be about my age . . . ' She stopped, unable to go on as the thought struck her that if Rafe had made love to *her* then why not to Tam — who he knew so much better — as well. But she couldn't say such a thing to Mark.

'What am I going to do, Mags?'

At last she brought her gaze up to his again. 'You can still be a friend to her, can't you?' she said a little sharply.

'She's got nowhere to go, Mags.'

'She has a home — at the Ivory Tower.'

'But Ava Thorne's disappeared.. Nobody knows where she is. The last Tam saw of her was when she was being carted off to hospital, and Ava said she would follow the ambulance in her own car.'

'And nobody's seen her since?'

'Only what I told you — she passed me coming out of Shorecross — driving like a bat out of hell. And then I found the note shoved under the garage door.'

Maggie shook her head, mystified. 'It doesn't make sense. Ava and Tamsin were such close friends — living together, working together.'

'You don't think . . . ' Mark began uneasily, 'I mean — Ava and Tam, surely they wouldn't be in some sort of relationship?'

'Lesbians! Heavens, no. I don't think so. There seemed nothing like that between them, Mark. Anyway — Tam's proved that isn't true, hasn't she? She wouldn't have got pregnant in a relationship with Ava, now would she?'

'We-e-ll, no, but stranger things have happened.'

'I just don't believe there was anything like that between them.'

'There never seemed to be any man in Ava's life though,' Mark mused.

Maggie was suddenly impatient with him. 'Does everything have to come down to men and women and sex?' she snapped. 'Oh, Mark. Grow up. Ava was first and foremost a business woman. All her interest was concentrated in her work — in her work and in her brother.'

'It must have been him, Mags. There was just nobody else, was there?'

'You told me Tam had once been to a rave. You picked her up on the road that night. She could have met somebody there.'

'Her reaction to me the following morning wasn't the kind that led me to believe she went in for casual one night stands,' Mark said. 'Honestly, Mags. She accused me of kidnap and rape, and God knows what — and just because I'd taken her home with me and chucked her on to a bed in a spare room and left her there. Cross my heart, Maggie — I did nothing — absolutely nothing. I never touched her.'

'This is getting us nowhere.' Maggie rose to her feet, feeling bewildered and uneasy. She didn't want to think badly of Rafe, but all the evidence pointed to him being the one who had got Tamsin into trouble and had then blithely gone off and left her to cope with pregnancy alone. She turned to Mark and asked, 'Where is Rafe Thorne now? Surely he ought to be told about his sister's disappearance — and about Tamsin.'

'All Tam will say is that Rafe went off to stay with Oscar Herrick while they do some tests on the cars. Tam's okay now though, and won't even think about telling Rafe what's happened. If he was the father of her child, then she's being very loyal. Oh, I don't know.' He hauled himself out of the chair and stretched. 'The thing is, she says she's not going back to that damned lighthouse. And I don't know what to do with her.'

'Couldn't you look after her? Take her to your house. She's been there before so it wouldn't be like her going somewhere strange, would it?'

'Mags,' he sighed heavily, 'Mags — what's it going to look like if I take her on? Folks are going to think it's a guilty conscience I've got. Your mother, for instance — she saw the state Tam was in. She took care of her, and it's still not clear what happened. Tam says she had a bad dream and fell down the stairs, but I can't help wondering — what if she did it on purpose to get rid of the baby?'

'Like I said before, Mark — this is one hell of a mess you're in. And I don't know how you're going to get out of it.'

'Couldn't Tam come here, Mags? I mean — not *here* to the lifeboat station exactly, but you've got that little house next door, and there's a spare room upstairs.'

'No,' she said quickly, too quickly. It just wasn't thinkable — having Tamsin under the same roof as herself and wondering all the time whether Tamsin and Rafe had . . .

'No!' she said again with vehemence.

'Why not?' he pleaded. 'Maggie — I thought you were a friend . . . '

'I am,' she said. 'But I can't have Tamsin here. Anyway, I won't be here myself. I've got a couple of days off and the second in command cox is taking Jim Farmer's place on the boat while Jim takes charge of the engines so that I can have a break. We don't have a stand-in full-time mechanic, more's the pity. This is the best we can manage.'

'Aw Maggie — don't be hard.'

'No,' she said. 'Don't ask me to take Tam in, Mark. I've told you — I'm going away.'

Suspicious, he said, 'Where to?'

'Look,' she said, 'I'm not answerable to you, Mark.'

'You're making it up. You're not going anywhere. You *never* go anywhere.'

'I went to France,' she said sharply.

'But that was a one-off . . . '

'I am going away,' she said, and it was true. In the last few minutes, she'd made up her mind. If Rafe *was* responsible for Tam's pregnancy — and in truth she couldn't think of anybody else being to blame — then Rafe ought to be told what had happened.

And it wasn't just something you could pick up a phone and do.

No! She wanted to be there. Wanted to see his reaction when she told him. And however unpleasant it was going to be, she was determined that Rafe should face up to his responsibilities.

★ ★ ★

From the scores of car auctions she'd been to all over the country with her father, Maggie had gleaned quite a knowledge of the different counties congregated around the middle regions of England. Northampton posed no problems for her. The motorway right down the middle of the county deposited her on what she hoped would be Oscar Herrick's doorstep. The actual doorstep itself was a little more difficult to find because the place where Starthe Manor was supposedly situated was way off any beaten track that she could make out on the map.

She drove down several leafy lanes in the vicinity, only to find out that each time, her progress was barred. She'd never in her life come up against so many rural cul-de-sacs!

The October sun was warm though, and on one of her detours she passed a black and white timbered pub which she made a mental note of. In a few hours' time, she realized, she might be glad of a bed for the night! It all depended though, she knew, on how long it took her to find Rafe, and to convince him that he *must* return to Heronsea and sort Tamsin out.

She wasn't intending drawing out the visit to Starthe Manor any more than she had to. She was doing this for Tamsin, she tried to convince herself. But in her heart, she knew there was more to it than that. Well, she might be doing Mark a favour, she reasoned, if she could get Tamsin off his hands, but looking at it another way, she knew if she were being entirely honest with herself, she wanted to see Rafe again, and know, one way or the other, whether he had been in a serious relationship with Tamsin or not.

He wouldn't lie to her, of that she was convinced. She could never imagine Rafe lying to get out of something that was his fault. As she drove carefully past thatched houses and a village green, she knew instinctively she was softening towards him. And it wouldn't do to start thinking like that, she told herself severely. Men were notorious bastards when it came to sex. She knew several who were.

But not Rafe, a little voice inside her cried. Not Rafe. Please not Rafe.

There was a village shop with a red post box outside. She drew up in front of it and went in to ask the whereabouts of Starthe Manor.

Back in the car again, her hands tightened on the wheel. This was it then. In another few minutes — according to the instructions she'd been given — she should see the buttressed wall with trees hanging over it, and then she'd be almost up to the long drive with 'crunchy gravel, my dear' that the shop-keeper had described.

'Two stone racing cars,' he'd told her, 'stand on pillars at the roadside. Turn sharp right — past those cars, and within minutes you'll see the house.'

She wondered if she'd get to meet Oscar. She hoped not. Not if those mean-looking cars were anything to go by, and resembled their keeper.

The house was red brick, with a red tiled roof. Red for danger, her heart told her. She said scathingly, 'Don't be stupid. He won't bite!'

At the top of the drive in front of the house was a large circle of grass. The drive went all the way round it, and she pulled up just short of the long, two storey building, on the left hand side beside clumps of purple Michaelmas daisies, cabbage headed roses, and shrubs whose leaves were turning to gold. The house, now she was up close, wasn't what she'd expected, even though it was set in what looked like several acres of park and woodland.

What she'd heard of Oscar had led her to believe he would live life on the grand scale. And maybe she'd imagined a long, low colonial type house. She didn't know. But this house, while being quite large, had been built in the style of a cottage. Not small though — not by any standards. Sitting in her little Anglia and gazing at it now, she guessed it must have five or six bedrooms at the very least — and then there was that small annexe built on to it just up ahead of her.

She found herself counting the windows. Four across the front, upstairs, three along the bottom. Lopsided, she thought, intrigued. Two windows on one side of the brick porch, one on the other. Each window had sixteen little square panes of glass. The door was solid wood and painted white. She wondered what she was going to say to him. Miles away, in Yorkshire, it had been easy to imagine herself coming here, asking to see him, then telling him plainly and directly what she thought of him.

In Yorkshire though, she'd been hurting like hell at the thought of him and Tamsin being an item. A pair. Lovers! That's right, she thought now. Come right out with it and say the word. Lovers! She murmured it under her breath, and felt a tightening in her throat. What could she possibly say to him that wouldn't sound condemning? How was she going to face him, and not sound accusing? He would know — he would know right from the start that she'd come here because she believed him capable of doing that dreadful thing to Tamsin . . . leaving her to cope with her pregnancy — alone.

She couldn't bear it. Couldn't bear to hear the truth from his own lips. It would tear her apart whether he were guilty or not. If he confessed it was true — that he had been having an affair with the girl, she knew she would never be able to face him again. And if he denied it all, well, what was left then? By her action in coming here, she had dug a pit for herself to fall in. He would know she had doubted him. He would never trust her again.

It was a two-edged sword she was playing with. She'd been staring down at her clasped hands, and she came to the only conclusion possible. She had to get away from here before anybody saw her. She had to get back to Shorecross and mind her own business. She had no right . . .

A tapping on the window had her head jerking up and staring into a face at the side of her, peering in through the window of the car. It was an elderly man, grey haired, thin faced, wearing a grey Arran patterned jumper, and leaning on a garden hoe.

She breathed a sigh of relief. A gardener. She could ask him for directions — tell him she'd lost her way. Nobody would be any the wiser then. She could just drive round the circle of grass and go back the way she'd come.

She wound down the window.

'Nice car!'

'What? Oh, yes.'

'What're you doing here?'

'Er — just passing through. I think I must have lost my way . . . '

'You don't pass through Silverdale. It's a dead end. It tells you so on the main road. Nobody loses their way through Silverdale. They come for a purpose.'

It was just her luck, she decided — to get an argumentative gardener. 'I'm sorry,' she said. 'I'm wasting my time . . . '

'Wasting *my* time, more like it.' Before she knew what was happening he'd grasped the handle of the door and yanked it open. 'Get out,' he said in a harsh voice. 'I don't like snoopers.'

'Look — you've got it all wrong . . . ' she began.

'I don't think so, lady. Get out.'

'No . . . '

'Want me to call the cops? I've got your car number — and you wouldn't get far in that little snazzy thing, would you? You'd stick out like sore thumb if you tried to go on the motorway. They'd pick you up straight away.'

'I'm not a criminal,' she cried.

'Prove it.'

'How?' She glared at him.

'Driving licence for a start. Show it.'

She fumbled in her bag aware that if he'd taken a note of her car registration, she was finished.

She handed over her licence.

He stared at it hard. Then he looked up at her, and said. 'Out! Get out!'

'No!' She sat tight.

'Okay,' he said. 'Let's get reinforcements.' And with the words he shot his hand in his pocket and brought out a mobile phone.

From inside the house she heard a shrill, insistent ringing. Then it stopped, and the man beside her spoke into the mobile, 'Oscar here!' he rasped. 'Get outside, Thorne. Front of the house. I think there's somebody come to see you.'

22

'Oscar Herrick!' she said, as Rafe — after he'd introduced her properly to his team owner — had led her away to the garden at the back of the house. 'I feel such a fool. I thought he was a gardener.'

'He likes to tinker around the place. It's Oscar's way of relaxing — pushing a hoe aimlessly in and out of the weeds.'

Rafe seemed ill at ease with her somehow, and who could blame him, Maggie thought. Their last meeting had been anything but amiable.

He stopped suddenly and faced her, his eyes searching her face for a hint as to why she'd sought him out. 'Out with it, Maggie — what brings you here? I think we both know that this isn't a social visit.'

They were well out of earshot of Oscar now. They'd left him at his own insistence, walking round her little Anglia, and rubbing his chin thoughtfully as he examined it. And his parting shot to them had been, 'I haven't seen one of these little dinkies in years; I thought they'd vanished off the face of the earth.'

Now she and Rafe were in a little paradise of a garden, set amid the parkland surrounding the house. There was a fish pond in front of a gazebo that had yellow roses trailing over it, and before she could reply to his curt question about her being there, Rafe said, 'Come on, let's sit down where we won't be disturbed.'

'She didn't want to sit there, where he indicated, in the gazebo with yellow roses crawling all over it. Those yellow roses were too reminiscent of another time, another place — a secluded villa set in magical mountains, where yellow roses in abundance had tumbled haphazardly over a wrought iron balcony . . .

She had no choice but to follow him though as he strode away from her — up two shallow steps to where a curved stone seat was set. He waited for her to sit down before he joined her, dropping down beside her and clasping his hands loosely together between his knees. He leaned forward, and she could see he was staring into the pond, but was seeing nothing of the bright orange fish dashing in and out of water lily leaves and long grasses. And seeing him so, she wondered if he too, was remembering the yellow roses — and France.

It wouldn't do to remind him of that time though.

Almost straight away, he said, 'It's important, isn't it? You coming here like this?'

'Yes,' she said, and came straight to the point. 'Tamsin's had an accident . . . '

'Tam?' Concern was there on his face, in his eyes as he lifted his head to look at her.

Quickly she said, 'She fell down the lighthouse stairs.'

'Oh, no!'

'It happened in the night. She said she had a dream . . . '

'Tamsin has these nightmares — since the accident last year.'

'Listen to me,' she cried. 'Don't keep interrupting. I don't know how to say this . . . '

'No!' His face went deathly white. 'She isn't . . . ?'

'Dead? No. Nothing like that. She's in hospital — or rather she'll be out today. Recovering. But she lost the baby.'

'Baby?' He looked at her as if he didn't understand the word.

'She was about eight weeks pregnant — or so Mark said.'

He was on his feet, staring down at her, hands clenched. 'Mark Langham. I'll kill him . . . '

'No,' she said. 'Mark wasn't the father. Tamsin wouldn't say who that was.'

He was very quiet for a moment, staring into space as if mentally he were adding something up, then he turned to her again and said, 'And — Tamsin was two months pregnant, you said?'

She nodded. 'As near as could be ascertained — according to Mark.'

'Two months,' he said softly, almost under his breath. 'Two months since . . . No! I can't believe this.' He swung away from her and smashed one clenched fist into his other hand.

'What?' she asked, not understanding exactly what he was getting at, but dreading having to hear him admit that he had been to blame, that he was the one responsible for Tamsin's pregnancy. 'What can't you believe, Rafe?'

'Vaughn!' he muttered, then said in an urgent voice, 'Maggie — come back to the house. There's something I've got to do — and it can't wait.'

She hurried at his side. Oscar was in the kitchen, but grim faced, Rafe swept past him, with a curt, 'Oscar — I need to use the phone.'

Jokingly Oscar said, 'Be my guest! I've told you before — use this place as your own.'

Down the hall, Maggie could hear Rafe impatiently moving his feet after he'd keyed in the number.

Oscar said, 'He's coming on well after that accident. I'm full of hope he'll be able to drive in the last race of the season.'

Rafe's voice, down the hall was raised. They both heard him talking on the phone. 'Vaughn! I'm with your father at Starthe. Get over here, will you?'

Maggie said with a frown, 'Does he want to do that? To race again, do you think?'

Oscar replied irritably, 'He'll drive — whether he likes it or not, providing of course that the damned circuit in Spain is finished by then. It's a new one, and they're having problems. It's giving everybody one hell of a headache . . . '

Rafe's voice — down the hall — was raised in anger now. 'I don't give a damn about your squabble with your father. I want you *here*! This is more important than just you and Oscar. Just get over to Starthe. Now. Because if you don't, I'll come and drag you over.'

He put the phone down and came, more slowly now, back to the kitchen.

'What's that all about?' Oscar wanted to know.

'I'll let your precious son explain.'

'I don't have a 'son'!' Oscar was incensed. 'And I don't like your attitude — just ordering that young fool to turn up here.'

'It's safer that way,' Rafe snapped. 'You can act as referee.'

★ ★ ★

Vaughn didn't deny he'd been having an affair of sorts with Tamsin when he arrived back at his childhood home.

'We're two grown people,' he said, with a nonchalance and lack of concern that amazed and worried Maggie.

They were an ill-assorted quartet. Oscar, standing with his back to them by the bay window of the sitting room, staring out over the garden, whisky glass in his hand, Rafe — pacing up and down, asking questions, demanding answers, and Maggie herself, trying to keep in the background, while Vaughn squared up to the man who had always been his friend.

'Tamsin might be 'grown-up' — as you put it,' Rafe replied in a tense voice, 'But you knew damn well she was still suffering the after-effects of the accident last year.'

Vaughn shrugged slightly and said, 'You were the one who hit her with the car. You're

369

the one she's always been obsessed with. But you couldn't — or wouldn't give her what she wanted — warmth, attention, love . . . '

'Love!' Rafe threw up his hands in despair. '*Love?* Is that what you call it — to get a girl pregnant and then leave her?'

Vaughn sighed and walked over to a comfortable sofa where he hurled himself full length across it, lounging there, then looking up and said, 'So? She's lost the kid. Is that any reason to get me over here on a wild goose chase? Slagging me off isn't going to make things any better is it?'

Oscar, for the first time then, turned round and intervened. 'No,' he said, before Rafe could make any retort, 'No! Nothing is going to make it up to that girl, is it? But even if she hadn't lost the baby, you would have abandoned her, wouldn't you? You'd have walked away and buried your head in the sand, wouldn't you? You never could take responsibility for your actions.'

Vaughn regarded his father in silence for a moment, then said softly, 'This is the first time you speak to me in years, and that's all you've got to say, is it?'

'Yes,' Oscar said with dignity. 'That's all I've got to say to you, Vaughn, except to remind you that you always were a spoilt little boy, and you haven't changed one bit.'

Vaughn sprang to his feet. 'Jade was the golden girl in your eyes,' he accused. 'How could I ever live up to her image? She was your favourite — your first born, and when I came along — I was a mistake as far as you were concerned. So what did you do? You did what you always do when something doesn't suit you. You ignore it. And that's what you did with me. You pushed me into the background and you ignored me.'

Rafe discreetly backed out of the conversation, looking shattered that he'd apparently stirred things up that had lain dormant for a quarter of a century. He sat, head bowed, beside Maggie, elbows resting on his knees, while recriminations flew back and forth, more vicious, more vitriolic than hammer blows or poisoned acid.

At last he looked up in the midst of all the turmoil, turned to her and said quietly, 'Let's go, Maggie.'

He held out his hand to her and she placed her own in it and they went out of the room. By now, outside, dusk was falling, and all at once he seemed to remember something. 'With all this going on, I never realized until now that you haven't even had a cup of tea.'

'It's okay,' she said a little sadly. 'I wish now I'd never come. I thought though that you ought to know what was going on at

Heronsea, and a phone call would have been so impersonal, considering what had happened.'

'Will you take me back there?' he asked. 'I don't have a car. I left it there, at the lighthouse before Monaco, and till now I haven't been able to drive, so there it stayed.'

'Now? You want me to take you back home, now?'

He nodded. 'I've got to find Ava. You said while we were waiting for Vaughn to arrive that she'd disappeared. What on earth is she playing at now, I wonder?'

'I don't know,' Maggie said. 'It all seems very strange.'

He looked at her wearily, 'No,' he said. 'It's not all that strange. There are things you don't know. Things you couldn't guess at in a million years. One thing's certain though — I've got to find Ava. And Tamsin needs somebody to take care of her too.'

'Tamsin's with Mark. We arranged it before I left to come down here. Mark was taking her to his home when they let her out of hospital.'

'Like hell he is . . . '

'Rafe!' She laid a hand on his arm. 'Rafe — it's not the first time she's been there. There's been an uneasy sort of relationship building up between the two of them for some time now.'

He drew in a deep breath, then slowly let it out and said, 'It seems there are a lot of things I don't know about.'

'It's nothing serious between Tamsin and Mark. Not yet. But it wouldn't be a bad thing . . . '

'But you and Mark . . . '

She cut in, 'There's absolutely nothing between Mark and me. We get on better now we don't have to work together, but as for anything resembling romance — well,' she gave a mirthless little laugh, 'that's not for us. Mark is completely smitten with Tamsin. I think he was from that very first day he met her.'

Anger flaring briefly again, he said, 'So why did she do what she did with Vaughn?'

'You heard what he said,' she replied quietly, 'he gave her what she wanted, attention, warmth, love. Things she couldn't get from anybody else.'

'Meaning me,' he said pointedly. 'Is that what you're getting at, Maggie?'

'I'm not blaming you,' she said. 'But even I could see that Tamsin was in love with you.'

'But I didn't feel that way towards her.' He shook his head, bewildered. 'She was Jade's friend. I felt responsible . . . '

In some small way, Maggie understood how Tamsin must have felt when Rafe showed no interest in her. She herself was beginning to think he was incapable of loving. She'd been so close to him in France, and then . . .

'It isn't what you think,' he said, moving away from her and walking to the kitchen door, then out into the warm October evening.

She followed, stood just behind him and said, 'Is it Jade? Do you still love Jade to the exclusion of all else? Will you never be free of her memory?'

Slowly he turned to face her. 'It's over a year, Maggie,' he said with a sigh. 'I loved Jade. But love — well, death changes everything. You still remember and feel sad, but somewhere along the way, you start to remember the good times, and though the regret's still there, you have to begin living again. It's a waste of two lives, not just the one, if you don't do that.'

'I'm sorry,' she said carefully, 'That things didn't work out for you and me.'

He came towards her, placed his hands on her shoulders and looked deep into her eyes. 'I love you, Maggie,' he said.

'You . . . love me?' She felt dazed.

'I couldn't admit to it,' he said, still holding her. 'I *can't* admit it to anybody else even now — except to you.'

'I don't understand.' She shook her head.

'You will. I promise — you will. Can you trust me, Maggie?'

'I don't know.' How could she trust him, she reasoned, when he was talking in riddles? If he loved her, why didn't he want to shout it from the rooftops instead of hiding it away so furtively?

'I have to find Ava. I *must* find Ava.'

At last she was beginning to understand. His sister was missing. That had to take priority over everything else.

She nodded slowly. 'Of course. You must find your sister . . . '

'No,' he said, his hands falling away from her. 'I have to find Ava — but there's something you have to know, Maggie. Ava Thorne is *not* my sister.'

23

Ava parked her car near the sea-front at Eastbourne on the south coast, then caught a bus.

Less than half an hour later she was at her destination, walking towards the edge of the towering cliffs. It was a damp day. Overnight it had poured with rain; she'd heard it pattering on the roof of the car as she'd reclined the front seat and dozed intermittently in a quiet spot near Ashdown Forest. She racked her brain now, trying to recall what she'd done the day before, and the night before that too. She must have eaten, she reasoned, because there was a packet of half-eaten sandwiches on the back seat, but getting out of the car and actually buying them? No, she couldn't remember that.

All that kept looming up in front of her was Tamsin's face, bruised, bleeding. And when she thought of the Ivory Tower, she could see nothing except Tamsin's blood on the landing outside the door of her own room.

She walked purposefully now, the wet grass along the top of the sheer white cliffs, soaking into her shoes. She knew where she was going although she hadn't been near the place in years. Her brows drew together in concentration. How many years? Twenty-two, she decided. Twenty-two years since she'd last been to Beachy Head.

She'd been nine years old.

'*Hold my hand, Mummy.*'

Mummy hadn't been listening. Ava had clutched at the short shift dress beside her. Mummy had dashed her hand away. 'Let go of me. Naughty girl. Mummy has something important to do.'

'*I'm scared . . . I don't like being so high up, Mummy.*'

A firm hand propelled her forward. 'Look — look at the lighthouse down there. Look at the band of red around its middle.'

'*I don't like it. It's not nice up here. We might fall . . .* '

'*Sit down then and wait. I'm going to look.*'

An impatient hand had shoved Ava down on to the grass, and she'd started to cry. Her mother was strange at times. But more strange than ever today, when, for instance, when she'd woken Ava up at dawn to get dressed. They were going to the sea-side she said. Today was a holiday. They'd catch a train, and then a bus . . .

Ava couldn't remember the exact spot now. She walked up and down in the wet grass. There was no way of remembering. She didn't want to see the red and white lighthouse down there on the rocks again though. It had made her feel dizzy that day. She just wanted to forget everything. And it would be so easy to do that — if only she could pluck up the courage — like her mother had done that day . . .

She stood and looked at the sea, then turned round full circle. There was nobody around at all. It wasn't the kind of day for picnics. It was October. Cool, blowy, and the rain was starting again. She checked there was nothing in her pockets. Ran her fingers round the back of her neck, satisfied that she'd made a good job of cutting the labels out of her clothes. They wouldn't know her — dressed like this. Chain store skirt and jacket, no jewellery. No purse, no credit cards. No identification. It was better that way. It would take time for the police to discover who she was. And by that time Rafe would have guessed what had happened. It wouldn't come as so much of a shock to him then.

No explanatory note either. He would know why she'd done it, because already he suspected that Jade's death had been no accident. And eventually, she knew, Tamsin would remember too. It kept coming back to the girl in those dreams, a little bit at a time. Tamsin would remember who had thrown Jade's scarf on to the track. Tamsin would remember the bride with the green face too — the bride with Jade's scarf pinned across her face, who hadn't been a dream at all . . .

But she'd meant no harm. No real harm. A year ago, she hadn't intended the other girl being killed. It was Jade — Jade who she'd known would rush out on to the track to stop Rafe crashing when he saw the scarf. Jade loved him. Jade would risk her life for him. But Rafe wouldn't be harmed. He was a good driver. He was strapped into that little car so tightly that nothing could hurt him — certainly not hitting something so soft and insubstantial as Jade. Those other fools — Rachel, and then Tamsin — they weren't part of the plan. They should never have been on the track.

A tear trickled down her cheek. In a few moments it would all be over. Mummy had known how to end the torment of years. Known how to rid herself of the silent enemy that had dogged her life — the illness that

379

had been locked into her mind. Mummy had known what she was capable of. And she'd done something about it before she could hurt someone she loved.

Ava was dry-eyed as she stared at the grey heaving sea five hundred feet below her. There was a way — a way to stop the torment. She walked forward, not caring when her high heels twisted and ricked her ankle, not caring about anything. Deliberately, she cleared everything out of her mind and concentrated on the grey sky above her, and the silent grey sea below her. There was an unfenced path — the nature trail. Now she remembered . . .

It was the only thing to do now that she'd killed Rafe's unborn child. She'd known of course that Tam was pregnant. Tam's pale face first thing in the mornings this past month, and her constant dashes to the washroom in the salon had soon opened her eyes as to what had happened between Tam and Rafe. But killing his child! How could she have done such a thing? Killed something so precious — a part of the man that she herself loved to distraction. It was worse than killing Jade — and even that had gone wrong, she hadn't planned to actually kill Jade Herrick. It would have been enough just to hurt her.

But killing *his* child — no! She couldn't live with that knowledge . . . she loved him so much.

Too much.

★　★　★

'Stay there,' Mark ordered as he got out of his car outside the house. 'I'm going to unlock the door. I don't want you out in this downpour for any longer than's necessary.'

'You're giving me orders.' Tam pouted. 'You have no right to tell me what to do.'

Mark stared down at her. 'Do as you're told,' he growled, but there was a smile on his lips, and Tam sat there, in the low little Porsche and waited until he came back to her, opened the door, then slipped one arm behind her and the other under her knees and lifted her out.

She gave a squeal of surprise. 'Hey . . . '

'Shut up.' He kissed her nose, and carried her, still protesting, up to the front door, kicked it open, then deposited her gently on her feet in the hall at the foot of the stairs.

'Don't I get carried up to my bedroom?'

'Nope!' His eyes crinkled with laughter. 'I'm going to see to the car. Put it away in the garage. I don't like it getting wet.'

'You're not turning into that kind of man

are you? The fanatic who treats his car better than he treats his wife?'

'Sweet Tam,' he teased softly, 'You are not my wife. I am merely your keeper until somebody else turns up to take you on.'

She grimaced at him, then waited, watching through the open door as he garaged the car, then came back across the drive to her, swinging her blue leather suitcase with clothes in it that he'd fetched from the Ivory Tower.

'Go and sit down,' he said as, drenched from the pouring rain, he came inside and closed the front door.

She went through to a large comfortable sitting room while he ran up the stairs with the suitcase, then came hurrying back down to her.

'You lit a fire.' Her eyes kindled as she turned towards him.

'And the central heating's on too. Your bedroom is warm as toast if you want to go and rest,' he said.

'I've been resting for three days. I don't want to rest, Mark.'

'Maggie's mother said you should rest.'

'Maggie's mother said I should be back to normal in no time at all.'

'Well then,' he said, 'Doctor Mark is telling you to rest.'

He went over to her and stood in front of her, on the rug against the hearth where coal was burning brightly in the grate. She looked up at him and said simply, 'Thank you, Mark.'

'What for?' he asked in a serious voice.

'Being there.'

He took his wet jacket off and threw it on to a chair, then flattened his fair hair to his head till the water trickled down his neck and dampened his shirt collar. 'I'll always be there,' he said. 'For you.'

'I'm not worth it.'

'Okay, you're not worth it. Shall I make a cup of tea?'

'Mark!'

'What?'

'You're a prat.'

'Yeah!' he said.

'Mark!' She reached out to him and grabbed at his hands. 'I'm grateful.'

'Silly bitch. You should realize I'm not doing this because I care. I just want to get you into my clutches. Maybe one day in the not too distant future then, you'll wake me up again by hitting me with a feather pillow like you did before.'

Her eyes were suddenly shadowed. 'You've never reproached me.'

'Why should I? Maybe I'm learning to

accept you the way you are.'

'I really fell for him.'

'Vaughn Herrick,' he said, the words bitter on his lips.

'Yes.'

'Well,' he sighed. 'If you can fall for a rat like him, maybe there's hope for me.'

'I was desperate for Rafe before Vaughn turned up.' She pulled a face. 'Why do I go and fall for all the wrong men? Why can't I be like other girls and know what's good for me?'

'Because you're not like other girls,' he said gently.

'I envied Jade Herrick for years,' she said. 'And when she died, it was like a pot of gold had dropped into my lap — especially when Ava and Rafe decided I needed looking after.'

'Envy?' he asked. 'Pot of gold?' he went on. 'You sure do paint a picture of a fortune hunter. I note the word 'love' doesn't seem to be high on your list of priorities.'

Looking forlorn, she said, 'You said something about making some tea.'

'The English answer to everything. A cup of tea!'

'I'd rather have a cup of tea than sex at the moment — if you don't mind.'

'You're hard,' he said, breaking away from her.

'About the baby?' She shook her head. 'No,' she said. 'It really doesn't matter. It wasn't a baby, was it? Not a flesh and blood one that cried and wet its pants. I never felt it move. It just made me feel sick, and wretched.'

'You're not cut out for motherhood,' he said, heading towards the kitchen.

'Maybe not,' she agreed. 'Perhaps I'm not normal, but I can't cry for something I never realized was there in the first place.'

He turned round at the door, and looked at her. 'And Vaughn Herrick?' he asked.

She tossed her hair back with an impatient gesture. 'It's over,' she said.

'Are you sure?'

'It was good sex. Last time was at the top of the lighthouse.' She grinned. 'Sex is sex though, isn't it? You can shut your eyes and imagine it's just anybody, can't you?'

'Hard bitch,' he said, with a short little laugh. And then he disappeared through the door and went to make a pot of tea.

24

As Maggie drove north up the motorway, Rafe, beside her in the passenger seat, said, 'My father married again after my mother died, and all of a sudden I had a ready-made sister. Ava was five years old when she came to live with us. I was an awkward ten-year-old who only saw her when I came home from boarding school in the holidays.'

Maggie said, 'So, in reality she's only your step-sister.'

'Yes. But what we didn't know for another few years was that she'd had a life of hell with her mother before she met my dad.'

'She had?'

'My new 'mother' had a history of depression. In those days, twenty-five years ago, you didn't think that somebody with an effervescent personality and lots of enthusiasm for life could possibly be a candidate for depression. But Ava's mother had lots of

386

problems. She ended up killing herself in front of Ava.'

'Oh, no . . . ' Maggie was horrified.

'At Beachey Head in Sussex.'

Maggie felt nausea welling up inside her. 'Oh, the poor little girl — to witness something like that.'

'Maggie . . . ' He was staring at her.

She glanced sideways at him.

'Maggie . . . ' he said again, hoarsely. 'Ava's disappeared. You don't think she could have . . . ?'

They were coming up to Services on the motorway. She counted the markers, three hundred yards, two . . . She began indicating and pulled off the motorway, parking the car under the glaring lights within sight of the restaurant and the bookshop. She sat back in her seat and stared at him.

'What do you want me to do?'

'It's late,' he said. 'Too late to go down to Sussex.'

'You could phone,' she said. 'The police?'

He nodded. 'It's the only thing I can do.'

He got out of the car, and she waited for him. He came back several minutes later, and she wound down her window. He leaned down to talk to her. 'They've found her car,' he said. 'Empty! At Eastbourne.'

She swallowed, not daring to ask the

question she dreaded to hear the answer to. 'Get in the car. We'll leave the motorway at the next junction and go south.'

'No. Not tonight.' His voice was hard. 'I want to go back to Heronsea first. Maybe I'll find an answer to what I'm looking for there. Will you come with me? To the lighthouse?'

She nodded.

'We should eat,' he said, jerking his head back towards the restaurant. 'You look all in. Let's grab a meal, then I'll drive the rest of the way back up north.'

She gave a shuddering little laugh. 'You'll drive this? Won't it be a bit of a comedown?'

He smiled grimly. 'It's got wheels and an engine. And that'll do for me.'

★   ★   ★

They arrived at Heronsea before ten that night. The lighthouse looked different in total darkness. Isolated. A towering chunk of whiteness against the black sea, with only one tiny bright light at the top giving a warning of its presence to any light aircraft that might be in the area.

Wind was whistling round the headland. Rafe shivered, and as he and Maggie hurried towards the Ivory Tower, he put his arm round her shoulders and held her close.

Tonight he needed to feel close to somebody. Tonight he needed Maggie as he'd needed and wanted her so often since that time in France.

With lights full on in the showroom, and the alarm switched off now, the place resumed its normality again, and he headed towards the stairs. And Ava's room.

He called to Maggie to follow him and she did. There were no tell-tale signs of the accident now, except for a slight staining of the floor outside Ava's door. Somebody must have been in to clean the place up, he decided.

They went into Ava's apartment and found it neat and tidy.

'What are you looking for?' Maggie asked, standing hesitantly against the door.

'Damned if I know. She might have left a note though.' He ran the fingers of one hand impatiently through his hair as he looked round the place. 'Goodness knows what I'm looking for,' he said at last. 'I just want a clue as to her state of mind, I suppose.'

But there was no note, no clue however elusive. They searched every surface, even going up to Tamsin's part of the lighthouse and looking there. Tam's bunk was still as she'd left it. Rafe looked in wardrobes and found gaps where clothing was missing.

'Her clothes have gone. Some of them at any rate.'

'Mark probably came for them. She'll need them if she's staying with him for a while.'

His dark brows drew together. 'I wish I could convince myself she's okay with him.'

'She is. She will be. Mark's not likely to hurt her.'

'Those dreams though. Will he be able to cope?'

'I don't know.' She went over to him when they'd gone back down to Ava's room and he was standing, not knowing what to do next.

'Darling Maggie,' he said softly, stroking her hair. 'At least I know where I am with you.'

'Do you?' she asked.

He laughed gently. 'Of course I do. I feel right with you. It seems like I've known you for ever.'

'That doesn't sound very romantic,' she said.

He took her in his arms and kissed her. Then kept one arm around her as they made one last check of the place. 'I still have this feeling that there should be *something* here,' he said. 'It's one of those feelings that you have just before a thunderstorm. You know? There's this whopping big cloud overhead, and you know it's going to split open with a great big bang and a flash of light.'

'I know what you mean.'

'I hate the thought of rifling through her things though . . . '

'Do you want me to look in the drawers beside her bed?'

It was a start, he supposed. There just had to be something, the way he was feeling. It was as if the Ivory Tower had a hold on him, and wasn't going to let him go until it had made him understand what had happened there while he'd been away.

He perched on the edge of the bed as Maggie made a thorough search of one chest of drawers. It revealed nothing except underwear, a couple of silk night-dresses, a sketch pad and pencil in the top one.

'She always kept a sketch pad handy — no matter where she went,' he said. 'She was always on the lookout for new ideas.'

'There are two sketch pads.' Maggie drew them out of the drawer and passed them over to him. Then she pushed the drawer closed again and went round to the other side of the bed.

'Maggie!'

She half-turned from the drawer that held gloves, stockings, pieces of sheer net, a green scarf . . . '

'Hmm?'

'Look.' He held out one of the sketch books.

She took it out of his hand and saw the name 'Jade Herrick' scribbled in a topmost corner.

She sat down on the opposite side of the bed to him. 'It belonged to Jade,' he said. 'These are her sketches. I remember them. There's even one in here of her own wedding dress — or there should be.'

'Can you bear to look?' she asked gently.

He knew she meant well, but what a question. At last he said, 'Yes. I can bear to look at it.'

She handed back the sketch book. He flipped through the pages, and while he did that, she looked through the one belonging to Ava.

All at once, he peered across the bed and said, 'Stop! Turn back a page or two.'

She did as he asked.

'Hold it there,' he said, shooting out a hand and flattening the pages out on the coverlet of the bed. Then he drew in a sharp breath and slapped down the book he held himself, the one that had belonged to Jade.

'Snap,' he said quietly.

The dresses portrayed on both sketch pads were identical. Only the names signed at the bottom of the page were different. One said,

Jade Herrick. The other one, Ava Thorne.

They compared several more sketches. Ava had copied most of them into her own book. 'Tell me I'm not seeing this,' she said.

'Ava's been copying Jade's designs.' Feeling sickened, he said, 'She's been putting her name to Jade's designs and selling them as her own.'

'But — does that matter?' Maggie asked. 'I mean — now Jade's not here . . . '

'It will to the folks who paid good money for a Jade Herrick dress,' he said. 'They were exclusive designs. Jade never made a copy of any one of her dresses.'

'And now Ava . . . ' She stared at him.

'Is selling them by the dozen probably. She has that workroom in Beverley and she's just taken on another half-dozen machinists.'

He closed the sketch book, picked both of them up, then stood up and placed them back in the top drawer. 'I think we'd better call it a day,' he said, turning back to her. 'I don't suppose we're going to find anything else.'

She closed the drawer she'd been looking in and a bit of green silk got trapped in it as she did so. She pulled the drawer open again and pushed the scarf more firmly inside, but he was right there beside her then, stopping her from closing it inside again.

'No,' he said, urgent now, because he'd recognized what she had not.

'What is it?' She glanced up at him. 'Hey — you look like you've seen a ghost . . . '

His hand dropped down on to hers and pulled it away from the drawer, then carefully he scooped out the green silk, and held it, lying across both his hands, just staring at it, and re-living again that day a year ago.

'It's Jade's scarf,' he said, hearing his voice beginning to crack, and feeling his heart hammering inside his chest. 'It's the scarf that got her killed. The one that plastered itself across my visor that day. Look . . . ' his hand slid to one corner of the long piece of silk. 'Look, her initial in this corner. Tam embroidered it on for her. A tiny J for Jade in white silk. Oscar-Jade colours — green and white.

He held the scarf to his face. 'I can still smell her perfume.' He sank down on to the edge of the bed again and buried his face in it. Beside him, he was aware of Maggie, watching him. He took one last long deep breath of the perfume, realizing that although it bore her scent, there was nothing else left of her. He looked up and held it out to her — the scarf. 'Here — look at it. I'd no idea Ava had still got it. I thought it had got blown away on the wind that day.'

She backed away from him, her hands held rigidly at her sides. 'It's all you've got left of her,' she said huskily. 'I couldn't touch it.'

He rose to his feet. 'Maggie,' he said thickly. 'Maggie — it means nothing to me. Don't you know that?'

She leaned against the drawer. Gently, he moved her aside. 'What else is there in there?'

She lifted her shoulders in a little helpless gesture. 'Gloves, stockings, some net, a torch.'

He pulled the drawer open again. 'The net,' he said. 'It's a bridal head dress, isn't it.'

She examined it. 'Yes. One of those kind that covers the bride's hair completely with a wide satin band.'

'And a torch.' Somewhere along the way back from Northampton, he recalled Maggie telling him about the dream Tamsin had had before she fell down the stairs.

'The dream,' he said, with incredulity in his voice. 'Oh, Maggie. That was no dream the girl had. It must have been absolutely terrifying.'

★　★　★

Rafe insisted on driving them both to Mark's house in his car. It had been nearly midnight when he and Maggie had arrived at Rothwold, and found lights still on in the living rooms downstairs.

'If you'd been in darkness I would have waited till tomorrow,' Rafe told Tamsin. 'I wouldn't have disturbed you . . . ' he glanced at Mark, ' . . . both,' he finished lamely.

Tamsin's tears were wet on the jade green scarf which she was still holding against her cheek, but she giggled a little hysterically and said, 'You wouldn't have disturbed anything, Rafe. Mark puts me in a separate bedroom when I'm here.'

'You realize what this means though?' Rafe said.

The girl nodded. 'I think I always knew. Deep down inside. It could only have been one of two girls who had pulled Jade's scarf off that day. She'd been standing between Ava and me, you see. And I knew it wasn't me.'

'But you never said a thing.'

'Rafe — darling Rafe — would *anybody* have believed me? And anyway, I never saw Ava throw the scarf on to the track. I just knew though.' She took the scarf away from her cheek and looked at it. 'It's over now. The mystery. And the scarf belongs to you, Rafe.' She handed it back to him.

In the hearth, the coal fire was little more than a glimmer now. Rafe looked at it, and then at the scarf in his hands. 'There's only one thing to do,' he said. 'We don't need it any more. We have to look forward now. Not backward.' He walked over to the firegrate and let the jade green scarf slip lazily through his fingers on to the hot coals.

It sizzled, then burst into a quick flame and was consumed within seconds.

Beside him, he heard Maggie's sharp intake of breath.

He looked up at her and said, 'It was only a scrap of silk, Maggie. Only a scrap of silk.'

25

Rafe drove her home, to the little cottage on the edge of the sea at Shorecross. It was half-past one in the morning, and the rest of Shorecross was sleeping. He stopped the car right outside the house and said, 'Somehow, we'll have to get your own car back to you from the lighthouse.'

'I have the keys,' she said. 'I'll pop over tomorrow for it.'

'You're sure you won't need it till then? I know how dependent you are on it if Edgar needs you to go out to a breakdown or anything.'

'Not any more,' she said. 'I don't work for Dad now.'

'I keep forgetting,' he said. 'But I suppose in an emergency he could call on you?'

'I have my other job,' she insisted. 'Here! At the lifeboat station.'

'But it's just a shop, Maggie. And there can't be much call for lifeboat mementoes at this time of year.'

'I keep busy,' she said, still reluctant to tell him she was part of the rescue team. He seemed to have built up this picture of her being incapable of running her own life, and it irked her. But to blurt out that she was actively involved with the running of the rescues would, to her way of thinking, sound as if she were boasting.

No, she decided. He was going to have to accept her as he imagined her to be — timid little Maggie Brand who had never taken a risk in her life. If he really loved her, that undercurrent of teasing derision would have to be tackled somehow. But she wasn't going to force the issue. She wondered uneasily though, how much of his wanting to keep their love a secret had any bearing on the fact that she was just an ordinary girl, and nothing special.

He turned to her in the darkness of the car, and said quietly, 'Maggie — I can explain now why I didn't want it bandying about all over the place that I loved you.'

About to get out of the car, his words gave her a jolt, and she sat back in her seat and regarded him uneasily, but said nothing.

'Ava,' he said, 'can be very possessive. And I knew her background was unstable. However, she never at any time showed any sign of being like her mother.'

'So?' she murmured.

'I was scared,' he said simply.

'Scared?'

'After Jade — Ava seemed on a kind of high — jollying me along, telling me I had all my life ahead of me — insisting all the time it was an accident and I should try and put it behind me. But accidents, especially that sort of accident, don't just happen. Accidents always have a cause. In the case of Jade's death, the cause was the green scarf. But again — no explanation was ever given for the scarf blowing on to the track. And it couldn't have happened accidentally, that scarf was part of Jade's outfit, it was buttoned tightly to the jacket Jade was wearing — underneath the collar. Only a close friend would have known that. And Ava was a close friend.'

'And you believed — all this time . . . '

'That *somebody* had it in for Jade.'

Maggie sat very still, staring through the car windscreen, out into the night. 'Oh, no . . . ' she breathed. 'You're not saying it was planned?'

His hands were fastened tight round the steering wheel in front of him. 'I don't want to think that. But it's been on my mind for so long now. Then, Tamsin started acting possessive around me too, and that really threw me. Both of them had been there that day — at the circuit. Both of them were close to Jade. Now, suddenly, both of them were trying to live my life for me.'

'I see,' she said in a calm voice. 'So when you met me . . . '

'When I fell for you,' he corrected gently, 'When we were in France and it became obvious to me that my little Maggie was carving a niche for herself in my heart — then I started to worry. I became uneasy. Obsessed almost, by the need to protect you — but I was laid up with a smashed ankle. I felt helpless.' He gave a harsh little laugh. 'When you climbed that hill to rescue Vaughn, I was incensed that I couldn't do anything except stand there and watch. And I hated it, Maggie — just being an onlooker. It came home to me forcibly then, that if anybody did want to harm you, I wouldn't be in any position to protect you.'

'I thought . . . ' she said awkwardly, 'I thought you didn't want people to know because you saw me as just an ordinary girl.'

He let go the steering wheel and his arm went right round her shoulders, dragging her towards him. 'Ordinary?' he whispered hungrily. 'Maggie — you are not ordinary.'

She leaned her head on his shoulder and lifted her lips to his. He kissed her in a hard and passionate way, and she felt an overwhelming happiness creeping over her like a warm wave.

'I was so scared,' she whispered. 'I thought you couldn't accept me as I was.'

'It's how I want you to be.' His mouth was close to hers. He kissed her again. 'I wouldn't want it any other way. I couldn't bear it if you were ever in danger.' He gave a little laugh. 'If, for instance you were the racing driver, I'd be frantic every time you took to the track. Yet for myself, I never see the danger.'

She pulled away from him a little and looked into his eyes. 'We do things every day that are dangerous,' she said guardedly. 'Everybody does.'

'And they're the only kind of risks I'd want you to take, Maggie,' he said, completely at ease with her now. 'I don't want a supergirl. I want to know you'll always be there. I want a settled home life, maybe kiddies in a year or two. I've had enough of never being in one place long enough to think of those things. And now I've fallen in love with a lovely girl who puts her mom and dad high on her list of priorities, who isn't a high flyer, and who doesn't put her life on the line at every opportunity.'

'You make me sound boring,' she pro-tested.

'Don't you want the things I want, Maggie?'

She sat still and thought of Jim Farmer, and all the lads at the lifeboat station who depended on her keeping the boat in perfect working order. She thought about the high seas and the thrill of ploughing into the waves when the boat was launched. At no time in her life could she ever remember being afraid of the sea. It had always been there, a part of her life, dangerous at times it was true, but she loved it. And before she'd joined the lifeboat, there had been other things too — scaling the cliffs under her dad's guidance when she was just a teenager, canoeing holidays, rallies where she'd raced her father's classics. She'd even, a year ago, done two parachute jumps, one for a local charity, the other for her mother's gynae unit.

And then, Rafe Thorne had come into her life again, just as it had been at a low ebb. Dad was recovering from his accident, things were hectic at the garage, and she'd of necessity been forced to put her own interests aside and get things on an even keel.

Rafe didn't really know her at all, she thought with a shock. He had this idealistic little picture of her, living at home, never taking risks . . .

If only he knew! But she couldn't shatter all his illusions.

She said quietly, 'I wouldn't be happy 'safe' all the time — and neither would you, Rafe.'

A clock somewhere near struck two. 'I oughtn't to be keeping you up,' he said. 'It's been one hell of a day.'

She needed to be alone. Needed sleep. 'Let me know if you hear anything about Ava,' she said.

He nodded. 'I will. Right away.' He drew his arm away from her shoulders and kissed her again. The kiss deepened into a longing. She wanted him to hold her again, wanted more than that even. And he felt the same way too. One hand was sliding inside her jacket, cupping her breast. She drew in her breath and closed her eyes. It could be so good. There was nothing for him to go home to. He could stay the night . . .

'No,' she said gently. 'No further, Rafe. I need some sleep.'

'All right,' he said with understanding in his voice. 'But I'll see you tomorrow, Maggie.'

She leaned towards him and placed her lips to his. 'See you tomorrow,' she agreed, and quickly, before she could have regrets about what might have been, she was out of the car and hurrying towards her own front door.

When she'd let herself inside, it felt lonely

in there. Fudge had been boarded with her parents while she'd driven down to Northampton, and she missed his enthusiastic welcome. She leaned back against the door, and listened to the distinctive noise of the engine, as the Ferrari roared away into the night.

★   ★   ★

The persistent ringing of her telephone dragged Maggie out of a deep sleep the next day. Sliding quickly out of bed, she raced down the stairs and grabbed it from its wall hanging in the tiny hall where there was scarcely room to turn around between the foot of the stairs and the front door.

It was Rafe, and she could tell at once he was on his mobile from the noise of background traffic.

'I'm half way to Eastbourne,' he said. 'Sorry about the noise at this end, Maggie, but I thought I'd better tell you — Ava's been found.'

She sank down on to the bottom stair, closing her eyes briefly as she managed a breathless, 'Found — you mean . . . ' and her heart began to pound.

'Alive! Thank God. In a guest house in Eastbourne. The police had issued a photo-fit and it was shown on the local TV stations early this morning. Somebody recognized her. I'm on my way now — I'm off the motorway and in a lay-by. I should reach Eastbourne by lunch time.'

'Rafe! Oh, Rafe — I'm so glad the news wasn't the kind we were dreading.'

'So am I, Maggie,' he said with a heartfelt sigh.

'Will you bring her back?'

'Lord knows. I keep wondering what sort of state she's in. She's obviously not been herself for some time.'

'Keep in touch — let me know what's happening, won't you?'

'Of course I will. Maggie — I'm going to ring off now. I want to get there as soon as I can.'

'I understand.' She stood up, prepared to put the receiver back in place.

'And Maggie . . . '

'Yes?'

'Remember what I said to you yesterday?'

'We said a lot of things,' she hedged.

'I love you, Maggie.'

'Yes,' she said softly. 'I remember that.'

'We'll sort things out.'

'Yes,' she said again, and he was gone.

26

He called her from the south of England several times during the next two weeks. Ava was having treatment. She was responding well. He wouldn't be able to get back to Heronsea however. Not yet. There was the last race in November — an extra one to those scheduled — it was the big one for him. The last one of his career, and already they were in trouble with it.

The track, so he said, was the problem. The circuit wasn't finished yet. It was in Spain, but there was talk now of holding the last Grand Prix in England. Panic everywhere. None of the teams knew what they were doing. Where to test! What kind of tyres to rely on! Oscar was going crazy.

'Where are you staying?' Maggie asked him on the phone.

He gave her the name and number of an hotel in Eastbourne, then said, 'But I'm having to go to Oscar's place whenever I can.

Every day when it's possible to leave Ava. We're testing at Silverstone some of the time. East Midlands others.' He laughed. 'I don't know whether I'm on my head or my heels, but we're all in the same boat. It's chaotic.'

'The East Midlands?'

'A place called Denning Park — a fairly new circuit out towards Lincoln. When we're there, we live in the motorhome. It's all work and no play at the moment. *Living* doesn't describe it! We exist. We exist for the cars.'

'Will Ava be coming back to Heronsea?'

'I hope so. She talks about nothing else but her Ivory Tower. Tam's on her own there at the moment, but quite happy. She's keeping the place going till Ava can return.'

'Do you know when that will be?'

'She's responding well — and there's an excellent doctor down here who seems to be getting her back on the right track. We're hoping perhaps in another week . . . '

Maggie laughed. 'In time for the Shore-cross Gala the week after Michaelmas?'

'The what?'

'It's held here every year — once the place is free of holidaymakers. People come from all over the East Riding for the day.'

'What on earth is it?'

She sighed. 'I've just told you — a gala day. For the kids really, a fairground, swings and a carousel, dog show, bonny baby contest, brass bands and umpteen stalls selling everything from home-made cakes to white elephants.'

Seriously he said, 'It might be a good time to bring Ava back. She always used to love fairgrounds when she was a little girl.'

'Does she know . . . '

'That Tamsin lost the baby? That we discovered what she'd been up to?' he said curtly. 'Yes, Maggie, she knows. And now she's on medication, she realizes the seriousness of the situation. Tam says she won't take the matter any further though, and with Jade — well it's too late now to do anything about that.'

'She could face charges though.'

'Unlikely. Tam's the injured party, and Tam says she can't do that to her friend. Some friend, huh? I don't think I would have been so tolerant of interference of that sort in my life.'

'But she's ill, Rafe. We don't know for sure that she knew what she was doing.'

'No,' he said, sounding incredibly weary. 'And this guy down here — the doctor — he says the paranoia isn't an over the top kind. It is treatable. Thank goodness.'

'You sound tired.' Maggie could understand the strain he must be under. With the race coming up and all the worry attached to that, he could well do without Ava's problems.

'I'll try to grab a few days to be with you, love. When did you say this gala thing was?'

'Next weekend,' she said. 'Dad's displaying all his classics on the cliff top. It'll be quite a show, he must have around twenty that are worth looking at.'

'You'll be there to help, no doubt?'

'Of course. And I'll be manning a stall selling lifeboat souvenirs too. Will you come and buy a badge from me?'

'I'll do that,' he said, 'But then I'll stick with Fudge, if you don't mind. I don't like carousels, they make me dizzy. Who could get any fun out of whirling round and round like that?'

'It doesn't remind you of a racing car going *round and round* a track by any chance, does it?' she teased.

He laughed. 'You've got it, Maggie.'

'Fudge won't be there,' she said. 'There's a dog show — and Fudge is either decidedly anti-social to the other dogs, or else over amorous to the bitches. I think it'll be better if he stays at home.'

He laughed again, and this time sounded more relaxed. 'You're good for me, Maggie,' he said. Then in a more serious tone, 'We're going to have to talk — make plans. I'm missing you like hell, Maggie.'

'Me too,' she said softly. 'Take care of yourself — for me.'

★ ★ ★

'Edgar's mad!'

Mark paced up and down the garage.

Maggie said, 'No he's not. He always puts the cars in the same place — every year. People like to see them on top of the cliffs.'

'The salt spray will ruin the paintwork.' Mark glared at her.

'It's one day,' she pointed out. 'Just one day, Mark. The cars might get a bit damp but that's only to be expected.'

'What's the point of it all anyway?'

'It's a charity day. All proceeds go to the hospital. Mark, you know quite well what the gala is all about.'

'I've never taken part in it before though,' he said with a glum face. 'Honestly, Mags, it's not my sort of thing, is it?'

Seeing the garage doors still open as she'd walked Fudge that night, Maggie had popped in and found Mark staring ponderously at the engine of his own car. 'The gears are playing up,' he'd told her. 'And there's a bit of re-spraying I want to do on the sills.'

'How's Tamsin?' She attempted to lighten his mood.

'Fine!' His face lit up. 'She's in complete charge at the lighthouse now Ava's away, and she's coping well.'

'She's bringing some publicity leaflets about the Ivory Tower to the gala, and she's going to make posies of flowers to give away with them,' she said.

The smile left his face. 'She is? She never told me.'

'Well — perhaps she's been too busy.'

'I see her most days.'

'You're getting on well together?'

He made a balancing kind of movement with one hand. 'So-so! You never really know quite where you are with Tam. I'm happy now she's moved out of that damned tower though. She's got herself a nice little flat in Heronsea now. She just goes to the lighthouse in the hours of daylight. To work. I don't think I'll ever trust that Ava Thorne woman again.'

'She's not still with you then? Tam?'

'No!' He let out a great sigh. 'She wants her independence, she says.'

'I'm sorry, Mark. I really thought you two had something going between you,' Maggie said. 'You seemed so well suited.'

'Tell that to Tam,' he said with a growl of laughter. 'She'll think it incredibly funny.'

'You should settle down, Mark.'

'Don't tell me I need a good woman. I like the bad ones best,' he joked.

'At least you've acquired a sense of humour, now that you don't have to work with me,' she said drily.

'You're better off with the boat,' he said. 'Boats don't answer back.'

'You'll help me with the cars on Saturday then. I can depend on you getting up at the crack of dawn and coming over to Shore-cross, can I?'

'Mmm.' he said. 'Yes. I'll be there, Mags.'

'What changed your mind?' she asked.

'Oh, I have this yearning to be a do-gooder and rake in lots of funds for the hospital,' he said.

'I thought you'd say that,' she teased. 'I never thought for one moment that your coming here next Saturday would have anything to do with the fact that Tamsin would also be here — with her posies of flowers.'

★ ★ ★

For the rest of the week the weather was foul, and it started to look like the Gala would have to be cancelled.

Rain hurled down, gales blew in from the north, and the sea smashed itself against the low boulder cliffs with a frightening ferocity. Even Fudge backed off, and took his walks along the cliff tops, keeping well clear of the edges which looked as if a giant jaw had bitten out great chunks of the coastline following one night's major storm.

By Friday though, the weather had calmed, but on the cliff tops, great puddles still lay, draining slowly through the boulder clay, and trickling streams of water down on to the beach. The streams cut channels through the sand, and Fudge examined every one, his nose trailing zig-zag paths down to the water's edge, where he jumped back every time a wave came near him.

Maggie laughed at him. He'd never liked the sea at close quarters. 'You're a coward,' she called to him, and he came bounding back to her, scuffing sand up and then rolling in it, and making a great fuss afterwards of shaking every bit of it out of his fur.

She heard somebody shouting. Looked round and saw a figure on the cliff top. He yelled again.

'Maggie!' He waved wildly at her.

'Rafe!' she squeaked. And then she was running towards the cliffs, with Fudge barking at her heels. 'Rafe!' She knew her face must be radiant. She could feel a smile spreading from one side of it to the other. She stood at last below him. The cliffs were higher here. He was fifteen feet above her.

'Maggie! Oh — I've missed you. You don't know what it does to me — seeing you again.'

'Come down,' she yelled, pointing, 'Look — there's a bit of a path.'

'The coast's taken a battering since I was here last.'

She laughed up at him. 'It's been awful this past week. Storms. Gales. We've had the lot.'

He strode out towards the path she'd indicated, and was nearly above it when the ground started crumbling under his feet.

'Watch out,' she shouted, her hand flying to her mouth in dismay.

Fudge came close to her side as rubble and soil started cascading down from the cliff top. She laid a hand on the big dog's head. 'It's okay,' she said. 'You're safe just here.'

Rafe regained his balance and ran easily down the jagged pathway, coming to a stop in front of her.

'Wow!' he said. 'That was a close one. I thought I was going to land in a heap down here.'

'It's been so wet,' she said, and showed him the rivulets running down through the boulder clay, and then across the sand to the sea. 'Fudge isn't at all happy about even more water invading his beach.' Her eyes lit up as they met his. 'It's good to see you again.' She ran into his arms. 'Oh, it's *great* to see you again.' She tilted her head back and gazed into his eyes. 'I love you,' she said breathlessly. 'Rafe Thorne, I love you to bits.'

Fudge didn't think much of all the kissing and the stroking. He wandered off to sniff at stones.

In his arms, Maggie couldn't get close enough to Rafe. They clung together as if it had been years, not just a couple of weeks they'd been apart.

'Maggie,' he said hoarsely against her hair, 'It's been hell without you. I've missed you.'

She wound her arms round his neck and pulled his head down to hers. Against his mouth, she whispered, 'I have needed this like somebody drowning needs a life-raft.'

'Maggie — let's go somewhere . . . '

'I'm on duty,' she said tremulously. 'I get an hour off for lunch and there's only twenty minutes left.'

'That damned shop! Can't you take the rest of the day off?'

'No,' she said, kissing him again. 'I have to be there. They pay me to be there.'

'Tomorrow then.'

'Tomorrow's Shorecross Gala!'

'Hell and damnation!'

'Tonight?' she asked. 'I'm off duty at five.'

'Maggie!' His arms went round her, he lifted her off the ground and spun her round till she was dizzy and helpless with laughter. He stopped then, held her as she wobbled till she'd regained her balance, then said, 'I'll come to the cottage, shall I?'

She nodded. 'Do you want to eat?'

'Yes,' he said.

'What's your favourite food?'

'You,' he said, pulling her to him again.

'You can't eat me.'

'We'll eat . . . afterwards,' he said.

Colour rushed to her face.

'Well?' he said.

'Yes,' she said. 'We'll eat . . . afterwards.'

27

Maggie's cassette alarm clock woke her the next morning, and she lay on her back, staring up at the ceiling, listening to a Chopin prelude. A voice beside her said, 'Do you always wake up this way?'

She hadn't forgotten he was there. How could she? 'In a couple of minutes,' she said, 'I shall go and make a pot of tea and bring it up here. That's the next step after Chopin.'

He leaned up on one elbow and stared down into her face. 'And the third step?' he asked softly.

'Ah, that's when Fudge comes up to keep me company,' she said with a wicked glint in her eye. 'That's when we share the bed and a piece of toast, and Fudge has a saucer of tea.'

'On the bed?'

She punched him. 'No. On the floor.'

'Thank goodness for that.'

'I hope he remembers you're here.' She began to laugh. 'He usually launches himself on to that side of the bed.'

'Tell him,' he said solemnly, 'that I did not intend to invade his territory, it was just something that happened.'

She pulled herself up in bed, self-consciously dragging the duvet up to her chest and covering her nakedness.

'Don't do that,' he said, pulling it down again. 'You have a lovely body — don't cover it up.'

She reached for her robe, on a chair beside the bed. It was the white silk one. She'd shoved the old chenille one into the back of a drawer before he arrived last night.

His hand closed over it. 'Don't go,' he said. 'Not yet, Maggie.'

'I have to. I told Dad I'd be there at eight o'clock to help move the cars to the cliff top.'

'Can I help?'

She leaned over and kissed his forehead. 'If you like. Dad will probably round you up with a shot-gun though if he thinks you've stayed the night here with me.'

'Darling Maggie.' His hand slid down under the covering and hooked round her waist. He moved nearer to her, pulled her down the bed, hovered above her, then swooped his head down and took possession of her mouth with his own.

'Maggie . . . ' he whispered against her lips.

'Maggie . . . ' and his hand moved down the side of her body, hard and insistent in the curve of her waist and over the sensuous thrust of her hip.

Downstairs they heard the plaintive whining of Fudge at the bottom of the stairs, and Rafe lifted his face from hers as he felt her stiffen beneath him. His expression was pained but full of understanding. They each held the other's gaze for a moment, then at the same time, both burst out laughing.

He rolled away from her then, and lying flat out on his back said, 'You never warned me he was a guard dog — and he's obviously put out because he's heard me here.'

She swung her long legs out of the bed and slipped into her robe. Tying it, she looked down at him and said, 'Aren't you glad he was tired out from his walk when you came up here last night?'

'Maggie Brand,' he said, his eyes never leaving her face for a moment, 'Maggie — we're going to have to make this arrangement more permanent.'

'You hardly know me.' She leaned on the bed with both hands and bent over him.

He grabbed at both her wrists and held them there so she couldn't move. 'Marry me,' he said. 'I'll get to know you later.'

'Let me go.' Her eyes danced with merriment.

'Give me an answer. It's not every day I propose to a girl.'

'Let me think about it,' she teased.

'What's there to think about?'

'Your insatiable appetite,' she said softly as her hair cascaded around her face and fell forward above him.

'You didn't complain last night.'

'Who says I'm complaining now. I said I was *thinking* about it. I was *thinking* about it as I fell asleep last night. I was *thinking* about it when I woke up this morning too. I like thinking about what happened, Rafe. I like remembering what it was like, having you make love to me, and me loving you.'

The Chopin prelude had finished, and as the last notes faded away, she wriggled a hand free, reached to the cassette and clicked it off.

'Maggie . . . don't go.'

'There's always tonight,' she said. 'And a million more tonights. But now I have to go.'

Reluctantly he released her other hand and she straightened beside the bed and pushed both her hands through her hair, lifting it away from her face, and then shaking it back over her shoulders.

'I really do have to go.'

'Did you mean it about all those 'tonights'?'

She nodded. 'I meant it, Rafe.'

★   ★   ★

The classic cars were set at a slanting angle, their rear ends towards the sea. They were a good ten to fifteen feet from the edge of the cliffs, allowing space for visitors to walk right round them to admire the gleaming chrome, the mirror-like polish they preened themselves with, and the spotless interiors oozing with the care that had been lavished on their real leather upholstery.

Edgar was well pleased with them when Maggie eventually left at around ten-thirty to go and set up her lifeboat stall on the adjacent field.

Rafe had said he'd meet her there, and he did. Jim Farmer appeared too with his Land Rover and two cardboard boxes full of items from the lifeboat shop. Rafe, to her surprise, took the whole thing seriously and helped her set up the stall with the good selection of things Jim had brought from the shop.

When it was finished, they covered the whole lot with a large sheet of plastic and pegged it down.

'What do we do now?' Rafe wanted to know.

She looked at her watch. It was lunch time and the Gala wouldn't be opening for another hour.

'Eat?' She looked up at the sky where angry clouds were gathering. 'I hope it doesn't rain.'

A cool wind was whipping up the waves into white water on the sea. The tide had turned and was racing up the beach. 'That tide is moving fast,' Rafe said with a frown.

Jim walked past them. 'I don't like the look of it, Maggie,' he yelled to her. 'Let's hope we don't get a call out. It could spell trouble.'

'What's the forecast, Jim?'

'Rain later. Squally.' He nodded towards the sea. 'Tell your dad to watch those cars, love. Sand's a killer to paintwork if it gets stirred up.'

'I'll mention it, Jim.'

'You're friendly with that bloke,' Rafe said conversationally.

'You could say he's my boss.' She grinned at him. 'Jim's the cox on the lifeboat.'

Break it to him gently, her conscience was saying to her. Get Rafe used to the idea, one step at a time. Let him see that the crew who manned the boat were mainly strapping big fellows like Jim so that he'd know she would come to no harm at sea with them.

'Ah, yes,' he said. 'The lifeboat house is right next to your little shop, isn't it?'

She nodded happily. 'You'll have to pop in and see the boat some time.'

'I'd like to.'

'How about that food?'

'Where do we go for it?'

'Back to my house,' she said. 'Fudge is a great timekeeper. He knows when it's time for his next walk, and he'll need one before we settle down for the afternoon up here.'

★ ★ ★

It was a good three quarters of the way through the Gala afternoon when the first huge spots of rain started to fall. At least it hadn't spoilt the whole day though, Maggie thought, and the evening's harvest supper was going to be held in the Church Hall so nothing would be spoilt there. There was a good crowd on the cliff top fields and with everybody routing for the hospital, money was flowing freely.

Jim came round frequently with small packets of loose change, and to collect the bulk of the money from the stalls and take it to the lifeboat station to lock it in the safe for the weekend. He was pleased with the collections. There was well over seven hundred pounds already in the safe, he told her.

She kept catching glimpses of Tamsin who was circulating in the crowd with her posies of flowers and advertising material for the Ivory Tower. Tam didn't have a stall, and she didn't take any money, but there was a hospital collecting box beside her enormous basket of flowers which stood right against the entrance gate. Mark was in attendance most of the time, doting on Tam, and helping her with the leaflets when Edgar didn't want him for anything.

The classic cars drew lots of attention, and Edgar was in his element. Maggie's mother came up to the lifeboat stall and said, 'Go and take a look at your father, Maggie — he's like a dog with two tails showing off his blessed cars. I'll hold the fort here for a while.'

Maggie introduced Rafe to her mother, and Sheila held out her hand to him and said, 'You don't need any introduction. I've seen you in the newspapers and on television hundreds of times. If we'd known you were going to be here, I'd have had you as the official opener, and we could have made a mint on signed photographs of you.'

Rafe's laughter rang out. 'Maybe next year, then.'

'If you're still around, hmm?' Sheila pursed her lips. 'You lead a busy life, Mr Thorne . . . '

As they walked away from her mother, Rafe said, 'She's nice. I hope she doesn't continue calling me Mr Thorne though when she knows I'm going to marry her daughter.'

Maggie caught at his hand and swung it as they walked in the teeth of the wind across the cliff top. 'You meant it then? It wasn't just pillow-talk?'

He pulled her round into his arms. 'Pillow-talk!' he said in disgust. 'Maggie Brand — I want to spend the rest of my life with you.' He looked down into her eyes. 'Tell me,' he said, 'that I am not wasting my time.'

Serious eyes gazed up into his. 'You are not wasting your time — Mr Thorne.'

'You sound like a Jane Austen heroine.'

They started walking again, and came upon Edgar who was making his way back to the garage in his wheelchair. He spun round as Maggie called to him.

'Maggie! Have you seen Mark?' He came back towards them looking worried.

'He was with Tamsin half an hour ago. But what's wrong, Dad?'

He nodded his head at the coastline. 'That darn sea for one thing. Already it's sending spray up the cliffs and high tide's not for another hour. I think we ought to move the cars, don't you?'

Rafe looked over at the boiling, threshing waves, and they were all silent for a few moments as they listened to the thundering boom of the ocean as it hit the boulder clay and sent resounding rumblings through the ground at their feet.

'Your dad's right, Maggie,' Rafe said. 'I'll help if you'll show me where to put them.'

Edgar pointed to the garage. 'There are two big workshops round the back. I'll go over there and prop the doors open.' He turned to Maggie, 'You bring the first one in and Rafe can follow and see where you go. Okay?'

'Right, Dad.'

Edgar handed her a great wodge of keys, and she started separating them quickly. Each one had a tag on it to show which car it belonged to. She handed Rafe half the keys.

'Lead on,' he said with a grin.

They moved the cars and got them safely tucked into the workshops nearly a hundred yards away from the cliff edge, and Edgar locked the doors securely, then thanked them both. It had barely taken fifteen minutes to accomplish the task, yet in that time the sky had darkened and the wind had turned into a gale force.

'There's one car left,' Rafe said. 'It was way

beyond the others — much nearer to the sea.'

'Not one of mine,' Edgar said. 'What sort?'

'Porsche. A Club Sport model. Not new exactly, but a nice looker.'

Maggie said, 'It belongs to Mark.'

'Well, I wouldn't leave it there if it were mine,' Rafe said. 'It's getting drenched with sea-water, and the ground it's on doesn't look all that safe.'

'Heck! I wonder where he is.'

They hurried back to the main Gala field as rain started pouring down. A mini-whirlwind was playing havoc with the plastic coverings of some of the stalls as people worked frantically to clear away books, cakes, fancy goods and bric-a-brac. Maggie raced to help her mother who had cleared the lifeboat stall and packed everything that was left over into the two large boxes Jim had left earlier.

Jim himself was crawling round the field in his Range Rover, collecting the remnants that were left from all the stall-holders. He yelled to her, 'I think we've got it all under control, Maggie.'

Rafe had his arm round her, holding her close as they were almost blown off their feet. Then they heard somebody screaming and saw a figure rushing their way.

'Tamsin!' Maggie cried, breaking away from Rafe and running towards the girl.

Tears were streaming down Tam's face as she tried to fight off Maggie's restraining hands. 'He's in the sea . . . ' She clawed at Rafe as he too tried to hang on to her. 'Mark . . . He went to move his car . . . ' The words were coming out in great sobs. 'It went into reverse . . . over the cliff . . . the waves just tossed it into the air . . . he's dead! I know he is . . . he disappeared under the water . . . and then he was thrown up again . . . a long way out and he wasn't moving. He's dead. I know he is, Maggie . . . '

28

Maggie's face was white. 'Show me,' she urged Tamsin. 'Show me where he is. It might be possible to reach him.'

'He was swept away,' Tam screamed again. 'That's what I'm trying to tell you. Somebody back there — they phoned the coastguard . . . they said they'd have to get the lifeboat out — but it'll take hours — absolutely hours to do that, won't it, Maggie?'

'No,' Maggie said swiftly. 'It won't take hours, Tam. If the station's been alerted we'll hear the maroons being fired . . . '

As if to add impact to her words, the pager in Maggie's jeans pocket suddenly started its shrill and persistent bleeping, and almost simultaneously there were two explosions high up in the air above the lifeboat station. As green stars plunged through the black clouds, Maggie saw Jim waving frantically to her from his Range Rover, and she started to run towards him, glancing back only briefly to yell to Rafe, 'Sorry! I have to go . . . no time to explain . . . '

The look on his face, the absolute incredulity, mingled with a growing dread, stayed with her as she flung herself into the Range Rover and hung on as it careered wildly across the tops of the bumpy cliffs, and then down the last field, taking a short cut to the station.

They were first to arrive, and into their uniforms and life-jackets in minutes. Almost immediately however, they came in a surge, men running from every direction, cars screeching to a halt outside as Jim, with the position made clear to him by the station secretary, made the decision not to launch the main boat, but to take the 'D' class inflatable — with two crew. 'I'll need you along to keep the engine going strong, Maggie,' he said, throwing her a grim smile. 'We'll need all the power we can get in that sea. But if he hasn't been swept too far out — and I wouldn't think he has because the tide hasn't turned fully yet — then this is the only way we're going to get him to safety.'

Maggie tried to keep calm and concentrate on Jim's instructions, but her fears for Mark's safety were growing all the while. 'He can't swim,' she told Jim.

'Oh hell! That's all we need.'

Maggie raced after him, and soon they were preparing to launch, with the help of two shore crew who would wait for them coming back and bring the boat in again. And then they were in the sea, and Jim as coxswain was in absolute command, Lloyd Rogers the estate agent navigated, and Maggie herself took charge of the powerful engine. All three of them were trained for this kind of work *and* in this kind of weather, but Maggie found herself hanging on for all she was worth in the heavy seas.

Jim yelled, 'Good girl, Maggie,' as they bounced through the surf, the little boat giving the best performance of its life in the most atrocious of conditions.

As they picked up more speed and hugged the coastline, it was relatively easy to see the crowd that had gathered on the cliff tops where the Gala had been held. For the first time then, Maggie allowed herself to wonder about Rafe. She could only guess what his eventual reaction to her hasty departure had been. All she could think about now was the expression that had registered on his face — first of all shock, and then suspicion! She wished with all her heart now that she'd prepared him for this, but the opportunity had never arisen.

The boat was being tossed about but the

sea held no fear for her. The engine was in tip-top condition. It sliced a way easily through the wind-torn waves as she kept it on course, and listened to Jim as he tried to pinpoint the spot in that dark forbidding ocean where Mark might possibly be.

She brought the boat round in an arc, as it became clear that Mark had been swept further out than they'd anticipated. There was no way of knowing in a swell like this though just how far out he could be.

They circled the area off shore where Mark must have gone into the water. Jim pointed to something near the foot of the cliffs. 'There's the car. Let's swing round again from here. He's got to be somewhere close.' But Jim's face was tense, and Maggie was seized with an unthinkable dread.

'He can't swim . . . ' she faltered again, and Jim shot her a fierce look and yelled, 'Then start praying. Now!'

That, and an ever growing sense of frustration, made her more determined than ever to find Mark. Maggie's teeth were clenched in concentration as they searched the area again, and anger started replacing the fear she was experiencing. What the hell had Mark been doing, she wondered? How had the car managed to go over the cliff? The sea was like a boiling cauldron. He should have been more careful.

Recriminations were not the solution though. Mark wasn't here to give her an answer to her questions. Jim ordered another sweep of the bay, then another, and they were on their third time round and Maggie was trying her hardest not to break down and howl. Mark had been in the water nearly half an hour now, and hope was fading by the minute.

And then Jim yelled, 'Over there, Maggie!' and pointed to something blue being lifted on the swell — lifted and submerged, lifted and submerged.

Mark had been wearing a blue sweatshirt, she remembered . . .

'We'll have to get a line to him.'

'Let me go out to him, Jim.' Tears were cascading down her cheeks now.

Jim shook his head. 'No, lass. Lloyd's the man for this. You stick with the motor. I need to know we can kick straight off again once we've got him on board. Just keep that engine steady, and ready for a dash back to the station.'

They made for the spot where Mark was being thrown about by the waves, and Lloyd went into the water with a line. Within minutes then, they had Mark's apparently lifeless body in the boat and Lloyd was bending over him.

There was no time to ask questions. Jim shouted, 'Now, Maggie. Give us wings, love. And if you haven't done already — start saying those prayers.'

★ ★ ★

There was an ambulance waiting, and although he was shivering and exhausted, Mark was adamant.

'I am not going anywhere in that!'

He did, however, allow the paramedics to check him out, and then to tell him he was one lucky man to have survived unscathed, such an ordeal as he'd been through.

Maggie's tears had been washed away by salt-spray and rain by now. They'd stopped the minute Mark had struggled to sit up in the boat, coughing and choking and swearing as they came into shore. And her anxiety had completely disappeared when Mark had yelled, 'My car! What happened to my car?'

She stood on the tiny promenade now, and Jim came and put his arm round her shoulders. She looked up at him.

'That was a near thing, Maggie. I thought he was a goner.'

She'd thought so too.

'And look at the bugger now! All cocky and

laying the law down to the ambulance crew.'

A big smile spread across Maggie's face. 'But he's got someone to answer to now,' she said, as Tamsin came racing down the road.

Mark saw Tamsin then, and hugging a blanket round him, came down the steps of the ambulance, beaming and waving. That was the Mark she knew so well, Maggie thought, brash, uncaring. Mark, the show-off.

He was. Until Tam got up to him and started laying in to him. It might have been relief on the girl's part, it might have been anger because he'd worried her so much. Maggie didn't know. All she did know was that Tamsin was absolutely livid.

Tam stood for a few seconds, hands on hips, the long skirt of her cotton dress soaked through and clinging to her legs, her hair a tangled mess. She stood just long enough to get her breath back — long enough for Mark to say, 'Hi, Sweetheart . . .'

And then she hurled herself at him, pummelling him with her fists, screaming at him. 'You fool! You utter idiot! What do you think you were doing?'

Mark looked taken aback and put his hands up to fend her off, but Tam's fingers hooked into the thin cotton shirt he was wearing now his soaked sweatshirt had been removed. She jerked on it, ripping it almost off his shoulders.

'Stop it,' he yelled, backing away. 'I didn't do it on purpose. The gears had been playing up all week. I thought I had it in first, but it went into reverse . . . '

'You could have been killed, you stupid great clown. I thought you had been killed.'

And then, as suddenly as the tirade had started, it stopped. Tam let go of Mark and panting heavily, backed away from him. 'I never want to see you again,' she hissed. 'Never! Do you understand?' And before he could answer she was marching away, back towards Shorecross village centre. Back towards the Gala fields. And it was then that Maggie saw somebody else coming down from the fields.

He had a purposeful swing to his step. He had a grim face and no welcoming smile. In fact, the frown he was wearing might have been carved out of stone, it was so rigidly fixed on his face.

He came up to her. Jim's arm dropped away from her.

'Maggie!' he said quietly as he stood in front of her.

'Rafe!'

She saw him swallow. The frown stayed put. She felt a mess. Water had trickled down her neck and her back was wet. She looked down at herself in the bright orange waterproofs. Yellow boots. She was still wearing her life-jacket with RNLI across the front of it. She'd taken her hard hat off. Jim was holding it.

Rafe gave a huge sigh. 'So! This is what you do when that little pager goes off? It wasn't something to do with the garage? A breakdown that needed attention?'

She faced up to him. 'I never said it was,' she said. 'You automatically jumped to the wrong conclusion.' Then she asked softly, 'Do you have a problem with that, Rafe?' as Jim discreetly moved away.

He was quiet for a moment, then he said, 'I wish you'd told me you did this sort of thing, it might have prepared me for that three-minute mile you performed this afternoon. But no, I don't have a problem with the job itself, Maggie.'

'You don't?'

The frown was lightening. 'You look like a half-drowned kitten, Maggie Brand. Let's get you home, huh?'

She glanced across at her little house. 'I'll have to go and strip these waterproofs off first.'

'Go on then,' he said. 'I'll wait for you.'

She stood and looked at him, not able to

tell what was going through his mind. 'Don't ask me to give it up,' she said. 'Because I won't.'

Slowly he said, 'You've never hinted that I should give up motor racing.'

'No,' she said, 'But when I watch you on television I sit on my hands to stop myself biting my nails.'

He started to laugh, softly at first, then he threw back his head and roared.

'I don't think it's funny,' she said, scowling. 'I worry like hell about you.'

He sobered instantly. 'You'll know how I felt then. This afternoon,' he said softly.

★ ★ ★

They sat together in front of a roaring fire at the cottage that night, with Fudge sprawled out across the hearth-rug. Rafe had raided her refrigerator and knocked up a hot meal for them both. Grilled haddock and parsley sauce had never tasted so good.

'I wanted to tell you about my work with the lifeboat, but I didn't know how.' She was curled up beside him on the sofa, with just a softly shaded lamp lit in one corner of the room.

'Am I so unapproachable?' His arm was round her. She felt it tighten.

She tilted her head back and leaned it against his shoulder. 'No,' she said quietly, 'but you'd somehow got this idea into your head that I always played things too safe. And then, the other night, you floored me when you said that was what you liked about me. I was safe, I never took risks — and you also made it very clear that you'd hate it if I did.'

'Maggie,' he said seriously, 'This afternoon, when I realized why you were racing away from me like you did, I was completely fazed. And then your dad came up to me and we watched the rescue from the cliff top together. He had his binoculars, and he was so proud of you. He handed them to me so I could see you, and Maggie — I was scared.' He suddenly went silent, and she glanced at him questioningly. 'I watched you though, and you knew what you were doing. You were a vital part of that team.'

'It has to be that way. Jim gives the orders, and we don't stand around arguing.'

He nodded slowly. 'I know what you mean. Your dad does too, Maggie. He was bursting with pride. And he turned to me and said, 'You and our Mags, you're both in the same game. The race against time game, and the name is the same — *winning* — no matter what the odds.'

She nodded and said, 'I suppose Dad's right.'

'Not quite, Maggie — yours is a game of life and death. It's more important that you should win.'

'Mark was lucky,' she said, staring into the fire. 'I'd almost given up hope of finding him.'

'It doesn't scare you, does it?' he said.

'No.'

'I love you, Maggie.'

She turned to him and said simply, 'It doesn't make any difference then? What I do?'

'I wouldn't be honest if I said it didn't,' he said. 'But I like to hang on to what Edgar said about us both being in the same game — just so long as we keep on the winning side.'

'There's no guarantee of that though.'

He said hesitantly, 'Maggie, it's my last race next weekend. Will you be there for me?'

'You've decided to drive again? One last time?' Suddenly she was uneasy.

He stuck out one leg and wiggled it around. 'The ankle's okay now. There's no reason why I can't race. I've kept in training, and Oscar needs me.'

'Are you really going to give it up, after this one, Rafe?' Her eyes searched his face. It had been his life for so long. It couldn't be an easy decision to have to make.

'It's like I said, Maggie — the last race. The very last race. The season's over after next Sunday. I don't intend racing next year.'

She shivered. It sounded ominous when he said it like that. 'Oscar Herrick will want to keep you.'

'While Oscar has me, he'll never take Vaughn back,' he said.

'Is that why you're quitting?' she asked sharply. 'Just to give Vaughn a chance?'

'Of course not. My contract has almost run out. I want something different. A new direction. But now we're on the subject of Vaughn, I have to tell you, this business with him and Tamsin, well it's come between us — Vaughn and me. I never would have believed it of him — that he could treat a girl like Tam that way.'

'You both live in the same world though. You and Vaughn. The world of motor racing. You can't let something like that break up your friendship, can you? That kind of enmity could be dangerous if it got out of hand.'

'I wouldn't ram him off the track, if that's what you mean,' he said with an attempt at a hard laugh.

'You can't just switch off though. The anger's still there.'

'Not quite so much,' he said. 'Now I've had time to think about it, I realize that Tam was just as much to blame. Vaughn's not the sort to have to force himself on a woman. They fall over themselves to get at him. He could have his pick of them. He does too. And the easier they are, the quicker he tires of them.'

She said, 'I'll be there, next week, if you want me to be.'

'I'd ask you to come for the weekend, but I'll be tied up qualifying in the afternoon and on Saturday night, Oscar's entertaining the sponsors — hoping to get more money out of them for next season, and he expects his drivers to be there. I won't be staying for the dinner, just to show my face, talk to a few people, that sort of thing.'

'I'll come if you want me to,' she said. 'I'd like to see what you do — up close, if that's possible.'

'Qualifying day,' he mused, 'I suppose you might find it interesting. I'll get you a pit-pass so you can come down to the paddock. If you get bored there's a good restaurant and a souvenir shop.' His eyes crinkled with laughter, 'You could wear your lifeboat shirt. Who knows what tips you might pick up for your own little shop? Have you thought about coffee mugs with lifeboats printed on the sides? I'm sure we have them for Hill and the Schumacher boys.'

She laughed with him, then said, 'I think I might enjoy it.'

'It's settled then. You'll come.'

She wriggled off the sofa and slid down on to the rug to ruffle Fudge's ears. From there, she could sit and look straight at Rafe, and that was something she'd never tire of doing, she told herself. Not in a million years. She nodded. 'I'll come.'

'And stay over on Saturday night at Denning Park?'

She said, 'Yes! I read about it being held here in England in the newspapers.'

'A pity it's not Spain.' He grimaced. 'It would have been nice — just the two of us in the sunshine there. We could have made a week of it.'

'It's the race that matters, Rafe. Not where it's being held.'

He sighed. 'I suppose so. Last minute switches are bad for business though. Just think of all those motor-racing fans who bought tickets for Spain. They're going to be disappointed — or sadly out of pocket if they have to fly over here.'

'Where would I stay overnight? Is it likely I'd get an hotel room at such short notice and with such a big race planned?'

'I'll sort it for you. Will somebody baby-sit Fudge while you come?'

'Mom and Dad. Fudge will be spoilt rotten at Fox Cottage.'

At the mention of his name, Fudge lifted his head off the hearthrug and thumped his tail.

'He's so intelligent, that dog,' Rafe said.

'He knows his name, that's all,' she said, laughing.

'Can I monopolize you next weekend then?' he wanted to know.

She didn't need to think about it any longer. 'Yes,' she said. 'I'd love to be there to watch you race.'

29

Ava was back at the Ivory Tower — subdued, but back in business. Rafe had wanted her to go over to the Shorecross Gala but she couldn't face it. She wandered round the deserted showroom and wondered how she was going to face Tam again. It wasn't going to be easy. She was glad the girl had moved out of the lighthouse though.

She went over to the door and pulled it open. The day was grey. She could hear the sea battering against the towering concrete sea wall below the headland. Rain was hurtling down, and the wind was whistling round the lighthouse.

There had been no customers all afternoon. Most folk would be at Shorecross though. It was a well-known annual event to raise money for the hospital. Heronsea's streets were deserted. The shops had closed early.

And then she heard the swish of tyres and

her heart leapt. She couldn't see the car yet, it hadn't come on to the coast road but it would be round the corner any second now. She hoped it was Rafe — come home early, though he'd told her he would be late in. He'd been cool towards her since fetching her back from Eastbourne, and who could blame him?

The car came round the corner. She had an overwhelming sense of disappointment when it wasn't the Ferrari, but Tam's little newly acquired Beetle. Ava stayed where she was, not caring that her black suit was getting a drenching from rain blowing in at the doorway.

Tam had seen her; she parked the car next to the lighthouse and got out.

Ava still stood in the doorway, waiting.

Tam came up to her. She looked a sight. Her hair was flattened to her head, her dress creased and crumpled.

'Are you going to let me in?' The girl stood out in the rain, unafraid, staring at her with hostility in her eyes.

Ava moved aside. 'Did you know I was here?'

Tam went inside the Ivory Tower, walked into the centre of the showroom then turned and said, 'For heaven's sake come on in and shut the door.'

Ava obeyed, then leaned her back on the door and said, 'Did you know?'

'Yes.'

Ava pushed herself away from the closed door and walked into the room. She didn't attempt to get near Tam though. She just stopped, several feet away and said, 'Tam! How can I ever expect you to forgive me?'

'You can't,' Tamsin said, throwing back her head. 'I'll never do that. You killed Jade, and you killed my baby.'

'Rafe's baby,' Ava said. 'I couldn't let a bitch like you have *his* baby.'

Tam started to laugh. It was an ugly sound. 'Fool!' she said. 'It wasn't Rafe's. It was Vaughn Herrick's. You did me a favour.'

'Vaughn!' Ava's voice was less than a whisper. She felt sickened at what she'd done. It had all been for nothing.

'Didn't you see the way things were going between us when Vaughn came to stay after Rafe was injured?'

Ava shook her head, she tried to speak, but no words were audible.

'No,' Tam said bitterly. 'You wouldn't see, would you? You're too wrapped up in this place. Obsessed with it, that's what you are. What you always have been. Obsessed. You don't have normal feelings.'

Ava felt a numbness creeping into her

heart. 'I do have feelings . . . '

'Unnatural ones. Again — an obsession, but with your own brother.'

'He's not . . . he never was . . . my real brother . . . ' Ava felt tears springing to the back of her eyes.

'No! I realize that.' Tam seemed to relent a little, then her chin came up defiantly again and she said, 'You should be ashamed of yourself. He's always been so good to you. Look at the money he poured into this place.'

'I was intending paying him back.' The tears came, trickling down her face and she was powerless to stop them. 'Tam — we have to make a go of it. I can't let him down. Not when I owe him so much money.'

Tam shrugged her slender shoulders. 'Go ahead then,' she said. 'Make a go of it. Prove that you can at least do *something* right, one way or the other.'

'We can make a go of it.' Ava held out a pleading hand. 'We will, Tam. We will.'

'You will!' Tam's voice was hard. 'On your own. I've had enough. I only came back to tell you what I thought of you. I'm going away.'

'No . . . '

'Yes.'

'I can't manage here without you . . . '

'Tough!' Tam turned away and walked over

to the glass topped counter, where she swung round again and said, 'Comfort yourself with the thought that it's all yours now — to do with as you please. I don't care any more.'

Ava tried to stifle her sobs. She succeeded to a degree, enough anyway to ask, 'But where will you go? What will you do?'

Tam observed her one-time friend carefully, then said, 'What a difference a day makes. Yesterday, I would have said I was going to settle down, become domesticated. I could have done it too, because yesterday I didn't care a toss for him. He was just useful to me. He took me in when I badly needed somebody to look after me. He picked me up off the road — oh, a long time ago when I'd done something stupid. He loves me. I know that now.'

'Who?' Ava asked, perplexed. 'Not . . . not Rafe . . . ?'

'No! Not your darling brother.'

'Then who?'

Tam said wearily, 'It doesn't matter. It's all over now.'

'You . . . you don't love him?'

Tam closed her eyes for a moment, then looked straight at Ava again. 'You just don't understand anything,' she said. 'I'm leaving him because I do care about him. I didn't know I did. Not until I thought I'd lost him.

And I never want to feel anything like that again — ever. I don't want to believe my life is ended, utterly and finally, like I did when I thought Mark was dead. I don't want to hurt inside, and feel raw, and bleeding and broken. No man is worth it.'

'I don't understand you,' Ava said.

'I knew you wouldn't. You never will. You can't love, you see. You're empty inside — empty except for your obsessions.'

Tam walked back across the showroom to the door again, took one long, last look around and said, 'Goodbye Ava.'

'No . . . ' Ava pressed the knuckles of both hands to her mouth. 'No . . . Tam — let's give it another try? We can make something of it, I know we can. We'll make it better than Jade's little empire.'

'Do it then. Do it on your own. Count me out,' Tam said, and opened the door and went out into the rain again.

Ava walked slowly over to the open door and watched as Tam climbed into her car again. Then she drove away, and never looked back once.

★　★　★

Mark woke to a cold dawn's early light filtering through the French windows of his

451

living room. He was stiff and cramped, slouched in the chair as he was, and for a moment he couldn't think why he wasn't in bed.

Then he remembered as his glance became fixed on the small table under the window, and the milk jug that had been hastily stuffed with flowers. Faded sweet peas — their scent filled the room. Where had she found sweet peas in abundance at this time of year, he wondered?

There was a note too. A card. The kind of card stocked by florists. This one had a black edge. There was one word on it. 'Goodbye'! It was propped up against the flowers.

It wasn't a joke as he'd first thought. Tam didn't make jokes like that.

He'd phoned for a taxi — gone haring over there to Heronsea, to the flat she'd settled into since coming out of hospital after losing the baby.

The flat was empty. Another card on the door. 'Gone away'!

It had been nearly ten o'clock last night when he arrived at the lighthouse. The Ivory Tower. Ava had answered the door. She'd invited him in.

'*Where the hell is she? You've got to tell me.*'

'*Gone away. She didn't tell me where.*'

He'd broken down then and told Ava about the flowers.

'Don't worry,' she'd said. 'Tam will be back.'

He didn't believe her. 'How do you know?' he said.

'The flowers,' she said. 'Sweet peas. Their meaning isn't 'goodbye', it's only 'au-revoir'!'

It was small consolation. He'd lost his car and his girl, all in the same day. He went home, paid the taxi driver, sat down with a glass and a bottle of whisky.

★ ★ ★

Edgar had hired a crane. They all stood on the cliff top as Mark's car was hauled up from the beach.

The tide was out and the sands were clean-washed from the storm of the previous day.

Mark shoved his hands in his pockets. 'I'm gutted,' he said morosely. 'Absolutely, gutted.'

'It's only a car,' Rafe said, standing hand in hand with Maggie.

Mark glared at him. 'You would say that. They're ten a penny to you. In your line of work you just have a new wing fitted, a new nose, or a whole new set of tyres. And how long does it take? Ten seconds to fill up with petrol in the pit lane and have four tyres fitted as well. Ten seconds if you're *unlucky* — seven if everything goes according to the book.'

'Mark, be reasonable,' Maggie pleaded.

'Leave him be,' Edgar said, 'He was married to that car.' He chuckled softly and Mark scowled at him.

Jack-O scratched his head as the car, with water streaming out of it, swung up over the cliff top and was gently lowered to the ground.

Mark groaned. 'Hell! Look at it.'

Maggie said to Rafe, 'Perhaps we ought to go.'

He nodded. 'I don't think I can take much more of this, can you?'

'Shh.'

'He won't hear. Anyway, he'll have his hands full now — playing doctors and nurses with the damn car for the rest of the day. It looks like a spot of intensive care wouldn't do it any harm though.'

Edgar was whizzing round the Porsche in his wheelchair, assessing the damage. 'Body's not too bad,' he shouted to Mark. Carpet's had it though. Sea-water plays havoc with carpet and upholstery.'

'Don't try to cheer me up,' Mark snapped.

'I'll buy it off you,' Edgar said.

'You will?'

Edgar nodded, and Maggie squeezed Rafe's hand and started to laugh quietly and helplessly. 'Watch this,' she said. 'Dad knows what he's doing.'

'How much?'

'Not what you paid for it.'

'*How much?*' Mark insisted.

Edgar tipped his head on one side. 'Nine hundred.'

Mark looked at him. 'Nine hundred? That much?' His eyes narrowed.

'Take it or leave it, lad.'

'What'll you sell it for — afterwards?'

Edgar fingered his chin, then said, 'Four thou. Thereabouts.'

'You can get it back looking that good? And road-worthy?'

'Not me, lad. You,' Edgar said grinning. 'You're the rubbing rag round these parts, I'm the engine driver. Remember?'

'You expect me to do all the hard graft on my own car — and then you'll step in and take the profit?' Mark stared at him.

'Why not? It's business. Anyway, you'd pick up a quarter share.'

'No way. It's *my* car.' Mark looked mortally offended.

'Get started on it then lad. It's Sunday. You can use the workshop at weekends, but don't let it interfere with your proper work on other days,' Edgar said.

Mark went up to his car and stroked the bonnet, then he turned to Edgar. 'I forgot to bring the garage keys,' he said.

Edgar chucked him his own.

'Mind if I fetch the pick-up truck and tow it in?'

'It's a quarter yours, lad,' Edgar said as the hired crane started crawling away down the road. 'I don't mind you borrowing my three wheels of the truck though. Just this once.'

30

All the colours of the rainbow were there, lined up in the race-paddock behind the pit lane garages, hulking transporters gleaming in the November sunshine, with aerial masts three times their height towering above them. Ferrari red, Jordan yellow, Williams — half blue, half white, the tartan ribbon of Stewart on a white background, black and white Tyrrell, and Benetton blue with primary colour slashes along the side.

And Oscar-Jade! The immense bulky vehicle glossy and shining, a rich dark green finish with the lightning flash of white down its side — contrasting oddly with the uniforms of its drivers and its engineers who wore stark white with a green zig-zag flash.

Rafe had sent a car to pick Maggie up from the nearest railway station to Denning Park. She sat forward in her seat, watching with interest the activity in the paddock. There seemed to be hundreds of people about, and between the parked transporter vans she caught glimpses inside the garages, and heard the constant revving of engines.

The taxi deposited her at last between the sleek impressive vans belonging to Oscar Herrick, and Vaughn's team — Blanchard's. It was not a good omen — Blanchard and Herrick being so close to one another; she hoped that Rafe and Vaughn would not have to come into too close a contact. Tempers had been frayed the last time they'd met, and she doubted that Rafe would ever forgive Vaughn for leading Tam on as he had done.

He came out of the back door of the garage to meet her, kissed her swiftly on the lips, then as the taxi pulled away, deposited her weekend case in the back of his own car which was parked beside the team vehicles.

She hadn't brought much in the way of a wardrobe, and had travelled on the train in casual trousers and sweat-jacket. He looked her up and down, holding both her hands. 'I'm glad you made it, Maggie. You look good enough to eat.'

Her eyes had lit up at the sight of him, so straight and tall and slim in his white driving suit. It brought back a memory of the first time she'd ever seen him, and she realized her love was so much stronger now that she really knew him.

'And you look . . . ' she paused and drank in the sight of him once more.

'Like what? Something the cat brought in?' he teased.

'Like Prince Charming,' she said happily. 'Why does a uniform — especially a sexy one like that, have this effect on me?'

'Come inside,' he said, 'I can show you twenty more guys who also wear uniforms.'

They went into the garage. 'Do I get to meet your other driver?'

'Stuart? Sure! He's out on the track at the moment though. We test drive from nine to nine-forty-five, and then again ten-fifteen to eleven o'clock. He's taken the first stint. I shall be out in the second half.'

'I'll see you race then?'

He looked at her lazily. 'Will you sit on your hands?' he asked, 'to stop yourself biting your nails?'

She gave a breathless little laugh. 'I'll try not to.'

Oscar was standing in front of two computer screens with figures and graphs on them. He wore headphones too. He turned to her and lifted a hand in welcome. 'Hi, Maggie!'

She waved back to him. It wouldn't be any use trying to talk to him, she realized, he seemed to be doing a dozen things all at once and giving three or four of the engineers his attention too.

The low, sleek racing car to one side of the garage didn't look like a car at all. 'What's wrong with it?' she asked Rafe worriedly. 'It's just a skeleton.'

It was true, the car was in bits and pieces all over the place — raised up on jacks, its wheels were missing, the back end shell was propped on a stand near the pit lane door, the nose cone was off, and a mechanic was lying underneath unscrewing something.

He laughed. 'This is what happens — every time the car comes back in the garage,' he explained. 'You'll see them all swoop on Stuart's car when he comes in.

Maggie was amazed at the cleanliness of the place. The car's bodywork, although in pieces, was gleaming, the floor clear of clutter and everybody seemed to know what their particular job was. No one person got in another's way. There was no rowdiness. The mechanics worked quietly, the engineers wore head-phones. And as she watched, every part of the car was checked over, and gradually put back together again. It was done in minutes, though the tyre blankets were left in place.

Rafe explained, 'We have to keep the tyres warm. They adhere to the track better. The blankets won't be taken off until I'm ready to go.'

When it did come round to Rafe's time for taking the car out, she was given a pair of ear protectors, but as he sat — almost unrecognizable — low down in the moulded seat of his car, his white fireproof balaclava obscuring most of his face beneath helmet and visor, she held the ear protectors in her hand. Rafe didn't look at her, his attention was taken by seat belts being fastened around him, Oscar gesticulating beside him, the starter motor being positioned behind him, and the tyre wraps being taken off the wheels.

When the engine fired, the noise in the close confines of the garage was like nothing she had ever heard before. It vibrated through the whole length of her body, up through her feet, along her spine, and reverberated through her head. She wanted to experience it all though, and to know first hand what it was like — for him.

The engine was a screaming roar of impatience long before the car took off, but when it did, it was out of the garage in a flash; out, and into the pit lane, accelerating, the noise pulsating, peaking, hurling the little car out of her sight in seconds. And Oscar was at her side then in the deafening silence, saying, 'Come on to the pit wall with us, Maggie. You might as well see everything.'

Most of the cars were out now, tearing round the track, the noise of their engines a mere whine while they were still a long way off, then altering to a drone as they came round the hairpin bend some distance away. The sound built up then, the nearer the cars came, working up to a threatened thunder, a strident caterwauling, and finally shrieking past the pit wall that the team managers, owners, and engineers were standing on, with an ear-splitting burst of high octane ferocity that wasn't merely sound-induced. The cars were power personified; the engines pulsating hearts of fire. Man and machine were forged together with invisible flux. Such men who drove these monsters were surely made of metal themselves.

In the silence that followed Rafe's first lap, Oscar said, 'You should wear those protectors.'

She shook her head. 'Not yet. I need to know what it's like. I want to feel the noise.'

'You're crazy,' he said, pulling his lips down in a grimace. 'But I know what you mean. I was just the same myself at one time. I've learned better since. I'm getting to be an old man, Maggie. I need to take care of the bits of me that are still working, and luckily my hearing hasn't suffered, despite being in this game for most of my life.'

She was getting to like Oscar. 'I appreciate you letting me come today.'

'You're not in the way, child. Do you like all you've seen, so far?'

She nodded enthusiastically. 'Love it.'

'Persuade that man of yours to stay with me then,' he said.

She shook her head. 'No! It's up to him. If this is what he wants, he'll find some way of staying with racing.'

'You think he wants to stay with it?'

'I know he does,' she said guardedly. 'But it's like Rafe says, he's thirty-six, and time he was doing something other than speeding round a track.'

'Management?' Oscar cocked an eyebrow at her.

She smiled helplessly. 'Don't ask me. I'm new to this game.'

'New, but loving every minute of it. I wish you were a man, Maggie. With that expression in your eyes when you look at the cars, you'd make a champion driver.'

'I was brought up on cars.'

'Ah, yes. I remember Edgar. Car crazy.'

She laughed. 'He still is. Classic cars through, not these little beauties.'

'Beauties, huh?'

'Beautiful monsters. They lure you, then

devour you. Look at them as they go round the circuit — the drivers are almost invisible — it's the car that everyone looks at, the car that everyone hears.'

'Well said, Maggie.'

Rafe had done two more laps. 'Come back to the garage,' Oscar said. 'You can look at the computers. We'll check his timing. It looks good from here though. Pole position after today's Qualifying, do you think?' he asked with a chuckle.

'It's what everybody wants. Pole position. First on the grid.'

'And first past the chequered flag,' Oscar said. 'That's what really matters. Winning.'

'The name of the game,' she said softly. 'Yes, Rafe has told me that many times.'

They hurried back across the pit lane and into the garage. Once there, he put a hand on her arm and said, 'Maggie — it's not just about getting in a car and pushing all the right buttons.'

'What isn't?' she asked.

'Winning.'

'Meaning?' she asked puzzled.

'Meaning — one day you'll maybe have to give him a push. And when that day comes, Maggie — push with all your might. Push him back into it, because if you do, he'll be right on track to becoming a real winner.'

'I don't understand you,' she said.

'No?' His eyes twinkled. 'You will. One day.'

★ ★ ★

Rafe came third in Qualifying. Oscar Herrick was over the moon. Next door in Blanchard's garage, things weren't going well. Vaughn was fourteenth, his team mate thirteenth. Tom Blanchard was furious.

'If that bastard next door can do it, how come we can't?' He turned to Vaughn. 'We have virtually the same engine, the same set-up. So what's going wrong?'

Vaughn rounded on his team owner. 'I don't know! I keep telling you, I don't know. The power's not there.'

'Or the motivation,' Blanchard sneered. 'Are you going soft or something? Or are you deliberately setting me up?'

'What do you mean?' Vaughn's confidence was in shreds. Blanchard never pulled any punches.

'Is he paying you to throw the race? That father of yours?'

'I could hit you.' Vaughn's eyes narrowed. 'You know damn well how things stand between me and my father. Nothing's changed. And as for throwing the race,' he laughed bitterly in Tom Blanchard's face, 'we don't stand a chance of coming in the first ten, let alone winning.' He threw up his hands. 'I've had enough. I'm through with it all.'

'Not until I say so.' Blanchard thrust his face forward. 'You go when I say you go. You don't walk out on me. Nobody walks out on Tom Blanchard.'

'Sell up. Buy a greyhound,' Vaughn said, pushing past the man.

Blanchard strode after him and grabbed his shoulder. 'Get him off the track,' he said. 'If you can't win, at least do that for me. Get Thorne off the track. I don't care how you do it.'

'You're sick!' Vaughn looked at him with contempt.

'And you're out of racing. Finished. Understand? I want Thorne off the track. If he finishes the race, I'll make sure you never get in a racing car again. Anywhere.'

'You're crazy, man. You expect me to do that? To the guy who saved my life at Monaco? Get real.'

Tom Blanchard drew himself up to his full height and towered above Vaughn. 'Oscar Herrick's nothing without his precious driver. I want to see him squirm. I want to see him in the dust. I thought that was what you wanted too.'

'Once upon a time,' Vaughn jeered. 'Once upon a time, maybe. But not now.'

'You'll be sorry. That's one promise I can keep,' Blanchard flung after him as Vaughn went towards the door.

'Make me sorry then.' Vaughn twisted his head round for one last look at his team owner. 'Do your worst,' he sneered. 'I couldn't care less any more.'

31

The hotel was comfortable — a couple of miles away from the Denning circuit, but then, so was everything. The new race track, like many more of its kind, had been sited where it would cause the least trouble with road congestion and noise pollution.

Rafe was picking her up at nine that night, after his formal meeting with Oscar's sponsors. They'd go for a meal, he said, but of necessity it was an early night after that, because tomorrow was the big day and, racing apart, meetings began in the paddock at eight-thirty sharp.

She'd packed only the minimum of clothing. Casual stuff had been the order of the day for the pit lane garages and Qualifying, and she'd arrived wearing the comfortable clothes that had been ideal for the purpose. Now, however, while Rafe had gone back to the Oscar-Jade motor-home she took a leisurely shower in her hotel room and afterwards dried her wet hair then brushed it till it gleamed.

She'd brought only one dress with her — silk jersey, midnight blue in colour. It was sleeveless with a high plain neckline, a deep 'V' at the back. It was svelte and simple, and she wore slender heeled shoes to match it.

Five minutes before she was due to meet him downstairs in the lobby, she looked at herself in the mirror and liked what she saw. Casual clothes were all very well, but tonight she wanted to look good for him. Tomorrow was an important day. It was his last day in Formula One.

His last race. Something to remember!

She touched a small perfume bottle to her wrists, then dotted perfume on her fingers before running them through her hair. She hadn't brought much make up with her, she'd used just a dab of matt stuff out of a bottle on her nose and cheeks. No lipstick, she decided, it wasn't needed, her colouring was good without it.

She picked up a small suede clutch bag and went out of the room.

He was just walking in through the door as she got to the half way point on the stairs. He looked up and saw her. She hurried down the rest of the stairs.

'Hey — I never saw you looking like this

before.' He took hold of her hand.

'Nor I you,' she said, a little breathlessly because that's what he did to her — he took her breath away, appearing like this, in a dark suit and tie, with his hair brushed back sleekly.

'I've got the car outside.' He hesitated a moment, then said, 'Maggie — I know this is an awful liberty — but could you put up with the pit lane just one more time before we eat?'

'The pit lane?' She looked questioningly at him. 'At this time of night?'

His laugh had a guilt-ridden note in it. 'No!' he said. 'It's idiotic of me. Not to say childish in the extreme. We'll give it a miss. Think no more of it. Forget I said what I did.'

'Hey — what is this?' she asked softly. 'Rafe — if we have to go to the paddock, then it's okay. Really it is.'

'We don't *have* to go,' he said. 'It's just that — well, it's something I've always done before every race. I've gone back down there, and stood in the garage in the semi-darkness, and most times it's been just me and dragonfly there. A kind of understanding between me and the car . . . ' he let go of her hand and lifted both his own in a helpless gesture. 'Talking about it like this — I don't know — it sounds crazy . . . '

She understood. Firmly, she said, 'We'll go to the paddock, Rafe. I insist.'

'Some of the guys from the other teams will still be there,' he said. 'Some of them work through the night if they've got a problem so it won't be creepy and lonely or anything like that.'

'It wouldn't matter if we were the only two people there,' she said. 'It's what you have to do, Rafe.'

'It won't take long,' he said as he saw her into the car.

'Look,' she said, 'we're together! That's all that matters.'

He slid into the seat beside her, and looked at her. 'I booked a table for ten o'clock.'

Seriously, she said, 'You *knew* I'd come with you then?'

'To see the car?'

'Mmm.'

He started the engine. Listened with a contented little smile playing around his lips, to the distinctive Ferrari sound of it for a moment, then said, 'I hoped you would.'

'I enjoyed it today — watching you race. I talked to Oscar. He took me on the pit wall and we watched you together. Maybe it's too late now for me to really get into this racing thing, it being your last race tomorrow, but I would've liked to have been a part of it before

— now that I'm getting to know what it's all about.'

He put the car in gear and drove away from the glaring lights of the hotel car park, and within seconds they were speeding along a wide and straight country road, heading towards Denning Park.

'Oscar likes you,' he said, glancing briefly at her.

'I like Oscar.'

'Oscar the team owner, or Oscar the gardener?' he asked, reminding her of the first time she'd met the man.

'Both.' She gave a soft laugh. 'He's straight, isn't he? You know where you stand with him.'

'Straight and tough. Like with Vaughn. He'll never back down over that.'

'No,' she said. 'It's sad. Do you think they'll ever come to terms with their differences?'

'No,' Rafe said, 'Because there aren't any differences. They're the same person, Oscar and Vaughn. They're so alike, it's uncanny. How can either of them give way? It's like having a fight with your reflection, isn't it? There can't be a winner.'

'I see your point,' she said, watching through the windscreen as the bright lights surrounding the circuit came into view. And then they were turning off the road and up to the security box at the top of the broad road belonging to the circuit. And there was no more time to try and analyze the problem between Oscar and Vaughn Herrick. Maggie knew in her heart though, that nobody could help either of them. They had to find their own solution.

★　★　★

They weaved in and out between the trailers, buses and motor homes parked in the paddock after getting out of the Ferrari, and it was exactly as he had said. The place wasn't deserted, not even at this time of night. There were lights showing in the half pulled up doors of some of the garages, and sounds of clinking tools being put down on concrete floors, men talking, and F1 engines starting up and then droning away again. Nobody was out on the track. All adjustments until tomorrow morning had to be made in the garages. The racing control tower was shut down. No lights gleamed out from its great octagonal dome of windows, from where the whole of the circuit could, in daylight, be observed.

Oscar-Jade garage was securely locked, but Rafe had the keys, and soon had the shutter-door gliding upwards with hardly any effort. Maggie was coming to know that in Formula One, everything worked with a well-oiled precision — even the doors!

They went inside, Rafe preceding her and switching on the strips of lights around the walls that made her blink at their brightness as she followed him out of the darkness. He closed the heavy metal door then, pulling it down to the floor and then walking past her.

The two Oscar-Jade racing cars each had a bay to themselves. Rafe walked straight over to his own. Both cars were shrouded under spotless white sheets that covered them completely. He threw back the one hiding dragonfly, then turned to her and held out his hand.

She hovered by the door, then shook her head. 'No,' she said, her voice echoing weirdly in the empty garage, 'I should have waited outside for you. This is between you and the car. I'm not part of that relationship, Rafe.'

He came over to her and took her in his arms, and she put her hands up to rest on his chest as she gazed into his face.

'Maggie — this is not the eternal triangle. It's a car, for heaven's sake, not a mistress. Now come over there with me and take a proper look, will you? You saw precious little of it this morning — it was all stripped down while you were here.'

'And then you were inside it,' she said softly, 'And it became a part of you, Rafe.'

He groaned softly at her words. 'Put like that, I suppose you could think of it as being a mistress,' he whispered hoarsely.

'Hadn't it ever occurred to you before?' Her voice was soft.

He raised his brows and shook his head at her. 'It would take a woman to see the comparison,' he said.

'I'm not jealous of dragonfly.' She reached her hands up to his shoulders, let them settle there for a moment, then ran them gently up into his hair and pulled his head down to hers.

Dragonfly was forgotten as they stood locked together and the kiss went on, for ever it seemed.

Two or three garages away from them, a Formula One engine suddenly burst into life, and their lips drew apart at the unexpected sound. Maggie laughed and said, 'Heck! That made me jump.'

The engine was being revved — unmercifully it seemed. Each time it was left to die, it suddenly sprang to vibrant life again.

Rafe held her close and she wrapped her arms right round him. He moved gently, swaying in time to the revving engine, rocking as it faltered, tightening his hold on her as it peaked and screamed. She tilted back her head and closed her eyes. Vibrations through the concrete floors and walls were sending shivers up her spine. It had a similar effect on Rafe too, she could feel him hardening against her, could hear the faltering breaths jerking through him as he fought to keep control.

The engine began losing power. Her head fell forward against his chest. She sucked in a great mouthful of air, feeling as if she'd been drowning before, and now had come a respite. She was trembling against him and the tension started mounting again then as the unseen car started a low grumble of sound once more, a long, rhythmic moaning that suddenly took hold and flared into a deepening growl, then increased in momentum, building up to a wide open sound that was filling the air of the night with a primitive, sexual, repetitive lament. It was like a thousand untamed tigers roaring for a mate, a frenzied burst of anger and pain, building to a crescendo of frantic excitement as the car screamed to be let free.

She clung to Rafe, her eyes wide now, and staring at the white car beyond him. Her head fell against his shoulder. Her arms were rigid, holding him tight, so tight it hurt.

And then, the engine died, and he whispered in a harsh voice against her ear, 'Maggie! We've got to get out of here . . . '

He kept a hold of her as he swept her towards the door again. He switched off the lights. They were in total darkness until he raised the door and they went out into the night.

There was activity in some of the transporters, laughter came out over the still air at them from a nearby motor home. She reached out to him and he took her hand in his again and pulled her into his arms. He smothered her face in kisses, holding her, then running his hands up the supple slenderness of her figure. She wanted him, she needed him. And his need of her was only too apparent.

Somewhere a clock struck ten.

'The restaurant . . . ' she whispered, and the words trailed off in a laugh.

'Oscar will kill me,' he said with a deep throated chuckle.

'Why?' She tipped her head back and looked at him.

'No food. No sex. Before a big race.' He pulled a face in the semi-darkness.

'We didn't have sex,' she pointed out.

'If that engine had started up again we would have.'

She started to laugh and couldn't stop. He joined in softly, then said, 'Are you hungry?'

She spluttered, sobered for a second, then bent over almost double to try and still the merriment welling up inside her. She said on a wobbly note, 'Not very. Are you?'

'Ravenous.'

'Really?' She was having trouble keeping her face straight.

'Really! I mean it, Maggie.'

'Shall we go then?'

He grabbed her and made her look at him again. 'Can I stay the night with you?'

'At the hotel?'

He nodded. 'To hell with Oscar and his rules.'

32

Oscar Herrick yelled, 'Come back here!'

Rafe spun round, his helmet swinging from his hand. 'No, Oscar.'

'This damned ritual . . . '

'So it's a ritual — wishing *your* son luck, is it? Well, if you want to break *my* little ritual, why don't you take it over yourself?'

Oscar made a fist and shook it at him. Rafe laughed.

'It's not luck he needs. It's a flaming good hiding.'

Rafe ignored the remark and kept walking towards Blanchard's garage next door to his own. Vaughn had obviously heard the commotion. He came outside, held out his hand to Rafe. His eyes were shadowed. He looked as if he hadn't bothered to shave that morning — or to sleep the night before.

They shook hands. 'It needs no saying,' Vaughn muttered. 'For goodness' sake don't mention 'luck'.'

Rafe was relaxed. 'It's *my* last race,' he said. 'I couldn't break with tradition. Good luck, Vaughn.'

Vaughn scowled. 'It's *my* last race,' he said. 'I've had enough.'

Rafe stared at him as their hands fell to their sides again. 'Don't be a fool, man.'

'You're not in a position to tell me what to do,' Vaughn said in a weary voice. 'In fact, you don't know what you're talking about.'

'Thanks!' Rafe gave him one more glance then turned away and walked back to his own garage where Oscar was standing in the doorway watching all that had gone between the two men.

'You never learn, do you?' he said. 'You never damn well learn. He's a complete waster. Why bother with him.'

'Because you *don't*! That's why I bother.'

'He's not worth it.'

'Maybe not.' Rafe shrugged and went over to the car, pulled on his Nomex hood and then his helmet. 'Ready?' he asked one of the engineers.

The man nodded. In the next bay, Rafe's co-driver was already in the cockpit and belted up, ready to get into place on the grid for the formation lap.

Oscar came up and looked pointedly at his watch. 'Are you going to bother,' he said, 'or shall we call the whole thing off?'

Rafe's visor was still up, he said, 'Come on, Oscar. What's riled you this morning? You're not your usual sunny smiling self.'

Oscar grimaced. 'Damn indigestion.' He rubbed his chest. 'Fried eggs never agree with me.'

Rafe grinned. 'You should be so lucky! Know what I had? Tea and toast.'

'You'll be able to celebrate your retirement with a slap-up meal,' Oscar said scathingly.

'The first decent meal in months — thanks to you.' Rafe grabbed the older man's hand, 'Come on you old moaner — wish me luck.'

Oscar's hand grasped his driver's and held on tightly. 'Break a leg, you mean. That's what they say in the theatre, isn't it?'

'That's what happened last time.' Rafe looked down at his boots.

'Ankle okay now? You're sure you can do it? Put on a good show for me?'

Rafe nodded, his eyes missing nothing of Oscar's anxiety. 'Don't worry,' he said. 'I'll give it my best.'

Oscar seemed to shrink in stature in that moment. He looked very tired, Rafe thought. Tired and getting old. But time was getting on. It was time to get into the car, and give Oscar what he wanted.

★ ★ ★

481

The cars were lined up and the red lights were on. Mentally, Rafe started counting the seconds down from five. Anything to keep his mind off *her*! Where was she? Oscar had told her she could go down to the garage, but she'd said no. Today belonged to Oscar — and to him. She had a seat — somewhere. Oscar had arranged it. Rafe was glad he didn't know where. It was better if he didn't start looking for her.

It was only two hours and then they'd be together — for always.

The red lights went out. The cars shot forward, but he was in a good position and was up behind the first two and the car sounded fine.

Don't think about last night. Think about the race. Think about winning. For Oscar.

Brake for the bend.

He checked his mirrors. He was pulling well away from the nearest car following him.

Foot hard down for the straight.

Maggie, I love you. A little smile played round his lips.

The track held no hidden terrors. He'd spent an entire week getting to know it. It was considered one of the safest.

The stands were full. The motorway had been jammed this morning with fans streaming into Denning Park.

Up to a hundred and sixty. Downhill. A hundred and sixty five and climbing.

He held third place. He was elated. If he could hold on to it . . .

Easy now. Watch the barriers. Brake . . .

The car in front spun crazily, and slid into the gravel trap.

Second place now!

Hell! Oscar would be having kittens. Second place held now for seven laps. Hold it. Don't get carried away. This is only the eighth lap coming up. Plenty of time left. Keep it cool.

Maggie! Was she sitting on her hands, he wondered?

He closed the gap between him and number one.

Difficult to pass. Narrow under the bridge.

Keep back, he told himself. Don't be over eager. It was going well. He'd passed Vaughn — somewhere. Way behind. He'd started fourteenth. Vaughn and his team mate — neck and neck. Five cars had been knocked out. It narrowed the odds. Mechanical faults. No injuries. The safety car hadn't been brought out. Most had spun off — he'd been pretty close to two — a loose wing — a blistered tyre.

Fatalities were rare nowadays. Safety was at a premium. It still happened though. A moment's loss of concentration . . .

'Blast!'

A magenta coloured car was in front of him. Rafe roared past Vaughn, who was merely crawling, his front wing loose and hitting the ground at every bump. Bad luck! But these things happened. They'd fix it in the pits if they could.

Out on the straight and another flash of magenta now. Vaughn's team mate in his mirror. Coming up fast, and closing in on him.

Too close.

'Hell!'

Accelerate! Foot down!

The magenta was slip-streaming, hanging on his tail. Rafe saw the bend coming up, the barriers of linked tyres, green and blue, making a splash of colour.

Brake. Slow. No more than a hundred and twenty for this one.

The car behind accelerated as he went into the bend, accelerated and advanced on him. Rafe felt the back wheels sliding, the whole car out of balance. The fool behind! He'd nudged his tail What was he trying to do? Kill them both?

Coming out of the bend now.

This time, more than a nudge — a jolt. Dragonfly was lurching, spinning, tyres screaming. The front end came round, hit the nose of the one behind. The magenta went up in the air, smashed into the bales of tyres. Rafe was fighting with the wheel. Spinning. Careering round and round, front wings sending up sparks. Gravel now. He let go of the wheel. The seat belts were holding him, cutting into him. He'd have some bruises. Only bruises?

Miraculously the car came to a stop and his head lurched sideways.

They were waiting to get him out. They were lifting the other driver out of the magenta.

Rafe removed the steering wheel, unfastened his belts and climbed out, carefully. No pain, no cracked ribs. Even the ankle was behaving itself.

The car was a mess. He went over to Vaughn's team mate who was sitting holding his head in his hands.

Rafe whipped off his helmet, stared down at him and said, 'What was all that about?'

The man looked up at him and ignoring the question, looked away.

Rafe stood a moment longer. The cars were being lugged away now.

Rafe said, 'Are you all right?'

The man looked up again. He nodded then scrambled to his feet and went after his car.

Vaughn took his time. He'd seen what had happened. It had come as no surprise. Nothing surprised him where Tom Blanchard was concerned any more. He blamed himself though. Tom had nurtured the rift between him and his father, Vaughn realized now. Tom and Oscar were old enemies. Vaughn didn't know the details, but it was nothing to do with motor racing. More to do with a woman. Vaughn had guessed it was his mother. Tom had known her first, but Oscar had lured her away, married her. It was hard to think of his dad as the romantic kind — the sort of man who would run after a woman.

Vaughn knew that he himself had played right into Tom Blanchard's hands in the past. He knew that now. Too late. A hard core of hatred had flared up between father and son. It had festered over the years.

Vaughn knew what he was going to do right now. He was going into the pit lane next time round. He was through with Blanchard.

The mechanics were ready. They'd had warning he was coming in. He stopped the car outside Blanchard's garage. Killed the engine, pulled off the steering wheel and climbed out, in no mood now to carry on even if the car could be fixed.

Blanchard yelled, 'Get back in there. What the hell . . . '

'I never thought you'd do it.' Vaughn pushed past him.

'You can't pull out of the race . . . '

'I've pulled out!' Vaughn whirled round to the man. He had his helmet in his hands. He flung it at Tom's feet with a resounding smash. 'There. Put it on a plate. You can imagine it's my head. That's what you want, isn't it? Not my head though. My soul, that's what you want.'

He strode through the garage and out into the paddock where the rows upon rows of transporter vans, buses and cars were parked. He kicked at a pile of slicks, and swore at them.

Oscar was leaning on the wall of his garage. Standing outside. His team manager was hovering. 'Can I get you something?'

Oscar seemed breathless. 'My driver,' he gasped. 'Rafe. Get Rafe. He should be here by now after that spin-off.'

Herrick's manager disappeared inside the garage, then ran back to Oscar. Vaughn just stood and watched.

'He's coming up the pit lane, Oscar . . . '

'Thank God!'

Something was wrong. Something was very wrong. Vaughn went forward quickly.

'Dad!'

Oscar slumped against the wall and stared at him. 'What the hell are you doing here?'

'I'm finished with it, Dad.'

Rafe came racing through the garage, pushing everyone aside who stood in his way. 'What's wrong? What's going on?'

Oscar held out a hand to him, and slid down the wall.

'Dad . . . ' Vaughn leapt forward.

Oscar tumbled to his knees and rolled over. People came running. Rafe was kneeling beside him. Vaughn stood helpless. Herrick's team manager had a phone in his hand. He jabbed out a number and while he was doing that yelled, 'Get a Medic,' to anybody within earshot.

'No pulse.' Rafe ripped Oscar's jacket open, shot his hand inside his shirt.

Vaughn saw his father's face turning grey, his lips white, eyes open and staring.

'No-o-o!' he screamed pushing his way through.

Rafe had Oscar's head tilted back now, he was giving mouth to mouth . . .

'No-o-o!'

The team manager had dropped on his knees, had one hand on top of the other and was giving compression. 'One, two, three, four . . . check!'

'No pulse. No heartbeat.' Rafe bent down over Oscar again.

The other man was still using compression, counting out loud each time he pressed down.

'One, two, three, four, five . . . breathe . . . '

Rafe's head swooped down again.

'One, two, three, four, five . . . breathe . . . '

Vaughn sank down beside his father and clasped one of Oscar's hands in his own.

In the distance a siren began to wail.

33

Maggie raced all the way across the paddock, almost skidding to a halt when she saw the crowd gathered around the back of the Oscar-Jade garage. Then she heard the siren and started to run again.

Had he been hurt in the crash he'd walked away from? Could it be delayed reaction? She'd heard of such things happening.

Her heart was pounding as she ran. She heard herself sobbing under her breath. 'The last race. The last race.' She was choking on the words. 'Don't let it be him. Don't let his last race end this way.'

They made a space for her to get through, and her knees went weak as she realized Rafe was unhurt.

He was all right, but Oscar wasn't, and even as she gazed down at the older man, she knew they would never revive him. Despite all their efforts, there was no response from the inert body lying on the ground.

She felt sorry for Vaughn, huddled by his father's side, clutching the old man's hand. Tears were streaming down his face. His shoulders were shaking with sobs.

She went over to Vaughn and crouched down beside him, putting her arm round his shoulders as the ambulance raced up between the colourful parked vans.

Paramedics took over then, giving injections, hauling equipment out of the ambulance and using paddles to try and shock Oscar's heart into starting again. They did their best, but nothing was going to bring Oscar Herrick back. At last they covered him over with something white, and took him away.

Rafe came to her then and helped her get Vaughn to his feet. Vaughn put an arm round each of them and buried his head on Maggie's shoulder. The little trio were still there when all the others had trailed back inside the garages.

When Vaughn stopped sobbing he wiped the sleeve of his racing suit across his face and said in a dull voice, 'I never told him I was sorry.'

And there was nothing anyone could say to comfort him.

★ ★ ★

Maggie returned home. After Rafe had seen Maggie on to the train, he went to Northampton — to Starthe Manor. He took Vaughn with him because Vaughn was incapable of thinking, or feeling, or existing on his own.

The weather turned icy, and Vaughn spent the first day after Oscar's death pacing round the garden and grounds, his head bent into the cruel wind that swept down from the north, his hands jammed into his jacket pockets.

In the afternoon, Rafe went out and found him, sitting on a wooden five-barred gate just beyond a wooded copse on the edge of Oscar's estate.

'This is not doing any good,' he said.

Vaughn barely looked at him, but Rafe saw his features were as pinched and wintry as the frost-whitened grass. His eyes behind the steel-framed lenses held a frozen stare too as he gazed out at a grey mist hovering over the bare meadows.

'Why?' Vaughn asked huskily. 'Why did it happen so suddenly?'

Rafe climbed on to the gate and sat on top, a foot on either side of it latched on to a lower bar, facing Vaughn. 'It was a heart attack,' he said. 'That's the way they get you, sometimes.'

'I came to my senses too late.'

Vaughn didn't look at him, Rafe noted, but it didn't matter. Who knew what Vaughn was actually seeing as he looked into that frozen landscape.

'Yes,' Rafe said, knowing there was no point in arguing or denying the statement.

Vaughn swallowed. 'I still can't take it in.'

'No. Neither can I.'

'You were more son to him than I was.'

'Blood,' Rafe said, 'isn't always thicker than water, no matter what anybody tells you.'

'You're not helping any.' Vaughn's gaze rested on him at last.

'Is that what you want me to do? Help you come to terms with Oscar's death?'

'Yeah! Sure it is!' Vaughn's voice was raised now. 'Tell me none of it mattered — all these years. Tell me Dad's forgiven me now. Tell me there's no more pain. That's usually what folks say to you, isn't it? When somebody dies?'

'You wouldn't believe me if I said all those things,' Rafe said. 'And I wouldn't say them anyway, because I don't believe them any more than you do.'

'One thing's true,' Vaughn muttered, 'There isn't any more pain, is there? Not for him?'

Rafe shook his head. 'No. That's a

certainty, but there's still plenty left behind, and you're going to have to find some way of dealing with it that doesn't tip you over into maudlin sentimentality.'

Vaughn cocked his leg over the topmost bar of the gate and jumped down to the ground. 'I can't find any way through this,' he said. 'It's too soon. First Jade, and now this.' He started walking back towards the house, and Rafe heaved himself off the gate and followed.

He caught up with Vaughn easily. Neither of them was hurrying. Vaughn was scuffing his boots in the crisp, hoary grass, and leaving footprints behind him. He looked up as Rafe walked alongside. 'He never even spoke to me at Jade's funeral. Did you know that?'

'I know. I was there.'

'Yeah!'

'I spoke to you.'

'Everybody spoke to me. Except him. It made it seem worse because everybody else accepted me being there, but *he* didn't.'

'He didn't turn you away though. Isn't that a form of acceptance?'

'You're talking a load of rubbish. Do you think he wants me at *his* funeral in two day's time?'

'I don't know, Vaughn. He never said. We never talked about things like that. Oscar was the sort of guy that never dies.'

'He just talked cars, I suppose.'

'Cars, yes. And you, sometimes. I did my best, Vaughn, but he was a stubborn old bastard.'

'Yeah!'

'He hated your guts because you stood up to him.'

'Yeah! Ditto. All my life — ditto!'

'There's something of him left then. Don't you think?'

'I don't want to be like him.'

'You are like him — whether you want it or not.'

'If I'd had the damned heart attack instead of him, what would he have done?' Vaughn stood very still and looked at Rafe.

Rafe said, in a perfectly normal voice, 'I think he'd be feeling just like you are now.'

'You think?'

'I know.'

'You knew him better than I did.'

'Yes,' Rafe said. 'So believe me.'

★ ★ ★

Tamsin headed towards Northampton. There was fog on the motorway making driving conditions hell. There were tailbacks for miles, and staring at fog and tail lights through the windscreen was making her eyes gritty and sore. She got to a point where she could take no more of it, and exited at the next junction.

She pulled into a lay-by then, and switched off the engine. There was a map in the glove compartment. She pulled it out, opened it up, and folded it so Leicester, Coventry, Kettering and Towcester made a neat diamond shape around the place she was at now as she traced her finger along a line to the right of the motorway. She was having to use a torch to see, it was getting so dark outside. She wasn't sure exactly where it was that Oscar Herrick lived, but she was determined to find Starthe Manor. Rafe would be there, and she had to see him — had to tell him to his face about that last meeting she'd had with Ava.

She wondered vaguely as she switched the torch off and stared out into the opaque darkness how the race had gone yesterday. She'd been so wrapped up in other things that she hadn't thought to switch on a radio or a television, or to buy a newspaper. The past week had been like something out of a horror film. She recalled now how she'd packed her belongings and left the flat after that fiasco at the Shorecross Gala, and she'd driven as if the wind were on her tail once she'd left Ava.

She'd gone south. On automatic pilot, she

supposed, because she knew that's where she'd find Rafe. But not till after the race. She wasn't going to worry him before that, so she had quite some time to kill.

She hadn't driven far. She'd been too tired to do that. She'd stopped at Nottingham and stayed there for five days. She couldn't remember what she'd done there. There had been shops, stone lions and a castle, that much she could remember though, and she'd bought some make-up on her credit card on the last day there.

Rafe was racing somewhere near Lincoln, so there was no point in going any further south till after Sunday. She drove to a little place near Leicester on Sunday morning, booked a room for the night, then went and withdrew some cash from a hole-in-the-wall bank machine. She paid her bed-and-breakfast bill late on Monday morning, and headed towards Northampton. Rafe would be at Oscar's place now.

She pulled out of the lay-by and into the fog again. It was a quiet road through little towns with brightly lit streets. The fog wasn't dense here. It just hung round the street lights, making them hazy. Rafe had once said how difficult it was to find Starthe Manor, it was so tucked away at the back of beyond. She went into garages and shops to enquire, and found it at just after five that night.

She drove up to the door. There were lights on in the house, but the curtains were drawn across so she couldn't see who was inside the rooms. One thing she was glad about though — there was no possibility of running into Vaughn here. He and his father had been at daggers drawn for years.

She got out of the car, went up to the front door and knocked very loudly.

Within seconds she heard footsteps coming down a passage on the other side. She hoped it would be Rafe. More probably though, it would be Oscar Herrick. Well, he knew her. He'd met her. At least she'd be made welcome.

The door opened and she gasped.

'Vaughn!' A tingle of shock went through her. She wanted to turn and run, but her legs refused to budge.

'Tamsin! What the hell . . . ?'

They stood and stared at each other, then she managed to stammer, 'I — I never expected . . . '

'Me to be here?' His face, she saw, was tense. His words were less than welcoming. 'What do you want? I suppose you'd better come in.'

She followed him inside and he closed the door then turned to her.

'Is it me you want?' he asked warily. 'Or have you come to see Rafe?'

'Rafe,' she said, her voice quiet. And as she looked at Vaughn, she wondered what on earth had possessed her to let him make love to her.

'Yes,' he said, studying her face. 'I can see I'm not the main attraction any longer.'

'Did you really think you would be?'

'No. I'm sorry you were hurt though.'

'Not sorry about the other thing though.'

'That,' he said, 'was a mistake. You're not cut out to be a mother, Tammy.'

'Just a bit of fun,' she said. 'That's all I ever was to you.' But there was no malice in her words. It had been fun. A little bit of her heart had been cracked in the process, but it had been good while it lasted.

'You'd better come through to the sitting room. Rafe's in there.'

She followed him down the long passage and as he hesitated at the door and swung round to face her again, she said, 'Have you made up the quarrel with your father then? You're the last person I expected to find here.'

His eyes, behind the round, steel-framed glasses, were very direct. 'My father,' he said, 'is dead.'

'Oscar Herrick,' she said softly, drawing in

her breath. 'Oh, no.'

'Yes,' he said. 'We didn't make up the quarrel. He died suddenly and left me with a conscience to wrestle with.'

'Suddenly?'

'While the race was on. Yesterday.'

'I'm sorry,' she said. 'I quite liked him.'

'Yeah!' he said. 'Lots of folks did. The damn phone hasn't stopped ringing all day.'

Tamsin felt absolutely stunned.

He pushed open the door, made a grand entrance by saying, 'A visitor for you, Rafe. Just look who's here.'

She went into the room. It was warm. There was a roaring fire — and radiators all over the house too. She'd not been in a house with a real fire since she'd been a little girl visiting her gran. She walked over to it and held out her hands to the flames as Rafe got up from a sofa and switched the television off.

She stared into the flames for a few moments, then slowly turned round. He was waiting for her to do that, she could tell.

'I had to come,' she said. 'I had to tell you I couldn't work with Ava any more. I don't want you to think badly of me.'

Rafe walked over to her and took hold of her hands. 'You could have phoned,' he said. 'You shouldn't have driven all this way just to tell me that, Tam.'

'I had to get away,' she said. 'I just didn't know what to do. I've been on the road since last Sunday.'

'Hell!' Rafe said. 'You're in no fit state — not after what you went through with Ava.'

'I'm okay,' she said. 'I couldn't stay there though.'

'Mark?' he asked.

'That's over.' Her voice was flat.

'I thought you two were getting on quite well.'

Vaughn said, 'Look — I'll go and make a drink.'

Nobody answered him, so he went out of the room, closing the door behind him.

'I don't know what to do,' she said, dragging her hands away from his.

'You have a home. In Heronsea,' Rafe said. 'You have a job. People depend on you there. You can't just walk away from your responsibilities.'

'I have done.' She dropped her gaze to the floor.

'You *must* go back, Tam.'

She brought her head up slowly and looked him in the face. 'No,' she said. 'I'm too scared. It took every ounce of courage I had in me to go and tell Ava I was finished with her.'

'You did that?' Rafe ran a hand impatiently through his hair. 'How did she take it?'

'Okay, I think. I didn't hang around to find out. Look, can I stay the night here?'

He nodded. 'Of course. Vaughn won't mind.'

'I'm sorry about Oscar. He was a better man than Vaughn.'

'Vaughn's young. He'll learn.'

'No,' she said. 'Vaughn's the sort who never learns.' She slipped out of her coat. 'I have an overnight bag in the car,' she said. 'I've been wearing the same things for a week.' She grimaced. 'I need a washing machine.'

'No problem.' He grinned at her. 'You never change, do you? Empty headed as usual.'

She began to relax. 'I *have* changed.' She went and sat down near the fire.

He folded her coat and laid it neatly over a chair. 'How?' he asked, going back to her and looking down at her as she stared into the fire again. 'How have you changed?'

'I found out I cared about somebody. Really cared. And it frightened me so much I ran away.'

'You didn't run away from Ava then?'

She looked up at him. 'Yes. I suppose I did. But that was different. I can't trust her, Rafe. I can never trust her ever again.'

'But you'll have to,' he said.

'No, I'm never going to do that.'

'Tam . . . what are you saying?'

'Just that. I'm not going back to Heronsea. But I couldn't think what to do. So I came to you. You'll take care of me, won't you, Rafe?' She lifted wide, expressionless eyes to him. 'There's nobody else, you see. I can't trust anybody else.'

34

'I'll be perfectly honest with you,' Rafe said. 'I'm going to marry Maggie Brand, Tamsin. I'll do what I can to help you get back on your feet, but Maggie comes first with me.'

He saw the girl's face flush as she replied, 'I haven't come here to ask you to sleep with me. I just need a breathing space.'

'I'm a guest here myself, Tam. This is Oscar's house, and I have to stay here until after the funeral on Wednesday.'

'There must be a guest bedroom.' She was stony faced.

Vaughn came back into the room then, carrying a tray with three cups and saucers on it. 'I made tea,' he said. 'It seems to always be what they make on films when there's a crisis.'

'This isn't a crisis,' Rafe said, though not believing his own words for a minute.

'Well, help yourselves.' Vaughn shrugged and threw himself into an easy chair, his legs sprawling out in front of him. 'Be my guests.'

'You look like you're enjoying being lord of the manor,' Tamsin said with heavy sarcasm in her voice.

'This is my father's house,' he came back at her, 'not mine. Dad promised me he'd cut me out of his will years ago — and he was never one to go back on his word. He's probably left everything to a charity for destitute Formula One drivers; I'm sure there must be one somewhere.'

Rafe picked up a cup of tea and managed a laugh of sorts. 'Oscar wouldn't do that. He'd be on the winner's side, not the loser's.'

'Perkins the lawyer wouldn't give anything away when he called this morning,' Vaughn said. 'He indicated it'd take about a month to wind Dad's affairs up, but he glowered at me as he said it. I got the feeling he thought it was none of my business.'

'You're heartless,' Tam said, 'talking about Oscar's will as if it were just a piece of paper. It doesn't seem to have occurred to you yet that your father is dead.'

Vaughn looked up at Rafe as he replied to Tamsin. 'Weeping for what's gone won't bring him back.'

Rafe winced as Tam said coldly, 'I never wept for your baby, Vaughn. I was glad it had gone.'

Calmly Vaughn said, 'Well, it solved a hell of a lot of problems for you, didn't it?'

Tam jumped to her feet. 'Just show me the spare room,' she snapped. 'Show me the spare room and I'll move on again tomorrow.'

'You have nowhere to go,' Rafe reminded her.

'I'll find somewhere. I have a bit of money.'

'You have a life,' Rafe said, 'back at Heronsea. Don't be a fool, Tam. Don't throw everything away.'

'There's poison at Heronsea,' Tam said stonily. 'Poison, just sitting there in her Ivory Tower, waiting to pounce. She'll never let you go, Rafe. Her obsession is disguised as love. Hadn't you ever guessed? Ava is in love with you. She always has been. I pity Maggie Brand — having Ava as a sister-in-law. If, of course, Ava ever lets the relationship get that far.'

* * *

The next morning, Rafe found a note waiting for him on the breakfast table. Tamsin had gone. Back to Beverley, she said. She'd get lodgings there. She'd look up a friend or something from the old days and find a job.

Vaughn came into the kitchen as Rafe was reading it.

'She's gone?' he asked.

Rafe nodded. 'Not back to Heronsea though. She's at least seen sense however and gone back somewhere she knows. She won't be wandering the country, which is a relief to me. I've got into the habit of feeling responsible for her.'

'You don't have to stay for Dad's funeral, you know.' Vaughn busied himself making coffee. 'Your sister probably needs you more than Tam did.'

'I tried to ring Ava this morning. There was no reply.' Rafe folded the note and dropped it on the table. 'I haven't spoken to her since Saturday so she doesn't know what's been happening here.'

'Look — it's hell just waiting around like this. Go back. You know damn well you want to be with Maggie.' Vaughn came over to the table, thumped it hard and said, 'Go, will you? Maybe a spot of solitude will do me good as well. I've blown everything with Blanchard's now so I'd better start thinking about what happens next.'

'You'll get another team. You're a good driver.'

'Yeah.' Vaughn didn't sound convinced. 'You've heard the phone ringing every few minutes these past two days, have you? Offers of a drive with all the top teams? Get real, man. Blanchard will have put the boot in good and proper by now. Vaughn Herrick will be the new dirty word on the circuits.'

'Blanchard's are bottom of the league,' Rafe pointed out patiently. 'Nobody's going to take any notice of rumours. Why don't you start making a few phone calls yourself? Invite some of the top dogs to Oscar's wake on Wednesday, then be on your best behaviour if they turn up.'

'Isn't that just a little bit sick?' Vaughn said.

Rafe grinned. 'Oscar would applaud it.'

Vaughn stood and stared at him for several seconds, then he said, 'You're right.' He spun away towards the door, pausing only to ask, 'Does Dad have an organizer anywhere, with all those phone numbers in it?'

★ ★ ★

As Rafe drove north that afternoon, his phone started ringing. He was off the motorway now and on a major A road. He pulled into a convenient spot and Tamsin said, 'What kept you?'

'I was in traffic,' he said.

'I decided to go back.'

'You said so,' he replied, 'in the note you left this morning.'

'I'm at Heronsea. In for a penny, in for a

pound, I thought. I decided you talked sense. I've put a lot into this business. Also, you don't want me hanging round your neck for ever.'

'Good for you.'

'The trouble is — Ava's not here, but the place is wide open.'

'Wide open?'

'Well, the outside door was shut, but not locked. The alarm system isn't on. But she's not here.'

'Have you looked in her rooms?'

'No!' Her voice trembled slightly and she gave a forced laugh. 'Don't ask me to go up those stairs again, Rafe. I stood at the bottom and yelled up though, but there was no reply.'

He looked at his watch. 'I'll be back there in less than an hour, Tam. Where are you now?'

'Outside the lighthouse — back in my car. And it's freezing cold.'

'It's November,' he said. 'It usually is cold on the north-east coast in November.'

'It's starting to snow.'

'Lock the lighthouse door,' he said. 'And go to the cafe at the end of the promenade. I'll meet you there.'

'Okay.'

'And Tam . . . '

'Yes?'

'Don't go back inside — just lock the door. Understand?'

'Message received.' She sounded relieved. 'We'll find her.'

'Yes,' she said.

★ ★ ★

Tam stayed behind him as he unlocked the door to the Ivory Tower and went inside.

'Brrr! It's cold in here.' He rubbed his hands together for warmth.

Behind him, Tamsin stamped a light covering of snow from her booted feet on to the recessed door mat. 'Ava always kept it cool. She said it was good for the dresses.'

'There's no heat on at all though.'

In a dull voice, Tam replied, 'That's how she liked it.'

'Well, she's not in here.'

'No.'

'I'm going upstairs. Are you coming?'

She nodded and looked terrified. 'I'll be okay with you in front of me, won't I?'

He held out his hand. 'Come on. Nobody's going to bite.'

They went up to Ava's apartment. It was clean and tidy.

'Not a thing out of place,' Tam whispered as he went inside and pushed open the bathroom door.

'She's not here.'

In Tamsin's room above Ava's, it was the same story. Things there were as Tam had left them the night she'd fallen down the stairs.

They searched cupboards, and behind the banana bunk curtains, but found nothing. There were two more narrow rooms, above Tamsin's. One was a tiny study where Ava did the books and kept invoices and things. The topmost of the two was merely used as a dumping ground for the bits and pieces that couldn't be fitted in anywhere else.

'There's nowhere else,' Rafe said, looking perplexed. 'Except . . . ' a thought hit him, and he stared at the ceiling of the final room. 'Up there?' he said. 'The lantern platform.'

'Why? Why would she go up there? And if she is there, why hasn't she come down? She must have heard us by now.'

'We'd better have a look.'

Tam's hand flew to her lips. 'Heights!' she said. 'You don't think . . . ?'

He looked grim. 'It affected her more than we thought — what her mother did all those years ago.'

They hurried to the last staircase that led up to the part of the lighthouse that had once housed the lantern. The door was firmly locked, the key still in it.

'Ava would have taken the key if she'd gone out there,' Tam said. 'She was always so fanatical about that. The door used to slam shut in the draught, you see. And you couldn't open it from the other side if . . . '

She stared at him in horror.

'Oh, no!' He grabbed at the key and unlocked the door, swinging it back towards him as he pulled it open and made as if to rush out on to the platform.

But something was barring his way. Something like a bundle of rags that had been heaped up, huddled against the door. It had a light covering of snow on it, but nothing could disguise the fact that it was Ava.

Rafe bent down and gently touched his step-sister's face. Then without looking up, he said, 'Tam — go and make a phone call, love.'

Tamsin backed away, down the stairs. 'Is she . . . is she . . . ?'

'Yes,' he said softly. 'She must have been here for some time. Since yesterday at least. Nobody can help her now.'

Tam went slowly down the stairs to the showroom, picked up the phone and dialled the emergency number.

Minutes later, she leaned on the glass topped counter and looked round the place. Now she could start to live, she decided. Now, there would be no more fear.

The final ghost had been laid.

35

Edgar was guiltily tucking a sprig of holly under the wiper blades of Mark's Porsche as Maggie walked into the garage on Christmas Eve morning.

'Dad! What are you doing here? I just called on Mom with the Christmas presents and she said you were working. What on earth are you doing?'

Edgar chuckled. 'Thought I'd been caught in the act when I heard your footsteps, love. It could've been Mark, see, and I wanted to surprise him.' He wheeled his chair back from the Porsche and said, 'What do you think of it? Like new, I'd say.'

'Better than the last time I saw it after its ducking in the sea.' She laughed. 'Mark's been busy. I expect he wanted it getting back in shape though. He likes to live it up a bit at Christmas, doesn't he?'

Edgar said, 'He's done most of the work on it himself, but being here till ten most nights has taken its toll on him. He was flaked out last night, and went early, so I came in and finished it off this morning — you know, gave it a real good going over inside, polished the seats, blacked the tyres . . . '

'And then added the sprig of holly for luck.' She grinned. 'Nice one, Dad. Holly's just the thing for Mark. He can be so prickly.'

'Never thought of that.' Edgar stroked his chin for a minute then said, 'Do you think mistletoe would have been more appropriate now that young lass is back at the lighthouse?'

'I wouldn't push your luck, Dad.' Maggie patted Fudge and said, 'Sit down, boy. If Mark's due in this morning, I'll wait and have a drink with you before I go back home along the shore with Fudge.'

'Kettle's boiled, love.' Edgar rubbed his hands together.

'Where's Jack-O?'

'Gone on a cruise for Christmas. Norway.'

'Really?'

Edgar nodded. 'He's on his own. Nobody to bother about. I told him he could come to us but the cruise won.'

'We'll see you and Mom, Dad? Sometime over Christmas?'

'Aye, lass. Course you will. Your mam's getting somebody else to take the urgent calls at the hospital from Boxing Day, so we'll have you and Rafe over for tea. Mam can make a trifle like the old days, eh?'

'And you're coming to us for New Year?'

'Aye! So your mam says. She's boss.'

'Rafe's had to go down to Oscar's place today. Vaughn rang him yesterday, said things had been sorted out now.'

'Hey — if you're on your own for Christmas . . .'

'No, Dad. I won't be on my own. Rafe said he'd be back this afternoon.'

'Well, you know where we are . . .'

She kissed the top of his head. 'I know, Dad. I know.'

'Things are working out, Maggie?'

'I think so.'

'Wedding bells, girl?'

She nodded, then said on a note of humour, 'I thought at one time I'd have to arrange my wedding day around next year's Grand Prix dates, but Rafe is determined he's not going to race again.'

Fudge gave a short, sharp bark and pricked his ears up as they heard a scuffling outside on the gravely yard, then the small door set into the large double doors was pushed open and Mark appeared.

He had to bend his head to get inside the garage, and then he just stood and looked at them, a wide smile appearing as his gaze alighted on the car.

'Edgar! You old wizard! You've finished it for me.'

'Aye, lad. I took pity on you — seeing as it's Christmas.'

'Mags! Are you okay?' Mark bent down and fondled Fudge's head as he spoke to her.

'Fine! Just going, in fact, but I'm glad I saw you to wish you a happy Christmas.'

Edgar said, 'You were going to stop and have a cup of tea, our Mags.'

'I'll get back home, I think. Rafe will probably be ringing me from Northampton.'

Mark said quickly, 'Don't rush off, Mags. I want your opinion about something. I'm glad you're here.'

'What is it?' she asked.

He fished into his trouser pocket and brought out a little blue box. 'This,' he said a bit self-consciously. 'Tell me what you think. I got it for Tam. I'm going to pop over there and just push it through the letterbox of her flat.'

Maggie smiled quietly to herself as she admired the tiny silver brooch in the shape of a cluster of lilies of the valley. 'It's lovely.' She looked up into Mark's face and what she saw there convinced her that Mark really cared for Tam.

'It's not much,' he said, off-handedly.

'It's lovely. It really is.'

'You think so? You're not just saying that . . . ?'

Seriously she said, 'No. I'm not 'just saying that'.'

He let out a huge sigh. 'Good. The flowers . . . ' he glanced at her, 'they all have a meaning you know.'

She nodded.

'And these . . . I asked the jeweller . . . and he said they mean 'return of happiness', so I thought it was right. Do you think Tam will know? What they mean?'

'She's sure to.'

There was a little silence, then Edgar broke it by saying, 'Eh, lad you are daft! Talking about pushing it through her letterbox. Why not go right in there and give her a whopping big kiss?'

Mark looked as if he didn't know whether to take Edgar seriously or not, then, seeing the holly tucked behind the wiper blades of his car, he swooped on it and said, 'Okay. I'll do that — if you think it might work. And I'll take this with me.'

'It's mistletoe you want — not holly,' Edgar said, roaring with laughter.

★   ★   ★

Back at her house, Maggie put the finishing touches to the little Christmas tree, then switched on its lights. The whole room looked cosy then, bathed in the flickering glow from the fire, and with diamond-studded dots of colour shimmering among the tinsel on the tree.

Fudge sighed in his sleep and stretched to his full length on the hearth-rug. Maggie stayed by the window, watching the road that led down to the sea front.

She didn't have long to wait before she saw the sweep of headlights coming down from the church. And then he was there, parking the Ferrari in front of the cottage. It was then that she moved away from the window and went to open the outside door.

He held out a potted plant wrapped round with gold foil to protect it from the cold. 'Vaughn's sent you this.'

She laughed softly. 'That was nice of him. How is he?'

'Fine!'

She closed the door as he went through to the kitchen, then she followed him.

'Smells good.'

She put the plant on the table, and he whisked her into his arms and kissed her.

'Me?' she asked, 'or the supper?'

'Both.' He held her away from him and she

placed her hands on his shoulders and said, 'You made good time. I wasn't expecting you for about another hour.'

'There was nothing to stay for,' he said, gazing down at her. 'I wanted to get back to you.'

He seemed as if he wanted to say something else, but didn't. He looked away, gazed round the kitchen. She could feel that he was slightly uneasy.

'What is it?' she said. 'There's something wrong. I can feel it.'

'I want Christmas to be perfect for us . . . ' His hands fell away from her. He walked to the other side of the room and flung his jacket on to a chair, then whirled to face her again. 'Maggie — I don't want anything to come between us. Ever!'

'It won't,' she said, but suddenly she was feeling edgy. 'Rafe . . . ' she said, and her voice was husky.

'Damn Oscar!' He strode back across the kitchen to her. 'That damn man,' he muttered.

'Hey! What is it?' Maggie was getting really het up now. 'Rafe — tell me. You've got to tell me what's wrong.'

His hands came up, then descended on her shoulders. 'Maggie,' he said, staring deeply into her troubled eyes, 'Maggie — this is something that's going to affect both of us. It's got to be your decision, just as much as mine. And if we don't agree then I'll say to hell with it.'

Her heart went cold. 'You're going to race again,' she said in a hollow voice. 'That's it, isn't it? You're going to race for Vaughn now he's taking over from Oscar?'

He stared at her. 'Worse than that,' he said.

'Worse?'

He tipped her chin up so she was looking straight at him and couldn't move away. He wanted to see her reaction, she knew. Her honest, no punches pulled, reaction.

'He's left me the damn lot,' he said. 'The house, the team, everything.'

Her first thought was for Vaughn. 'And Vaughn?' she whispered.

'Nothing!'

'Oh, no!'

He let her go. He threw up his hands. 'I told them. I told Perkins — the lawyer fellow — I told him I wouldn't accept it. It's Vaughn's. I said I'd hand it all over to Vaughn, and you know what they told me?'

She shook her head, unable to reply just at that moment.

'If I refused the legacy, it was all to go to . . .'

'Who?' she asked, mystified. 'There's

nobody else but Vaughn, surely?'

'Tom Blanchard!'

She gave a gasp. 'No!'

'So, I'm lumbered with it. Maggie — I couldn't let Tom Blanchard get the upper hand, could I?'

She smiled, then started to laugh softly.

'There's nothing funny about it,' he stormed. 'I want Vaughn to have what's rightfully his. But what can I do?'

'You can do what Oscar wanted you to do,' she said. 'Don't you see? You can't refuse — and Oscar knew that. It was the one way to make sure that you stayed with the team. That you were in charge, though, this time, not him.'

'The house name,' he said musingly. 'Do you know what it means?' Then without waiting for a reply, he said, 'Starthe Manor. Starthe is an old English word for the start of a sporting event. Oscar once told me that. Maggie — I feel so helpless. What can I do?'

'You know in your heart, don't you?' she said, some words of Oscar's coming back to her now, making her understand what he was getting at that time down in Northampton, when he'd told her that one day she'd have to push Rafe into winning.

'Oscar must have been out of his mind.'

'No,' she said. 'He wasn't. He knew what

was best for the team. Rafe — you can't let him down. You've got to do this one last thing for him.'

'To be honest, Maggie, I can't see any way out of it.'

'There isn't one.' She went to him and threw her arms round him and hugged him. 'Welcome to Oscar-Jade,' she said, looking up into his face, then tiptoeing and kissing him soundly on the lips.

'We could change the team name, I suppose . . . '

'No,' she said. 'Leave it as it is.'

'Vaughn fell about laughing,' he said.

'He's not so unlike his dad then, is he?'

'That's what I said to him. But he just laughed some more. But Maggie — it means you leaving Shorecross.' He placed both his hands firmly on her shoulders and held her away from him so he could look into her eyes. 'I'll have to be there, where the circuit is, where the team is most of the time.'

'Okay,' she said. 'We'll move.' She reached up and smoothed out the lines on his forehead. 'Don't look so worried — I liked Oscar's house. And Fudge will love all that open space.'

'Maggie!' He sighed, and his hands fell away from her. He moved from her, half turning away as he said, 'Think about it.

What it will mean. You won't have the sea on your doorstep, or your mom and dad, and the lifeboat . . . '

Softly, she said, 'I know I can't just walk out on Jim and the lads without any warning, Rafe, but I'll tell Jim right away to start advertising for a mechanic to take my place. With my little house so nice and cosy now, it might be an incentive for someone to move to Shorecross knowing there's decent living accommodation that goes with the job.'

He spun round, and with almost the width of the room between them now, said, 'You'll miss being with the lifeboat crew, Maggie.' There was a worried expression in his eyes.

'I'll have to find something else that's just as exciting to do then, won't I?'

'Like what?' he asked, his eyes telling her he loved her.

'Do you have to ask me that?' Her gaze came up to meet his.

His brow furrowed. 'Maggie? What do you mean?'

'Cars,' she said simply. 'It just hasn't occurred to you, has it?'

'Cars?'

She nodded. 'Tell me I'm completely mad,' she said, 'But you know as well as I do that, after you and Fudge, and Mom and Dad, the next greatest love of my life is a car engine.'

He stared at her, then closed his eyes, smacked a hand to his forehead before looking at her again. 'Maggie — are you serious?'

'I could learn about Formula One engines.'

The relief on his face made her laugh. 'Maggie!' he said. 'Maggie Brand, you never fail to amaze me.'

'Could I do it? Learn about Formula One? And be a mechanic for Oscar-Jade? Could you work with me, Rafe?'

He strode across the kitchen to her, pulled her into his arms and said, 'I could work with you, Maggie. I think it's a great idea.'

'And the other mechanics?' She tilted her head back to look into his eyes. Seriously asking the question now, 'Would they work with a woman?'

'Maggie — you've watched them working on the cars,' he said. 'We're a team, not a bunch of sexists. You know how dedicated they are.'

'Yes,' she said. 'I've watched them stripping the cars down. When they're in the pit garages they're totally in love with the car. I don't even think they noticed me — a woman standing watching, do you?'

He laughed softly. 'I think they might just have noticed,' he said.

'You'd give me a job then?'

'Consider it done.'

'You're still worried about something though?' Suddenly the laughter left her eyes.

'I'm short of a driver now I've given it up.'

'Yes,' she said. 'I realize that.'

'Any ideas?'

She nodded. 'They're the same ideas you're having yourself.' Her face lit up with amusement.

'Vaughn!' They both said the name in unison, and she laughed and said, 'Yes, go on. Ring him. Now.'

'He's still at the house. Oscar's house.'

'Your house,' Maggie said.

'*Our* house,' he corrected.

Impatient now, she said, 'So ring him before somebody else does. We need to start planning for next season.'

He walked over to his jacket, took the mobile phone out of it, then stood looking at it. 'You're sure. You're one hundred per cent sure about this? Because if not, Maggie, I'll say to hell with Oscar, and let Tom Blanchard have the last laugh.'

'I'm sure! A hundred and one per cent.'

He punched out the number, then stood and waited till he got an answer.

Then Maggie heard him say quietly into the phone, 'Vaughn. Maggie and me — we're getting married. I want you for best man.'

Maggie whispered, '*Ask him*! For heaven's sake, *ask* him . . . '

He covered the mouthpiece with his hand and said, 'Don't be impatient. First things first.' Then, speaking to Vaughn again, he said, 'Oh, I have something else to tell you too. We're taking on a new mechanic.'

From the phone, Maggie heard hard laughter that reminded her of Oscar Herrick, and then Vaughn yelling, 'Maggie! I knew it.'

Rafe looked taken aback and asked. 'How the hell did you guess?'

There was silence while he listened to Vaughn's reply, then he lifted his head, looked at Maggie, and said, 'Vaughn said it was a foregone conclusion. He also says to tell you never to forget the name of the game.'

She laughed. '*Ask him*,' she said. 'Never mind beating about the bush. Just ask Vaughn to . . . '

'Here!' He held the phone out to her. 'You ask him. It's the only way. He can't ever say no to a woman.'

She snatched the phone. 'Men!' she laughed breathlessly.

'I kept hearing you telling Rafe to ask me something,' Vaughn said. 'But he's already asked me to be best man at your wedding, Maggie. And I agreed.'

We do hope that you have enjoyed reading this large print book.

Did you know that all of our titles are available for purchase?

We publish a wide range of high quality large print books including:
Romances, Mysteries, Classics
General Fiction
Non Fiction and Westerns

Special interest titles available in large print are:
The Little Oxford Dictionary
Music Book
Song Book
Hymn Book
Service Book

Also available from us courtesy of Oxford University Press:
Young Readers' Dictionary
(large print edition)
Young Readers' Thesaurus
(large print edition)

For further information or a free brochure, please contact us at:
Ulverscroft Large Print Books Ltd.,
The Green, Bradgate Road, Anstey,
Leicester, LE7 7FU, England.
Tel: (00 44) 0116 236 4325
Fax: (00 44) 0116 234 0205

'It's not the wedding,' she said. 'It's the team.'

'The team?' Vaughn said.

'We want you,' she said.

'Me?'

'We need a driver. Don't be so slow on the uptake, Vaughn. We want you — Rafe and me. We want you to drive for Oscar-Jade next season, so how about it? And don't say you have to think about it or I'll . . . '

'I don't have to think about it,' Vaughn said. 'And I heard what Rafe said when he handed you the phone.'

'You did?'

He burst out laughing. 'He's right, Maggie.'

'He is?'

'I can't ever say no to a woman.'

THE END